There are worse things than vampires

Trudie Collins

DEDICATION

This book is dedicated to all the teachers around the world who continued to teach, either in person or remotely during the Covid-19 pandemic. Thank you for your hard work and dedication to your students.

ACKNOWLEDGMENTS

Thank you to Pete, Julie, Wendy, Terry and Jamie for their feedback

MURDER

For the first time since starting his career as a killer for hire, Virgil was questioning whether he should have taken an assignment. The thought ran through his mind once more as he did up his flies, having relieved himself against a tree. He had been waiting in the middle of nowhere for hours and was fed up. The man who had hired him had warned him he would need to wait around for the right opportunity, but he hadn't expected it to take this long.

He had been trailing his prey for weeks, well his car, anyway. He now knew the car so well he could recognise it from the sound of its engine. He had no idea why he had been hired to kill this man and he didn't care. He had a job to do; the reasons didn't matter.

He also had no idea who had hired him. That was something else he didn't care about, as long as he got paid. The only thing that had him concerned was his client's insistence that the victim be beheaded. Never before had he questioned a client, but this time he had asked why. The man refused to tell him, stating it was none of his business. Virgil could tell he was hiding something, but something about the man scared him enough to prevent him questioning him further. But he paid well. This one job was going to earn him enough that he wouldn't have to work for the rest of the year.

The other thing concerning him was the client's warning that he should make sure the victim was unconscious when he killed him. Virgil was a strong man, an ex-army vet who had been kicked out for insubordination. He kept himself fit by boxing and had earned a reputation for being a dirty fighter, so it wasn't as if he didn't know how to beat someone in a fight.

While he was good with a gun, he preferred to use his hands when killing. Getting someone in a headlock to cut off their air supply and then watching them take their last breath was much more satisfying than a bullet to the head. And a lot cleaner. But

1

he had been warned that he should not even consider doing so on this job.

He had also been told he wouldn't be able to use a gun. Even with a silencer, the victim would be able to hear it and get out of the way. He had trouble believing this for two reasons. Firstly, who could hear a gunshot when the gun was fitted with a silencer unless they were close by? Secondly, even if they did, somehow, manage to hear it, by the time it registered in their brain it would be too late; nobody could move fast enough to get out of the way. He had expressed his doubts to his client, only for the man to demonstrate how fast someone could really move.

Virgil had gone straight to the nearest bar, where he drank himself unconscious.

After that demonstration, he considered refusing the job, but the man had made it clear exactly what would be done to him if he did. He also pointed out failure was not an option. He either did what he had been hired to do or it was the last job he would ever take.

Which was why, as tempted as he was to go home, Virgil remained where he was, waiting for a call from his associate to say the car was on its way.

Virgil's target often used the backroad he was currently waiting on. He knew where the victim lived, where he worked and the places he often visited. He had seen him go to one of his usual places with someone else in the car and was working on the assumption he was going back later today to pick her up. Of course, he could be wrong, but if he was, he would wait for another opportunity.

While he waited, he thought about his victim and what little he knew about him. He had been provided with the address and car details, and that was it. He didn't even know the man's name.

But he was aware of what he looked like. He was tall and fit, but not overly muscular. He had dark hair, which was always neat, and, had Virgil been that way inclined, he would have found him more than just attractive. He could imagine women throwing themselves at him.

He assumed he was married, or at least living with the woman he often saw him with. They made a nice couple and seemed happy together. That would soon change; as soon as he completed his assignment.

His target was often with another man. They were either good friends or related. Occasionally a chubby woman joined them and from the way they behaved, Virgil assumed she was with the other man.

He hoped the car would go past soon, and his victim would be on his own. He had been warned to only make an attempt on his life when he was alone as, no matter how skilled Virgil believed himself to be, he would not be able to take on any of the target's acquaintances.

Just as he was considering going for another leak, his phone rang. He glanced at the caller ID and smiled. The wait was finally over. Whether it had been in vain or not, he would know as soon as he answered the phone.

"Well?" he said after hitting the right button. He didn't bother with any welcome or pleasantries; it would have been a waste of time.

"The car has just left. It's heading your way. There appears to be only one person in it."

Virgil hung up and smiled. Another few minutes and the job would be done. He got into his car and started the engine. He had positioned himself so he could clearly see vehicles approaching from either direction. Now all he had to do was wait for the car to come into sight. He would have to time it perfectly, but he had had lots of practice in his younger days when he caused accidents for insurance scams. The only thing that could go wrong now would be another car interrupting him. But it was a quiet road, so he was hopeful he would be lucky.

With his window wound down, he heard the car before he saw it. Soon it came into sight and he confirmed it was the right make, model and colour. He knew a lot about cars and could recognise most that were on the roads without having to see their badges.

He couldn't see the licence plate, but it was unlikely to be the wrong car.

He took off the hand brake and revved the engine, keeping his foot on the break until the last moment.

When he released it, the car shot forward at speed, hitting the oncoming car directly in the middle of the driver's door, sending it careening off the road and into a tree.

Virgil climbed out of his broken vehicle and looked at the steam pouring out of the crushed front end. It wouldn't be drivable in that condition, but it was stolen so he didn't care. His associate would pick him up as soon as he called him.

He went to the side of the car and opened up the rear driver's side door. He picked up the long knife which had dropped into the footwell and then made his way to the other car.

The driver's door was too damaged to open, so he walked around the front of it and got in the passenger side. His target was slumped over the steering wheel, unconscious. Virgil wasn't taking any risks. He pulled his gun from his jacket pocket and shot the man in the head. Twice.

Only then did he realise the hair colour was wrong. In a panic, he pulled the corpse's head back and swore. He got out of the car and walked around it, still swearing. He ran his fingers through his hair as he paced. What was he going to do? He had killed the wrong man. His client was going to be pissed.

Should he call him? No, of course not. He just needed to put this behind him. It was only a setback. He could still get his target; it would just have to wait for another day.

Then he remembered what he had been told about severing the head. Should he do it, just to be on the safe side, even though he had killed the wrong person? He had shot the man in the head at point-blank range, so of course he had to be dead, but was it safer to make sure?

He forced himself to enter the car once more. He placed his hand on the dead man's neck and felt for a pulse. As expected, he couldn't find one. He was dead. Of course he was dead. How could he not be?

He then looked at the knife he had dropped onto the passenger seat. Should he use it? Could he send his client pictures of the crashed car and a headless corpse and make out he had killed the right person?

No. It wasn't worth the risk. The client was bound to find out the truth and then Virgil was a dead man.

He continued to look at the knife, unsure, for the first time since he had become a killer for hire, whether he should follow his client's instructions. After all, it was the wrong man.

In the end, caution won out and he picked up the knife, placed it against the corpse's neck and began to cut.

I DON'T LIKE UNCLE CRAIG ANYMORE

JD looked out of his office window at his son playing in the garden and wondered, not for the first time, when his vampire traits would start to show.

At nearly five years old, Alexander appeared to be a normal human boy, despite having a vampire as a father.

Craig, Alexander's god-father and the best friend of JD's wife, Sarah, was keeping an eye on him while JD worked and Sarah spent time with her boss. Anna was visiting so Sarah could do an unofficial handover as her maternity leave was about to start.

Unlike JD, Anna was a greater vampire; she didn't age and was faster, stronger and better than JD in every way. But he wasn't jealous; he could have children, Anna couldn't.

But JD was unique. He was the only vampire who was also a vampire hunter. He trained his fellow hunters and had a reputation for being the best there was. Unlike most vampires, he didn't kill people. His team donated their blood to him, to keep him alive, and he would never take from someone against their will.

His mind drifted to his brother, Jonathon. He missed him. Jonathon and Katie, Jonathon's wife, were away training to be trainers. JD was proud of them; not many hunters were invited to become trainers. But that didn't stop him missing them. Alexander also missed his little cousin. He loved holding him, playing with his little toes and fingers. He would soon have a sister to play with, but he was impatient and didn't want to wait.

JD dragged himself from his memories back to his computer screen, but he couldn't concentrate. He could hear Sarah and Anna talking in Sarah's office next door and his mind drifted back to when he had first met Anna, back when she was human. It was thanks to her that he had met Luke and Gabriel and had found out about greater vampires.

JD smiled as he remembered Sarah's reaction when she complained about having to work with Gabriel, before she found out what he was. He was an egotist who used women for sex and then dumped them. Not unlike Jonathon, before he had become involved with Katie.

The vampire hunter society hadn't known there was such a thing as greater vampires, nor how hard they were to kill.

Luckily, Luke and his family weren't killers. They had the power to entrance humans so they could take some of their blood and then make them forget. They made peace with the hunter society and the head of Luke and Gabriel's family was now on the council.

A shudder ran through JD when he thought back to Anna deciding to become a vampire. It was not something he would have done, had he been given a choice. Not that Anna really had a choice, he supposed. Luke would never age, yet she would while she remained human. Her conversion had been a long and painful process and he was glad he hadn't had to witness it or listen to her screams.

He still didn't understand the bond that Anna and Luke shared. It was more than love at first sight, more than wanting or needing each other. They called it 'the calling' and it was supposed to only happen to greater vampires.

With great effort, JD forced his mind from the past and into the present. Somehow he managed to focus on his work long enough to finish it, before getting changed and going to the training room.

The room was large, providing enough space for his entire team to train together, with swords and bow staffs. One wall was covered with weapons of all kinds, most of them belonging to JD. A balcony ran around half the room, allowing people to watch.

JD took his training sword off the wall and removed it from its scabbard. Like all qualified hunters, he had two swords. His training sword was blunt, but could still inflict a lot of damage on an opponent. Referred to as a 'live' sword, its twin was razor sharp and was mostly used for hunting. It could slice through a vampire's neck or remove limbs.

JD performed some stretching exercises before he began one of his routines. He was part way through his second one when the balcony door opened. Two sets of footsteps entered the room, but he didn't let them disturb him. If whoever it was wanted anything important, they would call down to him. They remained silent, so he waited until he finished before looking up.

His eyes fell on Sarah and he smiled. She looked tired, but still had a glow about her. Her blonde hair was tied back in a ponytail and she was wearing a neck scarf, as had become her habit.

Not that she had needed to for a while. Sarah was the only person he drank blood from the neck from and he had not done so since they found out she was pregnant again.

Anna was with her, watching him with interest. She, Luke and Gabriel were such regular visitors to the Sanctuary that each had been given their own key.

"No matter how many times I see you training," Anna called down to him, "it still amazes me. I may be stronger and faster than you, but you have a grace and style that I'm jealous of."

JD liked Anna. She was impossible not to like. She was also a little different to other greater vampires. For some reason nobody could explain, she couldn't drink human blood. Luckily for her, Luke and Gabriel lived with a number of other greater vampires who were more than happy to provide her with the blood she needed. She could also drink JD's blood, but she didn't often do so.

"Want to join in?" he asked her, but she shook her head. Luke often took part in training sessions when he visited, but Anna always refused.

"We're here to let you know that we're going to watch a film, if you feel like joining us," Sarah said.

"Thanks Honey. I'll go and get showered."

He watched as his wife waddled out of the room. Not that he would ever tell her she was waddling. She may be pregnant, but she was still vicious with a sword.

The ladies had already chosen a film by the time he arrived in the TV room. He suppressed a groan when he saw it was a rom-com. It wasn't that he hated them, he just wasn't a huge fan. He much preferred action or horror or even a good murder mystery.

Resigning himself to at least ninety minutes of having to watch a 'chick-flick', he lay down on one of the sofas and moved back so Sarah could join him. He placed his arm around her, resting his hand on her extended abdomen. His daughter was active and he could feel movement inside.

Sarah gasped and he quickly moved his hand away, but he wasn't the cause of her pain.

"I'm sure this baby is going to be a footballer," she said as she moved position. "She's developed a habit of kicking me under the ribs."

She wasn't facing JD so he allowed his grin to show. He didn't like his wife being in pain, but found what she said amusing. He caught Anna's eye. She, too, looked like she was trying not to laugh.

Sarah settled down once more and JD drifted in and out of sleep instead of concentrating on the film. He was shaken awake to see the credits rolling up the screen. He had seen the film before and knew he hadn't missed much.

He manoeuvred himself so he could get off the sofa without making Sarah stand up and held his hand out to her. She needed help standing, which she was embarrassed about.

Just as she made it to her feet, there was a knock at the door and Craig entered, carrying a miserable Alexander. His eyes were red and there were tear-streaks down his cheeks.

JD held out his arms and Craig handed him over. "What's wrong?" he asked in the tone of voice he reserved for children.

"I don't like Uncle Craig anymore."

JD raised a questioning eyebrow at Craig, who was grinning.

"I wouldn't let him play in the pond," he said.

JD rolled his eyes. He remembered when Craig had thrown Sarah into the pond and she had gotten her own back by pulling him in when he held out his hand to help her out. Mentioning that in front of his son would not be a good idea, so instead JD explained why Alexander wasn't allowed to play in the pond.

The young boy pouted while listening to everything his father had to say. "Mummy would let me," he said when JD finished speaking.

"Mummy most certainly would not," Sarah said. "Come on young man, let's get you fed."

"Already done," Craig said. "It's not often you get to relax with Anna without Luke hovering around, so I thought I would leave you in peace."

"Thanks," JD said. He looked at his still sulking son. "Does that mean it's bath time?"

"No. Don't like baths."

"Tough."

JD carried his son up the stairs and into the nursery. Alexander would be moved to his own room soon, so the nursery could be ready for the new arrival. Alexander was looking forward to it, but JD and Sarah weren't, even though his new room was just across the hall.

JD placed his son on the floor and retrieved Alexander's pyjamas. Taking his hand, they walked to the bathroom. Each room had its own en-suite, but one of the bedrooms had been converted into a bathroom with a bathtub in it when Sarah fell pregnant.

While the tub filled, JD stripped the young man and put all his clothes in the wash basket. Alexander insisted he could do it himself, but it took him ages and JD wanted him in bed before dinner was ready.

Despite his claims to the contrary, Alexander loved bath time. He had different colour plastic boats he played with, each with a number painted on the side. JD and Sarah had used them to teach their son how to count to seven.

It didn't take long for JD to get Alexander clean and into his night clothes. He then carried him down the stairs so he could say goodnight to all the Sanctuary's residents. It took a while.

JD put his son to bed and left Sarah alone with him while she read to him. They took it in turns, both finding it an enjoyable experience.

While Sarah was reading, JD made his way to the dining room, intent on setting the table, only to find that Natalie had beaten him to it.

Natalie wasn't a hunter, though she had lived at the Sanctuary for a number of years. JD and his team had rescued her from a vampire who had used her as a blood bank for a few years and she had stayed there while she recovered. She fell in love with Craig and they married the previous year.

JD suspected she was pregnant, but didn't think it was polite to ask. When he was turned into a vampire, all his senses had been heightened, including his sense of smell, especially as far as blood was concerned. He was aware when each of the female residents were menstruating and Natalie was a few weeks overdue.

"Does anything else need doing?" he asked as she placed the last fork onto the table. She worked as a waitress at a local restaurant so she knew the best way to lay a table and had a habit of moving things to their correct position whenever anyone else did it.

"No, that's it. Unless you want to go to the kitchen to see if Silvia is ready for things to be brought in."

Silvia was married to Frank, the head of the Sanctuary. He was a fully qualified doctor so everyone called him Doc. She was short and plump and treated everyone as though they were her children. She was working as a nurse when she met and married Frank, but gave it up so she could help him run the Sanctuary. She was not from a vampire hunter family, but agreed to join the society so she could marry him.

"Need any help?" JD asked as he walked into the kitchen. The smells that assaulted his nostrils made his mouth water. Silvia did most of the cooking for the Sanctuary residents, but since Natalie moved in, she had been allowing the younger woman to do her fair share.

"You can take the pies through," Silvia said as she pulled a tray of roasted vegetables out of the oven. Two large pies sat on the countertop, steam wafting off them. They were a golden brown and traces of gravy could be seen escaping through the air-hole in the middle.

"The one on the left is beef and mushroom, the other is vegetable," Silvia continued.

11

JD grabbed a pair of oven gloves and picked up the nearest one. He passed Natalie on his way to the dining room and again when he returned to the kitchen. She had grabbed the other pie so Silvia handed him a large bowl of mashed potato.

By the time all the food was in the dining room, most of the seats in the room were occupied.

While they ate, JD looked at his friends. Every one of them had earned his trust and his respect. Doc sat at the head of the table, as always, with his wife beside him. Scott, their son, often sat there, but he was out on a date. He had met a lovely young lady while at medical school and they were both now doing their residencies, but at different hospitals. He had eventually told her about the hunter society and she had agreed to be a part of it. She was a regular visitor and now that they were engaged, JD thought it wouldn't be long before she moved in.

Sitting across from JD were Jane and Steve. Steve was a recent edition. He was from a different Sanctuary. He was dating Jane and hadn't wanted to move to 14, but JD refused to release her so he had reluctantly agreed.

As usual, Sarah sat beside JD, who watched with amusement the amount of food she was piling onto her place. She glared at him, daring him to comment. He wasn't brave enough. She was, after all, eating for two, as she kept reminding him.

Anna sat next to her and it felt strange to not have Luke there. He and Gabriel already had plans when Sarah invited all three of them over, so, for once, Anna was on her own.

Conversation flowed during the meal, as it always did, as well as laughter. They were more like a family than a group of friends and JD couldn't imagine living anywhere else.

When the meal drew to a close, nobody left the table. As the conversations continued, JD couldn't help looking at the empty seats Jonathon and Katie used to occupy. They would never live at 14 again. While they would come back and visit, as soon as they completed their training, they would be given their own Sanctuary and team of hunters. It could even be in a different country, though he hoped not.

JD's thoughts and the happy atmosphere were broken by a scream. All eyes turned to Anna, who was gripping the edge of the table, staring at nothing, as she screamed and screamed and screamed.

HE'S DEAD, ISN'T HE?

Gabriel was nuzzling Vivien's neck when his phone rang.

"Ignore it," she gasped as his hand ran down the side of her naked body.

Gabriel had no intention of turning his attention to anything other than the beautiful woman in his bed. He loved her as much now as he had all those decades ago when they first met, maybe even more. She was more than just his lover; she was his soulmate.

He kissed her, letting his tongue play with hers. He longed to be inside her, but he enjoyed the foreplay as much as she did, so he was in no hurry to satisfy his carnal desires.

The phone went quiet for a few seconds before ringing again. Almost instantaneously, Vivien's also began to vibrate. At least she had had the sense to turn hers to silent.

Sighing, Gabriel climbed off Vivien and picked up his phone. "Sarah," he said to Vivien.

"JD," she replied as she looked at her own phone.

"This had better be good," he said when he hit the green button.

"Anna suddenly started screaming and we can't get her to stop."

That got his attention. He put the phone on speaker.

"What do you mean?" he asked. "What were you doing just before this happened?"

"Eating dinner. We had just finished."

"Has she had any human blood?"

It was a stupid question, but it was the first thing that came into Gabriel's mind. Apart from her transformation into a vampire, the only time he had heard Anna scream was when she drank human blood. But she knew how it affected her, so she wouldn't be stupid enough to drink any.

Before Sarah could tell him he was an idiot, Vivien asked a more important question. "Why are you calling us not Luke?"

"I tried. Luke isn't answering."

Gabriel went cold inside. Luke always answered his phone, even while driving. He had Bluetooth so he just had to hit a button on his steering wheel. He glanced at Vivien, who nodded. She dialled Luke's number, but it rang and rang before going to voicemail.

"He left here to pick Anna up," Gabriel said. "He took my car as his is being fixed, but he should still be able to answer his phone."

"Maybe he broke down," Vivien said, "and he's looking at the engine or something so he can't hear the phone."

Gabriel could tell she didn't believe what she was saying any more than he did.

"Or maybe he's crashed," she continued.

That was a more likely explanation.

"We'll get dressed and see if we can find him." Gabriel wasn't panicking. At least that's what he told himself.

He'd never seen Vivien dress so quickly. He was still buttoning his shirt as she was putting on her shoes.

"I'm driving," she said.

Gabriel opened his mouth to argue, then closed it again. Not only would they be taking her car, but she was also calmer than he was, so her taking the driver's seat was a good idea.

They ran to the car and Vivien was pulling out of the garage before Gabriel had even closed his door. He swore at her, but she ignored him. He pressed the button to open the gate as they approached, but she still had to slow down to prevent a collision.

"You might want to go slower," Gabriel said as she pulled out of the driveway onto the road, leaving skid marks in the gravel. "We need to be able to see what's on the side of the road in case he's in a ditch or something."

She did as asked, but was still going over the speed limit. As they turned a corner a short while later, a long length of straight road stretched out in front of them. They could clearly see, about half-way down, two crashed cars. Gabriel's vampire-enhanced eyesight enabled him to recognise his own car as one of them.

Vivien had seen it too and raced toward it before slamming on the breaks and coming to a sliding stop, accompanied by a screech of tyres.

Gabriel was out of the vehicle before it had stopped moving. He raced to the driver's side and pulled on the badly dented door, but it wouldn't budge. He looked in the window and froze. Luke's headless body sat in the driver's seat and his head had been placed on the dashboard.

He felt sick. Not because of what he was seeing, he had seen more mutilated bodies than that, but because of who he was seeing. His brain refused to accept that it was real.

He had killed Luke many times, knowing he would come back to life. But not this time. There was no coming back from decapitation. They had been together for over a hundred years and now he was gone forever.

Vivien looked at what Gabriel was staring at and put her hand across her mouth.

She managed to pull herself together before Gabriel did and took out her phone. She called Gavin, the head of their household, and tapped her foot impatiently while listening to his phone ring. When he answered, she quickly explained the situation.

Gabriel could hear both sides of the conversation. He had never heard Gavin swear before. It was as frightening as it was unexpected. He promised that he would get there as soon as he could. They would have to collect the body; they couldn't risk any humans finding it.

Gabriel was still staring at his cousin's corpse. He was as still as a statue. Vivien told him Gavin was on his way, but he didn't respond. He couldn't make himself speak.

She checked the other car, but there was no sign of the other driver. She said Gavin would give the licence plate to one of his connections to trace the owner, but Gabriel knew it would lead to a dead end. This had been no accident; it had been an ambush.

She returned to his side and placed her hand in his. When he turned around and looked at her, it felt as though he had only just realised she was there. Then he took her into his arms, buried his head in her shoulder and began to sob.

By the time Gavin and Juliette, his wife, arrived, Gabriel had stopped crying. If either of them noticed how red his eyes were, they didn't mention it. Gavin glanced into the car before placing his hand on Gabriel's shoulder. "I am so sorry."

"Where's Anna?" Juliette asked.

"At the Sanctuary," Vivien said when Gabriel couldn't make himself respond. "Sarah called us to say she was screaming and she couldn't get hold of Luke."

Juliette nodded. "She would have felt his death through their bond, but probably doesn't know what it means. Someone has to go and tell her."

"I'll go," Gabriel said, making Vivien look at him in surprise. She probably thought he wouldn't want to leave Luke's side. She was right, but there was nothing he could do and Anna needed him.

"The others are on their way," Gavin said. "We'll make sure Luke gets home and the cars towed and disposed of." He smiled, but it was not a happy smile. "Then we are going to track down whoever did this and make them wish they had never been born."

Gabriel felt like he was in a daze as he was guided back to Vivien's car and told to get in. The journey was a blur. All he could think about was Luke. There would be no more fights in the empty swimming pool, which left cracks and dents in its structure. There would be no more laughter, no more teasing of each other.

He was overcome with relief that he had found Vivien again after all the decades he had spent searching for her. Without her, he didn't know how he was going to get through the next few days. Weeks. Months.

As Vivien pulled up to the gate at Sanctuary 14 and keyed in the access code, Gabriel's thoughts turned to Anna. He had no idea how he was going to be able to tell her the news. His bond with his cousin was strong, but it was nothing compared to what Luke had shared with Anna, thanks to 'the calling'. They weren't just in love, weren't just soul mates, they were connected in a way he would never understand. They never argued, never disagreed, always did what was best for the other person as if it was a compulsion, as if they had no choice.

He had no idea how, or even if, she was going to survive. He knew what if felt like to lose the person you loved more than life itself, but he had still had hope that he would see her again one day. Anna would not have that hope. She would have nothing but the loss.

He felt numb inside as Vivien pulled up outside the house instead of driving around the back to the garage. He barely heard her telling him he had to get out of the car.

He could sense her by his side as he walked up the steps to the front door. She had to ring the bell as Gabriel's key was on the chain for his car keys, which were in his smashed car.

He looked up as the door opened and saw JD looking at him. Something in his face must have betrayed how he was feeling because instead of saying 'hello', JD said, "Oh no."

"Where's Anna?" Gabriel forced himself to ask.

"In the infirmary. Doc was forced to give her a sedative, but it hasn't had much effect."

As soon as Gabriel stepped into the house, he heard Anna's screams. Her voice sounded raw, as if it was giving out.

Unbidden, his legs took over his body and he sprinted down the corridor. Having been to the infirmary before, he ran straight there. He burst through the door and found Anna lying on a bed. Sarah was beside her. All blood seemed to have drained from her face.

"Thank God you're here," she said. "We can't calm her down."

Gabriel didn't acknowledge that she had spoken. Instead, he made his way over to the bed. Anna didn't react to his presence; he didn't think she was even aware he was there. Only when he took her in his arms did she react. She buried her face in his chest, using it to muffle her screams.

"Ssssh," he whispered. "It's going to be okay."

He was lying to her and hated himself for it. How was it going to be okay? It was never going to be okay ever again.

He glanced up at Doc, who was standing nearby. "You know the tranquilizer you made for me to give to Luke when Anna was going through the conversion?" Doc nodded. "Anna needs it now."

Doc nodded once more and set to work. He soon had a syringe filled with liquid and waited until Gabriel nodded before he lifted up the sleeve of Anna's t-shirt and injected the concoction into her arm.

It took a few minutes to take affect and the entire time Gabriel held her trembling body. Only once it went limp in his arms did she stop screaming.

"She'll sleep for a few hours now," he said. His voice sounded dead to his ears. "Though I have no idea if she will start screaming again when she wakes up."

"What's causing it?" Sarah asked.

Gabriel opened his mouth, but he couldn't find the words. It felt as though Luke's death would be made more real if he told someone.

"Maybe we should go somewhere more comfortable," JD said from behind him.

He had no idea how he made it to the lounge. The next thing he knew, he was sitting on a sofa with a glass of whisky in his hand.

He gulped it down, relishing the feel of the amber liquid burning his throat. He held out his glass and it was refilled. Only once he had emptied the glass twice more did he feel up to talking.

He leaned back into the sofa and felt Vivien take his hand in hers. It wouldn't stop the pain that what he was about to say would cause, but it did calm him a little.

"Luke is dead."

The words struck him like a blow. Even though he was just saying what he already knew, speaking the words made it more real, more final. The words couldn't be taken back, they couldn't be made untrue.

19

Sarah gasped.

"How?" JD asked. "He's a greater vampire, for God's sake. I didn't think he could die."

Gabriel smiled a sardonic smile. "Of course we can die. I mean permanently die. We don't age, we don't get sick, we come back to life if we get stabbed or shot or poisoned. But we can die. The same way lesser vampires do."

"Someone cut off his head?" Gabriel could hear the incredulity in Sarah's voice. He nodded. "How? Nobody is that good they can get through Luke's defences."

"It was an ambush," Vivien said. "Someone ran the car off the road. He may well have been unconscious when he was killed."

"Murdered, you mean," JD said. "There is no other word for it. This was murder."

"But who would want to murder Luke?"

Gabriel couldn't answer Sarah's question; he had absolutely no idea. Luke didn't have an enemy in the world. Everyone who knew him, liked him. Few people were aware he was a vampire and those who did, saw him as a friend, a colleague, someone worth knowing.

"Was it a hunter?" JD asked. "If it was, I promise you the hunter society will not protect them. We have a peace pact with your family and anyone who breaks that will be going against our laws."

Gabriel didn't answer. He couldn't answer. He heard Vivien call Gavin, heard both sides of the conversation, and breathed out a sigh of relief.

"Unlikely," Vivien said. "It doesn't look like a sword was used. Probably a big knife, based on the ragged cuts. It wasn't done by an expert, according to Brian and Cassy and they have investigated enough vampire deaths to know."

Brian and Cassy, while not related by blood to Gabriel, had lived with him long enough for him to class them as family. He trusted their judgement. If they said hunters weren't responsible, then they would need to look elsewhere.

Vivien hadn't finished with her news. "Also, he had been shot in the head, point-blank range. They think that was what killed him and whoever did it removed his head later."

"Then it was someone who knew he was a vampire," Sarah said. "Why else would he have been decapitated?"

"To send a message?" JD suggested.

Gabriel shook his head. "No. Whoever did this knew that removing Luke's head was the only way to make sure he stayed dead." He didn't know how he knew, but something was telling him he was right.

"We need to let the council know," JD said. "Even though hunters weren't responsible, they need to know that someone is out there killing vampires, so we can find them and put a stop to it. Luke may only be the first."

Gabriel hadn't thought of that. Maybe JD was right. Maybe all his family were in danger.

"Leave it with Gavin," he said. "After all, he is on the council. He will contact them as soon as he has finished processing and cleaning up the scene."

JD nodded, confirming he would not interfere.

"Is there anything we can do?" Sarah asked. "For you or for Anna?"

Gabriel shook his head. There was nothing anyone could do to take his pain away. His numbness had gone, replaced by a cold ball of tension in the base of his stomach. And there was an empty space inside him that would be there for the rest of his life.

Craig arrived, carrying Alexander, who had been woken by a nightmare. JD took his son back to bed while the rest talked about other things, anything to take their mind off waiting for Anna to wake up.

It was a few hours later that Doc escorted her to the lounge. She was pale, but at least she had stopped screaming. Her eyes scanned the room, coming to rest on Gabriel.

"He's dead, isn't he?"

Part of Gabriel was glad all he had to do was confirm what she already knew. He nodded. He couldn't make himself tell her any other way.

Her legs gave way and Doc had to grab her before she fell to the floor. He helped her onto the sofa, next to Gabriel, who took her hand, but didn't speak.

"I feel empty," she said. "As though a vital organ is missing. Something that has been inside me for years has gone."

Gabriel had thought his voice had sounded dead, but it was nothing compared to Anna's. She sounded like she had never been alive.

When she looked at him, there were tears in her eyes. "I can't go on without him," she said and the tears started to fall.

He hugged her tight as she wept, tears falling unnoticed down his own face.

How long he held her, he had no idea, but when he looked around, he and Anna were alone in the room. She had finally stopped crying and had drifted off to sleep.

He didn't want to leave her, so he manoeuvred his body so he could retrieve his phone from his pocket and sent a quick text to Vivien. Within minutes she was in the doorway, car keys in hand.

"Let's get her home," she said.

The drive home was slow. Gabriel sat in the back of the car with Anna cradled in his arms. There had been a time when he had been in love with her, before he had found Vivien once more, and he had longed to be able to hold her, but now all he felt for her was brotherly love. She and Luke hadn't married and Luke was only his cousin, not his brother, but he looked upon Anna as his sister-in-law.

She didn't wake when they arrived home and he was able to carry her to her room and put her to bed without her stirring. He assumed she was suffering from stress exhaustion. He hoped that was all it was. He would have to ask Juliette. He had no idea what the death of a bonded partner did to a greater vampire. He was about to find out.

He was exhausted, but there was no point in going to bed; he wouldn't be able to sleep.

He found everyone in the dining room. Enlarged photos were spread out on the table and Cassy was explaining them. All eyes turned to him as he entered the room.

"You should get some rest," Juliette said, but he shook his head.

"What do we know?" he asked.

He saw Cassy glance at Gavin and scowled. Gavin nodded, so Cassy proceeded to tell him all they knew so far.

"The car was stolen a few days ago from a different city, so that's a dead end. No prints, no murder weapon, no bullet casings. This looks to have been a professional hit."

"Human or vampire?"

"Human, we think. A vampire would have made a cleaner job of the decapitation. One man at the scene, at least we are assuming it was a man. But he had an accomplice, someone who picked him up."

"Do you think it was personal? Someone had a grudge against Luke? Or is it someone who is out to get vampires?" Gabriel asked.

"We have no way of knowing," Cassy said.

"But he was driving your car," Brian pointed out.

Gabriel shuddered. Had he been the intended target? Was someone out to get him instead of Luke? Was Luke's death his fault?

Almost as if she could hear what he was thinking, Vivien interrupted his thoughts. "I don't think that means anything. You can see who's driving a car, so whoever did this would know it wasn't Gabriel. Even if he did crash into the car before he had chance to see who was driving, he would have known he had the wrong person either before he shot him or just after. He wouldn't have gone ahead with the decapitation. No, this is not a case of mistaken identity. Either Luke was the target or the killer was just going after any vampire."

Gabriel couldn't tell if Vivien believed what she was saying or was just trying to make him feel better. He didn't ask her; he didn't want to know the answer.

"The other question we should be asking is how did the murderer know he was a vampire?"

It was a good question, one none of them could answer.

"I need to phone the hunter society council," Gavin said and left the room. The discussions continued, but no more conclusions could be drawn from the evidence they had. When Gavin returned, he said the council sent their condolences and would help with the investigation in any way they could.

"They also told us to be careful. If this wasn't a one off, we could all be in danger. I know we are all more than capable of looking after ourselves, but so was Luke. Whoever did this knows a lot about us. We need to take a few precautions. Nobody goes out alone, watch out for anyone following you, that sort of thing."

Gavin glanced at his watch. "It's late. We should all think about getting some rest. We need to be bright-eyed and bushy tailed in the morning, as the saying goes. Anna is going to need us more than she ever needed anyone before."

Gabriel raised a questioning eyebrow at him. He wanted to know exactly what the statement meant. It was Juliette who responded.

"I've done some research and in a lot of cases, if one of a bonded pair dies, the other one soon follows."

YOU'RE NOT THE ONLY ONE SUFFERING

Gabriel punched the side of the pool, narrowly missing Martin's head. If Martin had been a lesser vampire instead of a greater one, he wouldn't have been able to get out of the way in time. A new crack formed and Gabriel wondered when he was going to be asked to fix it.

"You can do better than that," Martin said, deliberately goading him.

Gabriel snarled. He wasn't trying to actually hurt Martin, but fighting was a good way of releasing his pent-up anger and Martin had volunteered.

Martin's sister was dating Anna's brother, who was still human, so even if he wasn't another member of the household, Gabriel would still class him as family.

Gabriel's thoughts were on Anna, as they always were these days. It had been over two weeks since Luke's death and she had hardly taken any blood from any of them. Gabriel had to almost force her to drink his blood a few days ago and even when she had finally agreed, she hadn't taken much. It was almost as if she was trying to starve herself to death.

He didn't know if it was possible for a greater vampire to die that way and he didn't want Anna to find out. He had to do something to make her want to live again, but he had no idea what.

Martin took advantage of his distraction and kicked at him. Had it landed where it was aimed, Vivien would not have been happy, but Gabriel was much faster than Martin and caught his foot before it made contact.

Twisting it around, he spun Martin's body and slammed him into the concrete floor of the pool. Had he been human, Martin would have been seriously injured, but he just burst out laughing.

Gabriel backed away, giving him time to regain his feet. He liked Martin. When he and his sister, Helen, had first joined Gavin's extended family, he had struggled to only take what he needed from humans, but with everybody's help, he had learnt to control himself.

Gabriel always thought of it as Gavin's family. He was the patriarch who had formed the group, vetting everyone before he allowed them to join. At over three hundred years old, he was the oldest and everyone believed him to be the wisest as well.

Martin ran at Gabriel, slamming him into the side of the pool. The sound of his head hitting the concrete echoed around the pool. For a moment, Gabriel was dazed, but his head cleared when he shook it. He suspected it was bleeding, but he didn't bother checking.

He smiled at Martin. He was having fun. It wasn't enough to take his mind off his loss, or his concern for Anna, but it was helping his mood.

He was about to attack Martin when Vivien called from above him.

"When you boys have finished playing, we need to talk."

He looked at Martin, who shrugged, indicating he was happy to stop, if that was what Gabriel wanted, but had no issue with continuing for a while longer.

"Thanks for the stress relief," Gabriel said and jumped out of the pool. He could easily jump twice that height without any real effort and he landed lightly on his feet.

"I'm worried about Anna," Vivien said as they walked back to the house. "She's not eating enough to keep a sparrow alive."

As a vampire, Anna didn't need to eat food, though she often did in order to keep up appearances, but that wasn't what Vivien was referring to.

"I know," Gabriel said. "She also cries herself to sleep each night."

Vivien winced. "I was hoping I was the only one to have heard that."

Gabriel shook his head. "Sweetheart, everyone in the house can hear her. We just haven't mentioned it to her in case she doesn't know."

"I think we need to take her away," Vivien said. "This place has too many memories of Luke. Everything she does, everywhere she goes reminds her of him."

"Maybe she should move into the Sanctuary for a while. I know none of the hunters would mind."

"It wouldn't help. She has a lot of memories of Luke there as well. She needs to be someplace she has never been with him."

"And you know where." It wasn't a question. Gabriel knew Vivien well enough to know when she had already formed a plan.

"I lived with a couple of greater vampires on the other side of the country at one point when I was searching for you. I've stayed in touch with them. They would be more than happy to put the three of us up for a while. There is also a large community of greater vampires nearby so there would be no worry about Anna having a food source."

Gabriel stopped walking and waited for Vivien to also do so before he spoke. "You've already spoken to them, haven't you?"

Vivien smiled at him. "You know me too well. I've explained the situation and everyone there would be more than happy to be used as a blood bank."

Gabriel thought about what Vivien was suggesting. It was a good idea. Getting away for a while might be exactly what Anna needed. It would mean the investigation would have to continue without them, but Cassy and Brian were better at that sort of thing than Gabriel, anyway.

"I'll speak to her about it," he said. He had no idea how Anna would react, but it was worth trying.

"While you're at it, you should also speak to her about Luke's ashes. Is she planning on scattering them? It's what he always said he wanted."

Gabriel grimaced. That was one topic he really wanted to avoid, but Vivien was right; the conversation needed to be had sooner rather than later.

Ever since they had been turned, Luke had always insisted that he wanted to be cremated, not buried. The hunter council had offered to hold a full hunter funeral at their church and have him buried in their graveyard, but both Anna and Gabriel declined the offer; it wasn't what he would have wanted.

Instead, they went to a regular crematorium. Many hunters attended the ceremony, not just those from Sanctuary 14. Since learning that Sarah, Craig and JD were hunters, both Luke and Gabriel had befriended many hunters from a number of different Sanctuaries, including 12, where hunters practiced hunting in the dark. Training against real vampires was a great benefit and the two greater vampires were more than happy to help out.

As soon as they got back to the house, Gabriel and Vivien parted ways. This was something Gabriel was going to have to do on his own. He went straight to what used to be Luke and Anna's room, but was now just Anna's. The thought caused Gabriel's grief to surface once more and he forced himself to push it aside.

He knocked on the door and walked in without waiting for an answer. Anna would be there; she hadn't left the room, other than to attend the funeral, since Luke had died. She had resigned from her job and was refusing to see anyone outside the family, even Sarah and JD.

He didn't care that it was impolite to enter the room without her permission; he would have been waiting forever for her to respond. She no longer spoke unless directly asked a question, sometimes not even then, and never opened the door to anyone.

She sat on the bed, staring into space. At least she was still taking care of her appearance. She showered regularly and wore clean clothes, stating that Luke would be unhappy if she didn't. Gabriel had pointed out to her that he would also be unhappy if she starved herself to death, but she insisted that was not what she was doing. She took blood when she felt the need, which she hadn't felt since Luke's death.

"We need to talk," Gabriel said and sat down beside her. He looked around the room, his eyes falling on the urn beside the bed. He took a deep breath. "It's time to scatter Luke's ashes."

"No."

He didn't know what he had been expecting her to do or say, but the outright refusal took him by surprise.

"It's what he wanted," he said.

Anna turned her head to look at him. It was the first time she had looked him in the eye since they had lost Luke.

"You have no idea what he wanted." The venom in her voice made him flinch.

"We often talked about it. He wanted his ashes scattered in the lake and you know it."

"That was before he met me. Things changed."

He should have been glad that there was finally emotion in her voice, but he wasn't. It was full of hate and he felt like it was directed at him. He did his best to ignore it.

"Not that. We often talked about it, what we wanted to happen to our bodies if we ever died. Ever since moving here he has loved the lake and only a few months ago he said it was still what he wanted."

"Get out." The words were said with such viciousness they stung.

Something inside Gabriel snapped. All the hurt and anger he was feeling, but did his best to hide, burst out of him.

"You're not the only one suffering," he yelled at her, loud enough for the entire household to hear, even Martin who was still in the grounds. "I lost him too."

He grabbed the urn and with his free hand, took hold of Anna's arm. He dragged her from the bed and pulled her out of the room. She almost fell as he went down the stairs, towing her behind him. She tried to release his grip on her, but it just made him squeeze harder. He may have been hurting her, but he no longer cared.

People rushed from all directions to see what was going on.

"Stay out of this," he shouted at Paul, Anna's brother, when he moved toward them.

"Leave them be," Gavin said to Paul before he had chance to respond.

"But—"

"I said leave them," Gavin snapped.

Gabriel was out of the front door, dragging Anna behind him, before Paul could argue.

He didn't say a word as he pulled Anna along. He ignored her protests and the nails which were digging into his hand as she tried to free herself.

Only once they reached the lake did he stop. He released her and pointed at the water.

"Do it."

"No."

"This isn't up for debate."

"I can't."

"Why not?"

"Because then I will have truly lost him. This is all I have of him. I can't just throw it away."

The pain in her voice brought tears to Gabriel's eyes. He took her in his arms and held her close while she sobbed.

"You haven't lost him," he said soothingly. "You can never lose him while he is still in your heart, still in your memories. You need to do this, Anna. You need to let go. You need to start to live again."

"But I can't. How can I live without him?"

Her tears were soaking into his shirt, making his chest feel cold.

He stroked her hair. "You have to find a way to go on. This isn't what he would have wanted. I don't know if there is a heaven. I don't know if there is any sort of afterlife. But I do know that he is watching over us both and wishing we would move on."

Anna was trembling in his arms, so he held her tighter.

"How did you do it?" she asked. "When you lost Vivien. How did you start over again?"

Though it had been a long time ago, Gabriel could still remember how he had felt, how he had fallen into a black pit of despair.

"Luke forced me to move away. To put her behind me. Not to forget her, for that was something I could never do, but to try to find something else to live for."

"I don't think I can do that," Anna sobbed.

Gabriel let go of her and stepped away, just far enough that he could raise her chin and make her look at him.

"Yes you can. You are strong, stronger than you realise. You need to spend some time away from here, somewhere that doesn't make you constantly think about Luke. If Vivien and I leave, will you come with us?"

She nodded and Gabriel pulled her into his body once more. "Thank you," he said as he hugged her tight.

They stayed like that for a while, finding comfort in each other's arms.

"Are you ready to scatter the ashes now?" Gabriel asked and felt her nod her head. He phoned Vivien and asked her to gather the family. He wanted them to be present and having people who loved Anna with her when she finally said goodbye to Luke would help her.

It didn't take long for everyone to arrive. Vivien walked up to Gabriel and slipped her arm around his waist while Paul hugged Anna.

"Are you okay?" he whispered in her ear.

"No, but I think I am going to be."

When Paul released her, Gabriel handed her the urn.

Giving him a half-smile, she took it and walked to the water's edge. She unscrewed the top and flung the contents into the air, where the wind took them and dropped them onto the surface of the water.

Nobody said anything; words were not needed. Each silently said goodbye to Luke, knowing it would be for the last time.

After a few moments of silence, Gabriel announced that he and Vivien were going away for a while and were taking Anna with them.

"Are you sure about this?" Paul asked as he took Anna's hands in his. When she nodded, he hugged her. "Then I wish you luck. Keep in touch."

"I will."

"When do you leave?" Juliette asked.

Gabrielle looked at Vivien, who shrugged. "Immediately," he said. "It will take us a few days to get where we are going. We'll

31

take Vivien's car and arrange to have Anna's shipped to us if we decide to stay for more than a few weeks."

As the extended family made their way back to the house, Vivien assured Paul that Anna would be well looked after and they would not let her out of their sight, except when she requested her privacy. They promised everyone they would make sure she got enough blood and that they would keep in touch.

Vivien and Gabriel both wrote resignation emails to their respective bosses, apologising for the lack of notice, citing the need to get away after Luke's death. If their bosses didn't like it, they didn't care; there was nothing they could do about it.

Then they packed. They packed everything, not just clothes for a few weeks. They had no idea how long Anna would need to be away, or if any of them would ever return. They didn't, of course, mention that to anyone.

Helen helped Anna pack, making sure she had clothes for all weathers. She also made sure she packed all the things which Luke had given Anna, but she put those in a separate bag so Anna could choose if and when she wanted to see them.

The car was jammed full by the time they had finished loading it up and some boxes would have to be shipped up later. Gavin promised to take care of it.

Before they left, Gabriel noticed that Anna had taken Paul aside and couldn't resist the urge to listen in. She was making him promise that he would not decide to let Helen turn him into a greater vampire while she was away and that, if that was what he wanted, when he was ready, he would give her a call so she could fly back and support them both through the ordeal.

He gave her his promise, though whether he would stick to it was anyone's guess.

Before heading to the highway, Vivien took a detour to the Sanctuary. Everyone was sad to see them go, but understood their reasons. Sarah promised to let them know about the baby when it arrived and refused, once again, to name the baby after Gabriel. He brought it up every time Sarah saw him, saying Gabrielle was a great name for a girl.

Soon they were on the road once more, heading into the unknown. Well, it was the unknown for Gabriel and Anna. For Vivien, it was a case of catching up with old friends.

During the journey, Vivien told them a little about their destination. It was a quiet town where the weather was usually pleasant and the locals were friendly. When she had stayed there, there had been over a dozen greater vampires living in the vicinity, but they didn't live together as a family like Gavin's group. She was still in contact with a number of them and most of her old associates still lived there.

"You don't need to worry about finding work," Gabriel told Anna. "Unless, of course, you want to. Luke left you enough money to last you a number of human lifetimes."

"I can't touch his money."

"Why not? Everything he had is yours. It was the moment you moved in with him."

He didn't mention he had arranged with Juliette for all Luke's clothes to be given to charity as soon as they left. Sorting through his things was something Anna had refused to let anyone do and he wasn't sure how she would react to finding out.

It took them two days to reach their destination, with both Gabriel and Vivien driving and taking lots of breaks on the way, as well as a few detours to look at the sights. They stopped twice in hotels, with Gabriel insisting they only use five star ones.

Anna seemed to be getting a little better, joining in conversations occasionally without needing to be specifically asked. But both Vivien and Gabriel heard her crying herself to sleep each night, even though she was in a different room. They thought it would be a long time before that stopped.

Gabriel took a lot of interest in the sights as they approached the town which would become their home for a while. He couldn't help thinking how much Luke would have liked how many trees and animals there were. He almost voiced his thought out loud and stopped himself just in time. He didn't want to mention Luke in front of Anna unless he had to.

The town seemed quaint, if that was the right word. He hoped he wasn't insulting anyone by saying that. There were people about, but not many. Vivien drove through what Gabriel assumed was the town's high street, as it was lined with shops, and continued into the countryside.

"All the vampires live on the outskirts," Vivien explained. "They do mingle with the humans, but prefer to keep to themselves. They tend to head toward one of the bigger towns to feed."

"Is anyone expecting us?" Anna asked. She seemed stressed. Maybe it was the thought of meeting new people, people she may have to rely on to keep her alive by supplying her with blood.

"Yes," Vivien said. "I called Will when we last filled up the car. That's who we'll be staying with. Nice enough bloke. Was turned about fifty years ago when he was in his mid-twenties. Not bad looking if you ask me."

Gabriel saw her looking at him out of the corner of her eye, so he refused to react.

"He's who I stayed with last time I was here. Him and Marie."

"I look forward to meeting him." He said 'meeting', but he meant 'assessing'. He decided to ignore the smirk on Vivien's face.

A short time later, she pulled off the road, which was little more than a dirt track, onto a driveway paved with bricks. It was straight and led to a cottage, which appeared older than Gabriel. Smoke was pouring out of the chimney, even though it was a pleasant spring day.

Vivien drove to the side of the house and parked the car inside a barn, next to a collection of others. Gabriel spotted a Ferrari, a Porsche, a Lamborghini, as well as a Mercedes and a Ford Mustang.

"Will likes cars," Vivien said.

"Shouldn't he keep these locked up?" Gabriel asked.

Vivien shook her head. "It's a safe area. Plus the barn is usually alarmed and booby-trapped. If anyone gets in here without permission, they aren't getting out again unless Will wants them to."

Leaving the car in the barn, Vivien led them to the house. Before they could get close, they were greeted by growling. Gabriel couldn't see the dog, but it sounded big.

"Oh," Vivien said, "there's also a guard dog that you don't want to mess with."

As she spoke, the largest Rottweiler Gabriel had ever seen came into sight. It had an impressive set of teeth, which it was happy to show them. Anna froze. She wasn't the only one.

"Hello Cujo," Vivien called out and the animal stopped growling. He, and it was definitely a he Gabriel noticed, turned his head to one side as if trying to decide why he recognised Vivien.

Then he bounded toward her. Gabriel was about to jump in front of her to protect her, when the dog lay down in front of her and rolled onto its back, exposing its belly.

"Meet Cujo," Vivien said as she rubbed his chest, making him whine with pleasure. "He was just a puppy when I was last here. He's every bit as vicious as he looks and is fiercely protective of this house and anyone who lives here. Once you have been introduced, that will include you."

Vivien introduced Anna and Gabriel to the dog, the former happy to give him some fuss and attention when she was given permission, the latter more reluctant to do so.

"Cujo," a voice called out from the direction of the cottage. "You're supposed to keep people out not invite them in."

Gabriel looked over and saw an average-sized man standing in the doorway. He was smiling, which suggested he wasn't as angry as he sounded.

Vivien ran over to him and threw herself into his outstretched arms. Gabriel lied to himself that he wasn't jealous. As Vivien had stated, he was an attractive man.

"Good to see you, Vivien," the man said as he put her down.

"Let me introduce you to my husband and sister-in-law." The terms weren't, strictly speaking, true as she and Gabriel hadn't bothered to get married; they saw no need.

Vivien turned to look at Gabriel and Anna and moved her head to indicate they should come closer. "Come on."

The man held out his hand to Gabriel. "I'm William, but you can call me Will. Most people do. I'm delighted to finally meet you. Vivien talked about you a lot when she stayed here. I'm glad you found each other again."

Gabriel wasn't sure if he was speaking the truth or just being polite, but he decided to give him the benefit of the doubt.

He took Will's hand and shook it. Will's grip was firm, but not domineering and Gabriel made sure his was just a touch firmer. It was petty, he knew, but he couldn't help it.

"And you must be Anna," Will said, turning his attention away from Gabriel. "Welcome to my home. You are free to stay for as long as you like."

Anna looked nervous as she took Will's hand.

"Come into the house," Will said. "I put the kettle on as soon as I heard a car pull into the driveway. Tea or coffee?"

They gave him their orders before going into the house. Will informed them where the rooms he had set up for them were.

"You're in your old room," he said to Vivien. "I hope you don't mind."

"Are you kidding? It's the best room in the house."

Will showed them into the lounge before heading to the kitchen. He soon returned with a tray full of steaming cups.

"Any changes I should know about?" Vivien asked as she picked up her cup and blew on it.

"Other than Marie leaving me, you mean?"

Vivien winced. She hadn't mentioned the split to Gabriel, so he assumed she had been so caught up in Luke's death and looking after Anna that she had forgotten Will had told her the sad news. Will sounded bitter. And a little depressed. Maybe bringing Anna here wasn't such a good idea after all.

Will straightened his shoulders and seemed to pull himself together. "Sorry. It's still a little raw. I'm fine. These things happen. We're still good friends."

The look Vivien gave Gabriel told him she didn't believe Will. Marie might be good friends with Will, but Will certainly still saw their relationship as more than that. Gabriel vaguely remembered Vivien mentioning that she thought Will always had been more invested in the relationship than Marie was. While Vivien liked her, she believed she was making do with Will, using him for a while until she tired of him. Gabriel wasn't surprised that she had been proven right.

Will took a sip of his coffee. "No, nothing much has changed. The usual births, deaths, marriages and divorces among the humans. Some have moved away. Some have moved in. Nobody exciting and nobody for us to worry about."

"What about hunters?" Gabriel asked. He had sought permission from Gavin, who in turn had spoken to the council, for him to notify other greater vampires of the existence of the hunters and about the truce which had been agreed upon. Most already knew about them and had been keeping their distance, but had then reached out to them, offering their friendship and assistance.

"Those at the local Sanctuary are friendly enough. Once we demonstrated our abilities and told them all we already knew about them, they were happy to have us as allies. We're far enough away from any big towns to attract many lesser vampires and we're more than happy to deal with those who do invade our territory."

Gabriel nodded. It was what he had expected to happen. Given how well he, Luke and the others got on with hunters, he suspected it would be the same for most greater vampires. There would, of course, be those who wouldn't approve of the peace agreement, but those sorts mostly kept to themselves anyway.

He glanced at Will and noticed that he looked thoughtful, as though he was trying to decide whether he should mention something or not.

Vivien was also looking at Will. "Spit it out."

"It's just that we have some new neighbours. They moved in about a year ago. You know the old estate down Bridge road?"

Vivien nodded. "It was some sort of boarding house or hotel when I was here."

"Well," Will continued, "it was purchased by a corporation which nobody seems to know much about. Someone appears to have moved in, but nobody has ever seen who. Cars come and go, but all have blackened windows so we can't see inside."

"Sounds intriguing," Gabriel said. "Anyone gone up to the house to take a look?"

"Some of us did when the furniture vans first arrived, rang the bell on the gate, introduced ourselves and said we were there to welcome them to the neighbourhood. The man on the other end thanked us then said goodbye. The gates never opened."

"Someone famous wishing to remain anonymous?" Vivien suggested.

Will shook his head. "I don't think so. There's something about that place. It gives off a vibe now. I feel strange whenever I'm near it, as though instead of the hunter, I have become the prey."

Vivien laughed and Gabriel smiled. Even Anna looked amused, though she remained quiet.

"Laugh all you like," Will said. "But I suggest that while you are here, you avoid the place. There are things in this world which are more deadly than even greater vampires."

Gabriel wasn't impressed. "Like what?"

"I don't know and I never want to find out."

"You're winding us up," Gabriel said, even though Will looked like he was serious.

"The walls aren't that high," Vivien said. "You could easily jump them. Surely one of you has tried."

Will leaned forward in his seat. "Once. Some new arrivals, young men who had only been turned a few years, got drunk and decided to ignore our warnings. A number of people saw them jump the wall. They told them they would shortly be back, with an account of what they found."

"So what happened when they did make it back? What wild and fanciful stories did they have to tell?"

Did Gabriel sound sarcastic? He certainly hoped so.

Will looked at him and with a strange look on his face said, "They were never heard from again."

VAMPIRES AREN'T REAL

Joseph slammed his fist down on the desk. He couldn't believe what he was hearing. He thought he had hired a professional, but first the man killed the wrong person, now he was admitting that he had lost track of the intended target.

"What do you mean you have not seen him in over a week?" he yelled into his phone. "You know where he lives. You know where he works. You even know the places he visits. How can you not know where he is?"

He barely heard Virgil's excuses. His whinny voice was getting on his nerves. He had failed in his mission and failure had to be punished. He had been lenient, giving the man a couple of weeks to correct his error, but he had failed to do so. He had become a liability, one that would need to be dealt with.

The man was an idiot. As soon as he realised he had the wrong man, he should have left him. But no, the fool killed him and then beheaded him, making sure he couldn't come back to life; not that he realised that was what he was doing. He might as well have placed a sign on Luke's body saying, 'I am out to get you Gabriel.'

The element of surprise had been lost. Of course Gabriel had gone into hiding; what sensible person wouldn't? So now he had to track him down. But first things first; he had a human to dispose of.

"Meet me in Riverside park tonight at nine," he said into his phone. "I have something that may be of use to you."

Would Virgil be stupid enough to turn up? Probably, seeing as he had yet to be paid anything and, if nothing else, the man was greedy. If he didn't, Joseph knew where to find him. Whether he showed up or not, the man would be dead by morning.

Joseph disconnected the call and dropped his phone onto the desk. He felt a pang of regret for what had happened to Luke. From what he had found out, he seemed to have been a decent person whose only crime was being related to Gabriel.

At least something good had come out of Luke's death. Gabriel was suffering, suffering the way Joseph had been made to suffer when his sister ran away from him. And why did she run away? Because of him. Gabriel. She was determined to find him again.

Still, Joseph had managed to steal her away from him once, he would be able to do so again. Only this time he would make sure he was no longer alive for Vivien to go back to.

The thought of what he would do to Gabriel when he got hold of him made Joseph smile. He had originally intended to just kill him, which was why he hired the human, but now he wanted more. He wanted him to hurt, and not just emotionally. And he planned on making his traitorous sister watch. He would make sure she had nightmares for the rest of her life. She would never defy him again.

With regret, Joseph pushed thoughts of revenge from his mind. He had work to do. He had a business to run and he couldn't afford to neglect it while he concentrated on his personal interests. He had a deal to close, but once that was done, his hunt for Gabriel would begin. And this time he would do it himself.

-----------------------∞-----------------------

Virgil looked at his phone, as though he couldn't believe what he had just heard. His client had agreed to meet with him. Something in the back of his mind told him it was a bad idea, but his pushed the thought aside. He would take a couple of his associates with him for backup. Between the three of them, they would have enough firepower to make the man hand over the money he was owed. It had been a while since they had met, so the feeling of dread the man gave him had fallen from his memory.

So what if he hadn't completed the task. He had done more than enough to receive a down payment, hadn't he? It was hardly his fault his target had not been driving the car. And how was he to know that killing the wrong person would drive his target into hiding?

He had been diligent, watching him carefully, waiting for an opportunity to finally get his prey, but the opportunity never arose. He was always with the woman and his client had made it more than clear to him that the woman was not to be harmed.

And then they had disappeared. He had no idea when they left or where they had gone. After all, he couldn't be expected to watch them twenty-four-seven.

He licked his lips. The amount of money the client had offered to pay him showed how rich the man was. Someone like that would never carry any amount of cash on them, but he would be able to access his funds through his phone and with three armed men pointing guns at him, he would be more than willing to comply with Virgil's demands, no matter how fast he could move.

Yes, he had misgivings about meeting the man at the location he had chosen, but the pay-out would be worth the risk. Besides, it was a public location. It wasn't as if he was going to meet him in an abandoned warehouse in the middle of nowhere.

Virgil phoned a couple of buddies, both of whom agreed to help him out. For a cut of the payment, of course.

The wait for nightfall seemed to last forever. Virgil was itching to get his hands on some money and then get as far away from the job as he could. Never had he failed to kill his target, but he had no intention of wasting weeks, even months, looking for him. If the client couldn't tell him where the man was, that was his problem. Virgil was an assassin, not a manhunter. The client had resources, surely he could employ someone experienced in finding missing people. If he did, then Virgil would consider finishing the contract.

Darkness descended and he drove to the park. There were a few cars in the carpark, but not many. It was too late for parents to be there with their children and there were no streetlights, not even on the running track which surrounded the park, so it was unlikely there would still be joggers. Maybe it was teenagers, having a quick romp in the dark.

It never occurred to Virgil that he wouldn't be the only one to bring backup and that the cars could be owned by friends of his client.

He didn't have to wait long before his two buddies arrived. From the smell of them, both had been drinking, but that didn't bother him. As long as they looked like they were able to shoot straight, it didn't matter whether they could or not. It wasn't as if they planned on actually hurting the guy. The threat would be enough to get him what he wanted.

The hour of the meeting was fast approaching so the two men moved into the park, positioning themselves just out of sight in the trees, where they had a good view of the carpark.

Virgil leaned against the driver's door of his car and tapped his foot impatiently. He watched a couple come out of the park, hand in hand, get into one of the cars and drive away.

He glanced at his watch. His client was late. That would cost him another ten grand. He looked over to where his buddies had hidden themselves, but he couldn't see them. They were there though, watching, waiting.

He took a packet of cigarettes out of his pocket, lit one and took a deep, soothing drag. It was a habit he should give up, but trying seemed too much effort. Maybe next year. Then again, maybe not.

He had almost finished the cigarette when he heard movement behind him. The moment his eyes fell on the man approaching him, he realised he had made a big mistake.

--------------------------∞--------------------------

Joseph watched in fascination as two men arrived, got out of their car and approached Virgil. Before hiring him, he had done his research. Joseph was a careful man who liked to know who he was dealing with before a deal was even discussed.

Virgil was a low-life with no class and no ethics. But he was reputed to be good at what he did. Not good enough, apparently.

Joseph watched the two new arrivals enter the trees where they thought they couldn't be seen. Both pulled hand guns from their pockets and checked they were loaded. Joseph rolled his eyes. As if guns were going to be any good against someone like him. They wouldn't have chance to even point their weapons at him, let alone fire them.

He thought about disposing of the two sidekicks immediately, but decided to wait. Keeping Virgil waiting was going to irritate him and Joseph was in the mood for annoying the failed assassin.

Once Virgil started to smoke, it was time for Joseph to act. He would be distracted and while Joseph believed he could dispose of the two men without making any noise, there was no harm in being cautious.

The numerous clouds in the sky meant there was no moonlight to illuminate the park, but Joseph had no trouble seeing all he needed to. He crept up behind his targets and broke their necks before they even knew he was there.

He smiled at how easy it had been. Usually he would make it last longer, would drink from them first, while their hearts were still beating, but they weren't who he was after. They were a mere inconvenience which had now been taken care of.

Looking down at their bodies, a thought occurred to him which made his smile even wider. He was going to have a little fun with Virgil.

A short while later, he walked out of the trees, making enough noise that it would be impossible for Virgil not to hear him. The look on his face when he saw what he was holding gave Joseph immense pleasure.

While the park was not illuminated, the carpark was and Virgil had parked under one of the few working lights, giving Joseph a good view as all the colour drained from his face.

Joseph raised his arm, bringing the severed head to the height of his chest before throwing it at Virgil, who instinctively caught it. Joseph watched with fascination as Virgil turned the head around to see the face, before dropping it and screaming.

Virgil took one look at Joseph before turning to his car and opening the door.

"I would not do that if I were you." Joseph didn't raise his voice; he didn't need to.

Virgil paused, but only for a second. He climbed into his car, but before he could close the door, Joseph was beside him, holding it open.

"Get out and we can have a nice chat."

Virgil was shaking, too scared to move.

"Either get out of the car or I will make you and trust me, you really do not want me to do that. Who knows how many bones I will break in the process."

With obvious reluctance, Virgil exited the vehicle.

Without warning, Joseph attacked, sinking his teeth into the man's carotid artery and injecting him with a small amount of his venom. He did it so fast, Virgil probably didn't know what he had done.

"Come with me."

Virgil obeyed, not that he had a choice. Unlike lesser vampires, greater ones had the ability to control humans. While a lot of venom would turn a human, a small amount made them a vampire's puppet. He had heard of those who kept humans as pets, using just enough venom to keep them willing. He once had a human describe it to him when he had injected her. She said it was terrifying having no control over her own actions, knowing she could be made to do something even if she didn't want to. She had been a friend, so he didn't make her do anything she would regret, but it had been an interesting experiment.

Joseph walked into the park, leading Virgil away from all signs of human activity. Once he was satisfied they were somewhere it was unlikely that anyone would see them, he told Virgil to stop.

Joseph didn't need to take any blood, as he had fed the previous day, but why not take the opportunity when it presented itself?

"Have you worked out what I am yet?" he asked Virgil, who shook his head. "Let me give you a clue. I am going to drink every drop of blood you have in your body."

Joseph didn't think it was possible for Virgil to go any paler, but somehow he managed it. He wrinkled his nose in disgust as a wet patch appeared at the front of the man's trousers.

"That's not possible," the terrified man stammered. "Vampires aren't real."

Joseph smiled, showing his fangs. "In that case I am just a figment of your imagination, this is just a dream and you are going to live through this night. Now do not scream."

He plunged his fangs into Virgil's neck once more, but this time, instead of putting venom into him, he drew some blood. He would never get used to how good blood tasted, even after all these years. He didn't take too much; he wanted to play with Virgil for a while first.

He had always planned on killing him, but it was going to be quick and painless. That was until he had found out that Virgil had brought armed backup with him. Now he was going to suffer.

He took enough blood to make Virgil weak, but not enough to do him any real harm. He was aware of hunters and that they could somehow pick up when a vampire was feeding, but he also knew how far away the nearest Sanctuary was and how long it would take them to get to the park; it was one of the reasons he chose it.

"You made two mistakes," he said as he stood back. "The first was killing the wrong man. You should have let him live, let him believe it was just an accident. The second was thinking you could betray me."

Virgil didn't move, but Joseph wasn't surprised; he hadn't given him permission to.

"Take off your jumper," he ordered. Virgil obeyed. He was wearing a t-shirt with a picture of some sort of spaceship on it. Having never watched Star Wars, Joseph had no idea it was the Millennium Falcon. That would have to come off too. He needed Virgil's bare chest for what he was planning.

It wasn't a cold night, but as soon as his torso was exposed, Virgil shivered. Maybe he knew what was coming. Joseph withdrew a knife from his pocket. It wasn't particularly large, or sharp, but it would meet his needs.

"Keep quiet and do not move."

He could see the pain in Virgil's eyes as he cut a message into his chest. Blood dripped down, staining the pale skin red.

Joseph stood back to admire his handywork. It was crude, but would do. The message would get back to those Gabriel lived with. He hoped it would draw him out of hiding.

"I could torture you some more," Joseph said, "but I am growing bored and hunters will be on their way. I plan on being long gone by the time they get here."

It was a lie. He intended to stick around and watch what happened. He was good at concealing himself and even if he was spotted, he would be able to avoid capture.

He moved closer to Virgil and sank his fangs into his flesh once more. He began to drink his blood and this time he intended to take it all.

------------------------∞------------------------

JD collapsed onto a sofa. He was exhausted. For the last few weeks he had been juggling work, training, hunts and a newborn baby and he wasn't sure how much longer he could keep it up.

Since he had been turned into a vampire, his stamina had increased, but he was still affected by the sleepless nights. To be fair, Sarah was the one to get up every time young Charlotte cried, but that didn't mean JD got much sleep. With his enhanced vampire hearing, he found he could hear his daughter every time she so much as murmured, even though she was in the next room.

He was debating whether he should force himself to do some training, or if he should have an early night, when the hunt alarm went off.

He groaned. He was not in the mood for it. All he wanted was some rest. But duty called.

Craig entered the room, took one look at JD and said, "Sanctuary 7 said they are only picking up one vampire. We can handle this without you."

JD shook his head. While Sanctuary 7 were rarely wrong in their estimation of vampire numbers, it was impossible for them to know if more were there, but weren't feeding. His team were also down on numbers. With Katie and Jonathon gone and Sarah out of commission for a while, they were down to only four hunters, if he didn't include himself, and it was too risky to send so few.

Sarah would go on the hunt, if asked, but he refused to let her. He had allowed her to start training again, but while she was breastfeeding, he would not permit her to put herself in danger.

He should replace his brother and sister-in-law, as they wouldn't be coming back to Sanctuary 14 once they had completed their training, but he couldn't bring himself to do so. It had taken him a long time to get his team to be as good as they were and having someone new join would disrupt that. Jane had only just reached the level of Craig and Scott and Steve had a long way to go. He had to concentrate on him, get him to be as good as he could be before he let anyone new join them. Yes, there were plenty of experienced hunters who would willingly join 14, but JD was the best trainer the society had ever had and his standards were far higher than any other trainer.

"Get changed," he said. "I'm coming with you."

Craig left the room and JD forced himself to stand up. He went to his room and removed his hunting gear from his wardrobe. It was made of a tough leather that protected the body, but was supple enough to not restrict movement.

He was lacing up his boots when Sarah walked in.

"The alarm woke Alexander, but he's back to sleep now." She walked up to JD and gave him a quick peck on the lips. "Be careful."

He smiled at her. "Aren't I always?"

"No, you're not. You take risks. You rely on your vampire skills too much."

He didn't argue; she was right. He took a lot more risks than he did before he was turned, but when he was human he was a lot easier to kill.

"I promise I will be careful," he said and kissed her cheek. "Don't wait up for me."

He didn't know why he bothered to say it seeing as she always did. She could never sleep when the team was out on a hunt, even if JD wasn't with them.

Craig, Jane, Scott and Steve were already waiting by the front door when he arrived, as was Doc. Doc gave them the address of the park they needed to go to and Scott and JD both grabbed keys from the bowl.

Although everyone had their own cars, they always took the plain cars on hunts. They were basic and forgettable, with fake licence plates so they could never be traced back to the Sanctuary or any of the hunters. They also contained fake driving licences for everyone, should they ever be pulled over by the police for any reason.

By the time JD, Steve and Jane arrived at the park, Craig and Scott were already there. JD made a mental note to talk to Scott about obeying speed limits.

"Spread out," he said once everyone had retrieved their swords from the cars.

They split into pairs and headed in different directions. As usual, JD went off on his own. He hadn't even left the edge of the carpark when he heard Craig calling his name.

"This is unusual," Craig said as JD approached. JD looked down at what Craig was pointing to and was forced to agree. Usually they found either dead bodies or live victims and, more often than not, vampires who needed to be disposed of. Sometimes they got to the victims in time to save them, but not often.

Never had JD found a severed head.

"See if you can find the rest of his body," JD instructed. "Then try to ascertain if he had been bitten or not. We need to know if this was the result of a vampire attack. If there's no sign of vampire activity on the body, then we should leave it for the police."

Craig nodded and he and Scott headed off. JD examined the head more closely, checking the teeth for any sign of fangs. This was a human not a vampire, so he had no idea why he had been beheaded. It looked like a knife had been used, though he couldn't be sure. It made him think back to Luke's death and he wondered if there could be a connection.

It didn't take Craig and Scott long to find the body. There was another one alongside it, this one with his neck broken. One pistol lay on the ground while another was in the hand of the man whose body was still intact.

"No sign of bites, but I wouldn't rule out it being a vampire," Scott said. "We all know how easily they can break someone's neck."

"What do you want us to do?" Craig asked.

"Nothing, for now. Let's see what else we find, then we can decide."

He said 'we', but the decision would be his.

He headed off to look for Jane and Steve and found them in the center of the park, where a playground was located. Between swings and slides was a roundabout and it was this the two hunters were looking at. It was still turning and something was laying on it.

"We were just about to call you," Steve said as JD walked up to them.

As the object came into view, JD could see it was another body. He stopped the roundabout from turning and moved closer to the corpse.

The man wasn't wearing a shirt and a message had been carved into his chest. JD gasped when he saw it. He quickly examined the man's neck and found the puncture marks made by fangs. There were two sets. Either there had been more than one vampire or the victim had been bitten twice by the same one. Either way, the marks weren't small. They could have been made by an inexperienced vampire, but JD didn't think so. Whoever had attacked this man had wanted it known that he had been bitten.

"There may be more than one vampire," JD said, "and they are probably still here. Roundabouts don't keep spinning for long. Search the rest of the area, but be careful. I have a feeling they know we are here. They may well be watching us."

49

He wasn't worried about his team's safety; they were experience hunters and always assumed that vampires were still in the vicinity. Still, there was no harm in reminding them.

Once they had departed, JD took out his phone and called Sanctuary 1, who were always on-call to dispose of dead vampires or their victims. No hunting team ever left behind a human who had been drained of blood. He told them there were three human victims; he didn't believe the other two were unrelated. He let them know there were no signs of any vampires, yet, but that his team were still looking.

Sanctuary 1 had a number of vans which were made to look like mortuary vehicles, so if they were pulled over by the police they wouldn't wonder why there were dead bodies in the back.

Nobody asked how the bodies were disposed of, just in case they didn't like the answer.

Next he called Gavin, who answered on the second ring.

"I was called on a hunt," JD said into his phone. "You may want to get down here." He gave the details of exactly where 'here' was.

"Why?" Gavin asked.

"One of the victims has a message carved into his chest. It says, 'I killed Luke'."

I AM HIS MUSE

Anna looked out of her bedroom window and sighed. There were trees as far as the eye could see and the sun was just beginning to set behind a mountain in the distance, but she couldn't enjoy it. She missed Luke. Every waking moment she thought about him. Part of her was missing. She had a hole inside her that nothing would ever be able to fill. Some days she wondered why she was still alive when there was nothing worth living for.

She had only been in her new home for a few days, but already she believed moving there had been a mistake. Being away from everything that reminded her of Luke wasn't helping. She didn't think anything ever would.

She found herself thinking of ways to kill herself, which wasn't easy for a vampire, especially a greater one. Gabriel hadn't managed it and he had tried many different ways when he had first lost Vivien. Poison, drowning, stab wounds, bullets, nothing would cause her to stay dead. The only thing that would work was removing her head and she had no idea how to go about doing that.

She considered trying to contact the local Sanctuary to see if they would assist, but as soon as Gabriel had told JD where they were, JD had contacted them to explain the situation. They would be of no help to her.

She could always get them to hunt her down. Maybe they would kill her before realising who she was. But that would involve attacking a human and that was something she couldn't bring herself to do. She wouldn't be able to drink their blood, so she wouldn't appear on the hunters' radar. She could still remember the agony she had experienced when she tried to ingest human blood and she was not going to put herself through that again, not unless her death was guaranteed.

"Thinking about killing yourself again?" a voice asked from behind her, making her jump. She had been so engrossed in her thoughts she hadn't heard Gabriel enter the room.

She turned around and saw him smiling at her, but it was a knowing smile rather than a happy one.

"How could you tell?"

"I could see the look on your face in your reflection in the window. I've seen that look many times, though not for a while, and mostly it has been when I was looking in a mirror."

"How are you coping so well?" Anna asked.

Gabriel sat on the bed. "I'm hurting, a lot, but I'm doing my best not to show it unless I'm alone or with just Vivien. I've found physical exertion helps. Will's woodshed is full to overflowing and he has started giving it away to his friends."

"Killing trees helps?"

"I take my anger out on them. And before you say anything, yes I am planting a new one for every one I chop down."

"Do you think it will help me?"

Gabriel took one of Anna's hands and turned it over so he could see the palm. "Your hands are too soft and will blister. You'll have to think of something else. Let's start by going for a run."

Anna didn't feel like doing anything, especially running, but Gabriel was doing a lot for her and she didn't want to disappoint him.

"Okay." If he could hear the reluctance in her voice, he didn't say so.

He left her alone so she could get changed and met her by the front door a few minutes later.

As soon as they were out of the house, Gabriel challenged her to keep up. He took off, going so fast that to human eyes he would be a blur. She felt like going back into the house, but he would track her down and drag her out.

Sighing, she ran after him. There were running tracks covering a lot of Will's land and she had no problem finding Gabriel. He had stopped not far from the house and looked as if he was deciding whether to go back and look for her or not.

Without saying anything, he took off once more. Anna had no trouble catching him and ran past him, yelling at him that he would have to do better than that.

She should have known he wasn't going full speed and he soon raced past her. He pushed her to go faster than she had ever been before and nearly an hour later, when they finally made it back to the house, she was exhausted.

It wasn't until she was doing some stretches in the front garden that she realised that, just for a while, she hadn't thought about Luke.

Part of her felt guilty, but most of her was glad. She had been able to enjoy running without thinking, but now that was over and the weight of her loss came crashing back down.

She thanked Gabriel before going for a shower. She was drying her hair with a towel when there was a knock on the door. She called out, giving Gabriel permission to enter, but it wasn't Gabriel who walked in.

"When did you last eat?" Will asked.

Anna liked Will. He was one of those people it was impossible not to get along with. He was inquisitive, but not intrusive, friendly, but not overbearing. He seemed genuinely pleased to have visitors in his home and made them more than welcome.

On top of that, he was a great cook.

But it wasn't food he was talking about. He was aware of her problem with human blood and that Gabriel and Vivien had been complaining that Anna wasn't taking enough of their blood to keep a sparrow alive, seeing as they said it not only in front of her, but in front of Will as well.

"Yesterday," she said, but she wasn't sure if she was telling the truth.

"Liar," he said, but he was smiling as he said it. He held out his arm to her, showing her his exposed wrist. "I can't remember the last time someone drank my blood."

Anna shook her head. "I'm not hungry."

"Irrelevant."

"You sound like a Borg." She had no idea if he was a Star Trek fan, but his grin widened, suggesting he got the reference.

"You need to keep taking blood."

Again she shook her head. "I'm fine."

The smile dropped from his face. "You are far from fine. You are starving yourself. Even I can see that. Is this what Luke would have wanted?"

Anna gasped. She wouldn't have been shocked for Gabriel to say something like that to her, but Will didn't even know Luke; he had no idea what Anna was going through. He had no right to talk about Luke at all.

She opened her mouth to shout at him, but it wasn't Will she was angry with; it was Luke. For leaving her. For making her suffer. For dying. It wasn't his fault, but she was still angry with him.

She burst into tears. The next thing she knew, she was in Will's arms and he was whispering over and over again how sorry he was for what he said.

It took a while, but eventually she stopped crying. Wiping her eyes on her sleeve, she told him there was nothing for him to apologise for; what he had said was the truth.

She opened up to him, telling him about her anger and how unreasonable it was. It felt good to get it off her chest. It wasn't something she could say to Gabriel or Vivien; they would hate her for blaming Luke.

Will sat quietly beside her, listening but not interrupting. When she finished he told her there was nothing wrong with what she was feeling, that it was perfectly normal.

"When my girlfriend left me," he said, "I was devastated. I know it's nothing compared to what you're going through, but I found that distraction helped. I needed something to occupy my mind as well as my body and after a while I found myself thinking about her less and less. Now we are good friends."

He took her hand. "Come on. Let me show you what helped me."

He led her out of the house to a shed behind the building she had never been in. It contained a number of motorbikes. Some seemed to be in good working order, others were in pieces.

"I'm restoring bikes then selling them. Not to make any money, just to keep me busy in my spare time. I'm not saying it's something you should do, but it's what helped me through the darker times. Give some thought to whether there is anything you might enjoy doing, or something you used to do and wouldn't mind doing again."

Anna walked up to the nearest bike and ran her hand along it. It was sleek, black and shiny. She had ridden bikes when she was younger and enjoyed it. Her boyfriend at the time got her into it, but she stopped when she overheard him talking to a friend of his about how she looked like a whale in her leathers. She threw them out and never rode a bike again.

"I used to ride," she said. "When I was much younger."

"Want a go?" Anna nodded. "Let me see if any of my spare helmets fit."

He had a few on a shelf and took them down, one at a time, for Anna to try. While a couple seemed to fit her, Will wasn't happy that they were quite right. There was one left on the shelf, which he seemed reluctant to take down.

"This was Marie's," he said as he handed it over. He breathed an audible sigh of relief when it didn't fit.

"I guess we are going shopping. After you have fed, that is."

Anna hadn't forgotten that she hadn't taken the blood he had offered. The craving was becoming painful, but she liked the pain; physical pain distracted her from her emotional ones. She had hoped Will had been distracted enough to forget, but it appeared not.

He held out his wrist and she took it; she wasn't in the mood for an argument. She took from him the bare minimum she thought she could get away with, but he wasn't satisfied and refused to take her to buy a helmet until she took more.

"That's blackmail," she said.

"No, it's bribery."

Once he was satisfied, he drove her into the town, which she was surprised to find had a motorbike shop. Twenty minutes later she had a helmet, gloves, boots and a leather jacket.

"You look quite the professional rider," Will said as he looked her up and down.

Anna laughed, then immediately stopped. It was the first time she had laughed since losing Luke and it felt wrong.

"You are allowed to enjoy yourself," Will said in a serious tone. "I'm sure Luke wouldn't mind."

"You're right." The beginning of a smile tugged at the corners of her mouth.

Will placed a hand on her shoulder. "Come on. Let's get coffee and cake."

"That would be great."

Leaving Will's car outside the bike shop, they walked across the road to a café.

"This place sells the best cream buns in the state," he said as they walked in, loud enough for the girl working behind the counter to hear. She smiled shyly when he winked at her.

The array of cakes behind the counter was mouth-watering and it took Anna a while to make up her mind. The carrot cake was as delicious as it looked and she finished it before the coffee arrived, so Will ordered another slice for her.

They chatted while they ate and drank, mostly about the local people Will knew, and Anna felt relaxed for the first time in weeks.

They had just started on their drink refills when a couple entered the café. Will turned around to see who it was and Anna saw his face darken. He replaced it with a smile so quickly she thought she had imagined it, but the smile seemed somehow forced.

"Will," a cheerful young lady said and rushed over to him, placing her arms around his neck and kissing him on the cheek. "This is a nice surprise."

Anna couldn't help thinking of a Barbie doll when she looked at the new arrival. She was tall and thin, with dazzling blue eyes and long blonde hair. Dumb blonde jokes ran through Anna's mind and she had to force herself not to smile.

The Barbie doll had a hint of a French accent and Anna wondered where she was from.

The look on Will's face almost made Anna laugh. He looked like he couldn't decide if he was embarrassed or excited to have this woman so close to him. Anna didn't need an introduction; Will's reaction alone told her all she needed to know.

'Good friends, my foot,' Anna thought to herself. 'She may be good friends with you, Will, but you still see her as more than that.'

Anna wasn't in the least surprised when Will said, "Anna, meet Marie."

Marie plonked down on a seat as though she had been invited. There wasn't another spare chair so the man who accompanied her stood beside her, looking awkward and out of place.

Marie ignored him and focused her attention on Anna. "You must be Vivien's friend." She held out her hand for Anna to shake. It was pale and her skin was cool. "Will told us about your little problem. Don't worry, we are more than happy to help."

Anna wasn't sure she liked her inability to consume human blood being described as a 'little problem', but the woman meant well, so she remained quiet.

Almost as an afterthought, Marie added, "This is Kurt, by the way." She flicked her hand in the man's direction, but didn't look at him. Anna glanced up and saw him frowning. She didn't blame him; Marie was being rude. She expected him to say something, but he didn't.

"Pleased to meet you," Anna said and held out her hand for Kurt to shake. He had a firm grip and was much warmer than Marie. She couldn't help wondering if that applied to his personality as well as his skin temperature.

He was tall, wide and ruggedly handsome with a strong jaw and muscles his tight-fitting t-shirt failed to hide.

"Be a dear and get me a coffee," Marie said. She was looking at her fingernails, admiring the polish, so Anna had no idea who she was talking to. "And one of those cinnamon doughnut things."

Kurt must have been used to Marie's attitude because he headed off to the counter to place her order.

"I don't know why you are dating him," Will said quietly.

"For his body," Marie replied loud enough for Kurt to hear her. "He's great in bed, but he's as thick as two short planks, as the saying goes."

Anna glanced at Will to see how he reacted to the comment. The look on his face didn't change. Anna was offended on Kurt's behalf and she wondered why Will wasn't. Maybe he was used to hearing Marie put Kurt down. Maybe he was jealous and was hiding his emotions. Or maybe he agreed with Marie's assessment. From what Anna had seen so far, she wasn't sure if Marie had any more intelligence than Kurt.

"Marie is a lecturer at the local university," Will said. "Biochemistry, or something like that."

"Bioengineering," Marie said. She sounded displeased that Will had got it wrong.

So Anna had been wrong. She had assumed that because Marie looked like a typical dumb blonde, she didn't have a high IQ. It was wrong of her to have made that assumption. She was used to people judging her by how she looked and here she was doing the same thing. She felt ashamed of herself.

"So what do you do?" Marie's voice dragged Anna away from her thoughts.

"I am, well was, an IT project manager. I quit when I came here."

"Why are you here?" Anna wasn't sure if Marie was being nosey or was genuinely interested. Either way, she was pleased Will hadn't been going around telling everyone her life story. She understood why he had mentioned her need to drink vampire blood, as she would probably have to rely on some of Will's friends at some point, but she was glad he hadn't told them everything about her, especially her reasons for leaving home.

"Her life-partner died," Will said before she could speak. She had never heard that phrasing before.

"Life-partner?" she asked.

"Sorry. It's a common phrase where I come from to refer to the person you are bonded to due to 'the calling'."

"Where are you from?" Will hadn't told her much about his past and she was curious.

Kurt returned so Will waited for him to grab a spare seat from a nearby table before responding. Anna noted how polite Kurt was to the other patrons when he asked if the seat was free, thanking them when they said he could take it. Something told her Marie wouldn't have been so nice. She would probably have just taken it without asking.

Anna chided herself. She was making assumptions again. So Marie hadn't given a good first impression, but what did that matter? She should get to know her better before deciding what sort of person she was.

"I was born in England in the nineteen fifties. I was turned when I was in my twenties and decided to travel Europe for a while. That's where I met Marie. She was still living in Paris at the time. I moved to this country just after the turn of the century. Travelled about a bit and finally settled here a few years later. Marie came for a visit about fifteen years ago and never left."

'She left me though,' his eyes said, but he didn't speak the words.

"So what do you do for a living?" So far she had not seen him leave the house long enough to go to a job, but he may have taken some time off to help her settle in.

"Will here is a famous author," Marie said. The way she said it sounded like she was bragging, or gloating, even though Will's achievements were his own, not hers.

"What do you write? Anything I may have read?"

Will seemed uncomfortable with the conversation, as though his was embarrassed about what he did. "Erotica." He went red as he said the word. "My pen name is Gemma Lovejoy."

Anna choked on her coffee. Gemma Lovejoy was the hottest author on the market and had a few number one bestsellers. Anna had read them all.

"You're kidding."

Will shook his head. "I've just finished my latest novel. It's with my editor."

"I love your work," Anna said. "I even brought one of your books with me. Will you sign it for me?"

Again Will shook his head. "I don't do book signings. I don't do promotional tours. I don't go to speaking events. So far my identity has been kept secret and I intend to keep it that way."

"Because you're a man or because of the other thing?" Anna didn't need to say what she meant by that. The waitress was approaching with Marie's drink order, so she didn't want to say the word 'vampire' out loud.

Will grinned. "Both."

Marie didn't thank the waitress, but Kurt did, earning him a smile. The young lady was cute and Anna wasn't surprised when Kurt's eyes followed her back to her place behind the counter. Marie didn't notice and Anna couldn't help wondering if she would have cared if she had.

With her mind still on Will's books, thinking about Marie made Anna realise something.

"Oh my God, you're Elise."

Will wrote historical romances with detailed sex scenes which, unlike other authors Anna could think of, were realistic and enticing. His main character was a young French woman called Elise Cadieux, who got involved with at least one different suitor each book.

"Correct. I am his muse," Marie said and twirled her hair with her fingers.

"Wow. So tell me, how much of Elise's adventures are true?"

Marie let go of her hair and looked at Anna with a serious expression. "Every single one of them."

Anna wasn't sure whether to believe her or not until she saw Will give a slight shake of his head.

"It's been great seeing you, Marie, but we really should get going," Will said as he stood up. Anna had no idea what the rush was; it wasn't as if they had any plans for the rest of the day, other than taking a couple of motorbikes for a spin, which could be delayed.

Marie turned her head so Will could kiss her cheek, but he ignored her. He nodded a goodbye to Kurt, whose attention still seemed to be focused on the waitress.

"It was nice meeting you both," Anna called over her shoulder as Will almost dragged her out of the café.

"Sorry about that," he said once they were in the car. "But I wanted to get you out of there before there was any trouble. Kurt seemed a little too interested in the waitress for my liking."

"I can hardly blame him. She was attractive and it wasn't as if Marie was paying him any attention. Besides, isn't it her problem if he is interested in another woman, not yours?"

When Will looked at her, he wasn't smiling. "That's not the sort of interest he has in her. I'm sure Marie can handle it, but I wanted to get you away from there just in case."

"Thank you. Can I ask what the issue is?"

Will started the car and pulled out onto the road before he replied. "Marie turned Kurt a couple of months ago and he's having a few problems regulating his blood intake. He hasn't killed anyone, yet, but there have been a couple of close calls. There was hunger in his eyes when he looked at the waitress, but not the sort of hunger most men would be feeling."

Anna gulped. She remembered how she had felt when she had first been turned, how she had almost attacked her own brother, but that had been before she found out she couldn't consume human blood and it hadn't taken her long to get herself under control.

"Why is it taking so long for him to learn self-control?"

Will sighed. "He isn't the sort of person who suits being a vampire. Marie should never have turned him. Don't get me wrong, I have nothing against the guy, but he was a jock. Captain of the school football team. Dated his way through the entire cheerleading squad. He could have got a university sports scholarship, but he wasn't interested. He enjoyed playing, but did it as a way to attract girls rather than being interested in the game. He was used to getting what he wanted so never had to control his urges when he was human."

"Why did Marie turn him, if you don't mind me asking? She would have known he would have trouble."

"Because she likes having a pet." Will sounded bitter. Anna wondered what had caused their breakup, but didn't want to ask.

"Sorry," he said. "Can we talk about something else?"

They chatted about what life was like for Will, growing up in England, until they reached Will's house. They went to the motorbike shed and Will told her to pick whichever one she liked. He had three ready for sale, but hadn't put them on the market yet. He had been too busy finishing his latest novel to think about it.

While Anna liked the black one, her eyes were drawn to the Ducati. It was bright red and exuded power.

Will grinned at her. "I thought you might like that one." He went to a desk sitting in the far corner, opened a draw and took out a locked box. He unlocked it and withdrew a set of keys, which he threw at her.

"It's all yours, for as long as you want it."

They changed into their riding gear and headed out. They were travelling the back roads so didn't drive at excessive speed, but for the first time since Luke's death, Anna felt alive.

WE HAVE SOME NEWS

Craig was tingling with excitement, as he always was just before a hunt. The last couple of months had been worryingly quiet, in regard to vampire attacks, but only in the area that Sanctuary 14 covered; all other Sanctuaries had been called out on a regular basis.

JD had discussed it with Gavin, who also found it odd. He sent his fellow greater vampires to investigate, but none of them could find a reason.

Not that JD had complained. It gave him undisturbed time with his wife, son and newborn daughter.

Craig couldn't help smiling whenever he thought of Charlotte. Sarah was already back at work, though she was working from home most days. Natalie and Silvia were sharing child-minding duties while Sarah worked. It was good practice for Natalie. They hadn't mentioned her pregnancy to anyone yet, and wouldn't until she was further along.

Craig was dragged from his thoughts by JD arriving. The entire team had been waiting by the front door for him. It was unusual for him to keep them waiting.

"What took you so long?" Craig couldn't help asking, grinning as he did so. JD had a reputation in the hunter society that had most hunters a little scared of him, but those who knew him well knew that, while he was strict, he also had a sense of humour and didn't mind being teased.

JD frowned. "I had just got changed and Charlotte started crying. Sarah was in the bathroom so I decided to pick her up. Big mistake. She puked all over my hunting suit, so I had to get changed again."

Craig wasn't the only one grinning by the time JD finished talking. Scott was laughing out loud.

JD growled at him, revealing his fangs. Craig thought it was on purpose, though Scott wouldn't take the implied threat seriously. While JD had used physical discipline against them in order to bring them in line, and had broken Scott's arm when he was younger, everyone was confident that he would never use his vampire abilities against a human.

"Let's go," JD said and grabbed a set of keys. Scott took hold of the other set before Craig had the chance.

"Where are we going?" JD asked as they walked to the garage.

Craig gave the address. It was a large house sitting in the middle of a number of acres. They had been there before, a few years previous, when a group of vampires had decided to move in and use it as their den. If Craig's memory served him correctly, they had rescued a couple of young men who had been there for a while, having their blood regularly drained. They had arrived too late to save a third. To the best of his knowledge, the property had never been sold and had been vacant ever since.

"How many?" JD asked.

Craig didn't need to ask how many what. Sanctuary 7 always provided an estimated number of vampires whenever they called a group out on a hunt.

"Five."

JD didn't respond. It meant the number of hunters and vampires were even, but the hunters had skill on their side. And JD. This was going to be easy.

Taking two cars, they quickly drove to their location. Craig had been expecting the gate at the top of the driveway to be closed, but it stood open, so they drove inside.

Parking in front of the house, they retrieved their weapons. Looking up at the house, Craig could see no sign of lights inside.

"I'll take Steve and Scott through the front, if you and Jane want to head around the back," JD said to Craig. "We'll take the second floor and the attic, if there is one."

Craig nodded and led Jane around the side of the house. There were no lights at the back, either, and the back door was locked. But that didn't pose much of a problem. He was efficient at picking locks and soon had it unlocked.

It creaked as he opened it, making him wince. He had just announced to anyone inside that there were intruders. Still, it couldn't be helped. And it did mean he would be able to turn the lights on, assuming the electricity was still switched on.

Fumbling on the wall beside the door, he found a switch and flicked it up and down a few times, but nothing happened. So much for having lights.

He didn't let it bother him. He had practiced in the darkened basement at Sanctuary 12 many times and was used to hunting in the dark.

He moved slowly forward. He had his sword drawn, ready for an attack. Thanks to JD, they now knew that though vampires night vision was better than a human's, it wasn't as good as they had feared. While Craig could not see much in the dark, a vampire would be able to see him, but if he was standing still, they wouldn't know if he was a vampire, human or shopfront dummy or even a piece of furniture. They would not be able to make out his hunting suit, though they would see the shape of his sword, if he was holding it in front of him.

Despite the lack of light, Craig could see that he was in a kitchen. It was large, with a table and chairs in the middle, and counter tops around two sides. A fridge stood against one wall, but the door hung open, revealing a bottle containing something which Craig assumed used to be milk, and nothing else. There were two doors in the room. One probably led to a pantry and the other to the rest of the house.

Jane and Craig split up, one going clockwise around the room, the other anti-clockwise. There was a kettle sitting in one corner and touching it showed it had not been recently used. Then again, how could it have been if there was no electricity?

Jane investigated what was behind one of the doors, confirming it was a pantry. It was empty. No food. No drinks. No cooking equipment. No vampires.

They reached the other door at the same time and Craig opened it, revealing a hallway. He could make out a number of doors in front of him. "I'll take the left, you take the right," he said to Jane. She didn't reply, but he thought he saw her nod her head.

Jane was dating Steve, but that didn't mean they always partnered up. The group didn't have regular hunting partners as it was dangerous to get used to being with one particular person.

He opened the first door he came to and then stepped back in case there was a vampire inside. Nothing came at him, so he glanced into the room. Moonlight was pouring through the open curtain, providing enough light to show he was looking at a formal lounge. The sofas looked like they were there for show, rather than comfort, and were dark, though the light was insufficient for him to be certain of the colour.

He moved slowly into the room, carefully placing one foot in front of the other, making sure one was firmly on the ground before raising the next, as he had been taught. He couldn't see any signs of a vampire in the room, but that didn't mean there wasn't one and he didn't want to be caught unprepared.

He could hear movement coming from the front of the house, followed by the creak of someone climbing the stairs. Either the rest of the team had gained entry through the front door, or they weren't alone. Either way, Craig and Jane would need to concentrate on the ground floor.

As he slowly searched the room, looking everywhere in case a vampire was hiding in one of the darkened corners, he listened for any sign of movement. He couldn't hear Jane in one of the other rooms, but he could make out three sets of footsteps coming from above him.

Other than behind the sofas, the only other place a vampire could hide was behind the curtains, which were full length. They were drawn back, but would still be able to hide a person, provided they were not too overweight.

When he was close enough, he pulled the first one aside, revealing nothing. He repeated the process on the other one before relaxing. There was nobody in the room, human or otherwise.

He sniffed the air, but couldn't detect any trace that it had recently been occupied. There was no scent of aftershave or perfume. Or blood.

Between them, he and Jane methodically checked every room. One of the doors revealed stairs which led down. Craig closed it again; the basement would be searched once they were sure there was nothing to find on the ground floor.

"After you," Craig said to Jane when he opened the basement door for the second time, indicating with his arm that she should precede him down the stairs.

She shook her head. "No, I insist. Age before beauty."

Craig grinned at her as he pulled a small hand torch out of his pocket and switched it on. The small beam didn't provide much light, but it was enough for him to safely descend the stairs.

Jane did the same, shining her light on the walls before pointing it downward so she could see where to place her feet.

Craig put the handle of the torch in his mouth so both his hands were free to use his sword, should they encounter anyone on their way down. He had practiced this many times in the past so had no problem positioning the torch so it illuminated what he wanted it to.

If there was anyone hiding in the basement, the torchlight would give away the fact that he and Jane were descending the stairs, but so would the creaking that each step seemed insistent on making, so it was prudent to see where they were going.

As Craig got closer to the bottom, the smell hit him. Blood. Either blood had been spilled while the vampires were feeding or there was at least one dead body down there.

When he reached the bottom step and had both feet firmly planted on the ground, he shone his torch around, illuminating the walls. He moved out of the way so Jane could stand beside him and she did the same.

The basement was large and they would have to go further in to find out exactly how big it was. First impressions were that it covered the entire footprint of the house.

Being underground, it was cool, but not cold. Craig's torch illuminated a wine rack, but it was devoid of bottles. Other than that, it looked like the basement had been used for storing junk.

"Be careful," he whispered to Jane. "There are a lot of places to hide down here." 'A lot of places to hide dead bodies, as well,' he thought, but didn't voice.

He wasn't looking at Jane so didn't see her roll her eyes.

Once again, they took different sides, searching each section of the room completely before moving on to the next.

It didn't take them long to find the bodies. There were eight in total. Three, obviously human, were pale enough to suggest they had been drained of blood. The other five had been beheaded, their headless corpses neatly laid out on the floor.

"What the hell?" Jane said, but Craig just shook his head; he had no idea what was going on. Who could have done this? Why had they done it? Were they still here?

It couldn't have been another hunting team as Sanctuary 7 would have let them know if they were sending other hunters.

"Keep looking," Craig said. "These may not be the vampires we were sent to kill. Or there may be another vampire here."

This time they stuck together. Neither wanted to admit that their discovery had unnerved them, but it had. They were used to finding bloodless corpses and had no problem beheading vampires, but unexpectedly finding headless bodies was a different matter.

They shone their torches around, stopping when their beams fell onto a workbench. The five missing heads had been placed there, their mouths hanging open, revealing their fangs.

"Well that answers one question," Craig said.

"Should we let JD know?"

Again Craig shook his head. "Not yet. Let's finish checking the rest of the basement."

"What do you think did it?"

"I have no idea." He noted that she had said 'what' not 'who'.

There was no sign of anyone else's presence in the basement and no more bodies, or body parts, were found. They headed back toward the stairs, but just as they got there, something came out of the darkness so quickly Craig could not make out what it was. It slammed into Jane, knocking her to the ground. Craig ran over to her, shaking her while calling her name, but she was unresponsive. He shone his light on her head, looking for signs of blood, but there were none.

He opened his mouth to call out for JD, but before he could make a sound, he felt a hand covering his mouth and a voice whispered in his ear, "You are going to do everything I tell you."

His head was pulled to one side and he felt fangs entering his neck.

Terror flowed through him, not because he was worried about being drained of blood, but because he could feel venom being injected into him. Before meeting Luke and Gabriel, the hunter society believed that any amount of venom in the bloodstream could turn a human into a vampire and the only treatment was blood transfusions. This was why every hunter regularly donated their own blood, just in case they ever needed it.

The greater vampires informed them that they were wasting their efforts. If enough venom had been pumped into a victim to turn them, there was nothing anybody could do; blood transfusions would have no effect.

However, if only a small amount of venom was used by a greater vampire, the human was in no danger of being turned, but it did make them the puppets of the vampire until the effects wore off.

Twice, Craig had experienced this. While Sarah was pregnant with her first child, she had been kidnapped by a greater vampire. Craig had been with her at the time and had been given enough venom that when ordered to forget what had happened, he had done so. He returned home, believing he had been out alone. He had no memory of Sarah being with him or who had taken her. Even after the effects wore off, his memory did not return.

The only solution was for Luke to inject him with enough of his own venom to make him remember. He had been forced to use a lot and he had almost used too much; it had been a close call. Craig could still recall the excruciating pain he had felt as dose after dose of the venom was injected into his body, yet he still insisted on having more until he was able to remember.

"You will stay silent until I tell you to speak," the voice said. "And you will not move."

Craig wanted to scream, to call out a warning to the others, but he was unable to do so. He had no idea what was going on. If this creature wanted him dead, why didn't he just kill him?

He looked at Jane's inert body on the floor, wondering if he was going to be forced to watch her die.

Almost as if he read his mind, the man said, "She will be alright. I just knocked her out. She may have a headache when she wakes, but nothing more. I am not going to hurt her." The greater vampire, for that is what Craig was certain the man was, was speaking calmly, as though they were old friends having a pleasant conversation.

Then it turned more sinister. "Unless, of course, you do not tell me what I need to know."

Craig was under no illusion that he would not answer every question he was asked. He would not be able to stop himself. He also wouldn't be able to lie. He wanted to ask the vampire what he wanted, but he hadn't been given permission to speak.

"Before you ask, yes I did lure you here. I have been watching you and your group for a while. I have seen what you do to vampires. Or should I say, lesser vampires. I am not here to stop you or get revenge. If you ask me, you are doing the world a favour. They are trash that needs to be disposed of."

That confirmed Craig's suspicions. He had no idea who was holding him hostage, but he was definitely a greater vampire and seemed to like the sound of his own voice.

"For the last few months I have been finding them and killing them on your behalf, after interrogating them, of course. But none could tell me what I needed to know, hence having to lure you here."

That was another question answered. This was why they hadn't been called on a hunt for a while; this greater vampire was doing the killing for them.

"Now, are you going to answer my questions?"

Craig nodded. Why had the man bothered to ask? It wasn't as if he had a choice.

"We do not have long, so make sure you answer quickly. How do you track vampires? I have worked out that you only seem to be able to detect them when they are feeding, but I have no idea how."

Craig had no problem answering that one. "We don't know. A different Sanctuary monitors for activity and puts out a call to the nearest team, but they keep how they do it a closely guarded secret."

In the darkness, Craig could just about see his attacker shrug his shoulders. "No matter. It is of no importance. I was merely curious."

Craig momentarily wondered what would have happened to him if the man hadn't liked his answer, but didn't have long to think about it before he was asking his next question.

"What is your connection to Gabriel and Luke?"

Craig frowned. He wanted to ask why the vampire wanted to know about his friends, but all he could do was answer the question.

"I work with them. At least I did, before Luke died and Gabriel went away." He didn't mention that they had become good friends with all the members of Sanctuary 14, or that Sarah also worked with them. He didn't say that Gavin was now on the hunter society council, nor did he mention Anna. He had no intention of giving this creature any information he didn't specifically ask for.

"There is more to it than that. You must know what they are."

Craig nodded. "They're vampires. Greater vampires to be precise."

"Yet you have not killed them."

It wasn't a question, but Craig felt compelled to speak anyway.

"We couldn't even if we wanted to. They're too strong, too fast. We wouldn't stand a chance if we went up against them."

"You are right, especially as there are so many living together. But Gabriel no longer lives with the others, so why do you still see them?"

"We've become friends. The hunter society has an agreement with the greater vampires. They leave us alone and we leave them alone. We even work together sometimes, to dispose of the 'trash'." Craig deliberately used the same word for lesser vampires as his captor had.

"So you and Luke were friends. His death must have upset you."

It was hard, but somehow Craig managed to stop himself nodding.

"Where is Gabriel?"

The question took him by surprise. He had no idea what the man wanted, but the direction the questioning had taken was completely unexpected.

"I don't know." He wondered if the vampire would believe him. It wasn't as if he could lie, but did this man know that? Would he accept his answer?

"Why did he go away? Did he know I was after him and that he should have been the one who died, not Luke?"

Craig felt his jaw drop. This was the person responsible for Luke's death? And he had been mistaken for Gabriel? If he lived through this ordeal, he would have to warn him.

"No. He took Anna away. She wasn't coping with Luke's death and he thought she would be better off being somewhere that wouldn't remind her of him."

"Who is Anna?"

"She also worked with me. She and Luke met while she was still a human and he turned her. They were bonded."

He heard a loud indrawing of breath. "The 'calling'? They were bonded?"

Craig nodded. The man began pacing the room, clearly agitated. "I did not know. I never meant for Luke to die. I knew I should never have relied on a human. I will not be making that mistake again."

He stopped and looked at Craig. "Next time you speak to her, please tell her I am sorry."

Craig couldn't believe what he was hearing. This man had arranged for Luke to be murdered and now he was sorry? Something told him Anna wouldn't forgive him.

"Craig. Jane," a voice called out from somewhere on the ground floor.

"It appears we are out of time," the greater vampire said. "Thank you for your co-operation. I just wish you could have told me more. You will be able to move and speak again as soon as your friends find you."

With that, he was gone. Craig assumed he had gone up the stairs, but he hadn't seen him move. He tried to call out, but he was still unable to speak.

Torchlight entered the room, but he couldn't move toward it. It came closer and he could see JD holding the torch.

"No sign of any vampires or victims," JD said. He abruptly stopped and looked at Craig, as though he realised something wasn't quite right. "Are you okay?"

"I am now." Craig immediately went over to Jane's still form.

"What happened?" JD asked. Craig could hear the concern in his voice.

"I have a lot to tell you. Let's get Jane to Doc. She's been knocked out, but I don't think she is seriously hurt. We'd better call Sanctuary 1 as well. There are three human victims and five dead vampires."

JD raised an eyebrow, but didn't say anything. Craig knew him well enough to know he would wait to ask questions. JD picked up Jane and carried her out of the basement. Once they were outside, Craig called the clean-up squad, giving them details on where the bodies could be found.

Scott volunteered to stay behind and wait for the van to arrive while JD drove the others home. Jane was placed on the back seat with Steve, who held her close. While JD drove, Craig phoned Doc, letting him know what had happened to Jane.

Once Jane was being cared for, JD took Craig aside.

"What happened? How did you and Jane kill all five vampires without me hearing you?"

"We didn't. I'll tell you everything, but you may want to get Gavin over here first. He is going to want to hear this."

As soon as he got JD's call, Gavin agreed to make his way to Sanctuary 14. By the time he arrived, Scott was back and Doc had finished treating Jane, who had awoken and appeared to have no signs of concussion.

73

Everyone went to the lounge, including Natalie and Silvia, eager to hear what Craig had to say. He told them everything, from the moment Jane had been attacked, to JD arriving and asking if he was okay.

His tale was rewarded by stunned looks and sounds of disbelief, not that anyone doubted what they were being told.

"Have you heard about another greater vampire being in the area?" JD asked Gavin when Craig had finished his explanation.

"No. And there have been no signs. Is it worth sending Cassy and Brian to the house you were in to investigate?"

"Probably not," Craig said. "I got the impression he was only there to kill the vampires and meet us."

Gavin drummed his fingers on the coffee table as he thought. "I wonder who he is and what he has against Gabriel. I hate to say it, but it makes a lot more sense that someone wanted to kill him rather than Luke."

Nobody disagreed with the statement. While everyone had grown to like Gabriel, he did have a habit of winding people up the wrong way, though he had changed a lot since getting back together with Vivien.

"There's only one way to find out," Gavin continued and took his phone from his pocket.

He dialled a number and waited for it to be answered. "Gabriel. We have some news."

SHE'S NOT ONE OF US

"Sorry!" Anna yelled. "He killed Luke and now he says he's sorry! He has got to be kidding. I'm heading straight home and when I get there I am going to hunt him down and make him pay."

Gabriel winced, more from Anna's tone than her words. He was regretting telling her about Gavin's call the previous evening. She had settled into her new home well and Gabriel thought she was getting better. She was drinking blood more often, taking it from the local group of greater vampires, not just from himself and Vivien. She had started to socialise, with both the vampires and the humans, and had even found a job she seemed to be enjoying.

Now her progress had gone to waste. She would be back to square one. There was no way he could let her go back home now. At least she wasn't blaming him. Yet.

He had no idea who it was who wanted him dead. Yes, he had pissed off a few people, but not enough for anyone to want to kill him and especially not a greater vampire. They didn't hold grudges. If they had a problem with someone, they dealt with it there and then. If he had caused a problem with a greater vampire, he would have known by now. He would either be dead, or they would.

"Anna, please calm down."

It was the wrong thing to say.

"Calm down! How the hell am I supposed to calm down?" She was screaming so loudly he was sure everyone in the town could hear, despite the distance.

Will came running in. "What's going on?"

"Not now, Will," Gabriel snapped. He had to focus on Anna and Will was just a distraction. Out of the corner of his eye, he saw Vivien guide Will out of the room; she would tell him all he needed to know. Gabriel kept his attention on Anna, who was pacing. He could almost see steam rising from her and her anger hit him in waves.

Not that he could blame her. He was angry himself. More than angry. At the assassin, who had killed Luke by mistake. At the vampire who had hired him. At himself.

"Anna, please. This isn't doing you any good."

His words had no effect, but he hadn't expected them to. He had no idea what he could say to make things better.

"Does he know where we are? This person who is out to get you?"

It wasn't a question he had been expecting. Was it a good sign? Was she worried about his safety? Or her own?

"I don't think so. He questioned Craig, but only JD knows where we are."

"Then maybe JD should find him and tell him."

Gabriel was shocked. "What! Why?"

"So we can flush him out. If he comes here we can be ready for him."

As his shock receded, his mind started working. It wasn't a bad idea. There were enough greater vampires in the area and they would all help out. What harm could one do against a whole group of them?

"You mean use myself as bait?" Anna nodded. "It's worth thinking about."

"Like hell it is," Vivien said as she stormed back into the room. Whether she was eavesdropping or not, Gabriel didn't know. "You are not, I repeat, not going to put yourself in that sort of danger. Do you hear me? Anything could go wrong."

"Luke would have done it for Gabriel," Anna said.

Vivien rounded on her. "Maybe, but you wouldn't have let him."

Anna glared at her before striding from the room, slamming the door behind her.

"That could have gone better," Gabriel said and attempted to smile, but his heart wasn't in it.

"I mean it, Gabriel. You don't know if this person, this vampire, is working alone. He could have an entire army of greater vampires for all you know. At the moment we are safe here and we are going to keep it that way. Do I make myself clear?"

"This isn't your decision to make."

"Fine. Have it your way. Invite this maniac here to try to kill you. Who cares who gets hurt in the crossfire. Last time it was Luke. This time it might be Anna. Or me."

Gabriel flinched. Vivien's words stung, and not only because she was right. It had been a foolish idea. Getting revenge was not worth risking the lives of others.

His response was interrupted by the sound of a motorbike speeding down the driveway.

Will walked in. "Want me to go after her?"

Gabriel shook his head wearily. All his strength seemed to have seeped out of him. He collapsed onto the sofa and hung his head in his hands.

He looked up at Vivien. "You're right. Letting him find out where we are is an insane idea. So what are we going to do?"

Vivien sat beside him and squeezed one of his shoulders. "I have no idea.

Anna was seething as she sped down the road. She was going too fast, but she didn't care. So what if she got into an accident; it wasn't as if it would kill her. She wasn't that lucky.

She hated Gabriel; it was his fault Luke was dead. She had never hated anyone before and it felt strange, wrong. Deep down, she knew her feelings would change when she calmed down. It was the man who had hired the assassin that she should hate, but it was easier to feel that way about someone she knew rather than some mysterious person she couldn't even picture.

It would have been easier if Gavin had provided a description, but it had been too dark for Craig to see him. All he could do was give an overall impression of his build, which fitted most adult greater vampires, and describe his voice, which was meaningless.

She pulled back on the throttle, increasing the speed. She was on a little used road so was not worried about meeting other traffic. It had a lot of bends in it, but she had no trouble navigating it.

A creature ran across the road in front of her. It was far enough away that she wouldn't hit it, but the thought of doing so shocked her into slowing down.

She lost track of time as she rode around, not paying attention to where she was or where she was going. When she found herself driving past a large estate, she pulled over to the side of the road. It was the estate Will had warned her about when she first arrived. She had never been tempted to see what was inside, until now.

She had been told it was dangerous, but she didn't care. What was the worst that could happen? It was unlikely she would be killed, but she could always hope.

She contemplated going up to the front gate and pressing the buzzer, but decided against it. She wanted to look around without anyone knowing she was there. She parked the bike on the grass verge, close to the surrounding wall, and removed her helmet. After putting her gloves inside it, she put it on the seat. It would be safe enough from thieves. The entire neighbourhood avoided this estate so it was unlikely anyone would stop next to it. She looked up at the wall, estimating its height, and then jumped over it. It was high enough to deter humans, but to a vampire, it was easy to get over.

She bent her knees as she landed, so it wouldn't jar her, and looked around. She was close enough to the driveway to see it on her left. On her right, and in front of her, were trees as far as the eye could see.

She could hear no alarms going off and saw no sign of movement, other than birds in the trees, so started walking, following the direction of the driveway.

She hadn't gotten far when she heard a voice to her left say, "Stop where you are and put your hands in the air."

She turned to see two men, both pointing guns at her. She smiled at them, waved, and took off, running into the trees. It wasn't as if they were going to be able to catch her.

How wrong she was. It took less than a minute for one of them to get close enough to her that she had to increase her pace. What were they? No ordinary vampire could keep up with her and if these were greater ones, why didn't they introduce themselves to Will and his friends?

She was still thinking about that when someone slammed into her from the side, tackling her to the ground. She had been concentrating too hard on the two men following her to worry about anyone else joining in the chase. It was a rookie mistake and she cursed herself. She struggled to get free, surprised that her superior strength seemed to have no effect against her captor. They must be greater vampires; there was no other explanation.

"Keep still," a female voice whispered in her ear. She decided to ignore it until she felt two pairs of hands grab her arms and the woman's bodyweight lifted off her.

"Who are you and why didn't you just ring the buzzer at the gate?" the woman asked.

Anna looked her up and down. She didn't look like she was anything special. Of average height and build, she was no Olympic bodybuilding champion. Anna should have been able to get away from her, so why hadn't she been able to?

"She's not one of us," one of the men holding her arms said.

Anna had no idea what the comment meant, but it seemed to confuse the woman.

"What the hell is she then?"

"There's only one way to find out."

Anna didn't like the way the man was grinning.

The woman nodded. "Let's take her to Elias."

Anna struggled, but the grip the men had on her was too strong. Had she been human, they would have been leaving bruises. The woman led them through the trees and the two men followed behind her. Anna went along willingly; she had the feeling that if she didn't, they would drag her or, more

79

humiliatingly, carry her. She had no idea who Elias was, but she would meet him standing on her own two feet.

It didn't take them long to reach the house, which was so large it could only be called a mansion. The woman opened the door and walked in without knocking. She made her way down the corridor to a large oak door and knocked.

"Come," a strong voice sounded from within.

"I have the intruder," the woman said as she walked in.

"And why are you not dealing with her?"

"Because I don't know what she is."

Anna was pushed into the room, which appeared to be an office. A tall man, who she assumed to be Elias, sat behind a desk, his eyebrows raised as he looked at the woman. He ignored Anna.

"Explain."

"She's fast. Almost as fast as us. But she isn't one of us."

"Interesting." Only then did the man turn to look at Anna. "Sit." He pointed to the chair on the opposite side of the desk to him and something told her arguing would not be a good idea.

Once she was seated, he glanced at the two men and the woman. "You may go."

If they were concerned about leaving their boss alone with her, they didn't show it; they merely obeyed his command, shutting the door behind them.

"Look at me." His voice was compelling, rather than harsh, and she found herself obeying once more. She should have been scared, but she wasn't.

He was an attractive man, with neatly trimmed brown hair and the greenest eyes she had ever seen. She found herself gazing into them, unable to look away. There was a fire in his eyes which made her feel like he was reaching down into her soul, assessing her.

"What are you?"

"I'm a greater vampire," she immediately answered. She hadn't wanted to, but she was unable to stop herself. Was this how a human felt when they had been injected with venom in order to be controlled? She had no idea. Not only had she not asked, she had never used her venom on a human. Seeing as she couldn't drink their blood, there was no point. She didn't even know if she could produce any.

"How did you make me answer you?" At least she still had some control over herself.

"My kind have the ability to control others. Humans, our own kind. And, it appears, vampires."

"Greater vampires," Anna said. She had always hated the snobbery, the way greater vampires looked down on lesser ones as though they were beneath them, yet here she was correcting a stranger when he called her just a vampire. She felt hypocritical.

"My apologies." Elias smiled at her. It was a friendly smile and she found herself warming to him. Until she remembered that he was controlling her. "What is the difference, if you don't mind me asking?"

What difference did it make if she did mind? It wasn't as if she had any choice about answering. She told him everything she knew, from the fact that, unlike their lesser brethren, greater vampires didn't age and couldn't have children, that they were stronger, faster and better in every way. She even told him about being able to control humans with their venom and described the process of being turned.

When she had finished, he said, "So greater vampires are a lot like us in many ways."

"What are you?"

"We'll come to that. First tell me more about yourself and why you are here."

She told him everything. He seemed fascinated. At one point he made her stop and took her to the kitchen, where he made coffee. The bond she had with Luke intrigued him and he asked many questions about it. This should have upset her but, seeing her distress, he forced her not to feel sorrow and, for the first time since his death, she was able to say his name without feeling any pain. Elias warned her it wouldn't last long.

When she finally stopped talking, he knew everything about her, the greater vampires she used to live with and those who she had now befriended. He knew about lesser vampires and those who hunted them and everything about all those who lived at Sanctuary 14. If he meant them harm, she had just told him everything he needed to know to destroy them.

But she didn't feel threatened by him. She suspected that, despite her vampire powers, he would be able to kill her easily, but she also thought that he had no intention of doing so.

"More coffee?" he asked.

Anna accepted the offer. She had no idea what beans he used, but he made the best coffee she had ever tasted.

She remained silent as he worked, watching as he moved about the kitchen with a kind of grace she didn't expect from such a large and imposing man. He was rich, based on the size of the house and the estate, yet he didn't appear to have any servants. He had people who worked for him, but not in a domestic capacity.

"Let's go to the lounge," he said as he handed over a steaming mug. "It's much more comfortable."

Anna wasn't sure if she had a choice, but saw no harm in following him. The lounge was large and tastefully decorated, but there were no personal items to be seen anywhere. No family photos, no knickknacks, no awards or trophies. Everything looked like it was in the room to make the room look good rather than because it held any personal meaning to the owner.

The sofa was comfortable and Anna found herself relaxing.

Elias kicked off his shoes and stretched out his legs, placing his feet on the coffee table. "As you have been so gracious as to tell me about yourself and vampires, I should return the favour. But let me assure you, while your tale may seem fanciful and far-fetched to some, my history is even more unbelievable."

He had a strange way of speaking. It was almost as if he had been brought up in Victorian times. She was soon to find out how wrong she was.

"My name is Elias Brandon and I am nearly six hundred years old."

Anna spat her coffee across the room. "You're kidding," she said when she stopped choking.

"No. I was born in 1434, I think. It was around then, anyway."

She had heard of greater vampires living for a long time. Gavin was over three hundred, but Elias had just told her he was nearly twice that. She couldn't even begin to imagine what it was like to live that long.

"How? What are you?"

"The official term is a neophyte, but many witches used to call us soul eaters. Some still do. My brother and I prefer to use the term 'infected'."

"Infected? Infected with what?" If there was an 'infection' you could catch that let you live forever, Anna was sure that a lot of humans would be interested in getting it.

"It's a curse, really. When my mother died, my father became obsessed with not dying and leaving me and Nick orphans. A witch said she could help him and turned him into a neophyte. He couldn't die, unless his heart was destroyed, but he needed to feed off others in order to live. He had to take their life force. By the time he found out that he didn't need to take so much his victim would die, it was too late. He had turned into a monster who enjoyed killing."

Anna shuddered. She envisioned a man placing his hand on someone's head and drawing an invisible force from them, slowly draining it as their body collapsed in on itself, leaving behind a desiccated corpse. She had seen far too many movies, she decided. Reality couldn't be like that, could it?

"How do you take someone's life force?"

Elias smiled at her, revealing fangs, not unlike her own. "We inject them with an enzyme. This allows us to draw a little of their life force. The witches thought we were taking someone's soul, hence they called us soul eaters."

"But you don't?" Anna felt stupid for asking as soon as the words were out of her mouth.

"Of course we don't. Souls, if they exist, are not the same as life force."

"So how did you become infected?"

"My father infected both my brother and I against our will. It was a very painful experience. Personally, I have never infected anyone. My brother has, but that was for personal reasons and he has never forced it on anyone."

"The people who brought me here. They're infected with this disease as well?" Elias nodded. "And there's no cure?"

He shook his head. "Unfortunately not. If there was, Nick and I would have taken it a long time ago. Some witches are trying to develop something, but so far, with no success."

Anna had a lot of questions about witches, but they would have to wait; she wanted to know more about Elias and neophytes.

"How many are there? Neophytes, I mean."

"Hundreds of thousands. They are in every country around the world."

Anna was shocked. If there were so many neophytes going around attacking people and stealing their life force, how had it never made the news headlines?

Her thoughts must have shown on her face. Elias chuckled. "You're wondering why you have never heard of us. How has the fact that we steal people's life forces never come to the attention of the authorities? That's simple. We can control people, remember. We can make them forget."

Anna went pale. If these people were that powerful, what crimes could they commit and get away with?

Elias chuckled again. "It's not as bad as it sounds. We have strict rules, which have to be adhered to. No infecting someone without authorisation, no taking someone's life force against their will, no controlling someone, except in an emergency, no killing, except in self-defence. The usual sort of thing. Oh, and if someone is injured, we can heal them. That is the only time we are allowed to give someone our blood. If they don't have our enzymes in their body, it will kill them."

Anna's head was spinning. There were so many questions that had to be asked that she didn't know where to begin.

"Heal them?" she asked lamely.

"Yes. Drinking a little of our blood heals wounds."

This was going too far. Given her own history, she had been willing to believe what Elias was telling her, but now she felt he was making fun of her.

"Bullshit."

Elias didn't seem bothered by her outburst. "Actually, I'm telling the truth. Look, why don't I show you? Though I have no idea if it will work on vampires."

"What are you suggesting?"

"Let me bite you and then you cut yourself before drinking my blood. You'll see what happens."

She wasn't sure she wanted to and was surprised to find there was no compulsion to do so. Elias was no longer controlling her.

"What if I refuse?"

Elias shrugged his shoulders. "Then a demonstration won't be possible. Currently, there are no humans living or working here. Even my chef is one of the 'infected'."

So he did have servants after all. For some reason, that surprised her. Curiosity overruling caution, she asked for a knife. She momentarily wondered why Elias carried one on him when he took one from its holder on his belt, but pushed the thought aside.

She held the knife against her arm, but he told her to stop. "I have to give you my enzymes first."

Before she had chance to protest, he moved closer to her and bit her neck. She didn't have time to pull away before he moved away from her. She hadn't felt him take any of her blood or inject anything into her.

"You may proceed," he said, indicating toward the knife with his hand.

Taking a deep breath, she cut her arm. It was long, but not deep, and she winced as she did it. Elias handed her a box of tissues so she could clean the knife before she gave it back to him. Blood was flowing and she used another tissue to wipe some off; she was worried about it dripping onto the light beige carpet.

He was about to use the knife on his own wrist when he looked up at her and grinned wryly. He held it out to her instead. "Help yourself."

She was nervous as she took hold of his hand. How would she react to his blood? He wasn't human, after all, so it might not cause her any pain.

Bracing herself, she allowed her fangs to extend before biting down on his wrist. The blood flowing into her mouth was exquisite, as it always was. She swallowed, relishing the metallic taste before taking some more.

It was hard, but she forced herself to stop and pulled away from Elias. She looked at her arm and stared at her wound, watching the blood flow lessen and the cut begin to close itself. Soon there was nothing to show it had been there, not even a scar.

"That's not possible," she said as she traced her fingers along her arm, seeing if she could feel any evidence of her wound. She couldn't.

Elias winked at her. "Anything's possible, didn't you know that?"

Anna sat back and regarded him. All her doubts about him had vanished. The demonstration had shown her he wasn't lying, at least not about his blood being able to fix injuries, so did that mean everything else he said was true? Were there really a group of people out there who were more dangerous than vampires? And if so, what did that mean for Anna and her friends? There was only one way to find out. Ask.

"You said there were rules. Who enforces these rules?"

"My brother and I." He tilted his head a little to the side, as though he was remembering something. "And the witches, I suppose. When my brother killed our father—"

"What!" she exclaimed, cutting him off.

"Long story. I'll tell you another time. Anyway, I took over as leader and made everyone sign their loyalty to me, literally. The paper was enchanted, so they are now bound to follow the rules. I travelled the world, tracking down every 'infected' and gave them the choice of signing or dying. Most chose to live. I now spend most of my time here, but do travel a lot to make sure there is nobody I missed."

Anna said nothing. This man was even more dangerous than she had realised if he would destroy his own kind in order to make them obey him.

Elias hadn't finished explaining. "As soon as they sign, a symbol appears on their arm. If they break the rules, it glows red and they have to go to myself or Nick to make it stop. We will only do that if we agree the rule breaking was justified."

"And if they don't come to see you?"

"We let the witches hunt them down and kill them."

Anna shivered. This man was ruthless.

"How many 'infected' are living here?" she asked, just to break the silence that had invaded the room.

"Only a handful actually live here, but there are a lot in the area. Our main headquarters is down south, on my brother's estate. Speaking of brothers."

He stopped talking and pulled his phone out of his pocket. He selected a stored number and held it up to his ear. Anna could hear it ringing the other end before a man answered.

"Hey Nick," Elias said into it. "Do you remember once when Sophie wouldn't let you into her house as she thought you were a vampire and you told her vampires don't exist?"

She heard Nick confirm that he remembered the occasion.

Elias winked at Anna and said, "You lied."

DON'T MAKE ME KILL YOU

Elias glanced at the woman sitting in the passenger seat of his car. She looked nervous, though he had no idea why. After his initial control over her had worn off, he hadn't bothered to renew it. She was now doing everything willingly.

Her visit had shocked him. How could vampires exist without him knowing, without the witches knowing? His brother had been equally surprised to hear the news. Ethan, Nick's step son, had been visiting when Elias had called, along with the witch he had married. Emma confirmed she had never heard about the existence of vampires and had called the head of her coven, who took some convincing that what Elias had told Emma was true.

So here he was, in the car with something that should not exist, on his way to meet more like her. Would his kind and hers come to an understanding, or was a supernatural war on the cards?

He wasn't worried about the outcome. If conflict did arise, he was confident the 'infected' would be the winners. But that didn't mean he didn't want to avoid any unpleasantness. Now that the two groups knew about each other, it would be impossible to forget what they had found out, but they could form some sort of truce, like the greater vampires had done with the hunters.

He barely gave the hunters a thought. They were well-trained, organised and knew how to kill vampires, but they were still only human. They wouldn't be a match for his kind. If there was a fight and they decided to get involved, they would die.

A lot depended on this meeting. Unlike the 'infected', greater vampires didn't have a recognised leader, so it wasn't as if it would be a disaster if it went wrong, but it would gauge how meetings with others were likely to go.

"What are you nervous about?" he asked as he glanced at Anna once more.

"I have no idea how anyone is going to react. I was warned to keep away from your estate and not only did I ignore that warning by trespassing and then revealing to you everything I know about vampires, but now I am taking you to meet them."

He could have lied to her and told her everything was going to be fine, but the truth was he had no idea how things would turn out.

"You could always say I made you bring me with you."

She gave him a scornful look. "I do not lie to my friends."

'No,' he thought. 'You just ignore what they tell you and neglect to tell them things. Would you have told them you had been to my estate if you weren't taking me to visit them? Somehow, I think not.' He thought the words, but didn't say them. They would only antagonise her and he seemed to be getting on well with her, so far. The last thing he wanted to do was get on the wrong side of her before he had met her friends.

She directed him to drive through the town, if that's what it could be called, and out the other side. Anna lived on the outskirts, far enough out for privacy yet close enough to quickly drive there should she need anything.

As he pulled into the driveway, he looked around, but couldn't see any sign of anyone watching his arrival. He was instructed to pull up in front of the house, but still nobody arrived to investigate who the visitor was.

"You still have time to change your mind," he said before he got out of the car. "I can take you back to collect your bike and nobody will ever know I was here."

"I'll know," she said and got out of the car.

She went to the front door and opened it without looking behind her to see if he was following.

"Will, are you home?" she called out as she walked into the house.

The house looked cosy, with a real fireplace. It was a warm day, so there was no fire going, but Elias could imagine how nice it would be to have one in the evenings. It was one of the things he missed about no longer living on Nick's estate.

He was still looking around the room when a man walked in, drying his hands on a cloth. He was shorter than Elias, but not by much. Elias couldn't help thinking he would look better when he got older and his light brown hair began to turn grey, to match his eyes. Then he remembered that he would never age.

"I was just washing up," he said and came to a halt when he noticed Elias.

"Will, this is Elias."

Elias walked up to him and held out his hand. "I'm pleased to meet you. I've heard a lot about you."

Will had a bemused look on his face as he shook it. "All good I hope." He threw a questioning look at Anna, as though expecting her to give him a clue as to who Elias was and why he was in his house.

Elias saved her the trouble. "Sorry to barge in like this, but I thought it was a good idea to meet now that I know your kind exist."

"My kind?" Will asked, raising an eyebrow.

Elias smiled. This was going to be fun. "Vampires."

Will laughed, but it sounded forced. "Vampires? Vampires don't exist. Everyone knows that."

"Really? That's not what Anna's been telling me."

Will glared at her and she looked away, her face going bright red.

"Don't blame her," Elias continued. "She didn't really have much choice. I had her under my control, so she had to obey my every command."

"Who exactly are you, if you don't mind me asking?" Will's tone of voice suggested he didn't believe what he had just been told.

"I'm sorry, did I forget to mention that? I'm the owner of the estate you told Anna to keep away from."

He found it strangely satisfying to watch the colour drain from Will's face.

"May I sit down?' Elias made sure he didn't show his fangs; Will looked frightened enough as it was. Despite his reputation, which was well-earned, Elias was no longer a violent man, except when he needed to be in order to keep the 'infected' in line, but he wanted to assess Will before letting him know that.

"Of course," Will said, though something told Elias he would have preferred it if he just left.

He took a seat on a sofa and waited until both Will and Anna had sat down before speaking.

"I am not your enemy," he began, but Anna interrupted him.

"Wait. There are others who should hear this."

She took out her phone and selected a contact. She tapped her foot against the bottom of the sofa while she waited for her call to be answered.

"Gabriel, where are you? We have a visitor you really need to meet."

Elias was aware who Gabriel was and was looking forward to meeting him. Anna had told him Gabriel had been a bit of a player until he settled down with Vivien. Elias, too, had slept around a lot, with both sexes, until he tried to make a go of things with Mike. It hadn't worked out, but Elias had yet to fall back into his old ways.

He didn't hear the reply, but when she hung up, Anna said, "They are in the grounds and will be here shortly."

The room was filled with an uncomfortable silence while they waited. Will kept glaring at Anna, which Elias felt was unfair.

"Don't look at her like that," he snapped, making Will flinch. "I have the power to control people. Would you like me to demonstrate?"

He didn't mention that he hadn't forced Anna to bring him to see Will. He didn't like lying to people and avoided doing so when he could, so he made sure he phrased his words so Will thought he was there against Anna's will even if he didn't actually say that was the case.

"No thank you." The words were polite enough, but the cold tone with which they were delivered showed that wasn't the intention.

"I'm not here to cause you any harm," Elias said.

Will grunted. "Is that what you said to the three young vampires who decided to take a look at your property not long after you moved in?"

91

Elias frowned. He didn't know what Will was talking about. "Until I spoke with Anna, I had no idea vampires existed. None have invaded my estate, to the best of my knowledge."

"Yeah right." Will then described them and a memory surfaced in Elias's mind.

"They were vampires? We all thought they were human. We had no problem capturing them as soon as they came over the wall. My men found them in a heap on the ground, giggling like schoolboys. I like my privacy, so I decided to get rid of them. I took control of their minds and told them to forget they had even climbed the wall. They were escorted to the gate and I ordered them to leave and never come back."

"So where are they? Why has nobody seen them since?"

"I have absolutely no idea."

Elias was telling the truth, but something told him Will didn't believe him. A quick glance at Anna showed him she, on the other hand, did.

Silence descended once more, only to be broken a few moments later by the front door opening. Two figures walked in, hand in hand. The infamous Gabriel and Vivien, Elias assumed. Anna confirmed the assumption by providing introductions.

Gabriel walked up to him and held out his hand. When Elias shook it, he took a mental note of how firm his grip was. This was a man who was used to being the most dangerous person in the room. Well that was about to change.

Elias looked him up and down, taking in his good looks and fit body. He could see how he could be a womaniser, but he did nothing for Elias. He had been expecting a more predatory feel about him. Maybe Vivien had softened him.

He turned his attention to the lady in question, kissing the back of her hand when she held it out to him. He could see what Gabriel saw in her. Not only was she beautiful, but her eyes held strength and intelligence.

"I am delighted to meet you both," he said as he released Vivien's hand.

"Who are you and why are you here?" So Gabriel wasn't one to beat around the bush. Elias liked that in a person. Direct and straight to the point. Anything else was a waste of time.

Elias explained who he was and was pleased that neither Gabriel nor Vivien seemed as concerned as Will was. Maybe they believed he was no threat to them, or maybe they were prepared to get to know someone before making snap judgements.

"You don't seem scared of me," he said. "Unlike Will here."

Gabriel smiled. "What is there to be scared of? Vivien and I are more than capable of looking after ourselves. Besides, Anna isn't scared so there's nothing to worry about. Also, there are four of us and only one of you."

Elias knew that wouldn't make a difference, but didn't say so.

"The only reason Anna isn't scared is because he's controlling her somehow," Will said.

"Actually, that isn't true. I could be, but I'm not. At least not at the moment. I'll admit I forced her to tell me everything about you, but right now she is free to act however she pleases."

Gabriel took a seat and pulled Vivien down onto his lap.

"Fascinating," he said. "I've never heard of a greater vampire being able to control another one before. How much venom do you have to use?"

"None. I'm not a vampire."

Vivien and Gabriel both stared at him. It was Vivien who found her voice first. "So what are you then?"

Elias told them everything he had told Anna, and more. He told them how he had been unable to contain his urges for centuries, killing people to keep himself alive. He held nothing back about the monster he used to be and by the time he had finished, Vivien was looking as pale as Will.

Gabriel, on the other hand, wanted to hear more.

Elias spoke of the 'infected' civil war, when he and Nick had taken on their father, how the infected had either chosen to join them or had been forced to side with their father. He told them about how he and his brother had formed an alliance with the witches, whose mission was to destroy all 'infected', and of the truce that had been declared once his father was dead.

"That's an interesting story," Gabriel said when Elias finished. "You make out that the 'infected' are even more powerful than us greater vampires."

"That's because we are."

"Are you ready to prove it?"

Elias liked this man. He was confident, maybe even a little arrogant, but was prepared to back it up. He didn't just tell people how dangerous he believed himself to be, he was happy to demonstrate.

"Of course. What did you have in mind?"

"My cousin and I used to fight in an empty swimming pool." Gabriel turned his attention to Will. "I don't suppose you have anything like that on your grounds, do you?"

Will shook his head. "No, but there is a clearing among the trees that you can use, as long as you promise not to cause too much damage."

"You're not seriously going to attack each other are you?" Vivien asked Gabriel, who was grinning with excitement.

"Of course. What's the worst that could happen?"

"I don't know. Maybe he'll kill you." Gabriel shrugged his shoulders, as though it was of no consequence. "Maybe you'll kill him and the other 'infected', as he calls them, will come here for revenge and slaughter us all."

"Will they?" Gabriel asked, raising an eyebrow at Elias.

"My brother probably would, but seeing as you have to either destroy my brain or my heart in order to kill me, I can't see that being an issue. And I do mean destroy. Remove my heart from my body and I will still live. I have personally put a heart back into a friend and he revived the next day."

He wasn't trying to brag or scare Gabriel; he just wanted him to know the facts.

Gabriel turned to Vivien. "See. There's nothing to worry about."

Vivien looked far from convinced. Will looked terrified and Anna seemed bored.

Elias stood up. "Shall we?" He indicated with his arm that Gabriel should lead the way.

"I'll stay here," Anna said. "I've seen enough fights between Gabriel and Luke to know I don't want to see him fight again."

Gabriel grinned at her before turning to Will. "You'll need to show us the way."

Will seemed reluctant to do so, but eventually he stood up. He led them out of the house and into the trees behind it. It took them a while to arrive at the clearing he had been talking about.

"Good luck," Vivien said to Gabriel and kissed him on the cheek. She then turned to glare at Elias.

"No removing of heads."

He smiled, put his hand over his heart and bowed. "You have my word."

He watched Gabriel move to the centre of the clearing and stretch his muscles as he prepared for the fight. Elias didn't bother. He wasn't planning on even building up a sweat.

"Ready whenever you are," Gabriel called out and Elias walking into the clearing. Gabriel charged at him. He was moving so fast he would have had him on the ground before he had even seen him start to move, had he been human. But to Elias it seemed slow. He stepped out of the way at the last moment and Gabriel sailed past him. Vivien gasped and Will started swearing.

Gabriel went for Elias again, this time faster, but again Elias avoided him. For his next attack, Gabriel changed direction at the last moment, throwing a punch at where Elias's face should have been, but once more Elias managed to avoid him.

"You're fast, I'll give you that," Gabriel said.

He was standing close to Elias and kicked at him before he finished speaking, aiming for his groin. This time Elias held his ground, blocking the kick before it made contact.

Gabriel threw everything he had at him, punching and kicking with such speed the two combatants were just a blur. Elias blocked them all.

Gabriel growled and let his fangs drop from his gums. Then he took off, out of the clearing, running fast. Elias stayed where he was, looking around him, waiting for the next attack.

Gabriel came at him from behind and jumped up at the last moment, hoping to grab Elias's head and force him to the ground, but instead Elias hit out, sending Gabriel's body flying into one of the trees. Vivien and Will both winced, but for different reasons.

"Gabriel," Vivien called out.

At the same time, Will shouted, "Don't damage the trees."

Gabriel stood up, shaking his head as though clearing it. "That was fun. I'm impressed."

"Want to end this now?" Elias called out, making Gabriel grin.

"Of course not. I'm just getting warmed up."

He attacked once more, but Elias was ready for him and moved out of the way.

Gabriel tried again and again, but failed to hit him. At no point did Elias fight back.

"I've had enough of this," he said and the next time Gabriel got close enough, he grabbed hold of his throat, picked him up and slammed him to the ground with enough force it would have killed a human. He held him in position while Gabriel struggled.

Gabriel tried to remove Elias's hand, but was unable to prise his fingers away from his throat. As he tried to breath, he thrashed about, hoping to dislodge him, but Elias's grip was so strong he couldn't get any air into his lungs.

"Do you give up?" Elias asked. Gabriel was unable to move his head or speak, so he moved his eyes from side to side, indicating he didn't.

"You can't get out of this. Don't make me kill you."

Gabriel glared at him, refusing to submit.

Elias called over to Vivien. "Is he always this stubborn?"

"Yes," came the reply.

"You will accomplish nothing by dying," Elias said to Gabriel. "I know you will come back to life, but what will be the point? Now do you surrender?"

This time Gabriel moved his eyes up and down, so Elias reduced his grip, allowing Gabriel to breath.

"Say it," Elias demanded.

"I give up," Gabriel said. He didn't speak loudly, but both Will and Vivien heard it.

Elias stood up and held out his hand to Gabriel, which he took. Elias helped him to his feet.

"Are all 'infected' that fast and strong?" Gabriel asked.

"No. My brother and I exceed them all, but most would still be able to beat you."

Nothing more was said until they arrived back at the house, where Anna was waiting for them. She looked both Gabriel and Elias up and down, taking in Elias's unruffled appearance and Gabriel's dishevelled one.

"Do I need to ask who won?"

"No, you don't," Gabriel growled.

"Tell me," Vivien said. "You said witches kill 'infected'. How?"

"They have spells which immobilise us and exploding bullets. A lot of witches have protectors and they are exceptionally good shots."

"How do I get in contact with witches?" Gabriel asked. "I think I might need to get hold of some of those bullets."

Elias burst out laughing. "Gabriel, something tells me we are going to get along well."

THE SANCTUARY IS UNDER ATTACK

Craig was about to kill the queen alien, which would win him the game, when an alarm went off. It distracted him enough to let the queen kill his avatar instead. Thirty minutes of play had just gone down the drain, but he had more important things on his mind. It wasn't the hunt alarm which was going off; that sound meant someone had jumped over the wall and there was only one thing that could do that. Vampires.

"The Sanctuary is under attack," Scott yelled out as he ran into the room.

"How many?"

"So far, there seems to be only one."

Only one? That was odd. What good did a lone vampire think it could do against a Sanctuary full of hunters? Maybe he or she didn't know where they were. Then again, maybe they did.

"Get your gear on and grab your sword," he instructed. "I'll find JD."

He ran up the stairs and knocked on the door to JD and Sarah's bedroom, but received no reply. He tried the nursery next door, but that, too, was empty, other than Charlotte, asleep in her cot. How the alarm hadn't woken her, he had no idea.

Then he heard voices coming from the bathroom. He knocked and JD told him he could enter. Sarah had Alexander wrapped in a towel and the look on her face suggested she and JD had been having a 'discussion'; at least, that was what they always called it when they argued in front of the children. Craig had never heard them raise their voices at each other when their kids could hear and marvelled at how pleasant they could keep their voices while disagreeing with each other.

"Tell him I will be needed out there," Sarah said, looking pointedly at Craig.

"Oh no," he said as he backed out of the room. "I'm staying out of this one."

"How many are there?" JD asked him.

He felt like pretending he didn't know as admitting that the sensors had only picked up one would give fuel to JD's argument that Sarah should not get involved.

But he had never lied to JD since he took over as his trainer and he wasn't going to start now.

"Only one, so far," he said, wincing at the look Sarah shot at him. She may be his best friend and they were as close as any platonic couple could be, but JD was his trainer and that overrode any loyalty he had to her.

JD turned to her. "Put Alex to bed in the nursery and then get into your gear. Grab your sword." Sarah's face lit up, but JD soon wiped the smile off it. "You are not going out there. Your job is to guard the nursery. If, by some miracle, a vampire gets in here, you are going to stop it getting to our children."

Sarah wasn't going to argue. It was her trainer talking to her, not her husband, and she always obeyed her trainer.

"Are the others getting ready?" JD asked him. Craig nodded. Scott would have told them. Not that they would have needed telling. Instinct would have made them drop what they were doing and get changed into their gear.

By the time Craig had collected his sword and put on his hunting gear, Sarah had taken up her position outside the nursery door. JD ran up the stairs and handed her her sword.

"Don't let anything happen to them," he said and kissed her on the cheek.

"I won't."

Neither of them showed any sign of concern because there was no need to worry. Only once had the Sanctuary been attacked and, despite the large number of vampires, the hunters had prevented the house being invaded. This time there was only one so it was going to be easy.

Scott, Steve and Jane were waiting by the front door when JD and Craig arrived. Natalie was also there. Unlike Sarah, she looked scared.

JD placed his hand on her shoulder. "There's nothing to worry about. We'll go out, find the vampire and kill it. We'll be back before you know it."

She nodded, but didn't look convinced. Craig put his arms around her and pulled her into a hug. "Listen to JD," he whispered. "When has he ever been wrong?"

He kissed the top of her head before releasing her.

"Lock the door behind us," JD said. "And don't open it again unless one of us is on the other side."

It was just a precaution, a precaution that none of them believed was necessary.

"Let's go."

Following JD's command, Jane opened the door and the five hunters left the house. Craig heard Natalie shut and lock the door behind them.

Without waiting for instructions, they split into three groups. Scott and Craig went left while Jane and Steve went right. JD went straight ahead. There was no need for him to tell them what to do. They were experienced hunters and the fact that this time they were hunting in their own back yard made no difference.

It was still twilight and there was going to be a full moon, so Craig could see well enough to do what needed to be done. He and Scott kept close together, their eyes scanning all directions, including up in the trees. That was how JD had been turned. Two vampires had jumped down on him from tree branches and had injected him with their venom before he had chance to fight back. Since then, it had become standard practice to look up, as well as around.

Scott and Craig slowly made their way around the house. They would keep moving in the same direction until they reached the back of the house and then they would turn back again and search further away. Jane and Steve would be doing the same thing. It was the most efficient way to cover all ground.

JD would be going wherever he thought best. He didn't need a partner to watch his back and could quickly reach any of them if they called out for his help.

Scott and Craig were nearing the back of the house when Scott tapped Craig's arm to get his attention. He had been looking behind him and when he saw what Scott was pointing at, he almost swore at him.

Steve and Jane were standing, looking at the house. He was about to call out to them when he realised what had caught Scott's attention.

They were both standing still, not looking around them for a potential attack. And neither had their swords drawn. Something was wrong, very wrong.

Craig looked around, scanning everywhere, but could see no sign of anyone else in the vicinity. He debated whether to call for JD, but something told him the vampire was close by and he didn't want to announce his location, just in case he hadn't been seen yet.

Scott signalled toward Jane and Steve with his head, asking if he should investigate. Craig nodded. He was sure it was a trap and they were being watched, but they had to find out what had happened.

He stayed where he was, watching Scott approach them. He was being careful, moving slowly as he scanned his surroundings.

Out of nowhere, a blur crashed into Scott and he stopped moving. Whatever had attacked him disappeared. Craig watched in disbelief as Scott put his sword back into its scabbard. Like Steve and Jane, he turned and stared at the house. It was eerie, reminding him of a scene from the Blair Witch Project.

A shiver went down Craig's spine. They must be dealing with a greater vampire. Either that or their attacker was something they had never encountered before.

There was only one rogue greater vampire in their area that they were aware of and that was the one who had killed Luke, the one who had bitten Craig and made him answer his questions.

Whoever or whatever this creature was, he must know that Craig was there, so there was no point in being cautious any longer.

"JD," he called out, hoping his voice would carry far enough. "It's a greater vampire."

At least he had done his best to warn JD. He then backed up, slowly stepping back until his back came into contact with brick.

He now had less space in which to fight, but at least nothing would be coming at him from behind.

He continued to scan the area, looking for any sign of movement, while he thought through the situation. This greater vampire didn't want them dead, or they already would be. So what did he want? Craig had already told him all he knew and the vampire didn't appear to be asking the others any questions.

He saw movement in front of him, in the treeline, and focused his attention there. It was a mistake. The attack came from the side. Craig was bitten, injected with venom and his attacker had moved out of the way before he even had time to register his presence.

Craig recognised the man standing in front of him, smiling at him. Another shiver went down Craig's spine. He was a hunter; vampires didn't scare him. But this one did. He was fast, perhaps even faster than Gabriel or Gavin. And he was ruthless, as Luke's death demonstrated. Whatever he wanted, Craig had no doubt that he was going to get it. Their only hope was JD, but what chance did a lesser vampire have against a greater one?

"Put your sword away then stay there and don't move until I tell you to," Joseph ordered. "And don't speak unless I give you permission."

Craig had no choice but to comply.

Without moving his head, he glanced over at Scott. Was he feeling as scared as Craig was? He was too far away to see his face clearly enough to know.

A sound caught Joseph's attention and he swung around. JD had stepped out of the trees and was casually walking up to him. Craig held his breath. What was he up to? Why was he letting him know he was there? Why didn't he take the creature by surprise? But he already knew the answer to that question. JD was smart enough to work out that he wasn't fast or strong enough to catch a greater vampire unaware, so he didn't bother trying.

"You must be Luke's murderer," JD said casually. "I've been looking forward to meeting you."

He stopped walking before he got too close, placed the tip of his sword on the ground and leaned on it. To any other observer, he would have appeared relaxed, but Craig knew he was inwardly tense, ready to move in whichever direction he needed to.

"An unfortunate accident. You just cannot get the help these days. It seems even hired killers make mistakes."

"Why are you here? What do you want from us?"

Craig couldn't believe JD was asking that. Did he really expect to receive an answer?

"I need to borrow your hunters for a while. Do not worry, I will not harm them. I promise to bring them back to you in one piece."

Craig had released the breath he had been holding and breathed in sharply when he heard Joseph's words. What could he possibly want him and his fellow hunters to do that he couldn't do himself? And would he be able to live with himself if he was forced to do it?

"Over my dead body," JD said and moved position so he was standing with his legs apart and slightly bent, his sword held out in front of him. He was preparing to fight. Didn't he realise he didn't stand a chance?

"An unfortunate choice of words," Joseph said and launched himself at JD. He was too fast for JD to defend himself and Craig watched in horror as the creature took hold of JD's head and twisted it to the side, breaking his neck.

Craig couldn't breathe as he watched JD's body slump to the ground.

His attacker turned around and looked at Craig.

"Do not look so worried. We both know he will come back to life. It is not as if I have permanently killed him."

He smiled, revealing his fangs. "All of you, come with me," he called out and started to move toward the front of the house. The four hunters followed him.

They congregated in front of the front door and Craig's stomach sank. He knew what was about to happen.

"Get them to open the door."

He didn't want to speak, but he couldn't stop himself. He knocked on the door and called out, "Natalie. It's me. Open up."

He wanted to scream as he heard the lock turning, but he couldn't.

"Hello, my dear," Joseph said as soon as the door was open and went for Natalie's neck before she could react. "Go the lounge and sit down. Do nothing for the next hour."

Craig watched as Natalie walked away. He saw the terror in her eyes and felt helpless. There was nothing he could do to protect her.

Joseph turned to address Steve, Jane and Scott. "Stay here. Craig, you are coming with me."

Craig glanced at the lounge as they passed it, but Natalie had closed the door.

"Who else is in the house and where are they likely to be?"

Doc and Silvia were out for the evening, so that only left Sarah. And the children. Craig began praying that they weren't this man's target. He couldn't live with himself if anything happened to them.

"Only Sarah. She is upstairs with the kids."

"Lead the way."

Never had Craig wanted to do anything less, but he wasn't given a choice.

Once he reached the top he could see Sarah standing in front of the nursery door, her sword held out in front of her.

"Craig, what's going on?" If she was scared, she was hiding it well.

Craig wanted to tell her, but he couldn't. He wanted to yell at her to get inside the room and lock the door, but there was no lock and, even if there was, he didn't think it would keep the vampire out for long.

"I am going to borrow the hunters for a while," Joseph said. "I promise I will not harm them."

"Who are you?" Sarah asked.

"You do not need to know that."

"Where are the others?"

"Outside, waiting for me. Do not worry. They are fine. Under my control, but unharmed." He shrugged. "Other than JD, of course. My venom will not work on him, so I had to kill him."

Sarah paled, but her sword arm remained straight. The vampire must have seen her reaction. "It is not permanent. He will come back to life."

"You are not coming near my children."

Joseph smiled. "I have no intention of doing so. I just want to make sure you do not send out a warning or let anyone know what has happened until I have finished my business."

Sarah opened her mouth, but Craig didn't find out what she was going to say. Joseph rushed at her, bit her neck and injected his venom.

"You will not call anyone. You will not speak to anyone other than your children until the hunters return. You will go into the nursery and stay there, unless you need something for your children. Now go."

Sarah obeyed. The look on her face when she looked across at Craig told him how much she wanted to attack. He knew just how she felt.

Joseph turned to Craig. "Come. We have work to do."

Before Craig was led out of the house, he was instructed to pick up his car keys. As he walked toward the garage, the other three hunters fell into step alongside him.

"You are going to drive us all to where Gabriel used to live."

And that was what he did. He fought against the compulsion, but to no avail. As he pulled up outside the gate, he was instructed to ring the buzzer and ask to be let in.

It was Cassy who answered and she had no concerns about opening the gate.

Craig was nauseated as he drove down the driveway. He felt like he was betraying his friends by delivering the man responsible for Luke's death to them. He wasn't a religious man, but that didn't stop him praying that enough of the greater vampires were home to overcome his captor.

He was ordered to pull up outside the house and everyone got out of the car. Cassy opened the door as they approached and was killed before she had chance to greet them.

"Wait for me here until I call you," Joseph said before he walked into the house.

Craig heard nothing. No called out warnings, no exclamations of surprise, no sounds of a struggle. He could only assume the vampire was systematically working his way through the house, killing everyone inside. He hoped their heads weren't being removed and that, like JD and Cassy, they would come back to life.

"Come in," Joseph's voice called out and Craig was forced to obey. "And shut the door behind you. I am in the dining room. Oh, and bring the dead woman with you."

Craig picked up Cassy's body, cradling it as if she were still alive. When he entered the dining room, he saw Brian, Martin and Juliette sitting in chairs. From the angles of their heads, he assumed their necks had been broken.

"Place her in a seat."

Craig did so, as gently as he could. She was dead, temporarily, so could not feel anything, but that made no difference to Craig.

"I have been told that Helen and Paul have gone away for a few days and Gavin will be back shortly, so make yourselves comfortable while we wait."

None of the hunters moved. They were more comfortable standing, ready to react, should they be given the chance. The vampire shrugged his shoulders, indicating he didn't care whether they sat or not. All four of them were glaring at him with undisguised hatred. None of them seemed scared, though Craig suspected they were. But they were hunters; they would not let their fear show.

They didn't have to wait long before they heard a car on the driveway and a short time later, a key in the front door.

"Now the show begins. I want each of you to stand behind one of the dead bodies. Draw your swords and place them against their necks. If I tell you to, you will behead them."

-------------------------∞-------------------------

The house was eerily quiet when Gavin entered. Something felt wrong, but he didn't know what. Craig's car was parked in front of the house, so he was aware they had visitors, but there should have been the sound of conversation from somewhere in the house.

"Is anyone home?" he called out, but received no reply. A cold feeling went through him. The lack of response was troubling.

Still, everyone might be outside somewhere, though Gavin found that unlikely.

He put his keys in their usual place and slowly walked down the corridor. He debated whether to go upstairs, but decided to check the ground floor first.

Each room he checked was empty. The dining room door was closed, which was unusual, so he turned the handle and stepped back, prepared in case anything sprang out at him. When nothing did, he chided himself for being foolish. It wasn't as if anything would attack him in his own home.

He strode into the room and stopped dead when his eyes took in the scene. Most of his family were there, all dead, their necks broken. A hunter stood behind each of them, swords at their throats, ready to cut. None of them looked happy to be there. Tears were flowing down Jane's face.

On the only other occupied seat was a man Gavin had never seen before. He had his legs stretched out in front of him, his feet casually placed on the table. Had Juliette been alive to see it, she would not have been happy.

"Who are you?" Gavin asked.

Joseph swung his feet off the table and placed them on the ground. He leaned forward as he spoke.

"That question is irrelevant. What you really want to know is why I am here and why your family is being held hostage by hunters."

Gavin didn't acknowledge that the man was right. He refused to give him the satisfaction. "I'll ask again. Who are you?"

His question was ignored. "I want to know where Gabriel is and you are going to tell me."

Gavin smiled. Whether this stranger had realised it or not, he had, in fact, answered his question.

"So you're the man who caused Luke's death," he said. "Which makes you a greater vampire." He casually looked around the room, keeping the anxiety he was feeling from showing. "So why are you relying on humans to do your dirty work? Not able to do it yourself?"

Joseph glared at him. "I find it amusing to use lesser beings, to force them to do things against their will. Besides, this way I get what I want without a fight."

Gavin raised an eyebrow. "Is that what you think? How old are you?" Like a good wine, greater vampires improved with age. Ascertaining how old this man was, was a good way of gauging his strength and speed. Gavin guessed he was old, based on the fact he had manged to kill everyone else in the house, but he wasn't sure which of them was the older.

"I was born in the eighteen hundreds," he said. It was a smart answer, only narrowing his age down to within a hundred year range, but it was all Gavin needed to know. Even if this man had been born in the year 1800, he was younger than Gavin. But would age give him enough advantage to get his family out of the situation without any of them dying?

"A mere toddler then," Gavin said.

His goading didn't appear to bother the other man. "Compared to some, perhaps, but not many. Now we should cut the chat and get down to business. Are you going to tell me where Gabriel is or am I going to have to start executing your friends and family? Should I start with your wife?"

Gavin looked toward Scott, who was holding his sword against Juliette's throat. He looked like he wanted to vomit. Gavin had no doubt he was there against his will and if this man forced him to kill his captive, Scott would never forgive himself. Gavin was confident he would be able to get Juliette away from him before the 'kill' order was given, but what about the others? He couldn't rescue all four.

He decided to give the vampire what he wanted, sort of. He didn't know where Gabriel and Vivien had taken Anna, though he was aware that JD knew.

"I can't tell you where Gabriel is because I don't know. All I know is that they took Anna to stay with some of Vivien's friends. I have no idea where. I have no idea when she met these friends or how long she stayed with them. They didn't say and I didn't ask."

It was mostly the truth. Gavin wasn't an accomplished liar and he hoped the fact didn't show.

"I think you might want to reconsider your answer. Scott, when I say go, remove Juliette's head."

The look of horror Scott gave Gavin was heart breaking. With his eyes, he was pleading with him to comply, to tell the man what he wanted to know. Anything to stop him having to commit murder.

"Wait," Gavin called out. "I'm speaking the truth. I cannot tell you what I don't know."

Joseph looked at him, as though assessing him. It was taking everything Gavin had to hold himself together. When the assessment was over, the vampire must have believed him because he said, "Very well. Give me your phone."

Gavin complied, taking his phone from his pocket and throwing it across the room. The man caught it, switched it on and then sighed in exasperation. "Code."

Gavin told him the six digit code needed to unlock the screen and watched as he scrolled through. He didn't need to know whose number he was looking for. He was momentarily confused when the man took down two numbers instead of one. Then he realised that the other one must be Vivien's.

Joseph held up Gavin's phone. "Thank you for this." He threw it back and Gavin caught it. "I have managed to trace Vivien's movements from the last moment I saw her, which is how I ended up here, so tracking her and Gabriel down should not be a problem. Now I have their numbers, I can have a trace put on them. Thank you for your help."

109

Gavin wondered what would happen now that Joseph appeared to have what he wanted. Would he leave or would he kill everyone, just for the fun of it?

"Who are you and why do you want Gabriel so badly?"

"He took something from me and I intend to get it back."

"What?" Gavin asked.

Joseph ignored him, instead turning his attention to the hunters. "In five minutes you will put away your swords and step away from your hostages. Once you have done that, you will be free of my hold on you."

Gavin heard each of the hunters exhale. Relief? Probably. He had never seen hunters look scared before, but these four had been terrified, not for their lives, well maybe a little, but mainly about what they were going to be forced to do.

It was the longest five minutes of Gavin's life. He could imagine the hunters all felt the same.

How they knew when the five minutes was up, he had no idea, but all four of them put their swords away at the same time before sagging in relief.

Craig was the first to speak. "I am so sorry."

Gavin waved away the apology. "It's not your fault. You weren't given a choice. You didn't stand a chance against him. Where's JD?"

"Dead." Gavin paled, but his colour returned when Craig said, "Not permanently."

"Everyone else is alright?" Craig nodded. "In that case, I am going to put the kettle on. You all look like you need caffeine. Or something stronger. Then I will have a phone call to make."

I WANT YOU TO TURN ME INTO A KILLER

"Gavin, how are you?" Gabriel asked as he answered the phone. He had been debating whether to tell anyone about the soul eaters and the timing of Gavin's call made him wonder if he could read minds.

"Not good," Gavin said. "You may want to take a seat for this."

"Is this something Vivien and Anna should hear?"

Gavin confirmed it was so Gabriel placed his phone in the middle of the coffee table and put it on speaker. Will was in the room with them, but he was being kind enough to let everyone stay with him, so Gabriel would not keep things secret.

"We've just had a visit from the greater vampire who is responsible for Luke's death."

Gabriel glanced at Anna, wondering if he should ask her to leave, but decided against it. If Gavin didn't want her to hear what he had to say he would have said so.

Gavin proceeded to tell them everything that had happened, from the attack at the Sanctuary to Joseph killing all the greater vampires and getting the hunters to hold their bodies hostage.

Nobody spoke until he finished.

"So he's definitely after me then," Gabriel said.

"It appears so. And he is prepared to go to almost any length to get to you. Though he doesn't appear to be a psychopath. He could have permanently killed us all, and the hunters, but he didn't. He just used everyone as bargaining chips."

"Did he say who he was?" It was a long shot, but Gabriel thought it was worth asking.

"No, but he did say you have taken something of his that he wants back."

Three sets of eyes turned to look at Gabriel.

"That must narrow things down a bit," Vivien said, with a grin on her face. "While I can understand the list of people you have pissed off enough for them to want to kill you being long, those you have taken something from must be a lot shorter."

"Unless it's his wife," Anna said, earning herself a glare from Gabriel.

"He also knows you, Vivien," Gavin said. "I had to tell him something, so I said you had taken Anna to stay with an old friend. He seemed to think that he could track you down and said he had arrived at my place because he had followed your trail from when he had last seen you."

Gabriel looked at Vivien and didn't like the look on her face. For the first time since he had known her, she looked scared.

"Describe him," she requested.

Gavin did so and by the time he had finished speaking, Vivien had gone white.

"Joseph," she whispered. There was no pleasure in her voice, just a grim acceptance.

"Your brother?" Gabriel asked and she nodded. "Shit."

"Would someone care to explain?" Will asked.

While Will knew a lot about Vivien's history, he didn't know everything. She didn't like talking about her brother, so she rarely spoke of him. Gabriel saved her the trouble.

"I may have mentioned it was Vivien who turned me, but I'm not sure. We were happy together for a long time and then suddenly she disappeared. I spent decades looking for her, but to no avail. I assumed she had left me and Luke persuaded me to move on. It wasn't until I met her again around five years ago that I found out the truth. She hadn't left me, she had been kidnapped by her brother and held prisoner. She managed to escape and eventually found me, though that was by accident as she had given up all hope of ever finding me by then."

"So it sounds like your brother wasn't happy about you getting away from him and has tracked you down again," Anna said.

Vivien nodded. "He's not evil, just old-fashioned. He thinks that as my older brother, it's his duty to protect me. Unfortunately, his version of protecting me is keeping me under lock and key, only letting me out when he can be with me to make sure I don't speak to anyone he doesn't deem suitable."

She sounded bitter. Gabriel could hardly blame her.

"And he blames me for you escaping," he said.

Vivien shrugged. "Not necessarily. But he will be blaming you for me staying away. I guess he thinks that with you out of the way, I would have no reason not to return to him. It's not true, but it's the way he thinks."

"So Luke's death isn't, technically, my fault."

"No," Vivien said sadly. "It's mine."

"No it's not," Anna snapped. "It's Joseph's and when I get my hands on him I'm going to make him wish he had never been born."

"Calm down," Will said. "From what I've heard, that won't be easy. He managed to overpower five hunters, one of which is a vampire. Now I have no idea how skilled hunters are, but from what you guys have told me, they're more than just good."

"They are," Gabriel said. "At least Sanctuary 14 is. But they could never take on a greater vampire, no matter how many there were of them. It's the fact that he managed to take out most of my family single-handedly that has me worried."

Anna seemed far from worried. "That's because he had the element of surprise."

"I think it's more than that," Gavin said, making Gabriel jump. He had forgotten he was still on the phone. "This guy is nearly as old as me, which makes him powerful."

"He's right," Vivien said. "Joseph isn't someone you want looking for you. If you go after him, you won't win."

Anna looked far from convinced. Gabriel hoped that she wasn't planning anything stupid.

"There is one more thing," Gavin said. "He has your phone numbers. I think he just has Gabriel's and Vivien's, but he may have Anna's as well. He thinks he can trace you through them. You might want to ditch them and get some burner phones."

"I can take care of that," Will said.

"That's it from me. Let me know your new numbers as soon as you have them." With that, Gavin hung up.

"What are your plans?" Will asked. "Do you think it's safe to stay here or will you move on?"

Gabriel didn't want to move. Anna had settled down well and he was worried that making her leave would undo all the progress she had made.

"I think Gabriel and I should leave, at least for a while," Vivien said. "I want to visit some old friends, ask around, see if Joseph has been about, asking questions. And if so, how long ago. It will lead him away from here, if nothing else."

Gabriel didn't argue. It was her brother she was talking about, so she would know the best course of action. He would go along with whatever she wanted to do. Anna, though, was another matter.

"I want to stay here," Anna said. "If that's okay with Will." The man in question nodded his head.

"Anna," Gabriel said cautiously. "You're not planning anything stupid are you? You're not staying just because you think he will show up here, I hope."

"Of course not," she said, though her denial had Gabriel far from convinced.

"Let's go pack," Vivien said as she stood up. "We'll leave in the morning." She took Gabriel by the hand and pulled him up.

"First thing tomorrow, I'll go and warn the others," Will said. "I'll provide Joseph's description and tell them to keep an eye out for him. If he does turn up here, I'm sure one of us will spot him. Some people will probably remember him from last time he was here, looking for Vivien. I can get your new phones while I'm out."

He then turned to Anna. "Want to come with me? We can take the bikes for a spin."

Anna shook her head. "Thanks, but no. There's someone else I should visit instead."

-------------------------∞-------------------------

Anna pulled up outside the gate and removed her helmet. She pressed the buzzer and waited for it to be answered. She had no idea if Elias was home, but she could always return later if he wasn't.

She didn't recognise the voice which sounded from the intercom, asking who she was and who she was there to see. She answered the questions and was told to wait. A few moments later, the gate opened.

She replaced her helmet before riding down the driveway. She didn't need it, as there was no law requiring her to wear one on private property and if she fell off, no matter how injured she was, she would recover, but it was easier to ride with it on her head than in her hand or hooked over her arm.

She drove slowly, taking in the grounds surrounding the house. The house itself was old, mid-eighteenth century according to Elias, and she was jealous that he got to live there.

She pulled up near the front of the house and as she was removing her helmet, the front door opened and Elias walked out. She looked him up and down. Dressed in casual trousers and a short-sleeved white shirt, he seemed much more relaxed than their previous meeting. He was a fine figure of a man and she would have been attracted to him, had her heart not still belonged to Luke. She wasn't sure if their bond would stop her loving another man and wasn't interested in finding out. At least, not yet.

"Anna," Elias said in greeting. "To what do I owe the pleasure?"

"I want to ask you a favour."

"Sure. What can I do to help?"

"I want you to turn me into a killer."

She didn't get the reaction she was expecting. Elias merely said, "Let's sit down and talk," and led her into the house.

"Coffee?" he asked as they walked down the hallway. Anna declined; she wasn't in the mood for it.

He took her into the lounge and told her to sit.

"So exactly why do you want to kill someone and do you mind if I ask who?"

Anna told him everything. He already knew about Luke's death, but she spoke about Joseph and what Gavin had told her. She told Elias who he was, why he was after Gabriel and what she planned on doing to him, if she got her hands on him.

Elias listened intently, not interrupting her with questions.

"So you want me to teach you how to kill this Joseph person," he said once she finished talking. "And I'm assuming you don't want anyone to know."

Anna had no idea how he knew that, but he was right.

Elias relaxed back into the sofa. She didn't like the way he was looking at her, assessing her. She felt like he was trying to get into her head, to read her mind.

"When did you last drink some blood?" he suddenly asked.

"I don't need blood."

He leaned forward and looked at her intently. "That's not what I asked. Don't make me force you to tell me."

"It was yesterday. Or maybe the day before." Did she sound convincing? Not to her own ears, she didn't.

"You don't know, do you?"

There was no point in denying it; he would get the truth out of her whether she liked it or not. She was beginning to regret visiting him. She shook her head.

"I'll make a deal with you. I'll train you but you have to take blood more often. You can start now."

He held out his arm to her, inviting her to bite his wrist. The small amount of blood she had taken from him on her previous visit hadn't caused her any pain, unlike human blood, but she wasn't sure what taking more would do.

"Don't worry. I can take the pain away if you react badly. And I don't think my blood will harm you, even though my enzymes aren't inside you, like it would a human. I can always quickly inject some in if I think I need to."

Seeing that he wasn't going to take no for an answer, Anna forced herself to take hold of his arm, opened her mouth and bit down on his wrist. Her fangs pierced his vein and his blood filled her mouth. The taste was exquisite and she savoured every mouthful.

She stopped long before she had drunk her fill, but he ordered her to continue. She drank more than she ever had in one sitting before he let her stop.

"How do you feel?" he asked.

116

"Good," she said. She was telling the truth. She felt more alive than she had in a long time. She was buzzing with energy. Ever since Luke's death, she had only been taking enough blood to survive, not enough to satisfy her. She had forgotten how good sating her thirst could feel. But something felt different. She felt more vibrant, more energetic than she could remember feeling before. Drinking blood always gave a vampire a buzz, but what she was feeling far exceeded anything she had felt by drinking vampire blood. If all 'infected' could make her feel that way, she would have to see if they were willing to become regular donors. Until Joseph was dead. After that, she didn't know if she would need them.

"How fit are you?" Elias asked.

She shrugged her shoulders. While Luke had been alive, they often went for long runs together, keeping themselves fit, but she had let that lapse since his death. Gabriel had tried to get her to be more active on many occasions, but she repeatedly turned him down.

"I could be better," she admitted. She was too embarrassed to say she had more or less become a slob in regard to exercise. She no longer saw the point in doing it.

"Well that's the first thing we will work on then. I'll get a couple of my guys to put you through your paces, test you out."

He took out his phone and made a call. A short while later, two people entered the lounge. Anna recognised them as ones who had 'arrested' her on her first visit.

"Thank you for coming," Elias said, which confused her. Didn't they work for him, so therefore had to obey his orders?

He looked her up and down, critically.

"Find her something to change into, something more suitable for a work-out."

"What sort of work-out?" the woman asked. Anna wasn't sure she liked the smile on her face.

"No, she's not ready for that yet. I just want you to test her basic fitness, for now."

"Come to my room," the woman said. "You look about my size. I'm sure there's something there that will fit you." She indicated toward the door with her head.

"I can go home and get some clothes," Anna said. Being handed over to these two strangers made her nervous, but she didn't know why.

"No need." This time when the woman smiled, it was warm and friendly. Anna started to relax. She stood up and followed her out of the room.

"I'm Patrice, by the way. Most people call me Pat."

"I'm Anna."

Patrice turned and looked at her, giving her a knowing smile. "Elias has spoken a lot about you. He's quite taken with you, well what you are, anyway. You intrigue him and it's been a long while since anyone has done that."

"Are you and he…." Anna didn't know how to finish the sentence. Patrice worked out what she was asking and laughed lightly.

"No. Just friends. I fought with him during the civil war and when he came back into the country, I decided to join him instead of staying with his brother."

"So you don't work for him?"

As they spoke, they climbed the stairs and Anna was led down the corridor.

"Not exactly," Patrice said. She stopped in front of a door on the right. "This is me."

She opened the door and waved Anna inside. It wasn't what she was expecting. She wasn't sure why, but she thought she would be walking into something like a hotel room, clean, practical and impersonal. This room was the exact opposite.

It was large, with a king-size bed and a small table with two chairs. There were two wardrobes, antique oak by the look of things, with a matching dressing table and a chest of drawers. The curtains were a soft pink, which matched the bedspread. There were paintings and photos hung on the wall and a small vase with some blue flowers which Anna didn't recognise on the table. It looked warm, comfortable and personalised.

"I work with Elias," Patrice said, continuing where she had left off while Anna stared at the contents of the bedroom. "We are one of the places 'infected' can come and be safe. I also schedule his travel, making sure he visits every country at some point each year, but also gets to spend time relaxing."

"So you're his PA," Anna said.

Patrice laughed again. "I suppose you could say that."

She walked over to the chest of drawers and opened the bottom drawer. While she searched through it, Anna wandered over to the window and looked out.

"Great view," she said, looking at the trees.

"I like it. Here, try these on." Patrice threw some leggings and a t-shirt at her. "I'll look for some shoes."

The fit wasn't perfect, but the stretch material of the leggings made them adequate and while the t-shirt was a bit long, it wasn't too bad.

Shoes, on the other hand, were an issue. Patrice was two sizes smaller than Anna so had nothing that would fit.

The problem was solved by Patrice raiding the room of one of the men. The trainers she handed to Anna were slightly big, but an extra pair of socks made them fit well enough.

"All set?' she asked once Anna was dressed.

Anna nodded, so Patrice led her back to the lounge, where Elias and the man were waiting for her.

Elias looked at her critically again. "You'll do," he finally said. "Pat and Ben are going to take you for a run. I want to know your speed as well as your stamina. Let's see if you can keep up with them."

"I can't," Anna said immediately. She was thinking back to how easily they had caught her before.

"They'll go slow, I promise."

Anna pulled a face, indicating she didn't believe him, which made Elias laugh. "Off you go."

Ben and Patrice walked out of the house, with a reluctant Anna trailing behind. When she had asked to be trained, this wasn't exactly what she had in mind. She was thinking more along the lines of how to shoot or create a bomb, though why she thought Elias would know how to do that, she had no idea.

As soon as they were out of the house, Patrice and Ben took off. Anna swore before running after them. She managed to catch them, so they must have been going slow for her.

An hour later, when they made it back to the house, Anna was exhausted. But she had managed to keep up. Patrice and Ben seemed winded, but not as out of breath as she was.

Elias was by the front door, waiting for them. "How did she do?"

"We didn't manage to lose her," Ben said. Was that surprise she heard in his voice? Probably not.

"How slow did you have to go?"

"We didn't."

"Huh," Anna couldn't stop herself from saying. "That's not possible."

Ben looked at her. "I can't explain it, but Pat and I were running as fast as we could at one point and you kept with us."

"I don't understand." Anna was both surprised and confused. "Why couldn't I get away from you the first time I was here then?"

"That is a good question," Ben said.

All Elias said was, "Interesting."

He turned his attention to Patrice and Ben. "Thanks for your help. That will be all for today. I'll let you know when Anna is back for more."

"Happy to help out," Patrice said and Ben winked at Anna.

"Come on in. I've got homemade lemonade on the table," Elias said. He walked into the house without checking Anna was following him. She guessed he was used to people obeying him without question.

When they got to the lounge, he sat on the sofa and indicated with his hand that she should sit opposite. He handed her a glass, which she happily accepted. The run had made her thirsty. She took a sip. It was not too sweet, so she took a refreshing mouthful.

"You know why I managed to keep up with them, don't you," she said after swallowing.

"No," Elias said. "But I have a theory."

"Which is?" Anna asked when it was obvious he wasn't going to continue.

"I think it's because you drank my blood."

Anna hadn't considered that. She had experienced no positive side effects from drinking the blood of greater vampires, but she was just as powerful. Elias could be right.

"Come back in a few days and we will test you again."

Anna agreed and then changed the topic to weapons training. Elias refused to teach her how to shoot, at least not for a while. He explained she shouldn't learn to rely on a weapon, that she needed to know how to defend herself in case she was unarmed when she met her intended target. She was forced to agree that it made sense.

Elias promised to teach her how to shoot, but only after she improved her fitness and learned at least the basics of unarmed combat.

The conversation turned to other, more casual topics, and it was much later than Anna had been expecting when she looked at her watch.

"I should go," she said. Elias reminded her where Patrice's room was and gave her permission to enter it so she could get changed into her own clothes.

Before leaving, they arranged when she would next visit.

Gabriel and Vivien were still at Will's house when she returned, waiting to say goodbye to her. She apologised for being gone so long, but she didn't say where she had been and they didn't ask.

They promised to keep in touch and hugged her tightly before they left.

"Make sure you take care of her," Gabriel said to Will before he closed the car door and Vivien sped down the driveway.

"I have a present for you," Will said once they were out of sight. He handed over a phone. "It's not connected to you in any way. I've already programmed Gabriel and Vivien's new numbers into it. As soon as you have transferred all the ones you want to keep from your old phone, give it to me and I'll dispose of it."

Anna thanked him and went to her room. She scrolled through her old phone, adding some numbers to the new one and ignoring others. She had them all stored on her computer so she wouldn't lose them, but she saw no point in uploading numbers she would likely not need.

She hesitated when she got to Luke's number. It was one she would never call again, but not having it on her phone seemed like a big step, one she wasn't sure she was ready to take.

In the end she realised she was being silly; it was just a number after all. She ignored it and continued down the list.

When she finished, she handed her old phone over to Will.

"Thanks," he said. He glanced at his watch. "Want some food? It's way past lunchtime."

"Sure," she said and followed Will to the kitchen.

Together they cooked up some omelettes and took them outside to eat.

"You don't need to worry," Will said when they had finished. "I will take care of you. And all the other vampires in the area will be happy to help out."

Anna smiled. She liked Will, a lot. From the moment she had first moved in, they had hit it off and had soon become good friends. She also got on well with the other vampires. All of them had welcomed her to the area and had offered to help her with her blood supply issue.

She placed her hand over his and gently squeezed it. "Thanks, but I don't need looking after. I'll be fine, I promise."

She felt she could trust Will, that she could speak to him about anything. Well almost anything. She would not be telling him about her visits with Elias or the fact that he had agreed to train her to kill Joseph. That was something she wouldn't be telling anyone.

BECAUSE IT'S NOT SAFE

"We need to talk," Doc said as he walked into JD's office, shutting the door behind him.

"This sounds serious." As the head of Sanctuary 14, Doc was the first point of contact for the hunter society council, so JD assumed it was something to do with that. He was wrong.

Doc took a seat opposite JD. "You have to let Sarah hunt again."

JD's good mood vanished. "You have no right to interfere between me and my wife."

"I'm not. This is between you and your student."

"That's just a technicality."

Doc leaned forward. "No it isn't and you know it. When you first got together all those years ago, you stated that you would be able to draw the line between being her partner and being her trainer. So far, you've done well, but now you're blurring that line."

JD waved away Doc's concern. "I'll talk to her, make her understand why she can't hunt."

"That's not good enough JD. She has submitted a formal complaint to me. I have the authority to deal with it myself, but I will forward it to the council if I have to."

This took JD by surprise. "What?"

"You heard me. Ask yourself this. If she wasn't your wife, would you be letting her hunt?"

JD didn't need to think. "Of course not. My personal relationship with her is irrelevant."

"Then why won't you let her hunt?"

"Because it's not safe," JD snapped. He rarely lost his temper, but he didn't like where this conversation was going.

Doc remained calm. "When has it ever been safe? What's changed? Why are you letting the other's hunt but not Sarah."

"Because the others don't have a newborn baby to look after."

Doc shook his head. "This is because of what happened here a couple of months ago, isn't it?"

JD nodded. "If I can't protect her here, how can I protect her on a hunt?"

"She doesn't need protecting."

"Of course she does. You know what happened. You know how easily that vampire could have killed her, or the children, had he wanted to."

"That was a greater vampire and that's not what you hunt."

JD ignored the comment. "And he managed to kill me, just like that." JD clicked his fingers as he said the last word.

It was Doc's turn to get angry. "Get over yourself JD. So there are creatures out there more powerful than you. So what? Now you know how the rest of us feel."

JD was stunned. Doc had never spoken to him like that before. He slumped back in his chair. He didn't want to admit it, but Doc was right. Ever since the attack on the Sanctuary, he had been scared. Not for himself, but for his team and his wife.

Doc sounded calmer when he next spoke. "Let her hunt JD. It's not more dangerous now than it was before the attack."

Again Doc was right. JD was aware how easily greater vampires could kill him. Gabriel had demonstrated when they first met, which had caused a bit of angst among the hunters and it had taken a long time before they trusted Gabriel. Before the attack on the Sanctuary, he had also known that there was a rogue greater vampire around, yet it hadn't worried him. So why was he worried now? He didn't know more now than he had before.

"You're right," he said. "I'm being an idiot."

Doc smiled. "I wouldn't go that far, though Sarah probably will."

He stood up and walked over to the door, but before leaving the room, he turned and looked at JD.

"Sarah's in the training room, in case you wanted to know."

JD took the hint; his work would have to wait.

If Sarah was training, the training room door would be locked, for safety reasons, so he went to watch her from the balcony instead.

She would have heard him enter, but she didn't let it distract her.

Leaning on the guardrail, he watched her work through one of the harder routines he had taught her. Even after all their time together, he still marvelled at how good she looked with a sword in her hand. She moved with grace and strength. Her fitness level had dropped while she had been unable to train, but not by much, and she was now more or less back to where she was prior to getting too heavily pregnant to train.

As soon as she finished the routine, he called down to her.

"You put in an official complaint about me to Doc?" He hoped his tone conveyed that he wasn't angry with her.

She smiled up at him. "It was the only way to make you see reason. Talking with you failed, so what choice did I have?"

"Fair enough." He went to the ladder, but instead of climbing down, he jumped, rolling over in the air as he did so.

"Show off," she said.

"I give up. You can hunt again. Now let's go over that routine together. You're not extending far enough on the second from last turn."

They trained together for the next hour, before heading up to their room and showering. The shower wasn't just about getting clean and lasted quite a while.

They were still drying off when the hunt alarm sounded. Sarah looked at JD expectantly and he nodded. When he said she could hunt again, he hadn't expected it to happen so soon, but it was too late to change his mind.

They put on their hunting suits, grabbed their swords and met the others by the front door. Doc was there and smiled when he saw Sarah in her suit.

"You're going to the woods," he said. "It's out of our area, but Sanctuary 12 requested back-up and specifically asked for you guys."

"It's nice to be appreciated," Scott said.

Doc gave them the address and Scott and JD both grabbed car keys.

Sarah sat in the passenger seat beside JD, as she always did. It wasn't until she placed her hand on his thigh that he realised how much he had missed having her with him.

It took a while to reach their destination and cars from Sanctuary 12 were already there. One hunter had remained behind, waiting for them.

Once he told them the directions hunters from his own Sanctuary were covering and where Sanctuary 14 should go, he started to head off, but JD called him back.

"It's not a good idea to go off on your own," he said. "Take Sarah with you."

The hunter nodded and JD watched the two of them leave. He issued instructions to Scott, Jane, Steve and Craig and waited until they were out of sight before he entered the trees.

He could hear birds above him, but nothing else. No fighting, nobody calling out. He scanned the trees, easily making out the feathered creatures, but there was no sign of a vampire hiding in them.

He continued going straight. Jane and Steve were to his left somewhere and Scott and Craig to his right. Sarah had headed off in the direction he was going, but could be anywhere by now.

It was a dark night, the moon hidden by clouds. He guessed it was one of the reasons Sanctuary 12 had asked for 14; his vampire sight exceeded a human's.

He lost track of time as he walked, keeping a constant lookout for vampires or fellow hunters. But he didn't rely on his sight alone; his hearing was just as important. As was his sense of smell. Like some humans, some vampires didn't follow good hygiene practices and JD could smell their body odour from a distance. He came across two headless corpses; the severed heads lying next to the bodies showed they had fangs. There was a human body next to them. JD didn't stop to take a closer look. If the human was still alive, the hunters who dispatched the vampires would have taken care of her.

He heard fighting to his left, but it was too far away for him to care about. If it was members of his team, they would call out if they needed him.

As he continued forward, he thought he could hear something ahead of him, but he wasn't sure what it was. As he got nearer, he realised it was singing.

He edged closer and when he moved out from behind a particularly wide tree, he could see a woman swaying as she sang, a bottle of brown liquid in her hand. The song was tuneless and kept being disrupted by hiccups, suggesting the singer was more than a little drunk.

JD had two options. He could leave the woman in peace, skirt around her and continue heading deeper into the wood, but that would mean she could still become prey if not all the vampires had been dealt with. The alternative was to escort her out of the wood, but that would mean he would have to stop hunting.

The decision was made for him when he saw movement to the right of the woman. A vampire was crouched down, ready to pounce. JD timed it perfectly, rushing forward and swinging his sword just as the vampire leaped. His sword connected with the vampire's neck, severing her head.

The dancing woman turned around in surprise and upon seeing the dead body, began to scream. JD grabbed hold of her and placed his hand over her mouth while his other hand held her nose. She struggled, but JD was much stronger. Her body went limp and he placed her gently on the ground.

"You're not supposed to kill the humans," a familiar voice said and JD looked up to see two hunters from 12 approaching.

"Is she injured?" one asked.

JD shook his head. "No, just drunk. Can you get her out of here?"

They nodded and one picked her up while his partner kept a lookout. JD headed off once more, looking for more vampires.

He didn't spot any more, but he did find Sarah. She and the hunter she had gone hunting with were taking on two vampires. JD could have intervened, but his help wasn't needed. It wasn't often he got to see his wife in action, so he stayed hidden and watched.

She was moving well, her sword strokes clean and precise, but the vampire she was fighting against was an experienced fighter so this wasn't going to be an easy kill.

The hunter from 12 quickly disposed of his vampire and turned to see how Sarah was doing. He took a moment to take in the situation and then ran toward her, his sword ready.

"Duck," he called out and Sarah immediately obeyed. Years of training had taught her to react to any instruction called out instead of questioning it. The hunter's sword sailed over her head and through the vampire's neck. JD watched in amusement as the vampire stayed upright for a moment. Then the head fell from the shoulders and the body crumpled to the ground.

JD had seen enough and headed off once more.

It took a long time to search the entire wood, due to its size, and by the time JD made it back to the car park, almost all the other hunters were there. The total body count was thirteen, three of them human. Five people had been saved. It was better odds than they usually got and no hunters had been injured.

One of the hunters from 12 approached JD. "Want to come back to our place?"

It was traditional that if more than one team went to a hunt, they would get together at one of the Sanctuaries to discuss how the hunt went and what could be improved, but JD thought about his children and decided to decline the offer. His team were out of their usual territory so it would take them a while to get home.

"Thanks, but I think we will head off. Will one of your team stay and wait for Sanctuary 1 to turn up to collect the bodies?"

The man nodded. "Your team have already given us the location of their kills and we already know about your one."

JD called to his team, telling them to go home. Those who were in conversation with other hunters finished their discussions before saying their goodbyes.

When Sarah walked over to JD, she was glowing.

"I've really missed this," she said.

He took her in his arms and kissed the top of her head. "I know you have and I'm sorry I was such a pain."

She placed her hand on his cheek. "I understand why you felt the need to protect me. Joseph's attack really shook you up."

"It did, but it shouldn't have. Besides, he's gone after Gabriel, so there is probably nothing to worry about."

They both knew he was lying. There was always something to worry about, but they couldn't let it consume their lives.

They were alone for the drive home as the other four decided to go in the other car. Natalie was still up, waiting for them, and had energy drinks on hand.

They gathered together in the lounge and talked about the hunt. JD liked to hear his hunter's opinions on how a hunt went. He was a leader, not a dictator, and was open to the views of others.

This time, everyone was in agreement. Nothing went wrong and there was nothing that needed to be done differently.

Sarah spoke about being partnered with someone from another Sanctuary and how she didn't feel as confident working with him as she did with members of her own team. While she had trusted him to protect her back, there was something missing in their dynamics.

JD took a mental note. It was understandable and should be looked into. Whenever more than one Sanctuary was called to a hunt, the hunters still partnered up with people from their own Sanctuary. Maybe that was a good thing, maybe it wasn't, but it was something that needed to be talked about. JD would see if Doc could get him an appointment with the council.

While the rest of his hunters continued to talk about the hunt, with Natalie eagerly listening in, his mind went to possible options for getting hunters to feel more comfortable working one-on-one with those from a different Sanctuary. Maybe they should do it more often when they went on joint hunts, or perhaps hunters should spend a few weeks each year working with a different Sanctuary. He would give it some more thought, and maybe talk to some other trainers, before approaching the council.

His mind was drawn back to the conversation when Sarah took his hand.

"Time for bed," she whispered when she leaned closer to him.

"Are you tired?" he asked. It was her first hunt since giving birth and she wasn't up to full strength or fitness.

"No," she said. The smile on her face told him exactly what she was thinking.

"We'll see you in the morning," JD said and stood up, pulling Sarah up with him.

As soon as they were in their room, they undressed each other. It wasn't the frantic ripping off of clothes that often happened. This time it was slow and sensual.

When JD was naked, Sarah's hand trailed down his chest, but he stopped it before it went too low.

"Shower first," he said.

They washed each other, softly caressing and kissing each other's bodies.

As water cascaded down her, Sarah put her arms around JD's neck and went onto her tiptoes so she could kiss him on the lips.

"I've been thinking," she said. "Maybe we should get in some practice, in case we decide we want baby number three."

JD had been thinking exactly the same thing.

AFTER ALL, VAMPIRES DON'T EXIST

As the months passed, Anna managed to juggle work and training without Will getting suspicious as to where she went. He asked occasionally, but didn't probe, stating it was Anna's business and if she didn't want to discuss it, she didn't have to. As long as she was staying healthy and was coping both mentally and emotionally, that was all he cared about.

Elias tested her speed, strength and endurance both after taking 'infected' blood and without doing so and analysed the differences. The results clearly showed the blood had a positive effect on her. She didn't take 'infected' blood too often, though, as it would mean taking less from the vampires and she didn't want to cause Will any concern.

She socialised a lot with the other greater vampires in the area and got on well with most of them, even beginning to class some of them as good friends. She would never have the same bond with them as she had with those she used to live with, who she regarded as family, but they were an adequate substitute. She missed Gavin and the others, but didn't dwell on it.

Work was going well and she had already been promoted. She enjoyed the work and the team she was in was filled with diverse and interesting characters, none of whom suspected she wasn't human.

One of her co-workers, though thankfully not one she had to spend much time with, kept hitting on her. She made it clear she wasn't interested, but it took Will posing as her boyfriend at a work function to get him to back off.

She heard regularly from Gabriel and Vivien. They managed to find some of the places Joseph had been in his hunt, but that was before he got to Gavin's place, so they were no closer to finding him. So far, he had failed to show up where Anna was, much to her disappointment.

Elias had finally started to teach her how to shoot. She hated it, but didn't let him know that. She was learning out of necessity rather than enjoyment so whether she liked it or not was irrelevant to her.

She got to know all the infected that lived on Elias's estate and some who were regular visitors. She was greeted warmly whenever she arrived and even went to social events with some of them.

Elias's brother and his wife visited for a few weeks and Anna was fascinated when they discussed their past. For a while, both brothers had been monsters, until they had fought against it and escaped their father's clutches.

Sophie, Nick's wife, brought her son with her and they explained that, despite using her as a sacrifice to bring Elias out of a spell which had been put on him, she was prepared to give Nick a chance because he saved Ethan's life.

Anna found the story of how they got together fascinating. She didn't ask why Sophie had agreed to become a soul eater, as the witches liked to say; after all, it was no different to her being turned into a greater vampire so she could stay with Luke forever. At least that's what they had all thought, at the time.

Ethan was married to a witch, who was also the daughter of one of Elias's step-brothers. The family dynamics were almost as complicated as the plots of the TV show 'Dynasty', which she used to watch when she was younger.

She found the young witch fascinating and spent a lot of time with her while she was there, finding out about the different covens, how they tracked down 'infected' and the spells they could cast. She was particularly interested in the enchanted bullets they used, which exploded inside the body. She almost asked if she could have some, but decided to discuss it with Elias instead.

Will continued to spend a lot of time with Marie. Anna would have found it amusing, if it wasn't so sad. The woman had no idea how Will still felt about her. While it appeared she was dangling him on a string like a puppet, treating him as a toy she could take out and play with when she was in the mood and discard when she wasn't, this wasn't the case. She saw him as a friend, oblivious to the fact he followed her around like a love-sick puppy, at her beck and call night and day.

Kurt was no better. Nobody was surprised when she grew bored with him and moved on to someone else, yet he was still hanging around, doing everything she asked of him.

Will commented on it once, saying how weird it was that Kurt spent so much time with her, despite their breakup. Anna just stared at him. The words 'kettle', 'pot' and 'black' sprang to mind, but she didn't voice the well-known phrase. She had tried to talk to him in the past about it, but her attempts had fallen on deaf ears. There was nothing she could say to make him realise he was behaving exactly the same way as Kurt.

It was 2 o'clock one morning when Anna was woken by movement in the house. She put on her dressing gown and went to investigate. She found Will by the front door, dressed in his motorcycle gear.

"Sorry to wake you. I'm just going out to see Marie."

"At two in the morning?"

"She just split up with her latest boyfriend and needs a shoulder to cry on."

Anna couldn't imagine why. It wasn't as if the decision to break up would have been the boyfriend's.

"Do you really think she will get back together with you after all this time? Just because she's lonely and wants some company for a few hours?"

She knew that was exactly what he was thinking, but, of course, he denied it.

"I'm just going to comfort her, nothing more. I would do the same for you."

She believed him. He had shown her nothing but kindness and compassion. She didn't try to talk him out of leaving. Instead, she bid him a good night and went back to bed.

He was grinning like a Cheshire cat when he returned late the next morning.

"Marie and I are back together," he announced.

Anna was sceptical. "Did she actually say that?"

"Not in so many words, but after what we did last night, three times, how could we not be?" He held three fingers up, emphasising his point.

Anna shook her head. It was obvious Marie had just been using him for sex, but she wasn't the one to point it out to him.

She was proven right a few hours later when he rang Marie and invited her over for lunch. She declined, stating that she had a date, and sounded completely bewildered when Will told her he thought they were back together.

He spent the next three days sulking, not talking to anyone other than Anna. His mood changed, however, as soon as Marie called him to ask for a favour, a favour he was more than willing to do.

It was getting close to the anniversary of Luke's death when Gabriel returned. Anna wasn't surprised to see him. After all, it was a date he wouldn't be able to forget.

What did surprise her was that he was alone. He explained that Vivien had wanted to visit some old friends who were reclusive and didn't like strangers. He said it was the perfect opportunity for him to return to see how Anna was. She suspected it was actually the other way round and him returning was the perfect opportunity for Vivien to visit her friends.

Once he was settled back into his room, he caught Anna and Will up on what he and Vivien had been up to. It sounded like they had travelled most of the country. They had paid Gavin a quick visit, but didn't stay long in case Joseph was still having the place watched.

There had been no sign of Joseph since his attack on Sanctuary 14 and life there had returned to normal, other than everyone being more watchful whenever they went out.

Anna's brother expressed a desire to visit, but Gabriel had managed to convince him to wait awhile, until they knew where Joseph was. Paul spoke on the phone with Anna and they video chatted often, so he knew she was okay, but it wasn't the same as seeing her.

Anna contemplated going to visit him, but it was just as dangerous as him visiting her, so she would have to put it off.

She also wasn't sure she wanted to spend much time with him. Unlike Will, he would give her the third degree about how she was spending her time and she didn't want him to know she was being trained to kill Joseph.

Gabriel would only be with Anna for a few weeks, as he couldn't risk staying in one place any longer. They made the most of their time together, going for runs, having coffee at the café, going out in the evenings, socialising with the other greater vampires.

While Gabriel was around, Anna had to stop her training sessions with Elias. He understood, but said he would miss her. She was surprised at how much she missed him. She had no romantic feelings toward him, but enjoyed their time together. She realised that she liked his company more than anyone else's, other than Will's.

One evening, Gabriel, Anna and Will headed over to Marie's house on the other side of the town. She had decided to throw a party, though nobody knew what the occasion was.

As instructed, they dressed up. Anna couldn't help admiring Gabriel in his black suit. Though she had never been attracted to him, she could understand why other women were. Will was more casual, choosing smart trousers and a jacket, which Anna wasn't convinced matched, and at the last minute, he removed his tie.

Anna couldn't help imagining him spending hours in front of the mirror, trying to decide what would impress Marie the most.

By the time they arrived, the house was crowded. And not just with vampires. A number of the local townsfolk were there, as well as people Anna didn't recognise.

Marie was chatting with a group of men, but as soon as she spotted the new arrivals, she walked over to join them. She air kissed both Anna and Will on both cheeks, before looking Gabriel up and down, admiring the view.

"It's good to see you again, Gabe," she said. "I hope I get to see much more of you while you are here." She turned her head, exposing her cheek, indicating that he should kiss her. He obliged, but didn't look happy.

135

"Don't call me Gabe," he said.

She smiled at him. "But Gabriel sounds so formal."

"Maybe, but it's what I like to be called."

Before she could respond, more people arrived and she left without saying anything.

"She hasn't changed," Gabriel said.

"She never does," Will said. Anna wasn't sure if he thought that was a good thing or not.

"Come on," he continued. "Let's get a drink. The bar's over here."

Kurt was at the bar, standing by himself, so Anna went over to talk to him.

"Any idea what this party is for?" she asked.

"Haven't you heard?" He slurred his words, indicating he was more than a little drunk. "She's celebrating being single again."

Anna hadn't, but she wasn't surprised. Marie's latest conquest had been no more suitable for her than Kurt had been. At least this one had already been a vampire so Marie didn't turn another human into a blood-sucker, as Anna sometimes liked to call it.

"You don't sound happy about it," Anna said.

"Why should I care? It's just another in the long line of men she has made a fool of."

She could almost feel the waves of bitterness that came off him as he spoke.

"Why are you here?"

Kurt put his drink down and turned to look at her. "Because she's a soul-destroying bitch who poisons your mind so no matter how much you hate her, she still somehow manages to get to you do whatever she wants."

His words disturbed her enough for her to seek out Will, who had disappeared. She found him talking with a group of young women, who all seemed to be flirting with him.

He didn't seem disappointed when she dragged him away for a quiet word.

"How's Kurt these days?" she asked. "Does he have good control of his bloodlust now?"

"He seems to be doing well. Why do you ask?"

Anna explained her conversation with him and mentioned the fact that he appeared to be drunk. Will said he understood her concern and would have a word with him.

A short while later, he returned to her, looking anxious.

"I can't find him anywhere."

"Let's split up and look for him," Anna said. "I'll get Gabriel to help."

The three of them searched the house from top to bottom, but to no avail. There was no sign of him, so they started asking around. Marie had no idea where he was and made it clear that she didn't care.

One young vampire told Anna he thought he had seen Kurt heading upstairs with a young human female.

Anna ran to find Will. Together they raced up the stairs and bumped into Gabriel, who had been searching the second floor. He had checked all the rooms except one, which was locked.

All three of them went up to it and Gabriel banged on the door. There was no reply. They could hear the sound of movement inside, but couldn't make out if it was a struggle or something more sexual.

Anna wasn't prepared to take the risk. Without waiting for the approval of either of the two men, she kicked the door, near the lock. The lock didn't break; instead, the doorframe shattered.

Kurt was on the bed, holding down a struggling woman. Both were fully dressed.

"What the hell?" he said as he turned to face them. His fangs were out, but there was no sign of blood. They had gotten there just in time.

"You take care of the girl, we'll deal with Kurt," Gabriel said to Anna before glancing at Will, who nodded.

They walked over to the bed and each took hold of one of Kurt's arms and dragged him off the bed. Anna put her arms around the trembling young woman, whispering to her that everything was going to be alright.

Anna had to half carry her from the room as terror caused her legs to be unsteady. She took her to another room and closed the door.

"Did he hurt you?" she asked and the woman shook her head. Tears were streaming down her face, leaving trails of mascara.

"When he invited me upstairs, I thought he just wanted us to be alone, to fool around a little. Over the clothes sort of stuff. You know what I mean?"

Anna nodded, though in reality she thought the woman was a bit naïve. If a man wanted to take you upstairs, they only had one thing on their mind. Of course, there were some exceptions, but not many.

"He's drunk," she said. "You should never trust someone who is drunk unless you know them well. They are not in control of themselves."

It wasn't the alcohol making Kurt unable to control himself, but Anna saw no reason to tell the woman the truth.

"He seemed so nice," she sobbed as she wiped her eyes with her hand, causing the dark lines to smear.

"He is," Anna said. "Usually. He isn't normally like this. If you're up to it, maybe we should find a bathroom and get your face cleaned up a bit."

The young woman nodded and stood up.

Anna had never been in the upstairs of the house before, but soon found a bathroom. She ordered the woman to sit on the edge of the bath while she wet the corner of a towel in the sink.

Using it on the woman's face, she removed the black smears. It was a white towel and the stain probably wouldn't come out, but Anna didn't care. It was Marie's fault the young woman had been attacked, so she would just have to live with the consequences. They could have been a lot worse.

When Anna finished her administrations, the woman's face was clear, but her eyes were still red and puffy.

"Do you need someone to walk you home?" she asked, but her offer was declined. The woman said she had come to the party with friends and she would get one of them to take her home.

After thanking Anna for her help, she got up to leave the room, but stopped and looked back at Anna before exiting the bathroom.

"Did Kurt have fangs?" she asked. "You know, like a vampire."

"Of course not," Anna said. "It must be the shock playing tricks with your mind. After all, vampires don't exist."

The woman thanked her once more before leaving.

Anna had no idea how she had made herself say the lie. Not only did vampires exist, but some of them were far more dangerous than fiction led humans to believe. And there were worse things than vampires living close by.

Anna returned to the room whose doorframe she had broken, but there was no sign of Will, Gabriel or Kurt, so she went downstairs.

She soon spotted Gabriel near the front door.

"Where's Will?" she asked. "And Kurt."

"Will's taking him back to his place so he can keep an eye on him. He'll stick him in the spare room. Hopefully, he'll just sleep it off. He's horrified by what he did, or should I say what he was about to do, and begged us to kill him. I think I've managed to talk him out of doing anything stupid. Will's there to make sure of that rather than to stop Kurt leaving and seeking out another human to attack."

"What's he going to do?" Anna asked. She knew what it was like to crave blood. But she had always had a vampire by her side to help her through it. She couldn't imagine what it would be like trying to cope alone. Marie had a lot to answer for.

"I think I talked him into going and staying with Gavin for a while, though whether he'll remember it in the morning, I have no idea. I might even drive him there myself."

It was a great idea. If anyone could help Kurt, it would be Gavin and his family.

Anna and Gabriel returned to the party and soon put Kurt from their minds. The humans started heading home sooner than expected and before long, the only remaining guests were vampires. They were sitting in the lounge, swapping amusing stories of their escapades over the decades.

They were a variety of ages, both physically and chronologically. Some had been turned within the last few years, while others had been vampires for over a century. Looking at them, they ranged from late teens to early sixties, if not older, though how they looked indicated how old they were when they were turned rather than how old they really were.

Anna couldn't help noticing the way Marie kept looking at Gabriel, though he seemed oblivious. Maybe he was so used to women eyeing him up that he no longer took any notice. It made Anna feel uncomfortable.

"You know Gabriel well," Marie said when there was a gap in the conversation. She was talking to Anna, but looking at Gabriel.

"I've known him for a number of years," she confirmed. "We're practically in-laws."

"Tell us more about him. How did you meet, for example?"

Anna didn't like being the center of attention, but she did as requested anyway. Everyone present had shown her nothing but friendship and all, except for Marie, had let her drink from them.

She talked about her job, how when she returned after an extended leave of absence, Gabriel and Luke were working there. She didn't explain why she took a sabbatical. She was able to talk about it without it affecting her mentally or emotionally, but she didn't like doing so. Being caught up in a siege and having to watch your parents die was not a good topic of conversation at a party.

She went on to explain her bond with Luke and how they had been drawn to each other. Gabriel hadn't taken it well. He soon came around, though, when he saw how good she was for his cousin.

She didn't mention that he had fallen for her, or talk about the problems it had caused. It was in the past and he no longer felt anything for her, romantically, and hadn't since Vivien's return into his life.

140

She talked about how Gabriel met the hunters from Sanctuary 14 for the first time. They already knew Sarah and Craig, as they worked with them, but they had no idea they were hunters and the hunters had no clue that there was such a thing as a greater vampire.

Anna described how Gabriel had demonstrated his ability to control a human by getting Katie to kiss him. Jonathon had not been amused and there was a lot of resentment between the two men for a while. It took Gabriel helping Jonathon's father when he had been falsely accused of a crime for them to forget their differences and become friends.

"I can still remember hearing how drunk both Gabriel and Jonathon got after the trial," Anna said. "I wish I had been around to see it."

"Can we talk about something else please?" Gabriel said. Not many things embarrassed him, but talking about that evening did.

The next hour or so passed quickly as Anna joined in the various topics of conversation. Marie remained quiet, other than to occasionally whisper in Gabriel's ear. She kept putting her hand on his thigh and he kept taking it off.

"It looks like Marie's gotten over her breakup already," a middle-aged vampire sitting next to Anna said quietly to her, while looking over at Marie and Gabriel. "He's a lucky man."

Anna was outraged. "He's spoken for. He's in a serious relationship."

"That makes no difference to Marie. Or to most men."

Anna didn't know what to say. Gabriel wouldn't cheat on Vivien, would he?

She shook her head, as though she was trying to shake her thoughts out of her brain. Of course he wouldn't. He had been in love with her for too long to risk losing her over someone like Marie.

Not long after, the few remaining people at the party decided it was time to call it a night. They bid their farewells to their host, who ignored them. Her attention was firmly on Gabriel.

"You can get home by yourself, can't you?" Marie said to Anna once the three of them were alone. "Gabriel will be staying here tonight."

Anna didn't know what to say. She looked at Gabriel, worried he might nod his head or wink at her, but instead he looked furious.

He grabbed Marie by the throat. "How many times do I have to say no?" he snarled. "My body, my heart and my sole belong to someone else. And even if I didn't have Vivien, I would never be interested in someone like you."

He pushed her away violently. Luckily, they were sitting on a sofa or her head might have hit the floor. Anna wondered if it would have cracked one of the tiles.

He stood up and straightened the sleeves of his jacket. "Let's go," he said to Anna. Then he turned back to Marie once more. "And if you even think about spreading lies about us spending the night together, I will kill you, slowly and painfully."

Anna shuddered. Gabriel meant every word he had just spoken.

Marie rubbed her throat and glared at him. Anna wasn't sure what she was angry about, being turned down or being spoken to like that. She couldn't imagine that either had happened before.

"Are you able to drive home?" Gabriel asked Anna once they were outside. "I feel like a run."

"Sure," she said. Then she placed her hand on Gabriel's arm. "Don't be too mad at Marie. It's just the way she is."

Gabriel grunted before taking off. By the time Anna arrived back at Will's house, Gabriel was already there. The run had calmed him down and he bid her goodnight as soon as she entered the house. He had only stayed up to make sure she got home alright.

The next morning, Gabriel packed his bags. While he wanted to be with Anna for the anniversary of Luke's death, he explained to her that he needed to put some distance between himself and Marie, in case he did something he would later regret. He didn't think Will would be happy to find her in pieces, literally. He also wanted to take Kurt to Gavin's place, just to make sure he got there.

He apologised to Anna for not being with her on the anniversary of Luke's death. She understood and assured him that she didn't need babysitting. It would be a sad day for Gabriel as well and he deserved to be with Vivien for it.

"I promise I will look after Anna," Will said to Gabriel just before he left. "Especially on that day."

It was a promise he didn't keep.

WE NEED TO TALK

Anna felt sick. Physically, mentally, emotionally. It had been a year since Luke died, yet it still felt like yesterday. There was a hole inside her which she had started to think would never go away.

She looked over at her clock. It was only 6am. Why did she have to wake up early, today of all days? Why couldn't she have stayed asleep as the day passed her by?

Trying to get back to sleep would be pointless. She decided to get up and take the bike for a spin. It might occupy her mind for a while. Though it was a week day, she wasn't going to work. She had booked a day off and was now regretting it. Maybe work would have occupied her mind. Or maybe it wouldn't and she would end up making mistakes or, even worse, having an emotional breakdown. Some of her colleagues knew she had lost her husband, as she liked to refer to him, but none knew the details. Nor the fact that today was the anniversary.

It was too early for Will to be up, so she made as little noise as she could as she left the house. She wheeled the motorbike down the drive, only starting the engine once she was close to the road, so as not to wake him.

She didn't ride for long; her mind wasn't on what she was doing. She wasn't paying attention to the road or other road users and tears kept blurring her vision. She was a danger, not to herself, but to others and she couldn't risk causing an accident where someone else might get hurt.

There was still no sign of Will when she got back to the house, so she made herself some breakfast and took it out onto the veranda. She needed blood and eating took the edge off the craving. She had purposely foregone drinking for a few days in the hope the physical pain would mask the emotional one, but it wasn't working.

She had no idea what would help, so she put her dirty things in the dishwasher and then went to the lounge. She turned on the TV, hoping she could find a good murder mystery, something which would make her think.

After channel surfing for what felt like hours, she decided the song was right, even if it was out of date. 57 channels and there's nothing on. It must have been at least 157 channels by now. Even with all the available pay TV subscriptions, she failed to find anything she wanted to watch.

She switched the TV off and threw the remote on the sofa in frustration. It was then she noticed the note on the coffee table. It was folded over and had her name on the front. She reached for it and read the contents. She was disappointed, but not surprised.

Anna

Marie asked for my help with something. I won't be gone long, but I probably won't be back by the time you leave. Have a great day at work and I will see you this evening.

Will

Had she told him she had the day off work? She couldn't remember. If she had, he had forgotten, just as he had forgotten what day it was.

Or maybe he hadn't forgotten and just didn't care. After all, didn't Marie mean more to him than anything else?

She felt like she should be angry with him for leaving her alone, or at least bitter, but she found she didn't care. Will couldn't take her pain away, or bring Luke back, so what did it matter if he wasn't with her?

She heard her phone ringing in the distance. She had left it in her bedroom when she had gone for her ride and hadn't bothered to retrieve it when she got back.

She knew who it would be and almost didn't go to answer it, but he would just keep calling so she may as well get the conversation over with.

She raced up the stairs and grabbed it before it went to voicemail.

"Hi Gabriel," she said, trying to sound cheerful and completely failing.

"How are you holding up?" he asked.

She shrugged her shoulders. When she realised he couldn't see her, she said, "Okay, I guess."

They both knew she was lying, but Gabriel didn't call her out on it.

"How are you?" she asked.

"About the same. What are your plans for today?"

Anna could have made something up, but she didn't see the point. "I have absolutely no idea."

"I know what you mean. Is Will looking after you?"

"Yes," she said, automatically. She didn't like lying to Gabriel, but didn't want to tell him the truth. If she told him Will had gone out and she was alone, Gabriel would probably drive over to see her, no matter where in the country he was or how long it would take him. She didn't want to see him. Speaking with him was bad enough. She couldn't cope with her own grief, let alone seeing someone else's.

Gabriel would think he would be doing the right thing, and he probably felt guilty for not being with her, but he was wrong. He was not what she needed. She needed Luke, not someone who would make her think about him even more than she already was.

She was polite to Gabriel, but kept the conversation short and hung up as soon as she could. She put her phone on her dressing table and noticed the candle she had bought. It was a memorial candle with Luke's name engraved on it. She purchased it months ago and had forgotten about it.

She went downstairs and found a box of matches, which Will always kept in the kitchen drawer in case of emergencies, and took it back to her room. She lit the candle and began speaking.

"Luke, I know you can hear me. I miss you. I miss you so much. I don't know if there's such a thing as Heaven, and even if there is, would vampires be allowed into it? I have no clue. It's not something I have thought about before. Wherever you are, I hope that you are at peace. I hope that you are happy. I don't believe in ghosts, but if they did exist, I know I would have seen you before now. You would have made sure of that. Yet I know that you are watching me, making sure I'm alright. As you can probably see, I'm surviving, but I'm far from alright. How can I ever be alright when you're not with me?"

A tear rolled down her cheek, followed by another. As she watched the flame, her vision blurred and she blinked her eyes, but it did no good. She wiped away the unshed tears with her hands, but they were soon replaced by more.

She let them flow, hoping they would make her feel better, but they didn't.

How long she sat there, watching the candle slowly burn down, she had no idea. Her phone rang a few times, but she ignored it.

Eventually the tears ceased and she looked at her phone. Gavin, Sarah, Craig, JD. All had left her voicemails, but she didn't need to listen to them to know what they would say. She should call them back, to thank them for their concern if nothing else, but she didn't feel like speaking to anyone.

What she felt like was a drink. The local bar should be open, so she grabbed her purse and left the room.

She decided not to go to the nearest one. It was Will's local and she had been there with him enough times for the landlady to recognise her. She wished to remain anonymous, so she chose one she had driven past a few times, but had never entered.

It was surprisingly busy for a morning, but it may have been the lunchtime rush. She didn't look for an empty table, choosing instead to take a seat at the bar. She intended to get drunk and having to keep walking from a table to the bar seemed like too much effort.

As a result, she didn't see the two people in the corner, having a quiet drink, but they saw her.

147

She ordered a whisky. It wasn't her usual drink, but she wanted something strong, something she would feel going down her throat. She downed it in one, somehow managing not to choke, and ordered another. The barman obliged, but looked concerned.

She had drunk five shots before she slowed down. They were beginning to have an effect on her. The sixth one she took more slowly, sipping it instead of gulping it. She knew what she had to do, but wasn't quite ready to go through with it.

While she looked at the contents of her glass, her mind wandered to her history with Luke, how they had met, the fun things they had done together, the pain of being turned into a greater vampire. Her screams of agony had caused him such pain that Gabriel had been forced to drug him in order to make him sleep.

She couldn't help smiling as she remembered the way he kissed her, how he made her feel when he made love to her.

She finished her drink and ordered another. Just one more and she would be ready.

"Are you sure?' the barman asked. He looked decisively toward her motorbike helmet.

"Don't worry," she said. "I won't be riding until I'm sober."

He looked like he didn't believe her, but poured her drink anyway.

"I would feel better if you handed over your keys," he said.

She had no problem with doing so. After all, she had remembered to bring the spares with her just in case this situation arose.

"Thanks," he said and put them under the bar. "They will be safe here until you are ready for them."

She smiled her appreciation, though in reality she didn't care. She would not be collecting them from him.

She slowly drank her last drink, hoping it would be her last drink ever. She contemplated what Luke would think of her plan. He wouldn't want her to go ahead with it, though he would understand. But he was no longer around to stop her; nobody was.

She drained the last of the liquid and swallowed it before placing the empty glass on the bar. She slipped a fifty under it, as a tip.

She called out to the bartender. "I'm going to get some fresh air. Keep an eye on my helmet will you?"

He confirmed he was happy to do so. Leaving her helmet behind emphasised the lie that she was not going to take her bike with her.

Once she exited the bar, she looked around, making sure nobody was watching her. The last thing she wanted was someone questioning her actions.

She got on her bike, started it up, put it in gear and rode out of the carpark before the bartender could check the noise he had probably heard wasn't coming from her bike.

She knew where she was going. She had been into the wood she was heading for a number of times. There were no official walking trails, but the trees were far enough apart for her to manoeuvre her bike between them.

She rode into the center, far away from the road, stopping when she got to the place she was aiming for. She killed the engine and dismounted. She took the wire she had remembered to bring with her and walked up to one of the trees. The wire was thin, almost too thin to see, and she tied it around the tree at what she hoped was the right height.

She had measured how high her neck was from the ground, when sitting on her bike, and then measured where that came to on her body when standing up straight on the ground. It wouldn't be exact, but it would be close enough.

She walked across a gap between the trees to another one and tied the other end of the wire around it, pulling it tight. She walked up to the wire, strung between the two trees, and remeasured its height, compared to her body. Satisfied, she returned to her bike.

She climbed aboard, started the engine and rode away. It was the only place in the wood where the trees formed a line, one she could ride down without having to swerve. She had practiced a number of times, so she knew how far away from the wire she needed to be to get to her desired speed.

She had been planning this for a while, but hadn't intended to do it yet. She had wanted to wait until after Joseph was dead, but today that no longer mattered. Today she no longer saw it as something to live for.

She pulled to a halt and turned her bike around.

She wasn't certain it would remove her head, but the trials she had done on things she held up as she ducked underneath it had worked well. Human flesh was vastly different to what she had experimented with, but all her research told her the plan should work.

The only thing causing doubt in her mind was Gabriel had never tried it when he went through a phase of trying to kill himself. If it was as likely to work as she believed it was, why had he never made the attempt? They didn't have motorbikes in those days, but she was sure a horse would go fast enough. She could have asked him, but then she would have had to tell him why she wanted to know and that was something she could never do.

"I'll see you soon," she said to Luke as she accelerated fast toward the wire.

She couldn't see it, but that didn't matter; she knew exactly where it was.

She held her breath, waiting for the feel of the wire biting into her flesh, but before she got close enough, something barrelled into her, pulling her from the bike. She hit her head on a tree and everything went black.

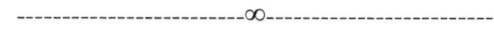

Anna opened her eyes and looked around. She was in a bedroom she didn't recognise. She tried to sit up, but the pain in her head caused her to give up. She gently touched it and felt a lump.

"Awake at last," a familiar voice said. Elias. Well that explained where she was, but not why she was there.

"If you wanted to die, you should have come to me," he continued. "I know plenty of ways to kill you."

"I come back to life, unless my head is removed, remember."

"You think that would stop me?"

He sounded amused. Anna didn't see what was so funny.

"Why am I here?" She rolled over so she could look at him. He was sitting in a chair beside the bed, his legs causally stretched out in front of him.

"Pat saw you drinking heavily in the bar and was concerned. She called me and I followed you. Do you really think I wouldn't know what day it is?"

Of course he would know. She had only told him once, when they had first met, but he seemed to remember everything.

She wasn't pleased he had interfered. She put a lot of effort into her plan, practicing everything from making the barman think she wasn't going to take her motorcycle, to the distance and speed she would need, and now it had all been ruined. She hadn't planned on it happening today, but that didn't mean she was happy she had been stopped. It wasn't as if she was going to be able to try it again. Elias would probably never let her out of his sight again.

"Are you going to tell anyone?"

Elias shook his head. "Of course not. It's nobody else's business. But I have to ask, why was nobody around to keep an eye on you? I don't mean to treat you like a child, but nobody should be left alone on a day like this."

Anna shrugged her shoulders. "Gabriel thought it best to stay away, and he was right. Having him close would only have made things worse."

"And Will?" There was a tone to Elias's voice that made Anna shiver. Elias didn't particularly like Will, but this sounded more serious than simple dislike. Was he blaming Will for her suicide attempt? She would have to put a stop to that. After all, it wasn't Will's fault.

"Will had to see Marie. And he doesn't know what day it is."

Elias spoke out loud the words she had been thinking. "He should have known."

151

She decided not to mention that Gabriel had made him promise to look after her, that he had reminded him only a few days ago.

"Come on," Elias said. "If you are feeling up to it, you are spending the day with me. Feel like practicing your shooting?"

She nodded and instantly regretted it, wincing as pain shot through her.

"Let's take care of your head first," Elias said. "It's not just wounds my blood can cure. Bumps and headaches can also be fixed."

He held out his wrist and she sank her teeth into it. She relished the taste of his blood flowing down her throat, but she didn't take too much. Her headache began to recede and when she placed her hand on her head, she could feel the bump had reduced in size.

"Thank you," she said. "Now I really should be going."

"I really don't think so, do you?"

Was she being held prisoner? Probably. But only for her own safety. There was nothing she could do, so she might as well stay and try to enjoy herself.

Elias took her to the shooting range he had set up on his property. Patrice was there, but she didn't drop her head. She didn't look ashamed or embarrassed. Instead, she held her head high and looked Anna straight in the eyes.

"I'm not sorry for ratting you out."

Anna wanted to be angry, but found she couldn't be, not at this woman, who she had begun to look upon as a friend. After all, Patrice had been looking out for her, making sure she was okay. How could she be angry for that?

"It's okay. I know why you did it. But I'm not going to thank you."

Patrice grinned. "I didn't expect you to."

Elias left the two ladies alone and they spent the next hour shooting at targets. Patrice was good, better than good. Every shot hit her target exactly where she was aiming. Anna was far from perfect, but at least she was now hitting the target every time, even if it wasn't exactly where she had aimed.

When she returned to the house, Anna found Elias in his office. "We need to talk," he said as soon as he saw her.

"About?"

"What you want to do. Will was supposed to stay with you today and didn't." Anna opened her mouth to protest, but Elias stopped her. "Don't even think about lying to me. We both know he should have been aware of the date and he shouldn't have gone off chasing after Marie. While he continues to drop everything the moment she whistles, he isn't being a good friend and that's what you need right now. I've spoken with my brother and I think you should go and stay with him for a while. He has better facilities than I do and a lot more 'infected' stay with him. You will be able to continue your training there and getting blood won't be an issue."

Anna thought about what Elias had said. She liked Will, a lot, but Elias was right; he couldn't be relied on. And she needed to be with someone who could. She had gotten on well with Nick and his wife when they had visited and moving to their place meant she could spend some time getting to know the witches. Maybe they could help her track down Joseph when she was ready to face him.

"Alright," she said. "I'll go."

Elias smiled at her. "I'll miss you. You'd better keep in touch."

"I will," she promised.

"I'll drop you off where you left your bike. If it's still in working order, take it to Will's place and pack. I'll come and pick you up in a few hours. You can have one of my cars for the journey."

Her own car was still with Gavin as there had been no need for her to ask for it to be delivered to her. Most of the time she used her motorbike and borrowed one of Will's cars when she needed to.

"I couldn't take one of your cars," she said, but Elias waved away her concerns.

"I have plenty and you can bring it back when you come for a visit."

153

"Thank you for everything," she said and hugged him tight.

--------------------------∞--------------------------

Will was not in a good mood. Marie's 'emergency' was she wanted to go shopping for a new dress and her car was in the garage, being repaired. She wanted a chauffeur and a pack horse to carry her bags. One dress quickly turned into half a dozen, along with accessories.

He was now in a ladies clothes shop, waiting for her while she tried on even more clothes. He couldn't believe she had taken a day off work just to go shopping.

Something else was troubling him. A voice in the back of his mind was telling him he was forgetting something, but try as he might, he couldn't remember what it was.

His phone rang, a welcome distraction from his thoughts.

"Gabriel," he said cheerfully. "How are you?"

"I could be better. How's Anna?"

Will frowned. Why was he asking about Anna? Why didn't he just call her if he wanted to know how she was?

"Okay as far as I know. I presume she's at work."

The silence that greeted his answer made him shiver, but not as much as the tone in Gabriel's voice when he eventually spoke.

"What do you mean 'as far as you know'? Aren't you with her?"

"No. Why would I be...." He didn't finish the sentence. He remembered what he had forgotten. He went pale. Today was the anniversary and he had promised to keep an eye on Anna to make sure she didn't do anything stupid.

He hung up on Gabriel and called her number, but there was no answer.

His swearing earned him a glare from the saleswoman, but he ignored it. As he ran from the shop, he could hear Marie calling after him, asking him where he was going. He didn't bother to reply.

He ran to his car, jumped inside and took off down the road. It didn't occur to him that Marie was stuck in the shop with heaps of bags and nobody to drive her home, but even if it had, he wouldn't have cared. There was only one person on his mind and it certainly wasn't her.

He broke the speed limits in his race to get home. Screeching to a halt in front of his house, he jumped out of the car as soon as it came to a complete stop. He searched the house, but there was no sign of Anna, not even a note letting him know where she had gone.

He raced to the bike shed, his heart beating fast. Her bike was missing. That meant she could be anywhere.

"Shit," he said. "Shit, shit, shit."

He had no idea where to even start looking. She could be anywhere. He had no idea how to contact any of her friends or work colleagues. All he could do was phone his friends, in the hope that someone had seen her.

Nobody had.

He sat down on the sofa to think. What would he do if he were in her position? There was only one answer: get drunk.

He tried their local first, but the bar staff hadn't seen her that day. He went to every pub, tavern and inn, but nobody had seen her.

He ended up in one close to where Elias lived. He could call Elias, to see if he knew where Anna was, but he couldn't bring himself to do it. He wasn't too proud to admit that Elias scared him. And it wasn't just the fact that he was more powerful. There was something menacing about him.

Will almost didn't go in, but forced himself to. And he was glad he did. Anna had been there, drinking heavily, but had gone out to get some fresh air. Quite a few hours later, she had returned, perfectly sober, to get her keys and helmet.

Will thanked the barman and ran out of the pub. He raced home. He had no idea if that was where she was headed, but there was only one way to find out.

He breathed a sigh of relief when he found her bike in the shed. It didn't mean she was alright, but it was looking more likely.

As he went to the front door, it opened. He was so relieved to see her, he didn't notice the suitcases beside her.

He ran up to her and hugged her tightly. "Thank God you are alright. I am so so sorry. I let you down. I should have been here."

She didn't return the hug.

"Yes, you should have been, like you said you would." Her voice was cold and uncaring.

Will winced. "Let me make it up to you."

"It's a bit late for that. I needed a friend today, someone I could rely on. I thought you could be that person, but I was wrong. You dropped me to run off to Marie, just like you always do. You're never going to change."

"That's not true," Will said.

Anna raised an eyebrow. "Really? Name me one time you put someone else's needs, even your own, ahead of hers."

Will opened his mouth, but nothing came out. He racked his brain, but came up blank.

"She needs me." Did he sound as lame to Anna's ears as he did to his own? He hoped not.

"She uses you." Anna didn't sound angry, more like resigned. She placed her hand on his cheek. "You're a good person, Will, just not a reliable one. Which is why I have to go."

Her words struck him like a punch to the stomach. "Go? Go where?"

"Somewhere where I have friends I can trust."

No, no, no, no, no. She couldn't be leaving. He was used to having her around. He liked having her around. He more than liked it.

"You can't go," he said.

"I can't stay."

"Please." He didn't care that he sounded like he was begging. He would do anything to get her to stay. "I'll change. I'll be a better friend to you."

She sounded sad when she said, "No, you won't."

Panic set in and he did the only thing he could think of to stop her leaving. Before she could move away, he took hold of her head and twisted it sharply sideways, breaking her neck.

I'VE BEEN EXPECTING YOU

Joseph looked at the house, trying to build up the courage to approach it. He had been watching it for over an hour. He told himself it was to make sure the owner was at home and didn't have any visitors, but the truth was he was just putting off what he had to do.

Not much scared Joseph, but for some reason, the witch terrified him. Not that he could prove she was a witch. The way she looked at him with her unseeing eyes made him feel like she was reaching down into his soul and didn't like what she found.

And she knew things, things she shouldn't. The first time he had visited her, she had told him she had no idea where Vivien was, even before he had introduced himself or explained why he was there.

A cold shiver went down his spine as he thought about his previous visit. It wasn't a sensation he was used to. Did he really have to see her again? Unfortunately, the answer was 'yes'. He was retracing Vivien's steps from the last time he had tracked her down so needed to speak to the same people.

He took a deep breath. He was better than this. One old woman shouldn't scare him. It wasn't as if she had ever threatened him or led him to believe she wanted to do him harm.

But there was something in her manner, something about the way she held herself upright when speaking to him and looked directly at him, even when she shouldn't have been able to tell where he was. She didn't like him. Usually that wouldn't bother him; he had never cared about what others thought of him. But something told him she was a dangerous enemy, one he would have to be careful with.

He slowly exhaled, and repeated the process twice more. His pulse slowed, yet he waited until it had nearly returned to normal before he exited the car. As he walked toward the house, it began to race again and he wondered if this was how others felt when they saw him approaching. Part of him hoped so.

He stood on the pathway, looking at the cottage. A hedge ran the entire length of the path, broken only by gates, leading to similar looking cottages.

Everything about this part of the village looked old, but well cared for. He half expected the gate to creak as he opened it, but it didn't. Rose bushes lined the path leading to the front door. It was the wrong season for them to be in bloom and he couldn't help wondering what colour the petals would be. Would they all be the same, or had the witch planted different colour bushes? It was something he wouldn't find out as he planned to never visit this house again.

A cat stretched out near the front door, sunning itself. The sight made him shiver once more. Was it an ordinary cat or was it a 'familiar'? Was it even the witch herself?

He shook his head. He had been reading too many fantasy books lately. There was no such thing as a witch, he reminded himself, and even if there was, they wouldn't have such a close bond with an animal as to class them as a 'familiar' and they certainly wouldn't be able to shape-shift.

He knocked on the door. Looking down, he noticed the cat had opened one eye and was glaring at him. He felt an overwhelming need to apologise for waking it up. He shook his head again; he was just being silly.

He waited impatiently for his knock to be answered. The cat continued to stare at him, making him feel uncomfortable, which he was sure was the intention.

He raised his hand to knock again, but he could hear movement from inside the house, so he let it drop to his side.

The door was opened by a short, plump woman with white hair and white eyes. Despite the lack of pupils or irises, she seemed to be looking directly at him, even though he had moved to one side, further away from the cat.

"Hello Joseph," she said. "I've been expecting you."

Fighting the urge to run, he asked, "May I come in?"

"You might as well," she said, "seeing as you're not going to leave me in peace until you do."

She stepped aside to let him enter. When she closed the door, he felt like a fly who had just flown into a spider's web.

"You remember where the kitchen is." It wasn't a question.

He made his way down the hall, ignoring the closed doors which led to the lounge, dining room, closet and downstairs toilet.

The kitchen was as he remembered it. There was a small round table with four chairs around it. On it was a pot of tea, with steam pouring out of the spout, and two cups. She hadn't lied when she said she had been expecting him.

He took a seat at the table. He hated tea, and he was sure she remembered that, but they both knew he would drink it; he didn't dare do anything to antagonise her.

"Be a dear and pour the tea."

He obliged and the smell hit him. It was even worse than he had been thinking. Earl grey. Of all the teas available on the market, it was the one he detested the most. He looked at the witch as he poured and he was sure she was trying to hide a smile.

She liked hers black, with no sugar, if his memory served him right. If he was wrong, she could always add whatever she desired.

To his own cup he added milk and three sugars. He looked down at the brown liquid and added two more; anything to take away the taste of the tea.

Reluctantly he took a sip. And almost spat it out. It was salt, not sugar. Had the old witch done it deliberately or was it an accident? He decided not to ask. She was looking at him with her unseeing eyes, as though challenging him to say something.

He took another mouthful and forced himself to swallow. He had tasted worse. He silently swore that he was going to make Gabriel pay for this when he got his hands on him, even though it wasn't his fault.

The witch took a sip of her tea. "You want to know where Vivien is," she said as she put the cup back on its saucer. "Again."

That was something else which annoyed Joseph. Who in this day and age used cups when mugs were available? A mug held a decent volume of liquid, unlike the cup he was being forced to drink out of. The china it was made from felt so thin and delicate he was terrified of breaking it.

He didn't ask how she knew why he was there. It was the only reason he had visited her last time, so why would this time be any different? He didn't acknowledge her statement, choosing instead to ask, "Where is she?"

The witch smiled. "What makes you think I know?"

She was playing games with him and he didn't like it. He was slowly losing patience.

"Look witch," he snarled. "Stop messing me around. You really do not want me as an enemy."

"No, Joseph," she said in a warning tone. "It is you who doesn't want me as an enemy."

Was it his imagination, or did the room suddenly go cold? He had had enough. He needed to get the information he wanted and get out of there. The quickest and easiest way to do that would be to inject some of his venom into her and make her tell him the truth. He was fast; it would be over and done with before she had even realised what he had done.

He let his fangs elongate, but kept his mouth closed; he didn't want to give her any warning of his intent.

Then he sprang at her. At least that was what he intended to do. He tried again, but couldn't move. He couldn't even breath. Every part of his body was frozen. Try as he might, he couldn't get his muscles to obey him.

His eyes locked on the witch. He tried to look away, but he couldn't. He couldn't even blink. He wanted to ask what she had done to him, but he couldn't move his mouth. All he could do was sit there, like a statue.

The witch looked at him smugly, even though she couldn't see him.

"Would you like to try that again?" she asked, her voice filled with amusement.

How was he supposed to respond?

161

"I didn't think so," she continued, as though he had answered. "Now here is what is going to happen. I am going to release you and then you are going to politely ask your questions. I will decide which I am going to answer. Once you have finished, you are going to leave and never come back."

She was right about one thing; he was never going to come back to this house, at least not while she was in residence. He planned on staying far away from this woman, but first he needed to know about Vivien.

As soon as he felt her hold on him release, he took a deep breath. He took two more before placing his hands on the table, palm down, and asking his first question.

"When did you last see Vivien? And don't lie to me. I can tell when someone is lying."

"It's been a while."

He watched her face carefully as she spoke. There was no sign she was lying and he was good at reading people. Very good. She could, of course, be the exception, but he trusted his instincts. If she was lying, it would be impossible for him to get the truth out of her, as she had already demonstrated.

"So you have not seen her in the last week or so?"

She shook her head. "No. I haven't."

He relaxed back and continued to regard her.

"When did you last talk to her?"

"Recently. Very recently."

So she had been in contact. This might lead somewhere.

"So you have her new number."

Again the witch shook her head. "No, I do not."

"You said she called you. Her number must be stored in your mobile. Let me see it." If he had her new number he may be able to trace her.

The witch laughed. It was a genuine laugh, full of mirth. "You really aren't very intelligent, are you? What use would I have for a mobile phone? Unlike most people, I still have a land line."

Joseph growled. She was right. What benefit would a mobile phone be to a blind woman?

"Where is she going next?"

162

"I have no idea. She didn't say."

Again, there was no indication she was lying. He was wasting his time. She didn't know anything useful and even if she did, he didn't believe she would ever tell him.

He stood up. "I will see myself out. I would say you have been most helpful, but I would be lying."

As he walked down the corridor, he could hear her following him. He didn't turn around. He had seen enough of her and just wanted to get out of her house. It took all his self-control to not run to his car. Instead, he walked calmly, but at a reasonable pace. He could feel her watching him with her unseeing eyes.

As soon as he was in the car, he started the engine and drove off. He could remember someone else Vivien had stayed with for a few days, years ago, so he would go there next.

A chill had seeped into his bones and it took a while for them to thaw out.

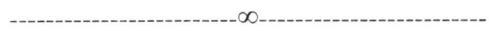

The back door of the house opened and Vivien and Gabriel stepped inside.

"Are you sure he's gone?" Gabriel whispered.

"I heard his car pull away," Vivien said. "It sounded like he was in a bit of a hurry."

"I'll put the kettle on."

While Gabriel was filling the kettle with water, the witch entered the kitchen.

"How much of that did you hear?" she asked.

Vivien took a seat at the table. "Most of it"

Gabriel collected the teapot from the table and threw away the contents before rinsing it out. He then put the used cups and saucers in the sink; the china was too delicate to go in the dishwasher.

While he worked, Vivien continued to talk to the old woman. "How did you lie to my brother?"

"I didn't lie. I just evaded the questions. He asked when I had last seen you. I took his question literally."

Vivien chuckled. It was a sound Gabriel liked hearing.

While he waited for the kettle to boil, he thought about the old woman. It was the first time he had met Maggie, though Vivien had told him a lot about her. She had first met her when she was young, before she lost her sight. Even then there had been something different about her. Vivien never believed any of the stories about her friend being a witch, but that was back when she didn't believe witches existed, before she met Elias and found out the truth.

Gabriel wanted to know if she belonged to a coven and, if so, if it was one of the ones the witch who was married to Elias's step-nephew had talked about, but Vivien had banned him from asking. It was Maggie's business and if she wanted to bring it up, she would.

Gabriel could understand Maggie wanting her privacy, but surely she could talk about it with friends.

As soon as the kettle boiled, Gabriel filled the teapot and took it to the table, along with three clean cups and saucers. Like Joseph, he would have preferred a mug, but Maggie didn't own any.

The conversation was still about Joseph.

"I don't think he likes me very much," Maggie said. She didn't sound like the fact bothered her.

"That's because he's scared of you."

"Why would he be scared of me?"

Vivien smiled and placed her hand across the table so it was on top of Maggie's. "Dearest Maggie. Everyone is scared of you. Just a little bit."

"He's not a bad person, not really," Maggie said. "He's just single-minded and prepared to do anything to get what he wants."

Vivien took her hand away. "And right now, that's Gabriel."

"Actually, it's not," Maggie surprised them both by saying. "Don't get me wrong, he blames Gabriel for keeping you away from him and wants to kill him, slowly and painfully, but he wants what he has always wanted. You. And he will forego killing Gabriel if he has to, to get you back."

Gabriel didn't ask Maggie how she knew this. He had been there a couple of days and had already given up trying to work out how she knew what she did. She had known Joseph was on his way to see her before he knocked on her door, giving him and Vivien enough warning to get out of the house. They had decided to stay in the garden so they could listen in on the conversation.

"He wants to lock me up in a cage," Vivien said. "He's sadistic."

"No, he isn't. Sadists enjoy inflicting pain on others. He gets no enjoyment out of it. He just believes it is necessary. Yes, he wants to kill Gabriel over and over again, but not because he is going to enjoy it. He wants revenge. He wants Gabriel to suffer like he has been suffering ever since you escaped."

Gabriel wasn't sure he liked Maggie talking about his death so casually.

"He's actually tracking you down because he loves you. He thinks the only way you will be safe is if he is protecting you. He sees Gabriel as a danger he has to save you from."

"Then he's delusional."

"Maybe he is," Gabriel said. "But at least he's gone now. Do you have any idea where he is going next?"

"He's going to keep following your trail, assuming you are ahead of him."

It made sense. He just wasn't sure where that left him and Vivien. Did they follow him? Did they go home? Did they go back to see Anna?

Thinking of Anna made him realise he should check on her. "I'd better give Anna an update."

Vivien smiled that knowing smile she seemed to save only for him. "Check up on her, you mean."

"Something like that."

Gabriel excused himself and called Anna. It went straight to voicemail. He didn't bother to leave a message; he would try her again later.

He called her again after an hour had passed, and again an hour later. After his fifth attempt to get hold of her, he was growing concerned. She wasn't responding to phone calls or text messages. He called Will.

"Gabriel," Will said as soon as he answered the phone. "How are you?" He sounded cheerful.

"I could be better. How's Anna?"

"Okay as far as I know. I presume she's at work."

Gabriel was shocked. Will knew Anna had taken the day off work, and the reason why.

"What do you mean 'as far as you know'? Aren't you with her?"

"No. Why would I be…." Will didn't finish the sentence. Instead, he hung up.

Gabriel swore, and then apologised to Maggie for his use of bad language.

"We have to go," he said to Vivien. "I'm worried about Anna. Will left her alone."

"He did what?" Vivien was as surprised as Gabriel was. Will had promised to look after Anna and they had both believed he would keep his word.

Gabriel leaned over and kissed Maggie on the cheek, making her blush.

"I'm sorry to rush off, but a friend is in trouble. Thank you for everything you have done for us."

Maggie took hold of his hand and closed her eyes. "Your friend is alright, at the moment. But I can see harm coming to her and soon. You had better hurry."

"We will," Vivien said and hugged the witch tightly. "Call me if you ever need anything. I have programmed my new number into your mobile."

That was another thing Gabriel realised Maggie had managed to mislead Joseph about without actually lying to him. She hadn't said she didn't have a mobile phone, she just asked what use a blind woman would have for one and Joseph had taken that as an answer. She really was crafty. He couldn't help admiring her.

He and Vivien quickly packed their bags and loaded them into the car. They had parked it in Maggie's garage so Joseph wouldn't see it. As soon as they were on the road, Gabriel slammed his foot on the accelerator.

"If anything happens to Anna," he said through clenched teeth, "Will is going to wish he had never been born."

SHE'S GONE

"Don't panic," Will said to himself. "Whatever, you do, don't panic."

He was panicking.

As he looked down at Anna's lifeless body, he had no idea what he was going to do. Yes, she was only temporarily dead, but what would happen when she woke up?

He was certain he had blown any chance he had of getting her to stay. After what he had just done, she would be insane to do so. And he was only beginning to realise how much he cared for her, how much he wanted her in his life.

"Think," he said. "Think. What are your options?"

Well the first option was to do nothing. He could leave her where she was, maybe go out and not return until after she regained consciousness. But that was the coward's way out. She would leave without him having to face her, or own up to what he had done. It was likely he would never see or hear from her again. That was not an option.

What else could he do? Carry her to her room, stay by her side until she awoke, and then apologise and explain his actions, explain how he felt about her? That could work.

He shook his head. Of course that wouldn't work. Knowing Anna, she would politely listen to everything he had to say, and then explain to him all the reasons she had to leave, why she couldn't stay. And she would be right. They would be valid, logical reasons. He was kidding himself if he thought he could convince her to change her mind in just one conversation.

No, what he needed was more time with her, more time to get her to see his side of things, more time to convince her that she should stay, that things would be different. And he was determined that things would be different. He was through being at Marie's beck and call. The sole focus of his attention would be Anna, as it should have been today and other days in the past.

There was only one thing he could do. He would have to lock her in the basement.

Like Gavin's house, Will's place had a secure room in the basement. It was designed to keep greater vampires inside. There were times when a greater vampire became a danger, to themselves as well as others, so it was good to be prepared. Will had only had to use it a couple of times, once when a newly created vampire couldn't control her urges and started attacking humans. She had remained locked up until he and Vivien had managed to calm her down and convince her to only leave the house with one of them.

It had taken many months, but they managed to teach her how to control herself. They never found out who had turned her and then abandoned her. If they ever did, he or she would be made to pay. She was now happily settled on the other side of town and made it her mission to help any fledgling vampires she found out about.

The other time had been when Marie had first dumped him. He had been so distraught he had one of his friends lock him up to stop him doing something stupid. It had taken two weeks of isolation before they let him out. It was the longest fourteen days of his life, only seeing someone when they brought him blood. But it had helped him; it had helped him a lot.

He felt guilty about locking Anna up, but he didn't see any alternative. He had to keep her there. He could phone her work and say she had had an accident and would not be able to go back to work for a few weeks. Vivien and Gabriel weren't there and if anyone else asked, he could say she had gone away for a holiday. If Gabriel and Vivien returned, which he was sure they would, he could tell them the same thing.

He would have to find a reason why she wasn't answering her phone when they called, though. Maybe he could say it broke and she promised to get in touch as soon as she had a new one.

As he thought his plan through, putting all the pieces in place, he realised how insane it was. He was no kidnapper. He couldn't keep her prisoner.

He decided to move her to the basement anyway, just in case he had to go out before she awoke.

The secure room was equipped with a fully functioning bathroom, a bed and a TV. He gently laid her on the bed.

He looked at her for a while, pondering whether he was doing the right thing. Deep down, he knew he wasn't, but he didn't see that he had any choice. He would only keep her prisoner for a few hours, a day at most. Just until he had managed to convince her his feelings for her were real, that he really could change for her. After that, if she didn't believe him, he would let her go, he would let her walk out of his life. It would kill him, but he would do it.

He had a while before she would wake, so he left her alone, making sure he closed the door behind him, bolting it top and bottom. Even if she woke before he returned, she wasn't going anywhere.

There was a phone call he needed to make. He had hung up on Gabriel and now he had to call him back, to assure him that Anna was alright. If he knew Gabriel, he was already on his way back. Will hoped it was going to be a long journey.

He took his phone out of his pocket and dialled Gabriel's number. He felt nervous as he listened to it ring.

"Anna had better be okay." Will could tell Gabriel was on speakerphone, which probably meant that not only was Vivien listening in, but that they were in the car.

"She's fine," he said. 'At least she will be when she comes back to life,' he silently added.

"What happened?"

To say Gabriel sounded unhappy was a huge understatement. Every word he spoke sounded like a threat.

Will took a seat on the sofa. He intended to tell Gabriel the truth, to admit what he had done, to speak about everything that had happened leading up to the point where he had returned home to find Anna had packed her bags. And that was where he planned to stop. He had no intention of telling anyone that he had killed her in a fit of panic.

"I have no excuse," he said. "I have no idea how I could forget what day it is. I'm sorry."

"It's not me you should be saying sorry to," Gabriel snarled.

170

"I've already made my apologies to Anna."

"Where did you go?" Vivien interrupted. "Why did you leave her alone?"

Will had been dreading being asked that question. He could predict how they were both going to react.

"Marie called, said she needed me."

He tensed, bracing himself for the expected explosion, but it never arrived. Instead, there was nothing but silence on the other end of the line.

"Well at least Anna now knows where she stands with you," Vivien eventually said. She made the words sound like an accusation. There was nothing Will could say in reply.

Over the phone connection, Will heard an indicator being switched on. Wherever they were, they were driving.

"Where did you find her?" Gabriel asked.

Will told him everything, from rushing home to find the house empty, to going everywhere trying to find her. He spoke of tracking her to a bar, only to find she had sobered up and ridden home.

"She had her bags packed by the time I got here."

"I don't blame her," he heard Gabriel say, but it was said quietly, so he didn't think he was supposed to hear. He agreed with the comment though.

Ignoring it, he continued. "I think I have managed to convince her to stay." At least he hoped he was going to. That wasn't something he was going to admit; it was better to pretend it was already a done deal.

"We're heading back," Vivien said. "We will be there in a few hours."

"And Anna had better be there when we arrive," Gabriel added. He didn't say what he would do if she wasn't. He didn't need to.

"She will be," he said and hung up. He held the phone in his hand, praying he was telling the truth.

The call had made him tense. He went to the kitchen and put the kettle on. He wasn't a big drinker, so it never occurred to him a beer might help. He made himself a coffee and by the time he finished drinking it, he had calmed down enough to return to the basement.

He unlocked the door and braced himself before entering. It was unlikely Anna would be awake, but if she was, she was going to be pretty pissed.

He exhaled slowly in relief when he saw her still form on the bed. He went over to her and felt her neck. He was no expert, but to him it felt like it had mended itself. Now all he had to do was wait until she woke up.

He kept a collection of books on the bedside table, in case he ever had to be locked in the room on short notice, so he retrieved one, sat on the bed next to Anna's prone form, and began to read.

He was a fast reader, but was still only half-way through it when she began to stir. He marked his page and placed the book back where he had found it.

It didn't take long for Anna to open her eyes and sit up. She looked around her and when her eyes fell on Will, she frowned.

"Where am I? What happened?"

Will stood up and began pacing back and forth. He couldn't bring himself to look at her as he told her everything; what he had done and why he had done it. He explained that he had feelings for her, real feelings, and it took the thought of losing her to make him realise how much she meant to him. She remained silent the entire time.

When he had finished, he plucked up the courage to look at her. She was staring at him, stony faced. He had been hoping she would be happy he had stopped her from leaving, pleased he wanted her as more than just a friend, but he had been dreading her being angry with him. What he wasn't expecting was indifference.

Finally, she spoke. "You killed me to stop me leaving?" He nodded. "And now what? I'm your prisoner?"

"Oh God no," he said. "Of course not."

He moved closer to her and took her hands in his. She didn't pull away from him, but she didn't squeeze his hands either.

"I could never do that to you," he continued.

"So I'm free to go?"

He wanted to say yes, but his need for her to stay overrode his sense of right and wrong.

"Stay," he said. "Just for a day or so. Give yourself time to think things through. Don't make any rash decisions."

Finally, she showed some emotion, but it wasn't the sort he was hoping for.

"Rash decisions?" she said incredulously. "You think me leaving would be a rash decision? Staying would be the rash decision, after what you have done."

Will said nothing. He knew she was right but didn't want to admit it out loud.

Anna pulled away from him. "I thought I knew you. I thought we were friends. I thought I could trust you." She shook her head. "I don't know you at all, do I?"

The conversation wasn't going as he had hoped. He could feel panic rising inside him once more. How could he convince her to stay, to give him another chance?

He didn't try to take her hand again; that would be a mistake. "I screwed up. Badly. I know that. Not just once, but twice, but I'm begging you, please, give me another chance. Let me make it up to you. Let me prove I can be the person you want to stay with."

Anna shook her head.

Before Will could say anything more, he heard a knock on the front door. He almost swore. He needed to get rid of whoever it was. It meant he would have to lock Anna in, but he didn't think he had a choice.

He left the room and closed the door, locking it behind him. As the last bolt slammed into place, he heard Anna calling out. "So much for not being a prisoner."

He winced. He had a lot of work to do if he hoped to change her mind about leaving.

He raced up the stairs to the front door and opened it. When he saw who was on the other side, the colour drained from his face.

173

Elias was the last person he wanted to see under normal circumstances and these were far from normal.

"I'm here to see Anna," Elias said.

"She left," Will said as he thanked the god he didn't believe in that he had remembered to move her suitcases to her room. "And I have no idea where she has gone."

"Really." Elias raised an eyebrow. "That's interesting seeing as she's borrowing one of my cars and I'm here to drop it off to her."

Will silently swore. This was not good. Elias knew Anna planned to leave and was even helping her. Will told himself to stay calm, that he could talk his way out of this.

"What can I say? She must have changed her mind. She left over an hour ago in what I can only assume was a hire car."

Elias smiled at him. Will didn't like that smile. Smiles were supposed to be warm and friendly. This one was cold and threatening.

"Why don't I just call her then?"

Damn. That was something he had forgotten. Where was her phone? Was it switched off or set to silent? He certainly hoped so.

He could feel Elias's eyes on him as he took his phone out of his pocket and dialled a number. Will help his breath. Then he heard ringing. It was coming from the direction of the bedrooms.

How good was Elias's hearing? He had enhanced strength and speed, but did he have vampire-like hearing as well? All Will could do was pray that he didn't.

His prayers weren't answered.

"I find it interesting that Anna left without her phone," Elias said. His voice was calm and conversational. For some reason, that terrified Will. He felt his legs shake and he had an overwhelming need to go to the bathroom.

"Where is she?" Again the words were calm and collected, as though they were acquaintances having a friendly chat. If Will didn't know Elias, what he was and what he was capable of, he wouldn't have thought he was in any danger.

174

But he did know Elias and was well aware that he might not live for much longer.

Keeping Anna prisoner hadn't been his brightest idea, but he hadn't foreseen the danger. Had he realised that Elias was involved, he would have let Anna go the moment she woke up. He would have liked to think he wouldn't have killed her, but he had acted instinctively, without thinking, so was sure that knowing about Elias wouldn't have changed that.

Realising he had no choice, he said, "She's in the basement."

Elias held his arm out. "After you."

Will had been hoping to make a run for it while Elias was freeing Anna, but it looked like that wasn't an option. Reluctantly, he led the way down to the basement. He undid the bolts and turned the key in the door. Then he stepped back to allow Elias to open it.

"Are you alright?" Elias asked as soon as he saw Anna.

"I am now," she said.

"Did this person hurt you?"

Will had never heard so much venom in the word 'person' before. Elias made it sound like an insult. Will began to shake all over. If Anna told him he had broken her neck, he was a dead man.

"No. I'm fine. He's just trying to convince me to stay and thought locking me up would work."

Will released the breath he was holding. Anna was defending him. It was more than he deserved.

"Do you want to stay?" Elias asked.

Anna shook her head. "I can't."

"Then let's grab your bags and go."

Will wanted to protest, to beg Anna not to leave, but he couldn't get his mouth to work. He watched Anna and Elias walk away, unable to make his legs move.

As soon as they were out of sight, he collapsed onto the floor. He held his head in his hands. He couldn't believe everything had gone so wrong. Not only was Anna leaving, but it was likely she would never speak to him again.

175

He heard them go into Anna's bedroom to pick up her suitcases and her handbag. He heard the front door open and close and a few moments later, the sound of a car going down the driveway reached his ears.

She hadn't even said goodbye.

He was still sitting there, hours later, when the front door opened again.

"Anna," a voice he recognised called out. "Will."

Just when he thought his day couldn't get any worse, Vivien and Gabriel had arrived. He was surprised that Elias hadn't killed him. He wasn't so sure Gabriel would show as much restraint.

Forcing himself to stand, he went to greet them.

"Where's Anna?" were the first words out of Gabriel's mouth.

"She's gone." Did he sound as defeated to them as he did to himself? He had no idea and didn't care. Anna had gone; what else mattered?

"Gone? Gone where?"

Will made his way over to the sofa and collapsed onto it. He didn't have the energy to stand up any longer. He felt drained, of strength, of emotion, of everything.

"I don't know. Elias gave her a car and she left. She didn't say where she was going or when she will be back."

'If she will be back,' he thought.

Vivien sat down opposite Will and took hold of one of his hands. "What happened?" Her voice was soft and gentle, the complete opposite of Gabriel's.

He pulled away from her. He couldn't bear her sympathy. He leaned back and began to talk. He told them everything, not even attempting to hide how stupid he had been. When he had finished, he braced himself, ready for the yelling and the threats.

Instead, Gabriel laughed. Will raised his head in surprise.

"You really are an idiot," he said. "Declaring how you feel about someone shouldn't be that dramatic. There are better ways of doing it."

Will said nothing. There was nothing to say.

"You probably don't know this," Gabriel continued, "but I was in love with Anna once, so I can understand how you feel. She was with Luke, so I hid my feelings. It wasn't until I felt 'the craving' coming on that I was forced to reveal the truth."

Will was shocked. His mind went back to the time he had experienced 'the craving', something that all greater vampires went through a number of times during their life, depending on how long they lived for.

He remembered the agony he had felt until a friend had realised what was happening and found a girl willing to have lots and lots of sex with him. Nobody he had spoken to could explain what caused it or why sex helped. It was the only thing that did.

Will had been lucky. He hadn't been in love at the time so any woman would have done. He couldn't imagine what Gabriel must have gone through. If he loved Anna, she would have been the only woman safe with him.

"What happened?" he asked, though he wasn't sure he wanted to hear the answer.

"Anna spent a few days locked in a room with me. Luke went to Sanctuary 14 so he didn't have to hear anything while the rest of my family monitored through cameras, ready to intervene if they thought Anna was in any danger."

Will didn't know what to say. He wasn't sure how he felt about Anna cheating on Luke, even though it was for a good reason. His thoughts must have shown on his face.

"Don't misunderstand," Gabriel said. "She didn't do it for me. She did it for Luke. He would have suffered, knowing what I was going through. He wanted to take Anna away, but she realised that the decision would cause him emotional pain for the rest of his life, so she took the decision out of his hands. It was the bravest thing I have ever seen."

Will was forced to agree. While it was usually safe for the object of a greater vampire's affection to be with him or her during 'the craving', they were not in total control of themselves and their lovers had been known to be seriously injured, or even killed.

"How did this affect your relationship with Luke afterward? And with Anna?"

"It didn't. Luke and Anna went away for a few days. This gave us time to put it from our minds and we never mentioned it again. This is the first time I have spoken of it since."

"He never even told me," Vivien said as she placed her hand over Gabriel's.

"So why are you telling me this?" Will asked.

"To convince you that I'm not angry with you. Not for what you did to Anna. I understand why you did it. I am, however, livid that you left her alone."

Will smiled sadly. "You're not the only one. I'm mad at myself. I would do anything to make it up to her."

He then looked at both Gabriel and Vivien. "What do I do now?"

Neither of them had an answer.

HE COULD DIE

JD put the phone down and smiled. His brother and sister-in-law were finally coming home. They had just passed their final assessment and were now fully qualified trainers.

Of course, they wouldn't be home for long. They would soon be given their own Sanctuary, though it would be the first time a Sanctuary had two trainers. If anyone could make it work, it was Jonathon and Katie. He wondered where they would be sent and hoped it wouldn't be far. There was talk that Oscar from Sanctuary 7 was going to retire, but those rumours had been circulating for years.

He couldn't wait to see them again. And their son. They had been away longer than the usual twelve months, despite JD beginning their training early, because they had been given permission to only train part-time, as they had their son with them.

He had really missed them. Alexander would be delighted to have his little cousin back, even though he now had a sister to play with.

He glanced at the clock on his wall. It would soon be time for dinner. He would make the announcement then.

There was a knock on the door and Sarah entered, the look on her face telling him how concerned she was.

"How is he?" JD asked. Alexander had been feeling unwell all day.

"Refusing to eat. He still has a fever and his hands are freezing."

The comment made JD smile once more. His wife was one of those naturally warm people so most people's skin felt cold to her.

"It's probably just a cold," he said and pushed back his chair. "Or a touch of flu." He hoped not as he could remember when he last had the flu. It hadn't been pleasant. He didn't have the energy to hold up a book so he could read.

He held out his arms and Sarah sat in his lap and rested her head against his shoulder.

"I know."

"If you're worried, get Doc to take a look at him as soon as he gets back from his shift at the hospital."

"I think I will."

They were disturbed by another knock at the door and Jane entered, announcing it was time for dinner.

Once everyone was settled around the dining table, eagerly eating, JD made his announcement. He wished Doc could have been there to hear it, but he wasn't due home for a few more hours. Silvia would tell him when he returned.

Everyone was pleased. Other than Steve, the hunters had lived with, trained with and hunted with Jonathon and Katie for a number of years and missed them.

"Any idea where they will be sent?" Craig asked.

JD shook his head. "Doc may know, but I don't. The decision may not have been made yet."

"Maybe they will be asked to take over here," Scott said. "I'm sure they will be easier to deal with than you."

JD didn't need to see the grin on Scott's face to know he was just trying to wind him up. Despite being a hard taskmaster, JD was well aware that his students not only respected him, but also cared for him. They wouldn't supply him with blood if they didn't.

"You'll never be that lucky," JD said. "I have an arrangement with the council that I will be your trainer for the rest of your life."

Scott faked being horrified.

Conversation continued and as soon as all the food had been devoured, Silvia announced that she needed to get rooms ready for Jonathan, Katie and their son.

"They won't be home for a few days yet, Mom," Scott said. "There's no hurry."

"And there's no harm in being prepared. A lesson you have yet to learn."

JD smiled once more. Everyone seated around the table was like family to him and he loved listening to their banter.

The smile didn't last long though, as the pleasant atmosphere was interrupted by the hunt alarm going off.

"I'll get it," Natalie volunteered and left the room. She would switch the alarm off and get details of the location and estimated number of vampires. It was usually Doc's job, but he wasn't there to do it.

All the hunters ran to get changed into their gear, except for Sarah and JD.

"Do you want to stay here?" he asked.

For once in her life, Sarah looked uncertain.

"I'll look after Alexander for you," Silvia said, as though reading Sarah's mind. "If you're not back by the time Frank returns, I'll get him to take a look." She was the only person in the house who called Doc by his first name.

"Alright," Sarah said, though JD could see she was reluctant to go.

"You don't have to come with us." He wanted to stay, but one of them had to go.

Natalie rushed into the room before a decision could be made.

"You'd better hurry. Sanctuary 7 have called you in as backup. After they had been dispatched, a lot more vampires turned up. It's like they're having a party."

That made Sarah's mind up for her. "I'm going."

They ran from the room and up the stairs. By the time they arrived at the front door, with their swords, everyone else was ready. Natalie provided the location and they headed off.

Everyone had heard of the abandoned mansion they were heading to. It was rumoured to be haunted and had been on the market for years. Nobody seemed interested in buying it. JD had never seen it close up and was looking forward to it. He wondered what state of repair it was in and whether it would make a good sanctuary, should a new one ever be needed.

He thought back to his brother's return. Maybe he should suggest creating a new Sanctuary for Jonathon and Katie to run.

There were a number of cars parked outside their destination when they arrived. The gates to the property were closed. Scott took a look, but shook his head; he wouldn't be able to open them from the outside. It had been a long shot anyway. If they could have been opened, it was highly likely Sanctuary 7 would have done so.

Which meant they would have to climb over. The gates weren't high, so that wasn't an issue, but the difficulty they would face was getting anyone out if they were injured.

JD put it from his mind. It was a problem he would tackle if he needed to. He deliberately didn't think 'when'.

As soon as all six of them were inside the walls of the estate, Craig took a look at the gate. It would be a good idea to get it open if they could.

He found the manual release mechanism, but the gate didn't slide across as it should have done. It was rusted in place and it took three of them to get it to move.

At least they had it open, which meant they could drive their cars. The cars from Sanctuary 7 were searched and they found keys to one of them, placed behind one of the back tyres. JD had spoken to Oscar many times about how unsafe it was leaving the keys where anyone could find them, but Oscar had always argued it was useful in an emergency and the risk of a car being stolen was low.

It looked like, this time, he had been proven right.

They drove the three cars down the driveway and parked in front of the house. There was no sign of any vampires or hunters and the front door was standing open. No light came from within the house, which wasn't surprising; the electricity had probably been switched off for years.

JD signalled that Scott and Jane should head to the back of the house while the other four cautiously made their way inside. As they approached the stairs, JD used hand signals to tell Steve and Craig to head up them. The sliver of moonlight that shone in through the open door provided enough light for them to see by, but wouldn't for long. As soon as they left its luminescence, they would be in the dark.

Sticking together, JD and Sarah checked each room. They found a few beheaded vampires and one dead human, but no sign of anyone or anything living.

Scott and Jane soon joined them, having gained entry through the back door. Once the ground floor had been thoroughly searched, JD sent them to join the others upstairs while he and Sarah headed into the basement.

He futilely tried the light switch, moving it up and down a few times, but nothing happened. The air became cooler as he slowly descended the wooden stairs, which creaked with each step. So much for the element of surprise.

Not trusting their integrity, he tested each step before putting his weight on it. Behind him, he could hear Sarah doing the same thing.

Before he reached the bottom, the smell hit him. Blood. His mouth filled with saliva and he had to concentrate to prevent his fangs from elongating.

After taking his final step off the stairs, he sensed movement beside him and swung out with his sword, making contact with flesh. He had no way of knowing if he had just attacked a human or a vampire, but experience had taught him that humans made noise, no matter how quiet they were trying to be, so he wasn't concerned. If it had been a human, he would have heard breathing. For some reason, though vampires still breathed, they made much less noise while doing so.

There was a thud as something hit the ground. The lack of exclamation from whoever he had attacked suggested he had been on target and had removed the vampire's head. Most hunters would have said it was skill, but JD put it down to luck.

The basement was vast, seeming to cover the entire footprint of the house. The house would be ideal for a Sanctuary.

JD soon discovered it was also divided into separate rooms. Using torchlight, he and Sarah checked each one, finding dead bodies, both intact and beheaded, but no-one living. JD checked each corpse which still had its head, checking for a pulse, just in case. One of the bodies was dressed in hunting gear.

183

The sound of fighting could be heard from the other end of the basement, but JD and Sarah didn't rush toward it. They had to make sure there were no vampires who could attack them from behind.

They found the body of another hunter, but this one was still alive, just unconscious. They couldn't afford to treat him or get him out of there, not while there were still vampires to kill, so they were forced to leave him where he was.

As they approached the last door, they could see light shining from underneath it. This was where the sounds were coming from. JD pushed the door open and stepped back, just in case anything inside rushed out at him.

It took him a moment to take in the scene. Dead vampires littered the floor, there were two hunters in the corner, obviously injured, and two more defending them, fighting off half a dozen vampires. Luckily, the vampires weren't armed or co-ordinated. The hunters were tiring, though, and needed help, fast.

JD didn't let himself wonder why the room was lit with oil lamps. He just thanked his lucky stars that there was light as he jumped into the fight.

The vampires hadn't heard them enter, so JD and Sarah were able to behead three of them before they even realised they were there. It was now four against three and the remaining vampires were quickly dealt with.

"Thank God you arrived when you did," one of the hunters from 7 said as he bent over and tried to catch his breath. "I don't know how much longer we would have lasted."

"Where's the rest of your team?" JD asked.

"We're all that's left," the other hunter said. "We were told that there were only six or seven, so we didn't see the need to have another Sanctuary join us. We had already arrived by the time we got the call to say that more had turned up."

"You should have waited for us," he said to the woman as he bent down to check on one of the injured. He recognised Oscar's grey hair. He was clasping his stomach and the amount of blood which was flowing past his hands told JD all he needed to know. Oscar was not going to survive.

"It was too late," Oscar gasped. He held out one of his hands and JD grasped it, not caring that it was covered in blood.

Oscar's grip was strong as he sucked in his breath, trying to cope with the pain.

"We had already been seen," he managed to say.

"Don't talk," JD said. Out of the corner of his eye, he could see Sarah tending to the other injured hunter. From the position of his leg, it seemed to be broken.

"Someone needs to phone Sanctuary 1," Oscar gasped. Like any good trainer, he was thinking about the hunt rather than himself.

"On it," the female hunter said and took her phone out of her pocket. It looked like she was having trouble getting a signal, so she left the basement.

"What's with the lamps?" Sarah asked the hunter who was helping her treat the injured woman.

"The vampires brought them with them. They were having some sort of party, like a vampire equivalent of an orgy, except they were drinking blood instead of having sex."

JD didn't try to picture it in his mind; it wasn't something he wanted to see.

Oscar took a sharp breath. His breathing was becoming laboured. He wouldn't last much longer.

JD talked to him, though Oscar wasn't able to reply. He didn't tell him he was going to be alright; they both knew he would be lying. Instead, he talked about other things, anything to take his mind off his pain. He told him that Jonathan and Kate passed their final assessment and would soon be home. He talked about his children and how Alexander wanted to start training.

He continued talking long after Oscar's eyes closed. He continued to speak to him after his breathing had slowed and then stopped. He continued talking because he didn't know what else to do. Oscar was more than just another hunter; he was a friend. They had worked together many times and JD would miss him greatly, as would the entire hunter society.

He felt tears in his eyes and blinked them away. He was a trainer and it wouldn't be good for hunters to see him cry. He didn't do it often and never in public.

The rest of the hunters from Sanctuary 14 arrived in the basement and told him the entire house had been cleared of any living vampires. Other than hunters, there were no human survivors. When Craig had given his report, he took in the situation, offered his condolences to the hunters from Sanctuary 7 and told JD he and the others would head home.

There would be no celebration between the two sanctuaries tonight, as was customary. Tonight was for mourning and remembering the lost hunters.

How long JD sat with Oscar, he had no idea. Sarah took a seat beside him, offering her silent support. He almost told her to leave when Craig said the others were going back to the Sanctuary, but he liked having her with him.

He had no idea how much time passed before one of the hunters from Sanctuary 7 approached him. "The clean-up crew from Sanctuary 1 are here. James has been taken back home to our doctor, along with Elizabeth's body."

'So that was her name,' JD thought to himself, assuming the hunter was talking about the dead hunter he had found.

"We'll take care of Oscar now," the hunter from 7 continued. It was the responsibility of a hunter's home Sanctuary to take care of the wounded and the dead.

JD placed Oscar's cold and bloody hand across his unmoving chest and said a quiet goodbye before standing.

He didn't reach for Sarah's hand. His own were covered in Oscar's blood and he didn't want to pass it on to her, not that she would complain.

It was a silent drive back to Sanctuary 14. Hunters didn't often die on a hunt and to lose two in one night was devastating. He would have to make a report, but he had arrived too late to say what had happened. All he could report on was his observations of the situation and what he had been told.

When they reached home, they were surprised to find Silvia waiting for them. She was wringing her hands, which was worrying as she only did that when she was anxious. While JD could understand her being upset, as the others would have told her the news, she looked worried rather than sad.

"You need to see Frank," she said.

A coldness settled in JD's stomach. He didn't look at Sarah; he didn't dare. This had to be about their son.

He ran to the infirmary at the back of the house, Sarah hot on his heels.

Alexander was on a bed, a drip connected to his arm. Doc sat beside him and looked up when they arrived. He didn't give a welcoming smile.

"What's going on?" Sarah asked.

"It's more serious than any of us thought. I'm going to have to take him to hospital."

"Hospital?" Sarah asked. "What's wrong with him?"

"I think he has meningitis, also known as meningococcal."

"Isn't that contagious?" JD asked.

Doc shook his head. "Only the viral kind. This is bacterial which, while less common, is more dangerous."

Without taking his attention away from Doc, JD reached out and took Sarah's hand. "How dangerous? Could he die?"

"I'm not going to sugar coat this. He could die. Or be left brain damaged or have to have limbs amputated."

Sarah gasped. "But he's just a little boy." JD could hear the tears in her voice.

"Unless you have any objections," Doc said, "I'm going to drive him to the hospital."

Of course they didn't have any objections. If Doc thought their son was better off there, then that was where he had to be.

Doc unhooked Alexander from the drip and JD picked him up. The young boy didn't even stir. JD looked down at him. He seemed so delicate, so fragile.

"He's going to be okay," he said to Sarah. "He has to be," he added, too quietly for her to hear.

They took Doc's Range Rover, with Doc driving and JD holding Alexander in the back, Sarah seated beside him. She held his small hand the entire journey.

187

They went to the hospital where Doc worked. It wasn't the closest, but it was where Doc could ensure Alexander would get the best treatment.

JD was impressed with how efficient the staff were. As soon as they walked into the A&E department, Doc grabbed the first nurse he saw and explained the situation. They were immediately taken into one of the examination rooms and a doctor called. Doc and the woman discussed the situation for a few minutes, with Doc describing Alexander's symptoms and his suspicions, and then they were all thrown out so the doctor could get on with her job without them in the way.

None of them wanted to sit in the waiting room, so Doc took them to his office. They just sat and waited. And waited. And waited.

JD stared at the wall, too numb to even think. Sarah clung tightly to him and he could feel her tense whenever anyone walked past the room.

When the doctor returned, she looked serious. Too serious. This was not going to be good news.

"I'm sorry to say that Frank is right. It is meningitis."

"How can he have it?" JD asked. "He's had the vaccine."

"The vaccine covers most of the strains. However, this is strain X, which it doesn't provide protection against."

"What's the treatment?" Sarah asked.

"We have him on antibiotics, but he isn't responding. I'm sorry, but there's nothing else we can do."

Sarah started to weep.

"Can we see him?" JD choked up as he spoke. They couldn't lose their son, they just couldn't.

"Of course. Come with me."

JD looked at Doc. "You should go home. There's nothing you can do here and Silvia will want an update."

Doc nodded. He looked like he was about to say something, then changed his mind. What could he say?

The doctor led them to a private room. Alexander was lying unconscious on the bed. A drip with a tube attached to a needle was in his arm. He looked like he was just sleeping.

Sarah sat in the seat beside him and took his hand. "Can he hear me?"

"Nobody knows for sure," the doctor said. "But there is no harm in talking to him."

Sarah sang softly. Her voice was cracking, but she kept going. She worked her way through his favourite nursery rhymes before going on to songs by the Wiggles that he liked. JD admired her. It wasn't something he could bring himself to do.

Emotions surged through him as he listened to his wife and watched his son's chest gently rise and fall. Sadness and despair gave way to anger. This could not be happening. Not today. Not after losing Oscar. His son had to get better. There had to be something he could do.

He didn't know why, but his mind went to Anna. He remembered her telling him about the 'infected' she had gotten to know, Elias in particular. His mind went back to that day, reliving the conversation.

She had spoken about Elias's brother, Nick, and the woman he married. He recalled her telling them how Nick and Sophie had met and how he had convinced her he wasn't the monster she had first thought. Her son had been in a coma for a year and Nick managed to cure him.

JD's mind raced. Could Nick do the same for his son? It was a different situation, but it might work. Nick only lived a few hours away. Would he be prepared to try? There was only one way to find out.

He kissed Sarah on the cheek and said there was a phone call he had to make. He wouldn't tell her what he was up to, just in case Nick was unable or unwilling to help.

He left the room, closing the door behind him, and found a quiet place down the corridor. He first phoned Anna, but there was no reply, so he tried Gabriel next. After apologising for waking him, he quickly explained the situation, all the while praying that Gabriel had a way to contact Elias or Nick.

"I don't have his number," Gabriel said, "but I know where he lives. I'll go there immediately."

JD thanked him and hung up. All he could do now was wait.

189

Gabriel tapped his finger on the steering wheel, waiting for someone to answer the buzzer. He hoped everyone inside the house wasn't asleep.

When a voice asked him who he was and what he wanted at such a late hour, he gave his name and said he had to speak with Elias urgently. He was told to wait.

A short while later, the gate opened and he drove down the driveway. By the time he got to the house, the front door was open and Elias was standing in the doorway, dressed in a red dressing gown.

"Is Anna alright?" were the first words out of his mouth.

"I'm sorry to wake you," Gabriel said as he jogged up the steps. "But this isn't about Anna. May I come inside and explain?"

"Of course." Elias led Gabriel to the kitchen, where he switched the coffee maker on.

While Elias made the coffee, Gabriel told him everything. "Will Nick be willing to help?" he asked when he had finished.

"Of course he will be willing," Elias said. "But I have no idea if it will work. When he tried to help Sophie's son, neither of us knew if he would succeed or not."

"But there is no harm in trying."

"No, there isn't."

Elias left the room and when he returned, he had his mobile phone to his ear. "Answer the damn phone," he kept muttering to himself.

"At last," he said when he heard his brother's voice. With his enhanced hearing, Gabriel could hear when the ringing stopped, but not what Nick said.

He listened in as Elias apologised for disturbing his brother at such a late hour and quickly summarised the reason.

Nick was more than willing to help and said he would head off immediately. Gabriel provided JD's number and Nick promised to give him a call as soon as he was on the road.

"How's Anna settling in?' Elias asked.

Gabriel couldn't hear Nick's reply, but he really didn't like Elias's response.

"What do you mean she's not there yet? She should have been there days ago."

If Anna wasn't with Nick, where the hell was she?

NOW, WE WAIT

Anna scrolled through her phone, looking at all the missed calls, while the sun beat down on her. The warmth of the afternoon was making her feel relaxed, rather than uncomfortable, and the need to seek shade never crossed her mind.

It had been over a week since she left and Will had been calling multiple times a day. She listened to every one of his voicemails, but never called him back. His text messages went unanswered.

Gabriel and Vivien had also been calling, a lot. They thought she had arrived at Nick's place and was settled in. It would only take one quick phone call to Elias, assuming he knew she hadn't arrived at his brother's, for them to find out she had been lying to them.

It wasn't that she wanted to deceive them; it was just that she didn't want them to worry about her.

And they had good reason to worry. She was so thirsty the pain was becoming unbearable, but she refused to take any blood. It wasn't as if she would have trouble finding a supply, seeing as she was close to Nick's place, but she didn't want to have any. She needed the pain. When she was thinking about how much she wanted to drink some blood, she wasn't thinking about Luke. Or about how much Will had let her down.

With a sigh, she resigned herself to the fact that she would have to give Gabriel a call. She hadn't been avoiding his calls all day, well not exactly, but she had somehow managed to just miss answering them in time each time he called. And he had been calling a lot, which was unusual. Either he had found out she wasn't where she claimed to be, or something serious had happened.

She realised she was being selfish by not speaking to him, thinking about her own needs rather than anyone else's.

She selected his number, which had been stored under a code name, just to be on the safe side, hit the dial button and put the phone up to her ear.

She could hear it ringing and it kept on ringing. Just when she thought it was going to go to voicemail, Gabriel picked up.

"Where the hell are you, Anna?" he yelled.

He wasn't angry; he didn't yell at her when he was angry. He only did that when he was worried.

But was his concern caused by him finding out about her lying in regard to her whereabouts, or just because he hadn't managed to get hold of her all day? There was only one way to find out.

"I've been out sightseeing. I'm on my way back to Nick's place now."

"Don't give me that bullshit. I know you aren't staying there. Why not? Where are you? Have you been getting enough blood?"

She heard him take a breath. "Are you okay?" he asked in a much calmer voice.

"I'm fine," she lied. "Getting blood hasn't been a problem." Of course it hadn't been a problem. She didn't want any, so not having any was of no issue.

"Talk to me Anna. I know you're lying."

What would he do if she told him the truth? That she had purposely been avoiding drinking blood just so it would cause her physical discomfort? Knowing Gabriel, he would drop everything in order to track her down.

Unlike Will, who would say he would do it, but wouldn't actually follow through.

Why did Will's actions bother her so much? It wasn't as if they were anything more than friends. And while he had let her down, he hadn't betrayed her.

"Will's not handling your departure very well, in case you're interested."

Was she interested? Not really, she told herself, but still asked what Gabriel meant.

"He's moping about. He's barely left the house. He's turning down every social invitation. He won't even go out for coffee with me and Vivien. He misses you. Won't you at least let him know that you're still alive?"

'Thanks to him, I almost wasn't,' she thought, but she didn't say the words. They were cruel and unfair. It wasn't Will's job to babysit her, to make sure she didn't do anything stupid, even though he said he would.

"I'll think about it," she said.

"Good. Now get yourself to Nick's. If I don't hear from him soon, I'm going to come and find you."

It was a promise, not a threat. The lack of blood had left her tired, too tired to argue with him.

"Alright. I'll call you as soon as I get there."

She hung up and sighed. She hadn't expected to be able to disappear for long and was surprised it had lasted for over a week. Now all she had to do was convince Nick and Sophie that she had been taking blood and pretend she was still doing so while living with them.

She wondered how long it would be before they noticed she was starving herself. She had no idea if there would be physical signs, other than the pain and the tiredness.

It only took her half an hour to reach her destination. She pressed the buzzer on the gate and it opened almost immediately. There was a camera on the gate, set to show who was in the car. Whoever had answered her ring must have recognised her.

It was Sophie who was waiting at the front door, not Nick. As Anna pulled up in front of the house, she thought about all she knew of the woman. They were alike in a number of ways. Both had given up a mortal life for the man they loved. Anna hoped that, unlike her, Sophie got to keep hers.

Anna put her at late thirties, early forties, though that was just the age she had become 'infected'. Her long dark hair was being blown about by the light breeze and, though she couldn't see them from where she was, Anna remembered being fascinated by her eyes. They were different colours and had been since birth; it was not a phenomenon brought on by becoming 'infected.'

As soon as Anna was out of the car, Sophie walked up to her and hugged her tightly, as though they were old friends not relatively new acquaintances. Sophie stated how worried she had been.

"Did you get lost?" she asked.

Anna could have lied and said she did, but she was too worn out to keep lying.

"No. I've purposely been staying away."

Sophie linked her arm with Anna's. "Come inside and you can tell me all about it."

Sophie whistled and two men appeared out of nowhere.

"Do me a favour and put the car in the garage and take Anna's things to the second guest room on the left."

"Sure thing," one of the men said and went to the car. Sophie thanked them before leading Anna into the house.

It was tastefully decorated and Anna was impressed with the wooden panelling. It looked old, but well cared for. The inside of the house was comfortable rather than imposing, as it could well have been.

Sophie took Anna to the kitchen. "Coffee? Or would you prefer something stronger? Are you hungry?"

"Coffee would be great." Anna declined the food. She didn't need it and since she had stopped drinking blood, even the smell of anything cooking made her nauseous.

"Where's Nick?" she asked as Sophie prepared the drinks. She chose to have a glass of red wine instead of coffee and Anna had to look away; it reminded her too much of blood.

After leading Anna to the lounge, Sophie explained about Nick's mercy dash to try to save Alexander the previous evening. "He's done all he can," she said. "Now all anyone can do is wait."

Guilt took hold of Anna. Sarah was her friend and she should have been there for her. If she hadn't been avoiding contact with everyone, she would have known about Alexander's illness and could have been by her side by now.

She was pulled from her self-pity by Sophie asking an unexpected question.

"So what's going on between you and Will?"

Anna was startled. "What do you mean?"

"You're interested in him, right?"

"No," Anna said immediately. "Of course not. We're just friends."

"Uh-hu." Sophie's response told Anna she didn't believe her.

"We are," Anna insisted.

Sophie lent forward. "I know I don't know you very well, so I could be wrong, but are you seriously trying to tell me that you have moved half-way across the country just because a 'friend' let you down?"

Anna didn't like the way Sophie had said 'friend'. She might as well have used her fingers to mimic quotation marks. She opened her mouth to speak, but Sophie held up her hand, her palm facing Anna.

"Before you say anything, I know what you have been going through. Elias told me. I hope you don't think he was betraying a confidence, but he felt it was important for me to know everything."

"So you can keep an eye on me." Anna wasn't happy, but she could understand Elias's reasons for talking to Sophie.

"Something like that. Now, back to Will."

"Can we talk about something else please?"

"No."

Even if Anna had never heard about Sophie's son, she would have known she was a mother. She had that tone of voice which only develops when dealing with a toddler. It was a no-nonsense mixture of patience and authority. Anna's own mother had used it on her, though sparingly, well into her teenage years.

Anna felt like a young girl again, being reprimanded. She had to stop herself from pouting, as she used to do frequently when she was younger and not getting her own way.

Sophie tucked her legs under her. She was looked like she was settling down for a long conversation. Anna resigned herself to it. Sophie was being kind to her, letting her stay at the house indefinitely, so enduring an unwanted conversation was the least she could do.

"From what Elias has told me, Will obviously cares for you." Sophie grimaced. "Though I have to admit, he does have a strange way of showing it."

Anna didn't disagree. She could accept that Will had feelings for her, but he was still too hung up on Marie for it to matter.

"And you have feelings for him," Sophie continued.

"I do not," Anna stated. "I'm still in love with Luke."

Sophie's voice softened. "I know you are, and you always will be, but that doesn't stop you caring for someone else. It doesn't stop you moving on. It's been a year. Wouldn't he want you to try to find love again?"

Anna said nothing. Sophie was right; Luke would want her to get on with her life instead of wasting it mourning over him. But was she ready? And even if she was, would it be fair on any man she could potentially get involved with? She would never be able to give all of her heart to him.

Then she thought about Sarah. Before she met JD, she had been engaged to Craig's best friend. He had died and the only reason Sarah got through it was that Craig stayed by her side, never letting her be alone, just in case she did something stupid.

Sarah had loved her fiancé with all her heart, yet that didn't stop her having a relationship with JD. Anna was aware that Sarah still visited her fiancé's grave, so she still cared for him. Instead of feeling like he was competing with a dead man, JD accepted Sarah's past and even went with her to the graveyard.

Would it be the same for Anna? Could she find someone who would accept that she would always love Luke? Could Will be that person? Did she even want him to be?

Anna could see Sophie watching her carefully, as though she was trying to read her emotions. She gave Anna time to process what she had said, before continuing.

"Do you think you should give him another chance?"

Anna shook her head. "I can't trust him. The minute Marie clicks her fingers, he'll go running to her. He always does."

"From what Elias has told me, according to Gabriel, Will hasn't seen her since you left."

"He won't stay away from her for long. I know he won't."

"Then why don't you put him to the test?" Sophie asked.

"What do you mean?"

Sophie told her what she was thinking and by time she stopped talking, Anna was smiling. It just might work.

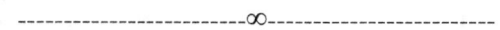

Gabriel hung up the phone and walked back into the lounge. Vivien raised a questioning eyebrow.

"Well?"

"Let's go for a drive," he said.

She didn't ask why he hadn't answered her question; he would have his reasons and would talk to her when he was ready.

Gabriel waited until they had exited the driveway before speaking.

"Anna has arrived at Nick's place and Sophie has persuaded her to give Will another chance."

"And you don't want Will to know this because?"

Gabriel smiled. "Because she and Sophie have devised a test for him. If he passes, she'll come home. If he fails, she will stay where she is."

"What's the test?" Vivien asked.

Gabriel told her and she agreed it was a good idea. A little cruel, maybe, but nothing Will didn't deserve.

"There is one problem though," he said.

Vivien was able to guess what that was. "We need to get Marie to agree to help out."

Gabriel nodded. He had told her about Marie making advances toward him, so she understood why he wanted to avoid her.

"I'll go speak to her," she said. While Marie wasn't her favourite person at the moment, she bore her no ill will. She could understand the other woman being attracted to Gabriel, but she should know better than to try to seduce someone's boyfriend. She should know, but she didn't. It wasn't that Marie was malicious or callous, she was just so used to getting her own way it never occurred to her there were times when she shouldn't try. She was so self-centred she didn't realise what she was doing sometimes. Her treatment of Will was a prime example.

They drove to Marie's house and Gabriel waited in the car while Vivien went inside. Marie welcomed her in as though she hadn't tried to steal her boyfriend, which was of no surprise to Vivien. She explained what she wanted Marie to do and Marie was happy to help out, though she did seem confused as to why her help was needed. Again, this was not unexpected.

"Will and I are just friends. Why would Anna think he would leave her for me?"

"Because he always does."

Marie frowned. "He comes to help me when I need it. That's what friends do. Why is that a problem?"

Vivien shook her head. There were some things Marie would never understand.

"I'll let you know when you need to make the call."

Vivien was about to leave the room, when Marie called out to her.

"Vivien. I am sorry you know."

Vivien stopped and turned to look at her. "Sorry for what?"

"For Gabriel leaving you for me. We both know he is going to."

Vivien couldn't be angry at Marie. She wasn't trying to hurt her. Her regret was genuine. She also wasn't making a threat. Marie honestly believed Gabriel choosing her over Vivien was inevitable.

Vivien shook her head once more and left.

"How did it go?" Gabriel asked when she was in the car and they were driving away from Marie's house.

"She's agreed to help out."

"And?"

Vivien liked the way Gabriel was able to read her. He always knew when she was holding something back.

"And she is sorry that you are going to leave me for her."

Gabriel slammed on the breaks. "What!"

Vivien smiled as she patted him on the cheek. "Don't worry. I know you have no intention of doing so, no matter what she may think."

Gabriel still didn't look happy. "If that bitch does anything to upset you."

He didn't need to finish the sentence. Vivien was under no illusions about how vicious Gabriel could be when he wanted to. But Marie wasn't in any danger. There was nothing the woman could say or do which would upset her. Marie would never understand what Vivien and Gabriel had and that even if she did try to split them up, it would never work. Vivien was not the jealous type where Gabriel was concerned; there was no need to be.

While Gabriel drove, Vivien called Anna to let her know everything was in place. By the time they got back to Will's, he had already packed an overnight bag and was about to leave. Vivien had never seen him looking so excited.

"Anna called. She wants to see me." His entire face lit up as he beamed at her.

"Calm down," Vivien said. "What exactly did she say?"

"That she's prepared to talk. She gave me a location and a time, two days from now." Will was talking so fast, he was barely coherent.

"Don't get your hopes up," Gabriel warned. "Just because she's prepared to talk, doesn't mean she's coming back."

Will looked at him as though he was an idiot. "I know that. But as least I am going to have a chance to persuade her."

He grabbed his keys and ran out of the door.

"Good luck," Vivien called after him, though whether he heard, she had no idea.

"So what do we do now?" Gabriel asked her.

"Now, we wait."

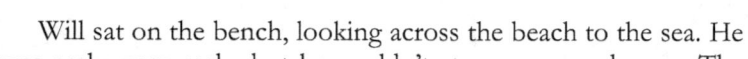

Will sat on the bench, looking across the beach to the sea. He was early, very early, but he couldn't stay away any longer. The anticipation was eating him up from the inside. He felt sick. What if she didn't show? What if she only wanted to speak to him to tell him to his face that she never wanted to see him again?

But he couldn't worry about 'what ifs'. If he went down that path, he could end up anywhere.

So he waited. And waited. The hour he was due to meet Anna came and went. He kept looking around him, but there was no sign of her.

He had no idea he was being watched. He didn't know Sophie had been waiting for him to arrive and had phoned both Anna and Gabriel the moment he turned up. He had no way of knowing that a few hours later, Vivien had called Marie to let her know it was time.

His phone rang and he picked it up, answering without looking at who was calling.

"Anna," he said expectantly. "Where are you? I'm here waiting."

"It's Marie," the voice on the other end of the phone said. She sounded annoyed.

"Sorry Marie. I was expecting a call from Anna."

"Obviously. Where are you? I need your help with something."

"I'm not home at the moment. You'll need to call someone else."

"But I need you," Marie insisted. "My father has asked to see me and I need you with me. He's planning on being in town tomorrow night and wants to meet with me."

Will was well aware of the strained relationship between Marie and her father. She had mentioned it many times, both while they were dating and after they had split up. He looked at his watch. If he left immediately and drove through the night, he would get there in time. Just.

He didn't even consider doing it. "Sorry Marie. I have something important to do. I can't leave yet. You will have to ask someone else."

He hung up the phone. Anna was late, but he would wait for her. He would wait as long as it took.

While he waited, phone calls were being made. Marie phoned Vivien, confirming she had asked Will for help and he had refused. Gabriel contacted Anna. Anna called Sophie.

Will spoke to nobody. He just sat and waited.

After three more hours had passed with no sign of Anna, he was growing concerned. Had something happened to her? He called Vivien, but was told neither she nor Gabriel had heard from Anna. He didn't know what else to do.

He was debating asking for Elias's number, even though he was the last person Will wanted to talk to, when someone tapped him on the shoulder.

He looked up at a woman standing next to him. She looked late thirties, maybe early forties, the trace of grey in her hair indicating the later. Though he had never seen her before, he knew who she was. Anna had talked about her, a lot, after she had met her at Elias's house. The different colour eyes gave her away.

"Are you Will?" she asked.

Will had no doubt that she knew who he was. "You must be Sophie."

She smiled and sat on the bench next to him.

"She's not coming, is she?" He was praying his assumption was wrong, but Sophie shattered his prayers.

"No, she isn't. She tried. She watched you for a long time, but she just couldn't face you. I am so sorry."

Will felt like crying. He wouldn't give up, not yet.

"She just needs time," he said.

Sophie placed her hand on his arm. "You're right. She does."

Will stared out to sea. "Then I'll wait."

Out of the corner of his eye, he could see Sophie shake her head. "She needs more time than that. Go home. She will be in touch."

"No." Will could be stubborn when he wanted to. It was one of the things Marie used to complain about.

Sophie shrugged. "Suit yourself, but you will be wasting your time."

Will said nothing. He continued to stare out at the sea, his mind completely blank.

He didn't turn when Sophie stood up.

"Goodbye Will. I hope things work out for you and Anna, I really do. You just need to be patient."

Will didn't respond. He was feeling too numb to speak.

He didn't see Sophie walk away. He had no idea that as soon as she was out of sight, she took out her phone and called Anna.

He just looked out at the sea, thinking about nothing while he waited to hear from Anna.

The sun had set by the time he realised she wasn't going to call.

I'LL BRING THE BLOOD TO YOU

"Well you look like shit," Gabriel said as soon as he saw Anna. Why she had knocked on the door instead of using her key, he had no idea.

"It's good to see you too," she said. She tried to smile, but didn't quite manage it.

Gabriel took her in his arms. He had never seen anyone looking so pale, so worn out. She looked like she hadn't slept or eaten in weeks. Or drank any blood.

He stepped away from her. "When did you last have blood?"

"Recently."

She wouldn't look at him, indicating she was lying.

"Don't give me that crap. How recently?"

When she raised her head, she looked scared of him. He was not going to like her reply.

"I haven't had any since I left here."

He couldn't contain his anger. "For God's sake Anna. You can't go that long without having blood. No vampire can. Are you trying to starve yourself to death? Trust me, it won't work."

He stepped further away from her and ran his fingers through his hair in frustration.

"Damn it Anna. You can't do this to yourself."

"Why not?"

The question shocked him. What could he say to that? Because you might die? Experience told him that wouldn't happen. Because it will cause you a great deal of pain? Like she didn't already know that.

"Because you may lose control," he finally said.

"I haven't so far. And it's not as if I would attack a human."

"Wouldn't you? Just because you can't ingest their blood doesn't mean the craving won't cause you to attack."

Anna shrugged. "I'm tired. It's been a long drive. I'm going to bed for a while."

Gabriel did nothing to stop her as she pushed past him.

"Anna," he called after her. She stopped, but didn't turn around. "I'm just worried about you."

Then she did turn around and look at him. "I know."

After she had gone, Vivien came out of the kitchen.

"I heard Anna arrive and thought I should give you some privacy. Does she look as bad as you made out?"

Gabriel sat down and clutched his hands together in front of him. "Worse."

Vivien sat beside him, placed a hand on his shoulder and gently squeezed.

"From what Luke told me, you've been through worse."

"I had Luke to help me through it."

"And Anna has us. And Will. He's on his way back. Maybe when he gets here, he'll be able to help Anna."

"I'll tell you one thing," he said, raising his head and turning it to look at Vivien. "He'd better not let her down again."

Will wearily opened the door. He wasn't happy to be home. He hadn't heard from Anna and he had no idea when, or even if, he would.

He felt drained, defeated. Why hadn't he told Anna how he felt sooner? Why hadn't he been there for her when she needed him? He only had himself to blame.

"You look terrible," Gabriel said to him as he glanced up from the sofa, where he was drinking coffee with Vivien as though they didn't have a care in the world. Maybe they didn't.

Then he remembered that Vivien's brother was out to take her back and kill Gabriel and reassessed his thinking.

"Are you alright?" Vivien asked.

"I've been better."

Been better? He struggled to think of a time when he had been worse. He hadn't felt this dejected when Marie dumped him.

"Go to bed," Vivien said. "Get some sleep."

Will nodded. It was a good suggestion, but something told him he wouldn't be able to sleep.

He didn't ask if either of them had heard from Anna; he didn't want to hear that she was happy to keep in touch with them, but not him.

He trudged to his bedroom, opened the door and froze. Anna was on his bed, asleep.

It took him a moment to realise he wasn't breathing.

He slowly exhaled. His heart was beating so fast he could hear it in his head. She was here! She was actually here!

Or was he seeing things? Was his imagination playing tricks on him?

As quietly as he could, so he didn't wake her, he closed the door and crept up to the bed. He reached out a hand and gently touched her arm. It was solid; it was real. He wasn't imagining things. Anna really was here.

He felt like crying in relief. Then he realised he had no idea what to do. Should he wake her? Should he leave her in peace?

He gazed down at her, taking in how pale she was. She didn't look well. He had to know what was wrong with her; how else could he fix it?

He sat on the edge of the bed and she stirred, but didn't wake. "Anna," he said softly, but she didn't respond.

He reached out to her, but withdrew his hand before touching her. Never before had he been so unsure of what to do.

How long he sat looking at her, he had no idea, but eventually he forced himself to shake her awake.

She murmured and slowly opened her eyes. They didn't widen in surprise, as he had hoped, and she didn't smile.

"Hey," he said, wincing when he heard how lame that sounded.

"Hey."

Her voice sounded like speaking was difficult, like she didn't have the energy to do it.

Then he realised that was probably the case. He knew what was wrong with her and it was something he could fix.

"You need blood."

She didn't deny it, so he took off his t-shirt, revealing his well-formed body. He hoped Anna was impressed, but something told him she didn't even notice. She was too far gone with blood deprivation for her to notice anything. And it was all his fault.

He moved closer to her and helped her sit up. It was concerning that she wasn't able to do it herself.

"Drink," he said and moved his head to the side, exposing his neck. She had only ever drunk from his wrist, but taking it from his neck would mean she would get more blood in a shorter period. Plus it meant he would be able to hold her close while she drank.

He sucked in his breath as he felt her fangs penetrate his skin, but the initial sting soon subsided and he relaxed. He placed his arm around her, holding her in position as she drank.

After only a few minutes, she tried to pull away, but he wouldn't let her. She hadn't had anywhere near enough. She continued to suck his blood for another minute before stopping.

He relaxed his hold on her so she could pull away from him.

"You have to have more," he said gently.

"Not from you. I've taken too much already."

"I'm fine. Take more. Please."

She shook her head. "If I take any more, I'm not sure I will be able to stop before I kill you. Did you know that a vampire dies if they lose all of their blood? Or so JD was once told by a vampire who was planning on killing him. I know that Gabriel tried it once. He slit his wrist and cut his throat, but he healed before he lost too much blood."

Will took Anna's hands in his and looked her straight in the eyes. He did his best to ignore how dull and lifeless they looked. At least a little colour had returned to her skin.

"I trust you. You won't kill me. Now drink."

He moved his head to one side, offering his vein again. He hoped she realised that he was offering her his heart with it.

She seemed reluctant when she placed her mouth on his neck once more. He wished she was kissing it instead of biting it, but that would have to wait. He didn't even know if she wanted a relationship or just friendship. It was one of the things they would have to discuss once her thirst was sated.

She drank a little more before pulling away again.

"I'm tired. I need to sleep."

Will nodded. He would let her rest and make her drink more when she woke.

She didn't push him away when he settled on the bed next to her. He placed his arm over her and they both closed their eyes. Will had a smile on his face. He couldn't remember when he had felt this happy. Or this exhausted.

The room was dark when he was woken by soft knocking on the door. If he hadn't been a vampire, he wouldn't have heard it.

Without waking Anna, he moved his arm off her and got off the bed. He glanced back at her before opening the door, making sure she was still asleep. He wanted to be with her when she woke.

He opened it wide enough for him to leave the room, closing it silently behind him. He was glad he had oiled the hinges. It had developed a squeak which only regular treatment with oil would silence.

Gabriel stepped back, allowing him to move into the corridor.

"How is she?" he whispered.

"Sleeping, but she has taken some of my blood. She needs a lot more."

"I know, but she refused to take mine or Vivien's. I'll try again when she wakes. Now that she has started to drink, maybe she'll be less stubborn."

Will shook his head. "No. I caused this and I am going to fix it. I will provide all the blood she needs."

Gabriel frowned as he looked him up and down. "That's not a good idea. You can only give her so much before it begins to affect you. When did you last drink?"

Will smiled. "Don't worry about me. I drank on my journey home. I'll be fine."

Gabriel continued to frown. "You'll still need more if you are planning on letting Anna drink all of yours. Go out and get some. I'll keep an eye on her."

"No," Will said through clenched teeth. "I am not leaving her."

Gabriel placed a reassuring hand on his shoulder. "I understand. Stay here. I'll bring the blood to you."

Will had no idea how he planned on doing that, but didn't ask. He needed to get back inside his room, back to Anna.

He didn't thank Gabriel. He just nodded and turned away.

Anna was still asleep. She rolled toward him as he lay down beside her, allowing him to hold her tight. He closed his eyes and went back to sleep.

When he woke, Anna was awake and looking at him. He tried to read her face, but failed. He had no idea what she was thinking or feeling. He could ask her, but he had other things on his mind.

"Time for more blood."

"Not from you." Anna shook her head.

"Yes, from me. I will be fine. Stop worrying."

"But—"

He didn't let her finish her sentence. "No buts. And no more arguing. Just do as I ask. Please."

Her thirst must have overpowered her stubborn streak because she said no more and latched onto his neck. He could feel the blood leaving his body, draining him of energy. Gabriel was right; he would have to replace his lost blood, and soon.

Anna didn't drink for long, but it was enough to make Will feel so weak he wasn't sure he would be able to get off the bed. Once she had taken her fill, she lay back down and went to sleep once more, making Will wonder if she had been avoiding sleep as well as blood.

He closed his eyes, but sleep wouldn't come. He was thirsty. He had no idea what Gabriel was up to in regard to supplying him with blood, but he hoped it didn't take too long.

After what felt like days, there was a knock on the door. Will forced himself to get off the bed to answer it, but it almost took more energy than he could muster. As soon as he was out of the room, his legs gave way and he would have fallen to the floor if Gabriel hadn't caught him.

A man and a woman were standing next to Gabriel, people Will had never seen before.

Gabriel gestured toward them with his hand. "Lunch."

They seemed scared, but didn't move away or even flinch when Will took hold of the man's shoulders. Gabriel must have put a little of his venom in them so he could control them. Will assumed that their memories would be wiped once he had drunk his fill.

He took blood from both of them, enough to leave them feeling tired, but not enough to cause them any harm.

"I'll take these two back where I found them," Gabriel said, "and will be back with more in a few hours."

Will nodded his thanks before stumbling back into the bedroom.

For three days, Will's life consisted of drinking blood, sleeping and feeding Anna. Her periods of being awake began to slowly increase and she was no longer pale and sickly looking.

On the third day, she made it from Will's room. She was placed on the sofa in the lounge with a blanket on her and a steaming cup of coffee in her hands. She wanted to bathe, so Vivien ran a bath for her and helped her into it once it was full of hot water. Will had volunteered to do it, but the looks both Vivien and Gabriel gave him had him backing away.

When Anna made it back into the lounge, she looked like a completely different person to the one he had found in his bedroom when he had returned from his trip to find her. Her hair had been washed and Vivien had applied a little makeup. Anna looked her old self again. Will couldn't help smiling.

"Do you want any food?" he asked. "I can make you an omelette."

Anna liked his cooking and had often commented on how good his omelettes were. While she didn't need to eat, Will knew she enjoyed it.

She shook her head. She was nearly fully recovered from her lack of blood, but wasn't quite there yet. Will wouldn't push her. He would let her start to do things again at her own pace.

"You've had a few visitors while you were sleeping," Gabriel informed her. "A number of people from Elias's estate, including Elias himself, have dropped by to check that you are alright They wanted to see you, but I didn't want you disturbed."

Will was glad Gabriel hadn't allowed them into his room. Elias was the last person he wanted to see.

"Thank you," Anna said. "I will give Elias a call later."

"Speaking of calls," Vivien said, "Marie has been trying to get in contact with you, Will."

Will had purposely left his phone in the lounge so he wouldn't be disturbed. He had heard it ring a few times, but ignored it.

He retrieved it from where he had left it and winced when he saw the number of missed calls and unread text messages. Someone had plugged it in for him instead of allowing it to go flat. He wasn't sure whether to thank them or not. If it wasn't charged, he could avoid the messages for a while longer.

Not all were from Marie. He spent some time going through them, responding to some. His literary agent had called and he made calling her back a priority. He apologised for being out of contact for a few days and promised to take her out to lunch the following week. It was about time he started on his latest book. Now that Anna was back, he might be in the mood to write once more.

A number of people had been in regular contact with Gabriel, asking about Anna's recovery. Gavin, JD, Sarah, Sophie, to name but a few. Will wasn't surprised to hear that so many people cared about her.

Once Anna finished speaking to everyone she needed to, she said she was feeling tired once more, so Will took her to her room. He liked having her in his, but there was no longer a need and she said she wanted her privacy. He wanted to argue, but didn't.

She surprised him, however, by asking him to stay. There were things they needed to talk about and she thought it was time.

Will wasn't sure he was ready for the conversation. He had convinced himself she only wanted to be friends and he didn't want to hear her say it.

"What are your plans now?" he asked before she could speak. "Are you going to go back to work?"

She nodded. "I didn't quit, I took a sabbatical. I just have to let them know when I'm ready to start again. They said I could take up to a year off before they would replace me."

"That's good." Will was pacing the room. He was too highly strung to sit down.

"I didn't ask you to stay so we could talk about work," she said as she watched him move about.

"I know." He forced himself to sit on the edge of the bed. "What I did was unforgivable. I know I'm an arsehole. You don't need to tell me."

Anna smiled. It was the first time he had seen her smile since her return and it warmed his heart. "I need to know how you feel about me. I need to hear you say it. To me. Face to face, not over text or voicemail, like you have been doing."

Will couldn't stop wringing his hands. Was he ready to speak to Anna? How would she react if he did? Was it better to say he respected her as a friend in order to keep her and not scare her off? Then again, if she had listened to any of his voicemails, she would know that he felt more for her than just friendship.

Honesty was the only course of action. But that didn't mean he was ready.

He couldn't look at her when he started to speak; he didn't want to see her reaction.

"I care about you, Anna. A lot. I didn't realise how much until you said you were leaving. I guess I took you for granted. And for that I apologise."

He paused, in case she wanted to say anything, but she remained silent. Was she even listening to what he was saying? He assumed so, but didn't look at her to find out.

"I love you Anna. I should have told you sooner. I should have shown you sooner. You leaving broke my heart and made me act in ways I am ashamed of."

Then he raised his head and turned to look at her. She didn't seem angry or upset. But she didn't look happy either. Maybe she was processing what he had said. But he had more to say and he wasn't sure she was going to like it.

"I love you, but I'm not in love with you. I think it won't take long, but I'm not there yet. I can't be devoted to you, the way Luke was, at least not for a while."

He was surprised to see her smile. "Thank heavens for that. The last thing I wanted to hear was that you're head-over-heals for me when we both know that's not the case. I don't like it when people exaggerate their feelings."

She looked away. Will had no idea what she was thinking or feeling. When she turned back to him, he could see the pain in her eyes. And the indecision.

"I don't love you, Will."

The pain cut him like a knife. He thought he had prepared himself to hear the words, but he was mistaken. Nothing could have prepared him for it. A cold sensation settled in the pit of his stomach and slowly spread its icy tendrils throughout his body. He wanted to run away, to put as much distance between himself and Anna as he could, but he couldn't get his body to move.

Then Anna placed her hand on his arm and he felt the warmth of her touch infuse his body, beating back the chill which had settled into him. When he looked at her, a trace of a smile touched her face.

"I like you, Will, a lot. But it hasn't turned into love yet. I cannot guarantee it will, but it is a strong possibility."

Will was sure his heart skipped a beat. Hope flared within him. He wasn't looking for guarantees; nothing in life was guaranteed. Other than death and taxes, he reminded himself.

He placed his hand over hers. "That's good enough for me."

"I should warn you, though. Luke will always have a piece of my heart. I will always love him and will always feel his loss."

Will let out a small laugh. Not because he found what she said funny, as it was far from it, but because he was relieved that she was concerned about how he felt.

"I have a confession to make," he said. "While you were away, I phoned Sarah. We had a long chat about how she felt when she lost her fiancé and how she struggled when she started having feelings for JD. I didn't know if you felt anything for me, but I wanted to try to understand, just in case you did."

"You did what?" She wasn't angry, he was sure of that. But he wasn't sure what emotion she was feeling. He could have been wrong, but he thought she sounded surprised. No, that word wasn't strong enough. Amazed sounded like a better word to use.

"That's....that's....incredible," she said in the same tone. "That you went to that sort of length to try to understand how I might be feeling."

Will couldn't keep the smile off his face. He had finally done something right.

"I'm not going to pretend to understand what you have been through, or what you will continue to go through, but I can accept that I can never have all of you. But I won't be competing against Luke. Your heart is big enough to love us both, should you choose to do so. I understand that, if you do ever fall in love with me, it won't be the same as the love you feel for Luke, but it also won't be any less."

Anna breathed out slowly, as though she had been holding her breath while Will had been speaking.

"So where do we go from here?"

"I'd like to kiss you, if you will let me."

It was Will's turn to hold his breath. Was he moving too fast? Would she turn him down?

"I think I would like that."

He leaned forward and placed his lips against Anna's. He kept the kiss soft and gentle, though it wasn't easy. He wanted to deepen it, to show her how much he cared, but he forced himself not to.

"That was nice," she said when he pulled away.

He placed his hand on her cheek. "You should get some sleep."

214

Leaving her alone was the last thing he wanted to do, but it was the right thing to do. He forced himself to remove his other hand from where it was still positioned on top of hers. When she, too, moved her hand, his arm felt cold.

"I'll come and see you in a few hours," he said as he stood up.

He hoped she would ask him to stay, but he knew she wouldn't. She looked like she really did need some sleep. She was no longer craving blood, but she still wasn't fully recovered from starving herself.

He kissed her on the forehead. "Sleep well."

He went to the door, but waited until she laid down before leaving the room. He closed the door behind him and leaned against it as he breathed a sigh of relief. The conversation had gone a lot better than he had been dreading.

He felt like whistling as he returned to the lounge, but refrained from doing so.

"Anyone want a coffee?" he asked as he walked in, but there was nobody there. He had no idea where Vivien and Gabriel were and he didn't care.

He went into the kitchen and put the kettle on. He was feeling happier than he had in a long while.

That feeling didn't last long, though. Less than an hour later, he heard a knock on the door. When he opened it and saw who was on the other side, his legs started to shake.

"Hello, Will," Elias said and smiled, revealing his fangs.

Will's mouth went dry. He couldn't speak, so he stepped back, indicating with his arm that Elias should enter.

"Anna is sleeping," he managed to say as he closed the front door.

Elias went into the lounge and sat on the sofa. He stretched his long legs in front of him, resting his feet on the coffee table.

'Why don't you make yourself at home,' Will thought to himself, but he didn't say the words out loud. He had no idea how Elias would react to sarcasm and he didn't want to find out

"I'm not here to see Anna," Elias said.

Will gulped. He didn't like the way Elias was looking at him.

"I'm here to see you," Elias continued. "I had an interesting call from Anna a while ago. She said she's decided to give you a second chance."

Will said nothing. What could he say?

Elias took his feet off the table and leaned forward.

"Hurt her again and it will be the last thing you ever do."

DO I WANT TO KNOW WHAT SORT OF THINGS YOU DID?

As JD looked down at his son, sleeping peacefully in his bed, tears filled his eyes. He had never been so scared in his life, not even when he and his entire hunting team had been surrounded by more vampires than was humanly possible to defeat and death to them all, including Sarah, was inevitable.

And now it was over. Alexander was getting better, was well enough to be allowed home. The doctors at the hospital thought it was a miracle that the drugs they had been giving him had suddenly started working, but JD knew better. It was nothing to do with traditional medicine; it had been Nick that had saved his son.

He reached out and stroked his child's head. There were insufficient words to voice the gratitude he felt. He couldn't help thinking about what would have happened if Anna hadn't been taken away, if she hadn't been curious about the place she was told to avoid. If she hadn't entered the grounds and befriended Elias, JD wouldn't know that 'infected' existed, or that they could cure human illnesses.

His thoughts went to Luke. If Luke hadn't died, none of the events he had been thinking about would have happened and it was likely his son would not have survived.

He looked up at the ceiling, but he didn't see it. His focus was above that, to a heaven he wasn't sure was real. If it was, he had no doubt that Luke was there, watching over Anna.

"Thank you," he said, though exactly what he was thanking Luke for, he wasn't certain.

He looked down at his son once more, smiled and left the room. Nick was waiting downstairs, talking with Sarah and Craig. He could have left as soon as he had done what was needed, but he decided to stick around and see what the outcome was.

When JD arrived in the lounge, he found the topic of conversation was how Nick had met Sophie.

"I'm sorry," Sarah said, "but can you say that again. You didn't really use her as a sacrifice, surely."

JD took a seat beside his wife and took hold of her hand. It seemed like he had interrupted an intriguing conversation.

"I did," Nick said after nodding a greeting to JD. "It was necessary, to bring back Elias."

Sarah shook her head. "I think you need to start at the beginning."

Nick grinned. It seemed like he enjoyed telling his story. Before he started speaking, though, the smile dropped from his face and he turned serious.

"You have to understand. Elias and I have done some truly terrible things. We have hurt people, have killed hundreds, if not thousands. And not all of them were so we could feed. It took a long while for us to realise what our father was making us do was wrong. When we did, we fled."

"Do I want to know what sort of things you did?" JD asked.

"No, you don't."

JD didn't push it. He was curious, but didn't want to get on the wrong side of Nick, especially after all he had done for his son.

"I learned to control my urges," Nick continued, "but Elias couldn't. He tried so hard, but always ended up killing the person he was feeding off."

'Not unlike vampires,' JD couldn't help thinking.

"Seeing no alternative, we had a witch put Elias into some sort of suspended animation."

Craig held up his hands, palms facing outward, and waved them about. "Hold on. I thought the witches were trying to kill you."

"They were, but we found one sympathetic to our cause. Can I continue now?"

Craig nodded, though he still looked confused.

"Decades passed and I got word that my father was raising an army. I knew of only one way to stop him. I needed Elias."

"Are you telling me that one man can defeat an entire army?" Craig asked. JD glared at him.

Nick didn't appear to mind the interruption. A smile appeared on his face once more. "Far from it. Elias is good, but not that good. What he excels at, though, is strategy and training. I needed him to help build my own army."

"So it was like a civil war," JD said.

"Exactly. While my father forced 'infected' to join him, we asked for volunteers. Hundreds sought us out as soon as they got word, and not just 'infected'. To bring Elias back, I needed a number of sacrifices and some gemstones which were used in the initial ceremony. And that is where Sophie comes in. Her boss had one of the gems I needed and wasn't willing to give it back when I contacted him. I went to her place of work to retrieve it. I had to shoot one of her colleagues in the head in order to make her boss hand it over."

JD glanced at Sarah and registered the shock on her face. Nick did as well.

"Hey, I never said I was perfect. I am still more than capable of killing, but now I only do so when it is necessary. In that situation I deemed it necessary. I do not regret my decision."

JD could feel how tense Sarah had become, so he squeezed her hand. "When did you last kill someone?"

He was hoping Nick would say that was the last person he killed, but he didn't. "That man was the last human I killed, but I still have to kill 'infected', when they break the rules."

JD shivered. This man was not only deadly, he was ruthless. He was suddenly glad Nick was a friend, not an enemy.

Then JD started thinking about his own life and what he did with it. Could he claim to be any different? He killed vampires just for what they were. He could say he was protecting humanity, but if he found a vampire who, like himself, only took blood from willing donors, would he give him or her the chance to explain themselves, to plead their case? Would he let them live? He wasn't sure and he didn't like where his thoughts were taking him. His mind was dragged back into the conversation when Nick continued to speak.

"Back to Sophie. One of my men was getting a little too friendly with one of Sophie's teammates and she stood up to him. Her bravery impressed me and I wanted to know more about her. I needed another sacrifice so taking her would kill two birds with one stone."

JD glanced at Sarah once more. She looked like she wanted to be sick.

"We performed the ceremony to bring Elias back and he took the life force of the sacrifices, killing them. All except Sophie. She didn't scream, which was how we discovered that it was the screaming that made Elias lose control. He now takes control of his victim's minds so they won't scream. He hasn't killed one since."

The tone Nick used suggested he was proud of his brother. JD, on the other hand, was disgusted. Taking life force in order to survive was no different to drinking blood, but at least his donors did so willingly; he didn't force anyone to do it against their will.

He didn't like the way Nick was looking at him. It was almost as if he was reading his mind. Were his feelings showing? He didn't think so. As a lawyer, he was used to hiding what he was thinking. He had perfected the 'poker face'. But he was at home, in a relaxed setting. Maybe he had slipped and no longer wore his emotional mask.

"Since I killed my father and we won the civil war," Nick said, his eyes still on JD, "things have changed. Both myself and my brother are now surrounded by people who are willing to donate some of their life force in order for us to stay alive. We no longer have to steal the life force from others."

JD relaxed his tense muscles. He had been misunderstanding both Nick and his brother. He had jumped to unfair conclusions and felt guilty. He let his head drop. When he raised it again, he found that Nick was still looking at him. He had a smile on his face.

"I know what you were thinking," he said. "And I don't blame you. Elias and I used to be terrible people, monsters even, but now we do our best to make up for that. We no longer harm people, unless it is necessary in order to protect others."

"Sorry," JD said, but Nick waved away his apology before he could finish.

"I understand. Now, where was I?"

"You were going to explain how Sophie became your girlfriend, even though you used her as a sacrifice," Sarah said.

"Ah yes. Her son was in a coma and had been for over a year The doctors said there was no hope, but Sophie refused to believe that. I cured him, the same as I did your son."

"And she was so grateful, she fell into your arms."

Sarah wasn't the only one to give Craig a withering look. He might be married, but JD thought he still had no clue about women.

"Far from it," Nick said. "To win her over, I told her everything about myself, and not just the good things. I have a sort of diary, written by one of the men I served with during some wars I took part in. It details some of the horrific things that were done. I wasn't personally responsible for most of them, but I was in command and did nothing to stop them. I let her read it."

"And she was still prepared to get to know you?" Sarah sounded like she didn't believe what Nick was telling her.

"Sophie is a remarkable woman. She was prepared to see who I am now, not who I was in the past. She said that everyone has things they are ashamed of in their history. In my case, it's a little worse than most. Well, a lot, actually."

Nick then looked at his watch. "I should really head off. I've been away from Sophie too long."

Everyone stood up. Sarah hugged Nick and both Craig and JD shook his hand.

"Thank you for everything," JD said. "Not just for saving our son, but for opening up to us as well, for letting us know who you really are."

"No problem. Keep in touch."

Everyone promised to do so. Once Nick left, JD collapsed down on the sofa. Sarah sat next to him and cuddled up beside him, pulling her feet up and tucking them under her.

"What has you so concerned?"

221

JD knew better than to try to keep things from his wife.

"Nick has made me think about things, that's all. About what we do."

Sarah sat back and looked at him. "What do you mean?"

"We kill vampires just because they are vampires. Is that really fair?"

"We don't kill greater vampires," Sarah pointed out.

"But that's because we couldn't if we tried. We have a truce with them to protect ourselves, not them."

"They are also our friends. Well, some of them are, anyway."

"And that's my point. Are there lesser vampires out there who don't kill people for their blood, who don't keep people prisoner just so they can have a constant blood supply? Are there vampires out there like me, who drink blood because they have to, not because they want to, who just want to be left in peace to get on with their lives without hurting anyone?"

Sarah took hold of his hand. "Maybe. But we haven't met any yet. Every vampire you have killed has attacked a human."

"I know, but I still think I should talk to the council, bring up my concerns."

"Why don't you give Gavin a call? After all, he is on the council."

It was a good idea and JD followed her suggestion.

Gavin answered after the second ring. After the usual pleasantries, JD got down to business. He explained his concerns and then waited for Gavin to laugh at him.

He didn't. He said he'd had the same thoughts himself from time to time. Were there lesser vampires who, like the greater vampires he lived with, didn't kill or enslave humans? He hoped so, but he had yet to meet any.

He promised to take JD's concerns to the council next time they met, which was scheduled to be the following weekend.

Nick, Elias and the other 'infected' would not be mentioned. It had been agreed that nobody outside of Sanctuary 14 and Gavin's group of greater vampires needed to know about them. The vampire hunter society had enough to worry about without finding out that there were things out there in the world that were more dangerous than even greater vampires.

As Gavin had said when he heard about how easily Elias had beaten Gabriel in a fight. "There are worse things than vampires."

YOU'RE TURNING ME DOWN?

"Are you sure about this?" Will asked as he pulled up outside the café. It was the first time they were going to be seen in public as a couple. They had been taking things slow, so it felt like a big step.

Anna nodded her head. He smiled at her. He had been doing that a lot, ever since she had agreed to give him a chance. It had only been a week, but already he felt more relaxed, more comfortable with his life. He had started writing again, much to his agent's pleasure.

He got out of the car and rushed around to the passenger door, but Anna was already out. He tried to be an old-fashioned gentleman, but she never seemed to give him the chance. He didn't let it bother him, though.

The café was nearly empty when they walked in, hand in hand. The owner was behind the counter, serving her only other customer, and raised her eyebrows when she noticed them. She indicated with her head that they should take a seat.

Will chose a table by the window. It didn't give them as much privacy as one near the back wall would, but they weren't there for privacy; they were there to announce their relationship. It was a small town and as soon as one or two people saw them together, holding hands, word would spread. It was one of the reasons Will chose the seat he did; he wanted to see who was walking past.

He and Anna had just settled into their seats when Cassidy walked up to them, notepad in hand. The smile she gave them was genuine. She worked long hours, but she loved running the café. She enjoyed spending time with customers, listening to, but not spreading, the latest gossip. She was the first person to make Will feel welcome when he moved into the area.

"Hi, Will. It's good to see you, Anna. I heard that you went away for a while. I'm glad you're back."

Will could see her eyes drifting to the table, where his hand holding Anna's was clearly on display. He knew Cassidy well enough to know she wanted to ask, but wouldn't. She never pried into other people's business.

"What can I get you?"

"The usual please," Will said. He and Anna often had coffee at the café and they always ordered the same thing.

"Have you got any apple turnovers today?" Anna asked. She didn't often eat at the café, but when she did, it was always an apple turnover. Will had tried to make them himself, once, but it had been a disaster. He was a good cook, but when it came to pastries, his skills had a lot to be desired.

"Sure," Cassidy said and looked at Will, waiting to see if he wanted anything.

To Will's eyes, she looked young for her age. He was aware her blonde hair came out of a bottle and it covered up the odd grey hair, but it made her look in her early thirties, rather than the late forties he knew her to be.

"Nothing for me, thanks," he said and she turned away with another smile. He watched her swaying hips as she returned to the counter. He wasn't sexually attracted to her, as he saw her as a good friend, but he couldn't help admiring how well she looked after herself. If he ran the café, he would eat all the profits and his waistline would suffer for it, had he not been a vampire.

He and Anna made small talk until Cassidy returned with their order. After thanking her, Anna took a large bite of her turnover and groaned with pleasure. While she ate, Will let Cassidy know that he and Anna were now officially a couple, though they wanted to take things slow.

Cassidy was delighted for them and wished them well. Before she could say more, another customer entered the café and she went over to greet him.

Will and Anna sat in silence while she ate. Will smiled as he watched her. He liked her doing things which gave her pleasure. She had gone through a traumatic experience before she met Luke and gave up all guilty pleasures, like eating sweet pastries, and it had taken her a long time to get used to doing so again. Will was glad it was all in her past.

225

He glanced out of the window and groaned. Marie had just pulled up. While she was a regular at the café, she was usually there in the afternoons, which was why he had chosen to take Anna there in the morning. He wasn't sure he wanted to see her, but it looked like he had no choice.

"Marie's just turned up," he said to Anna. "What do you want to do?"

"That's up to you, but we did come here to let people know about our relationship and she has to find out sooner or later."

Anna had been gracious in regard to Marie. She hadn't told Will he couldn't see her anymore and the few times in the past week that she had called him, Anna left it up to Will to decide if he would respond to her summons or not. He hadn't. It wasn't because he was worried about upsetting Anna; he no longer felt the need to do so. The pull she used to have on him had gone. He wasn't a puppet anymore and he was glad he had finally realised that was what he had become.

Marie hadn't been offended when he declined to meet her. After all, she had enough other male friends she could call upon for assistance in whatever task she wanted doing.

She entered the café like she was a famous movie star, calling out to Cassidy for her usual, completely oblivious to the fact that Cassidy was serving another customer.

As she walked toward her usual seat, she looked around the room and her eyes fell on Will. When she noticed that he was holding hands with Anna, her eyes widened. She changed trajectory and went over to them.

She was beaming when she said, "I see you two finally got your act together. It's about time. I always said you would make a great couple."

'Said it to who?' Will couldn't help thinking. As he looked her up and down, he wondered what he had seen in her. Yes, she was beautiful and he knew, from experience, what a great body her clothes were hiding, but her personality had a lot to be desired. Saying she was self-centred was an understatement. It wasn't that she was intentionally selfish, she just didn't realise the entire universe didn't revolve around her. She used people, but had no idea she was doing so.

"Would you care to join us?" Will asked. He didn't want her to, but it was the polite thing to say.

Marie waved his suggestion away, making him feel like he was a mosquito, flying around and bothering her, rather than a friend making her an offer. He pushed the feeling aside. It was unfair to think like that.

"I have a date." She looked at her watch and frowned. "And he's late. That doesn't bode well for this relationship, does it?"

It was a rhetorical question, so neither Anna nor Will replied.

Marie then turned her attention to Anna. "I'm happy for you, Anna dear. Take good care of this man. He's one of the best."

A few weeks ago, Will would have thought, 'Well why did you dump me then?', but all the bitterness toward Marie he hadn't even realised he had been harbouring, had disappeared.

"Thanks, Marie," Anna said, without a trace of irony. Will looked at her, but couldn't read any emotion in her face, other than happiness. It seemed she bore Marie no ill will.

Marie turned away and started back toward her own seat, but turned back. The look on her face told Will that she had just thought of something and he wasn't going to like what she was about to say.

"Let me throw a party in your honour," she said, clapping her hands together in glee.

"There's really no need—" Anna started to say, but Marie cut her off.

"Of course there is. What better way to announce your new relationship to the whole world?"

"Like the entire town isn't going to know within an hour, now that you know," Will said quietly enough so only Anna could hear him. He saw her lips twitching as she fought not to laugh.

"I'll make all the arrangements. All you have to do is turn up. Oh, and make sure you bring Gabriel with you."

She said the last part as though it was an afterthought, but Will wasn't convinced. Gabriel and Vivien had both mentioned

227

Marie's infatuation with him. That was the real reason for the party. Will would, of course, let him know about the invitation, but he doubted he would accept.

As soon as they finished their coffees, Will said, "Let's go."

Anna didn't object. They had done what they were there to do.

As they walked out, Will slipped his arm around Anna. It felt right to do so and he hoped he would be doing it for many years to come.

Marie was still sitting alone, tapping her foot on the ground. She wasn't one to hide her emotions.

As Will and Anna approached his car, a car came skidding into the parking lot. The young driver abandoned it rather than parked it and ran to the door of the café, stopping just before he reached it so he could try to straighten his dishevelled clothes and smooth down his hair with his hands.

"Marie's date, I'm guessing." Will didn't even try to keep the amusement from his voice. Anna laughed. It was a nice sound that pulled on Will's heartstrings.

"Something tells me he's in for a hard time," Anna said as she climbed into the car. For once, she had allowed Will to open the door for her.

Gabriel and Vivien were waiting for them when they got home.

"How did it go?" Vivien asked.

"Marie saw us."

Nothing more needed to be said. It was a foregone conclusion she would tell everyone she knew. And she knew a lot of people.

"Oh, one more thing," Anna said. "She's insisting on throwing a party for us. She asked us to make sure Gabriel knew that he was invited."

Will glanced at Anna. She had a smirk on her face. She had enjoyed saying that. She knew that Vivien wouldn't mind; she wouldn't have said anything if she even suspected it would upset her friend.

Gabriel rolled his eyes.

"Why don't you just bite the bullet and sleep with her to get her off your back?" Vivien said, her eyes lighting up with amusement.

"I would rather you killed me now." Will wasn't sure if he was joking or not. "Besides, we both know that I'm so good that if I sleep with her she'll keep coming back for more."

"Unfortunately, he's right," Vivien said. "It's not just his ego talking."

Anna turned her head away, trying to hide her face, which had turned bright red. Will was about to ask why, when he remembered Anna had forced herself to sleep with Gabriel, even though she had no feelings for him and was in a relationship with Luke, when Gabriel went through 'the craving'. It was one of the things he loved about her. She would do anything for anyone.

Gabriel looked at Vivien. "We're going, I take it."

"It would be rude not to."

Later that afternoon, Will received a call from Marie, letting him know the date and start time of the party. She was nothing if not efficient. If she set her mind on something, you could guarantee it would happen. Which left Will feeling uneasy about Marie having her heart set on claiming Gabriel for herself. To the best of his knowledge, Marie had never failed in a conquest.

When the evening arrived, they decided to take two cars, just in case one of the couples wanted to leave early. They timed it so the party would be in full swing by the time they arrived. Will hoped to make a quiet entrance, but Marie was by the front door, waiting for him and Anna, and made an announcement. While they were being mobbed by well-wishers, Gabriel and Vivien snuck in unobserved.

They headed straight to the bar, which was being run by one of the local publicans. Gabriel ordered whisky, which he drank straight down before asking for a refill and ordering Vivien a drink.

"Planning on getting drunk?" she asked with a glint in her eye. She was teasing him, not criticising him.

"No, I just need a few drinks inside me to fortify me against the inevitable encounter."

The evening went well and it was nearing midnight before Marie approached them.

"It's so great to see you," she said before air kissing Vivien on both cheeks. "You should have let me know when you arrived."

"You were busy with other friends," Vivien replied. "We didn't want to bother you."

"You are never a bother." Marie went onto her tiptoes so she could kiss Gabriel's cheek. He wanted to move away at the last moment, but it would have been rude.

"Do you mind if I borrow Gabriel for a little while?"

Gabriel waited for Vivien to say no, to point out how inappropriate the request was, given that Marie had already shown her intentions toward him. But she didn't. Instead she agreed. She addressed Gabriel, telling him to be a good boy, before walking away and leaving him alone with Marie. He glared at her retreating back. While he understood she was demonstrating to Marie that she believed she had nothing to worry about as Gabriel would never cheat on her, he still felt she was abandoning him to the situation.

"Come with me," Marie said as she took his hand. He wondered what she would do if he pulled away, but decided not to find out.

She led him up the stairs, passing many doors until she got to one near the end of the corridor. She opened it and dragged him inside.

He assumed it was her bedroom. The décor was so 'girly', as Anna would say, that it made him feel uncomfortable. While the pastel colours matched, he felt they made the room a little flat, a little washed out.

The room was dominated by the largest four-poster bed he had ever seen. He thought it was over the top, but refrained from commenting.

"What can I help you with?" he asked when he heard Marie close the door. He turned around to see her unzipping her dress. She let it fall to the ground before stepping out of it.

She was wearing nothing underneath.

Dressed in just her high-heeled sandals, the straps of which laced around her ankles, she walked up to him, slowly, seductively.

He couldn't help admiring her body. It truly was magnificent. It was a shame it was inhabited by an undesirable personality. If he had met her ten years ago, he would have gone to bed with her with enthusiasm, but now he had Vivien once more and he had no desire to have sex with any other woman.

When she reached him, she placed her arms around his neck. "You can help me reach orgasm," she whispered in his ear. "Multiple times."

He didn't know exactly how she expected him to react, but she was shocked when he pulled her arms off him and stepped back. "I don't think so."

Her mouth hung open. He now understood what people meant when they said their jaw dropped. It took all his self-control not to laugh.

"You're turning me down?" He had never heard anyone sound so incredulous. It must have never occurred to her he would say no.

"Of course I'm turning you down. I'm in love with Vivien. I have no interest in doing anything sexual with anyone else."

"You're turning me down?" she said again, this time emphasising the 'me'.

"Yes," Gabriel said and stepped around her so he could get to the door.

"Gabe."

He wasn't sure if it would be a mistake to turn around, but he did so anyway.

"You will change your mind." She made it sound like a foregone conclusion.

"No, I won't."

He had nothing further to say, so he walked out of the room, making sure he closed the door behind him. He may not like Marie, but he didn't want to embarrass her by allowing anyone who might walk past to see her naked.

He made his way down the stairs and sought out Vivien. She wasn't hard to find. She was propping up the bar, along with a vampire she had befriended the first time she had stayed with Will.

"What happened?" she asked once she made her excuses to her friend and took Gabriel to a quiet place where they wouldn't be overheard. She had a glint in her eye again. Gabriel wasn't sure he was happy about her finding the situation amusing.

He filled her in, leaving nothing out. He didn't keep secrets from Vivien.

"Do you think she got the message? Will she leave you alone now?"

"Not a hope in Hell."

They stayed at the party for another hour or so, but there was no sign of Marie. Whether she was avoiding them, had found another man to seduce, or was hiding in her room, Gabriel didn't know and didn't care.

Will and Anna beat them home and Gabriel and Vivien filled them in on what happened.

"You might want to make yourself scarce for a while," Anna suggested. "Seeing you might upset Marie."

"We were planning on leaving tomorrow anyway," Vivien said. "Now we know you are safe, we should keep an eye on Joseph's movements. We know he was heading north, so we will assume that he's still doing so."

The next day, true to their word, Gabriel and Vivien packed their bags and left. Before departing, Gabriel took Will to one side for a private chat.

"Look after Anna. And if you don't do a better job than last time, I guarantee you are going to regret it."

Will placed his hand on Gabriel's shoulder. "Don't worry. Now that I have her, I am going to do everything in my power to make sure I keep her." Gabriel gave him a dirty look, which made Will chuckle. "No, that doesn't include locking her in the basement."

When they returned to the women, Will slipped his arm around Anna as they both waved the couple goodbye.

"Is Marie going to cause any trouble for us when we come back?" Gabriel asked Vivien as he drove down the driveway.

"According to Will, she's never been turned down before," Vivien said. "So I have absolutely no idea."

IT HAS TO BE DONE

"What do you want to eat tonight?" Silvia asked as JD walked into the kitchen. "Seeing as it's just going to be the two of us."

She wasn't talking to him. Someone had their head in the fridge and he assumed it was Scott. It was Craig and Natalie's anniversary, so they were going out to dinner, Jane and Steve were planning on grabbing a bite to eat before going to the movies, Doc was working and JD and Sarah had been invited over to Sanctuary 7 where Jonathan and Katie were now joint trainers. That just left Silvia and her son who would be at the Sanctuary that evening, along with the kids.

JD was glad to have his brother and sister-in-law back, even if they were now living somewhere else. He and Sarah visited them often, with the children, and the cousins enjoyed playing together. This time, however, the children would be left behind. Silvia had volunteered to babysit for them, as well as look after Craig and Natalie's daughter. It wasn't often they had a child free evening, so they planned on making the most of it.

"Why don't you let me cook?" Scott suggested as he withdrew from the fridge, can of drink in hand, and closed the door.

Silvia laughed. "Because I don't want food poisoning. I still remember your disastrous attempt at cooking a simple stew all those years ago when JD thought it was a good idea for you all to learn how to cook."

A smile crept onto JD's face. The experiment hadn't lasted long and they ended up eating quite a few takeaways during those few weeks.

"I've improved since then."

"I'm still not taking the risk. How does steak with baked potato and green beans sound?"

"Perfect. Thanks, Mom."

JD couldn't help smiling at the exchange. He felt a pang of regret. Or was it jealousy? He had never had that sort of relationship with his parents. He and Jonathon grew up in a

Sanctuary which their mother ran and had their father as their trainer. Their parents did their best, but as they got older, both boys felt the Sanctuary came first. As a result, they spent a lot of time together and Jonathan really suffered when JD was sent away for training. While JD's relationship with his parents wasn't a bad one, he didn't see them much and he could never imagine having the sort of interaction he had just witnessed with either of them.

When Silvia turned around and noticed him, she said, "Are you here for the muffins?"

"Yes please."

When Katie had been living at Sanctuary 14, she had grown addicted to Silvia's chocolate chip muffins and put in a special request for JD to take some over with him that evening.

Silvia went into the pantry and instead of returning with a small Tupperware container, she handed over a large basket covered with a cloth. It looked like she had baked enough to feed everyone in Katie and Jonathon's new Sanctuary.

JD took the basket in one hand and used his other to lift the cloth. Silvia smacked the back of it.

"No eating any before you get there. They are not for you."

"Yes, Mom," JD said, with a cheeky grin on his face, which made her laugh. Both knew at least one, and probably two, would disappear before the end of JD and Sarah's journey. Katie wasn't the only one addicted to Silvia's baking.

"Are you sure you don't mind babysitting?" he asked for the umpteenth time. She did it a lot and he didn't like to think he was taking advantage of her.

"Of course. I love being with the children. It's good practice for when I become a grandmother." She raised her voice for the last sentence, speaking loud enough for her son to hear as he walked out of the kitchen.

He made a rude noise in response.

"Well thanks again."

"My pleasure. Now get going or you will be late."

JD bent down and gave her a kiss on the cheek before following her orders.

Leaving the basket near the front door, he went in search of his wife and found her in the nursery, reading to their two children. Charlotte was sleeping, but Alexander was avidly listening to every word. He loved books and refused to go to sleep at night without a bedtime story, preferably two.

"Are you ready to go?" he asked, winking at his son and making him giggle.

"Nearly. Two more pages then we're done."

JD stayed to listen to the end of the story. He had heard and read it so many times he knew it off by heart. Once Sarah finished, she put the book away, kissed Charlotte, who didn't stir, and picked up Alexander, ready to take him to his own room.

"Be good for your Aunty Silvia," JD said as he kissed his son and ruffled his hair.

"Yes, Daddy," the young man said and rolled his eyes, as if saying he would never be anything else. JD knew better. Alexander was starting to develop a rebellious streak, but Silvia wouldn't put up with any nonsense from him.

JD and Sarah shared one of the muffins on the journey, with Sarah breaking bits off and feeding them to him as he drove.

When they arrived, despite knowing the code to open the gate, JD pressed the buzzer. He felt it was rude to let himself in and only did so in emergencies.

They must have been expected as the gate began to open without anyone asking who was requesting admittance.

Jonathon was standing in the open doorway when they pulled up outside the house. He walked over to the car to greet them, pulling his brother into a hug and kissing Sarah on the cheek. He told them Katie was putting their son to bed. He wanted to stay up to see his aunt and uncle and wasn't happy he wasn't allowed to.

Jonathon took the basket from JD, muttering that he had better get at least one this time, causing both Sarah and JD to smile. They missed Katie and Jonathon and wished they were still at Sanctuary 14, but hunters went where they were sent. And Sanctuary 7 was in need of a good trainer to replace Oscar. They were lucky to get two.

They went into the lounge and the three of them spent some time catching up before Katie joined them.

"Sometimes I wish it was legal to chloroform children," she said as she collapsed into a chair. "I swear he's getting worse."

"It does get better, I promise you," Sarah told her.

Before Katie could respond, the gong sounded, announcing dinner was ready.

The two couples made their way to the dining room, which was full by the time they got there. Everyone seated around the table knew JD and Sarah. They had been regular visitors even before Katie and Jonathon had moved there. It was the first time they were eating there since Oscar's death and it felt wrong not seeing him at the table.

Conversation flowed as they ate. The usual questions were asked about the children and the other residents of Sanctuary 14 Sarah was sitting opposite Rob, one of the hunters who had embarrassed himself in front of her the first time they had met. It was something JD often reminded him about.

"I have a bone to pick with you, JD," he said when there was a lull in the conversation. "Your brother is almost as bad as you are. And Katie isn't much better."

"What do you mean?" he asked, though he had a good idea what Rob was talking about.

"Did you have to teach them to start training at such an early hour?"

"Hey, we start half hour later than JD does," Katie said.

"I know, but does it have to be every day? And do you have to make it so hard?"

JD was filled with pride for his brother and sister-in-law. If the hunters were complaining, it meant they were doing a good job. A trainer had to be tough and had to keep their students on their toes. It was what kept them alive on a hunt.

Sarah had no sympathy for Rob. "Toughen up you wimp."

Rob growled at her, but not in an unfriendly way. He wasn't brave enough to do that. Most people sitting around the table were a little scared of Sarah, and a lot scared of JD, even though they knew he would never harm any of them.

JD's phone rang. It was considered bad manners to answer your phone at the table, so he quickly glanced at who it was and frowned. Why would Doc be calling him? He was supposed to be at work.

"Sorry, I have to take this."

He left the room to answer it in the hall, closing the dining room door behind him.

"Hi Doc, what's wrong?" He knew it wouldn't be a social call.

"You need to come to the hospital. There was an explosion at the restaurant Craig and Natalie went to. Some sort of gas leak or something."

A chill passed through JD. For Doc to be calling him, it had to be serious.

"How are they?" he forced himself to ask. Part of him didn't want to hear the answer.

"Craig's unconscious and Natalie is being prepped for surgery."

At least they were alive. For now.

"Will you be operating?"

"No, due to my personal relationship, they won't let me. I'll be there to assist and the surgeon they have called in is one of the best. She's in good hands."

"And Craig?"

"We don't know yet. There's swelling on the brain. We won't know much more until the swelling goes down or he wakes up."

JD could hear what Doc wasn't saying by the tone of his voice. *If he wakes up.*

"We're on our way."

All conversation stopped when JD returned to the dining room and everyone saw the look on his face.

"What's happened?" Sarah asked.

"There's been an accident. Craig and Natalie are in the hospital."

JD was glad she didn't ask for details. "Sorry," she said as she stood up. "We've got to go."

Jonathon also rose. "We're coming with you."

"We'll take care of Nathan," Rob said, referring to Jonathon and Katie's son. One of the joys of living in a Sanctuary was there was always someone willing to look after your children for you, without being asked.

"Thanks," Katie said. "We'll keep you updated."

They practically ran from the house. Jonathon grabbed his keys from the bowl by the front door and he and Katie made their way to the garage, while JD and Sarah got into their car and headed off. There was no need to wait for them. Jonathon owned a Ferrari and liked to drive fast; they would soon catch up.

Jonathon knew the area better than JD and took the back roads, allowing him to arrive at the hospital first, but only just. They ran into the building and headed straight to the front desk. JD enquired after Craig and Natalie and was asked if they were family.

"Yes," Sarah said before JD could reply. It wasn't technically true, but they were the closest thing Craig had since he turned his back on his parents, blaming them for his brother's suicide. Their reaction to his death made Craig swear to never speak to them again. It was a promise he had kept. Some things could never be forgiven.

The receptionist told them to go to the waiting room and a doctor would see them as soon as they could. The plastic seats were uncomfortable and JD paced the room until Sarah told him to sit down; he was disturbing the other people waiting for news of their loved ones. Katie sat quietly with Jonathon, who was gripping her hand as though he never planned on letting it go.

A woman in a white coat entered the room and went over to them. "Are you the relatives of Mr. and Mrs. Blakley?"

Sarah stood up. "I am, yes."

The woman gestured to the seat Sarah had just vacated. "Please, sit down." She didn't wait for Sarah to comply before continuing. "I'm Doctor Harwood. I can tell you that Natalie is still in surgery and will be for a while. Her spine was crushed. She will live, but we are not yet sure if she will be able to walk again."

Sarah's hand went to her mouth as she gasped. JD took hold of her other hand.

"I'm sorry for being so blunt, but there is no easy way to tell someone something like that. I promise you will be kept informed of her progress."

"What about Craig?" JD asked.

"He suffered a head injury. There is swelling on his brain that we can't reduce. He's in a coma and we had to hook him up to a ventilator."

JD could feel Sarah shaking next to him. She and Craig were more than just friends. He had saved her life when she lost her fiancé and as she had told the receptionist, he was family to her. He was family to them all.

"Can we see him?"

"Of course," Doctor Harwood said. "Come with me."

Katie and Jonathon both stood up.

"Only two of you I'm afraid." The doctor's eyes were filled with regret.

She led JD and Sarah down a number of corridors until she reached the room Craig was in. She opened the door and JD heard the beeping of the machine which was monitoring his heartbeat. It wasn't strong, but was steady. The ventilator he was attached to sounded like it was breathing rhythmically.

Craig was a good hunter, strong but not overly muscular, yet lying in the hospital bed he looked frail and weak. Sarah was sobbing quietly. JD couldn't imagine how she must be feeling.

"When will he wake up?" he asked.

"We don't know. The next six or so hours are going to be critical. If we can't reduce the swelling by then, it is unlikely he will recover."

Sarah looked like she was in a daze as she slowly walked over to the hospital bed and took Craig's hand. "Hi Craig, it's Sarah," she said quietly. "I need you to get through this. You can't leave us. Alex and Charlotte need their uncle."

"I'll leave you alone," Doctor Harwood said to JD. The look she gave him told him all he needed to know; she didn't hold out much hope.

As soon as the door closed, JD grabbed a seat and placed it beside the bed so his wife could sit down. Tears were streaming down her face when she raised her head to look at him.

"You need to call Nick."

JD nodded his head. Nick had been able to save their son, so maybe he could do the same for Craig.

He left the room and stood in the corridor to make the call. As soon as Nick answered, he filled him in on the situation. Nick wasn't home; he had taken Sophie away for a few days and it would take him too long to reach the hospital for him to be of any use. He promised to contact someone who was living at his estate. None of them there were as powerful as he or Elias were, but it was the best he could offer. JD thanked him and hung up. Now all they could do was wait.

It would take a few hours for anyone to arrive and those hours were going to feel like days.

He returned to the room and placed his hands on Sarah's shoulders. She was still talking to Craig, reminding him of all the good times they shared. He had no idea if Craig was able to hear her, but the words were as much for Sarah as they were for Craig.

When she stopped, he told her the bad news. While help was on the way, it may not arrive in time and, even if it did, it might not deliver the miracle that was required.

For nearly two hours, JD and Sarah remained in the room. JD watched Craig's chest moving up and down as the ventilator filled his lungs then allowed them to empty. He wasn't really seeing it though; his mind was elsewhere.

Other than the sound of the machines, the room was silent. Sarah had talked herself out and JD had nothing to say.

When the sounds changed, it took JD a moment to realise what the difference was. The machine monitoring Craig's heartbeat was no longer beeping. He looked at it and saw Craig had flatlined. He was about to call out for help when it emitted a loud warning alarm.

Seemingly from out of nowhere, medical staff filled the room. JD and Sarah were kicked out. Through the open doorway, the room looked like it was in chaos, but it was organised chaos. Someone was in command, calling out instructions. A crash cart was wheeled in and someone said, "Clear."

JD pulled Sarah away. She didn't need to see or hear what was going on.

He held her tight, hoping his arms around her would stop her shaking, but knowing they wouldn't.

Then JD heard the monitor start its regular beeping again. Never had anything sounded so good. It didn't mean Craig was out of the woods, but at least he was alive.

He let Sarah know the good news and she pulled out of his arms. "We need to talk."

She took his hand and led him back to the waiting room where they had left Katie and Jonathon, who both stood up as soon as they entered the room.

"How's Craig?" Katie asked.

JD filled them in on the situation. Other than the four of them, the room was empty. JD knew what Sarah was going to say and wasn't sure if he was ready for the discussion.

"We need to make a decision," she said. "Should JD turn him?"

Turning him would make him a vampire, but would keep him alive. He would go through agony, but would survive. JD had never done it before and had never been faced with having to make the decision. Years before, everyone had let him know if they wanted to be turned or not and Craig had opted for JD to do it, should it be the only way to save his life.

Unlike all the greater vampires he had met, JD didn't like being a vampire. He tolerated it and didn't let it affect his life, but it wasn't something he would have chosen for himself.

But was this his decision to make? Craig had already made it, but that was years ago and it hadn't been discussed since. Under normal circumstances, he would ask for Natalie's approval, but these weren't normal circumstances and Natalie was in no position to offer an opinion.

He looked at his brother for guidance.

"He said it was what he wanted," Jonathon said.

242

"And he's given no indication that he's changed his mind," Katie added.

JD sighed and ran his fingers through his hair. It was all well and good for them to assure him it was the right thing to do, but they weren't the ones who had to do it. What if Craig couldn't cope with being a vampire? What if he hated it and resented JD for turning him?

On the other hand, if JD did nothing and Craig died, how would he feel? How would any of them feel? It was almost as if he was playing God and he didn't like the feeling. He was used to being responsible for his hunters lives, when they were on a hunt, but this was different. He had never been so unsure about something. Was there a right or wrong answer?

And would it even work? If he was a vampire, he would recover from his injuries, but would he succumb to them before the conversion was complete? Would he be putting Craig through agony for no reason?

His thoughts were interrupted by Doctor Harwood entering the room. All eyes went to her.

She didn't beat around the bush. "The prognosis isn't good I'm afraid. We managed to get his heart beating again, but it could stop again and if it does, we may not be able to revive him a second time. You should prepare yourself for the worst."

That was all JD needed to hear. He could not, would not, let Craig die if there was anything he could do to prevent it.

"Can we see him?" he asked.

"Of course. I wish there was more we could do."

JD thanked her and as soon as she left, he looked over at his family. "So are we decided?"

They all nodded.

"It has to be done," Sarah said. "We can't afford to wait for Nick's associate to turn up."

Hating what he was about to do, but knowing Sarah was right, JD stood up. He held out his hand and Sarah took it.

They walked slowly to Craig's room, neither of them in a hurry to arrive. The room was empty when they got there, other than Craig and the machines which were keeping him alive.

JD stared at the heartbeat monitor, watching its steady pulse and wondering what effect his venom would have on it.

Sarah grabbed her seat, which had been moved out of the way, and returned it to its place beside Craig's bed. She took his hand.

"I hope we are doing the right thing," she said to him, "and it's what you would want."

She looked up at JD, tears flowing down her face, and nodded. JD walked to the other side of the bed and took hold of Craig's other arm. It would be quicker to inject his venom into his neck, but the machines were in the way. He turned Craig's hand over, exposing the veins in his wrist, and opened his mouth, allowing his fangs to elongate. He could feel the venom in them, longing to be released.

Just as he was about to bite down, Sarah called out, "Wait."

He looked over at her, wondering what had made her stop him.

"He just squeezed my hand."

"Craig, can you hear me?" he asked. "Can you move your fingers?"

He held his breath as he waited for what felt like hours. Then a miracle happened; Craig's fingers twitched.

JD looked across the bed at Sarah, who was smiling. Were they reading too much into it? He hoped not.

Then the hand Sarah was holding squeezed hers tightly. The movement was unmistakeable. It couldn't have been an instinctive reaction; Craig had taken hold of Sarah's hand. He was aware of his surroundings, even if he hadn't yet woken up.

JD ran from the room, calling for doctors, nurses, anyone. A nurse entered the room and asked Sarah what had happened.

Sarah pointed to her hand, which was still being gripped by Craig's, as she explained.

The nurse went to find a doctor and when Doctor Harwood arrived, JD and Sarah were asked to leave. They returned to the waiting room where Katie and Jonathon were anxiously waiting.

"Is it done?" Jonathon asked.

JD shook his head before explaining why he hadn't injected Craig with is venom.

"What does this mean?" Katie asked, but JD had no idea.

While they waited, Doc turned up. He looked exhausted. The operation was over and Natalie was in a recovery room. They had done all they could, but the damage had been too extensive. He didn't think Natalie would ever walk again.

Everyone had been excited Craig had responded to Sarah, but all the excitement drained out of them, leaving them deflated.

Despite JD insisting he should go home, Doc waited with them for news about Craig. They waited for over an hour before Doctor Harwood arrived to give them an update. This time she was smiling.

"Craig is awake and responding to questions. He's not out of the woods yet, as there is still swelling on his brain, but it is reducing and all signs indicate he will make a full recovery."

JD took Sarah into his arms and let her sob into his chest. This time they were tears of joy.

JD felt his own eyes well up. It was the best news anyone could have delivered. Craig was going to be okay.

I'VE JUST HAD A VISITOR

Joseph slammed his hand down on the table, making the man opposite him jump. He didn't care that he had scared him. The man claimed not to have seen Vivien since she had last stayed with him decades ago and Joseph was sure he wasn't lying, which added to his frustration.

In his hunt for his sister, he was failing at every turn. It was looking more and more likely he was heading in the wrong direction. He was retracing her steps from when he had first tracked her down and it was becoming increasingly obvious he was using the wrong tactic.

This time she wasn't looking for Gabriel, so she wouldn't be moving about. She would have decided on a destination and gone straight there. It would be somewhere Anna would be safe and well protected. It would need to be a place where she would have an adequate supply of vampire blood.

He needed to give this some thought. He thanked the shaking man for his hospitality and left the house. He would need a hotel room for a night or two while he did some serious thinking.

He drove to the nearest town and checked into the first hotel he found. He didn't care that it wasn't five star; all he needed was a bed and somewhere to do his planning.

His next stop was a local bookshop. That proved to be harder than it should have been. With so many people buying ebooks, many bookshops had closed down. He eventually found one. It wasn't big, but it had what he needed.

He returned to his hotel room and opened the map book. With a pen, he began to mark every location he could remember Vivien staying at for more than just a couple of days.

It took him a few hours and by the time he finished, he was getting thirsty. The streetlight shining through his window indicated the hour was late, but the last remaining hues of sunset told him night had not yet fallen.

It was the ideal time for hunting. Not many people would be in the park he passed on the outskirts of the town, but enough would be going for a late jog or simply walking home that he wouldn't have to struggle to find food.

It didn't take him long to drive there. The carpark had a few cars, but not enough for him to worry about his attack being witnessed.

He strolled causally through the park. It was large with many trees. There was a soccer pitch marked out at the edge with a court close by. He wasn't sure if it was for basketball or netball. It wasn't currently in use.

Paths were laid out through the trees and he decided to follow one. To the casual observer, he was just another human taking a stroll before turning in for the night. Anyone watching him would see he was observing everything and listening intently, turning his head whenever he heard a noise.

A woman pushing a pram walked past him, her attention too focused on the baby inside to even notice him. He let her go, unharmed. He didn't take blood from parents who had their children with them, no matter how young they were.

Joseph carried on walking. He could hear footsteps ahead. Two sets, if he wasn't mistaken.

The footsteps stopped, but the heavy breathing didn't. Maybe the people who had been running were taking a break.

Night had fallen, but the local council had installed streetlights along the park's pathways. Not enough to light it adequately, in Joseph's opinion, but the light they emitted was enough for him to see two people dressed in running gear as soon as the path he was on straightened out.

One was bent over, his hands on his hips as he panted loudly. The other had one leg up on a bench and she was stretching. She wasn't breathing as heavily as her running partner, suggesting she was the fitter of the two.

Joseph walked up to them, both of them looking up at him as he approached.

"Sorry to bother you," he said, smiling at them in a friendly fashion which often worked in regard to relaxing a stranger's guard. This time was no exception. Both joggers relaxed their stances.

"Have you seen a woman?" he continued. "Short with blonde hair, tied back in a ponytail. Probably looked like she wanted to kill someone."

The man chuckled. "Would that someone be you?"

Joseph faked a grimace. "Unfortunately, yes. We had a 'discussion', as she likes to call it. I call it an argument. She walked off in that direction."

He pointed to where the joggers had come from. Like most humans, they automatically turned to see if there was anything where he was pointing. They would know there wasn't, as that was where they had just been, but that didn't stop instinct taking over.

Joseph wasted no time. As soon as their heads were turned, he bit them both, injecting them with just enough venom to make them compliant.

"Turn around," he ordered. Of course, they obeyed; they didn't have a choice.

He could have taken advantage of the situation, made them do whatever horrible things he could think of to themselves, or each other, but he wasn't a cruel man. He wanted some of their blood, nothing more. He had no interest in torturing them either physically or mentally.

"You are going to remain still and quiet while I drink your blood, then you are going to forget all about it. You will feel tired, but will soon recover."

The man's eyes were filled with terror, but the woman seemed more angry than scared. Joseph could imagine her trying to hit him, had she been able to move. If they were in a relationship, he suspected he knew which one wore the trousers, as the saying went.

He drank his fill, taking enough to quench his thirst, but not so much it would harm them. By the time they got home, they would be exhausted, but would put it down to the exercise, nothing more.

Once he finished drinking, he licked their necks, removing all trace of blood. He hoped there was none around his mouth, but he had never been a messy eater, so he was confident his face showed no sign of what had just taken place.

"Forget," he said, then changed the tone of his voice. "She was wearing black trousers and a pink blouse," he continued as though he was still talking about his missing girlfriend or wife or whatever.

"Sorry," the man said. "We haven't passed anyone tonight."

"Thanks anyway."

As Joseph began to move away, the woman called after him. "Maybe you should give her time to calm down before looking for her."

"Maybe I will. Thanks for the suggestion." Joseph waved to the couple before turning his back on them.

He set a steady pace as he walked back to where he left his car. He was in no particular hurry and moving too fast or too slow would draw attention, should anyone see him.

He met nobody else in the park and was soon back in his room at the hotel. He sat on the bed and opened the map book once more. He flicked through the pages, ticking some locations he had marked and crossing others. Anna would need to be close to vampires, if they were to keep her supplied with blood, so he ruled out everywhere that didn't have a number of vampires living in the vicinity. He was basing his decisions on old data, but he didn't have the time or the patience to visit everywhere. If he couldn't find Vivien in any of the remaining areas, he would go to those he had discarded.

He managed to narrow his search down to four potential destinations, spread throughout the country. He had no idea which one Vivien would be at, if she was at any of them, so he decided to start with the closest one. It would take him nearly an entire day to reach it, so getting some sleep was a good idea.

The following morning, the woman who was manning the reception desk when he checked out didn't seem pleased he was leaving a day early. The smile returned to her face when he insisted on paying for the two nights he had originally booked in for.

The drive was long and boring. He had been alive so long he no longer appreciated looking at beautiful scenes of the countryside as he drove through them. He often wondered when the joy of seeing the country's natural beauty stopped being enjoyable. No matter how hard he tried, he couldn't put a decade on it, let alone a year.

Maybe it was when his sister left him the second time, but he couldn't be sure. It felt wrong to blame her, but he did.

Streetlights lit the road he was on by the time he reached his destination. It wasn't so late the people he intended to see would be in bed, but he still considered it rude to disturb someone at such a late hour. It meant having to book into another hotel, but he could live with that.

The following morning proved to be unproductive. None of the vampires he spoke to had seen Vivien since she had stayed there. All of them remembered who he was from the last time he had interrogated them, so he didn't need to resort to threats or violence to get the truth from them.

One down, three to go. At least that was the worst case scenario. If he was lucky, he would pick up some clue to Vivien's whereabouts at his next destination, but so far, luck had not been on his side.

Looking at the map book, he had two options. He could head east or south, both locations being roughly the same distance from where he was. He didn't believe in making decisions by flipping a coin, so he went the way which felt right. East was calling to him, so he headed out.

-------------------------∞-------------------------

He should have gone south. East was a complete and utter waste of his time. Vivien hadn't been there in a few years. She had been back for a visit, taking Gabriel with her, but that had been before Luke had died. Nobody there could tell him about her current whereabouts. Wherever she was, she appeared to be keeping it secret from all her friends. Well most of them. Someone would know; he just needed to find the right person.

Going south, he was headed to a small town. He could have taken the scenic route, following the old railway track, but a new motorway had been built since he was last in the area, making the journey quicker, if not more enjoyable.

He arrived at lunchtime and decided to have a meal. He didn't need the food and wasn't hungry, but he had learnt that staff in eating establishments in small towns knew everything that was going on.

He drove down the high street, passing two restaurants, one pub, which advertised meals, and a number of cafés. Choosing one at random, he parked his car outside and went in.

"Take any seat," the woman behind the counter called out, "and I will be with you in a moment."

There were a number of tables and he chose one by the window. He looked over to the woman who had spoken to him as she served a customer. He took in her blonde hair, which needed re-dying as her roots were showing, and her friendly, easy smile. There was something about her which told him she knew everybody in the town and would be more than happy to answer his questions.

A menu, covered in plastic to protect the paper sheets, was on the table, so he opened it and browsed the options. There wasn't much in the range of main dishes, but they did a variety of snacks. In the end he opted for coffee and cake instead of a proper meal. He didn't have a sweet tooth, but the occasional slice of fruit cake went down well.

"What can I get you?" the woman asked once she finished with her customer and made her way to his table.

"Coffee, strong, black, no sugar, with a slice of fruit cake please." He closed the menu and handed it to her. "And some information, if you can spare me a few minutes."

"Sure. Let me get you your order first."

He thanked her and watched her walk away. She swung her hips, but it was natural movement rather than put on to try to get his attention.

She returned a few moments later with his slice of cake and promised the coffee wouldn't be long. She wasn't wrong. He had

251

barely started on his food when a large mug was placed on the table in front of him.

"So how can I help?" the woman asked.

Joseph put his fork down and held out his hand. "I'm Joseph."

The woman shook it and introduced herself as Cassidy.

"Will you join me?" He waved toward the empty seat and she sat down.

Joseph took his wallet out of his pocket and pulled a photograph from it. It was the only one he had of Vivien and him together. It was old, but Vivien hadn't changed her appearance much since it had been taken.

"I'm looking for my sister. Do you know if she has been through here?"

He handed over the photo and Cassidy scrutinised it.

"That's Vivien," she said almost immediately. "She and Gabriel were staying with Will for a while."

Joseph picked up on the word 'were'. It sounded like she was no longer living with Will, but at least he was now closer to finding her.

"Were?" he asked. "You mean she has moved away?"

"Yes," Cassidy said as she handed back the photo. "You just missed her I'm afraid. She and Gabriel left a few days ago. I have no idea where they have gone or when they will be back."

Joseph smiled his thanks to her. "Would you mind telling me where this Will person lives?" he asked. "He might know where they have gone."

He had met Will before, when he had been looking for Vivien and tracked her to Gavin's place, so he already knew where Will lived. At least he knew where the man lived at the time; it was possible he had moved.

Cassidy provided directions, rather than an address, as Will lived off the beaten track so the address would not be much help.

At that moment, the door opened and another customer entered. Joseph thanked Cassidy for her help and returned to consuming his slice of cake while Cassidy walked over to the new arrival, welcoming her in like she was an old friend, which she may well have been.

Once his cake had been eaten, he relaxed back in his chair to enjoy his coffee. He would never class himself as a connoisseur, but he knew what he liked and the blend Cassidy supplied was one of the better ones.

While he drank, he glanced over at the new customer, taking in her Barbie doll looks. She was wearing a short dress which, below the table, showed off her shapely legs. She was the sort of woman he would enjoy spending a night with, but no more. He wrote her off as a blonde bimbo and returned his attention to his coffee.

He debated how to approach Will. He would probably recognise him and he wouldn't put it past Vivien to have warned all her acquaintances about the likelihood of him showing up. Yet Cassidy didn't know Vivien would be avoiding him. It was a puzzle he was going to enjoy solving.

He drained the last dregs of his coffee and left the café, not bothering to look back at the woman, though he was aware she was watching him. He had more important things on his mind than a quick tumble in bed. Maybe after he finished his business with Will he would return, to see if she was still there, but he doubted it.

He drove directly to Will's house. If the man in question wasn't home, he would wait. He was a patient man and had no problem hanging around. If Will wasn't there, it gave him the opportunity to break into the house and search it for any sign of Vivien's destination. During his long life, he had become proficient at breaking and entering without leaving any evidence.

No vehicles were in sight when he parked outside the house, but he vaguely remembered there being a garage somewhere around the side, so the lack of cars didn't mean that nobody was home.

He wasn't sure if he wanted the house to be empty or not. He might find out more by searching than he would talking with Will, but on the other hand, Will might have some useful information he wished to share. Or information he would share, whether he wanted to or not.

His mind went to Anna. Cassidy hadn't mentioned her leaving with Vivien and Gabriel. In fact, she hadn't mentioned her at all. What if she had stayed behind and was living at the house? He wasn't ready to face her. While he liked the fact that Luke's death had hurt Gabriel, he was consumed with guilt whenever he thought of Anna.

It was early afternoon on a workday. He hoped Anna had found herself a job and wasn't home. There was only one way to find out.

He got out of the car, without bothering to lock it behind him, and walked up to the front door. Before he reached it, he could feel eyes on him and turned around. A large dog was watching him. It raised one side of its top lip, revealing a sharp fang, making him reconsider breaking in. Something about the dog told him he would regret it.

Turning his back on the animal, he raised his hand and knocked on the door.

---------------------------∞--------------------------

Will heard a knock and swore quietly to himself. He hated being interrupted when his creative juices were flowing. He finished the sentence he was writing and left his office to answer the door.

He opened it, prepared to tell his visitor to go away, but the moment his eyes fell on the man, his throat closed up.

He knew who he was looking at. He hadn't been worried when Vivien had warned him her brother might turn up on his doorstep one day, but now the moment had arrived, his nonchalance disappeared.

While Joseph oozed charm, there was an air of menace about him that Will remembered well. Now it was all he could see. The camouflage of the polite and respectable gentleman had been stripped away during his last visit and it wasn't something that could easily be put back in place.

"It is good to see you again, Will."

There was that smile, which was so deceptive. It said, 'you can trust me', but Will knew it was a lie. To be fair, Joseph had never actually threatened him, but he hadn't needed to; the threat was implicit in the way he spoke and the way he held himself. Everything about him screamed that he wasn't someone to get on the wrong side of.

Will had only ever met one person he was more wary of and that was Elias.

"May I come in?"

Will desperately wanted to say no, but instead stepped aside so Joseph could enter.

"Vivien's not here," he said as he closed the door. There was no point pretending he didn't know why her brother was visiting. The only question on Will's mind was whether he already knew she had been living at the house.

"So Cassidy told me."

That explained a few things. Vivien had warned all her vampire friends about her brother, but hadn't mentioned it to any of the human inhabitants of the town. He hoped it wasn't a mistake she would soon regret.

He sat on the sofa, not bothering to invite Joseph to do the same. If he wanted to sit, he would do so with or without an invitation.

Joseph sat down opposite him and stared at him intently. "Where has she gone?"

So much for small talk. Then again, Will hadn't really been expecting any. "I have no idea."

It was the truth. Vivien and Gabriel hadn't even hinted at a destination. It was safer for Will not to know.

Joseph continued to stare at him, making him uncomfortable, but Will refused to react. The urge to squirm in his seat was almost overwhelming, but he didn't give in to it.

It was Joseph who broke the silence. "What is her number? I will give her a call."

"She didn't give me her new number."

It wasn't a lie. He had obtained the new phones so it had been he who had given the number to her, not the other way round.

"Do you mind if I check?"

Joseph held out his hand so Will removed his phone from his pocket, unlocked it, and handed it over. He wasn't worried about doing so. He had stored both Vivien and Gabriel under aliases.

Joseph scrolled through the contacts list, frowning when he got to the bottom without seeing either Vivien or Gabriel's names.

He handed the phone back and Will put it away.

"Do you mind if I search the house?"

It was posed as a question, but something told Will it wasn't really. It didn't matter whether he minded or not; Joseph was going to do so with or without his permission.

"Go right ahead."

When Joseph stood up, Will remained seated. There was no point watching what Vivien's brother did.

His mind went to Anna and he was relieved she wasn't there. The thought of her coming face to face with the man who was responsible for Luke's death made him shiver.

Joseph wasn't gone long and he didn't look pleased when he returned.

"It looks like they took all their belonging with them. Are you expecting them to come back?"

Will shook his head. "Expecting, no. Hoping, yes. But I have no idea when, if at all."

Again it was the truth. When they left, they gave no indication of their future plans. Will suspected this was to keep him and Anna safe.

Joseph took a card out of his wallet and handed it to him. While it looked similar to a business card, all it had on it was Joseph's name and number; no email address, no company name. It didn't even contain a surname.

"If you do see them again, or hear from them, give me a call."

Will didn't agree. He had no intention of doing so, but wasn't prepared to lie to Joseph.

"I will let myself out."

Will waited until the door closed before exhaling. The visit had gone better than he had feared.

For a while, he stayed where he was, unable to convince his body to move. Eventually he returned to his study, but he was no longer in the mood for writing.

He waited another hour before calling Vivien, just to make sure Joseph had really gone.

His call went to voicemail, so he left her a message.

"I've just had a visitor. You need to call me. Now."

WE MEET AGAIN

As Joseph closed the door, the air was filled with the sound of a car racing up the driveway. Curious as to who was driving so erratically, he stayed on the doorstep, waiting for them to arrive. Well it was part curiosity and part self-preservation. He wasn't sure it was safe to walk to his car.

The dog was still there, watching him.

A car skidded to a halt near his and he thought he had seen it somewhere before, but he wasn't sure where, until the driver opened the door and stepped out.

He recognised the woman from the café. If she knew Will, maybe she had more uses than just warming his bed.

He approached her as she walked toward the house, meeting her half-way.

"We meet again."

She smiled at him. "We haven't met for the first time, yet, seeing as you took no notice of me in the coffee shop."

"Trust me, I noticed."

"Yet it was too much effort to come over and speak to me."

Joseph returned her smile. There was more to this woman than he had assumed.

"Then let me correct that mistake." He held out his hand. "I am Joseph."

"Marie."

Instead of shaking his hand, she held hers out, with the wrist slightly bent. Taking the hint, he kissed the back of it.

"So are you a friend of Will or Anna?" she asked.

"Neither actually. I'm looking for my sister."

Something played across her face, but he wasn't sure what. It wasn't fear. Unease maybe?

"So you are Vivien's brother. We were told you might be paying a visit."

Told or warned, he wondered. Knowing Vivien, it was the latter.

"It seems I have just missed her. Do you happen to be friends with her?"

Something about this woman told him she would say yes, even if it wasn't true.

"Of course. Why don't you come to my place for a drink and I can answer all your questions."

"I thought you were visiting someone."

She waved away his comment. "Nothing that can't wait. Shall we go?"

She didn't bother to wait for his answer, assuming he would follow her. He had learned a lot about this woman in a short conversation. She would be easy for him to manipulate, to get what he wanted out of her. And he wanted information. Anything else was a bonus.

Somehow he managed to follow her to her house. The speed at which she took some of the bends was frightening. It seemed she had no regard for her own safety. Nor that of anyone else.

She led him into her lounge and offered him a drink. When he told her how he liked his coffee, she laughed lightly.

"I said a drink. Wine? Red or white?"

It was too early in the day for him to be consuming alcohol, but it would be impolite to decline the offer, so he opted for white.

He didn't bother to ask what it was when she handed him the glass. His first sip told him it was something expensive. He had never seen the point in spending a lot of money on wine when he could find reasonably priced bottles he enjoyed just as much.

He took a seat on one of the sofas and made himself comfortable. "Tell me about yourself."

He wasn't surprised to find her favourite topic of conversation seemed to be herself, though he soon found out he had underestimated her. Beneath the body of a bimbo was an intelligent mind. This was a case of not judging a book by its cover. The only reason she wasn't at work was because it was the end of term so the university she worked at was closed for another couple of weeks.

She was a charming host who answered all his questions. As long as they were about her. The more he talked with her, the more he found her fascinating. She was probably the most self-centred person he had ever met, but she had no clue that she was. It wasn't that she was egotistical; she just believed that she was the most important person in the room, no matter who else was there. It didn't make her likeable, in his opinion, but it made her interesting.

He soon found out everything about her, including her favourite colour of underwear, though why she thought that would interest him, he had no idea.

"So you are good friends with my sister," he said before she could start talking about more of her history. The momentary flicker of annoyance that crossed her face didn't go unnoticed.

"Yes," she said. "Viv and I are like this."

She held up her hand and crossed two fingers. Joseph knew she was lying. For one thing, Vivien never got that close to anyone, except, perhaps, Gabriel. For another, she would never let anyone call her Viv. She detested having her name shortened. She thought it sounded vulgar. Joseph agreed with her.

"Though I'm not sure how much longer our friendship is going to last. I don't think she is going to cope very well when she returns and I take Gabriel away from her."

This got Joseph's attention for two reasons. Not only was she sure that Vivien would be returning, but she was also interested in Gabriel and her staking a claim on him didn't sound like an idle boast; more like a foregone conclusion. This was something he could use to his advantage.

"I never thought he was right for her," he said. He neglected to add that no man he had ever met would be good enough. His sister needed looking after, protecting, and nobody could do it as well as he could.

He expected Marie to agree with him, but she didn't. "Actually, they seem ideal for each other, which is a shame. For Vivien. He is going to be so much happier with me and I doubt she will ever find anyone as good for her as he is. It's a little sad, really."

Joseph couldn't believe what he was hearing. Marie wasn't being selfish or malicious. She just saw things differently to most people. She wanted Gabriel, therefore she would have him and everyone would just have to get used to it. She felt no guilt or remorse because she didn't see she was doing anything wrong. She was just claiming what was rightfully hers. She really was a fascinating creature.

"When are they due back?"

Marie waved away his question as though it wasn't important She had done it a few times already and he found it annoying, though he didn't let his irritation show. It wasn't something she wanted to talk about, therefore they wouldn't.

"No idea. Now enough talk. Let's go to bed."

Joseph had just taken a mouthful of wine and sprayed it everywhere. Never before had he met such a forward woman. At least not one who wasn't expecting payment and wasn't drunk or high on drugs. He made a habit of avoiding all three.

Marie was frowning at him. Was it because of his reaction or that he had made a mess of her carpet? Luckily, it was white wine, not red.

"Isn't that the reason you came here?"

There was no trace of sarcasm in her voice. She was being serious. Did she really believe every man she met wanted to go to bed with her? As soon as he thought the question, he realised that was exactly what she thought. And he wasn't convinced she was wrong.

"Actually I wanted to get to know you better," he said. He ignored her pout. "And I think that has been accomplished."

The pout disappeared and she held out her hand to him. He took it and she led him upstairs.

Her bedroom was just as he imagined it would be. It wasn't a room he would be comfortable sleeping in, but he didn't plan on doing so. He had no intention of getting any more involved with Marie than he needed to.

The sound of material hitting the floor reached his ears and he turned around to see Marie standing in just her underwear.

She hadn't been lying about the colour. It matched the décor so well it was almost as if she planned it that way.

He looked her up and down, admiring her body the way he would a statue or some other piece of art. It was something to be enjoyed, not viewed from a distance, so he stepped close enough to take her in his arms.

When he kissed her it was soft and sensual, not the frantic, passionate sort of kiss she was probably expecting. Decades of experience had taught him to take it slow, even when a woman was throwing herself at him.

As he kissed her, he ran his hand down her back, making her shiver. Only then did he deepen the kiss.

When he finally pulled away from her, she gave him a shy smile before placing her hands near his chest and slowly undoing his buttons. When she had his shirt open, she ran the tips of her fingernails down his hairless chest, hard enough for him to feel it, but not so hard it would hurt or leave red marks. He wondered if they were real, but doubted it. Most women with long nails these days wore false ones, or so he had been led to believe.

As she slowly undressed him, his body began to show its appreciation. The bulge in his trousers became noticeable, though she avoided paying it much attention, at least until the rest of his clothes had been removed.

Neither of them spoke until he was completely naked. She reached out her hand to grab hold of him, but he intercepted it with his own.

"Come and have some fun," he said and pulled her over to the bed.

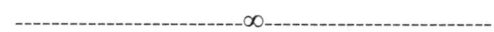

After an enjoyable sex session—well three, if you were counting, which he wasn't—Joseph and Marie lay in the bed, his arm around her and her head on his chest.

The evenness of her breathing told him she was asleep. He wanted to leave, to get out of the room which contained far too many pastel colours for his liking, but he had to remain. He wanted to know where Vivien was and Marie might be able to help him.

So he stayed where he was, passing the time by thinking about what he would do to Gabriel when he got hold of him.

It wasn't long before Marie stirred, though to Joseph it felt like a lifetime. He had come to the conclusion that if a man ever moved in with Marie, he would have to have his own bedroom. One with darker colours and no flowery patterns.

"What are you thinking about?" she asked before yawning. Some women could still look sexy when they yawned; Marie wasn't one of them.

"You." Joseph didn't often lie, but when he did, it came easy to him.

Her head was resting against his chest once more, so he felt rather than saw her smile.

"And my sister," he added.

"Why are you looking for her, anyway?"

This time he didn't have to lie. "She needs protecting and I don't believe Gabriel is as capable as I am."

She moved so she could look at him, supporting herself with one arm.

"So you don't mean any harm to Gabriel?"

"Of course not. All I care about is my sister and making sure she is safe. Do you have her number?"

She shook her head, making her hair move in a tantalising fashion. Once he had the information he needed, he might enjoy her once more before leaving.

"I don't, but Will probably does."

"I already tried him."

"What about Anna? I would be surprised if Gabriel hasn't left a way for her to keep in contact with him."

It was something he had already considered, but he didn't want to speak with Anna. The chances of her helping him were less than zero.

"Could you find out for me?"

"Sure. I'll be right back."

She didn't bother to cover herself as she left the room. He couldn't help comparing her to Cassidy as he watched her walk away. Even though Cassidy had been fully dressed, she had provided the more enjoyable view.

A short while later, Marie returned. The frown on her face told him all he needed to know.

She threw her phone on the bed. "She says she doesn't have a number for either Vivien or Gabriel, though I know she's lying."

"Then maybe she needs a little persuasion."

"What did you have in mind?" she asked as she slid under the covers.

"I'll tell you later," he said as he rolled on top of her and kissed her in a way that left no doubt of his intentions.

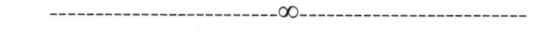

"It's Marie," Will called out to Anna as he picked up his phone and looked at the display. "Should I answer it?"

Anna's voice drifted in from the kitchen. "It's up to you. But she did call me earlier to see if I would give her a number for Vivien or Gabriel, so she may well be asking you the same thing."

Will couldn't help smiling. It had only been a couple of months, but already they had settled into what he liked to call 'domestic bliss'. Okay, so they still slept in different rooms and hadn't passed second base, but he didn't mind taking things slow. He was happy, and he believed she was too. What else mattered?

He hit the green button to answer the call and immediately Marie's voice sounded. In typical Marie fashion, she didn't ask after him or Anna, instead she went straight into what she needed.

She was getting the decorators in and was calling on every strong, able-bodied male she knew to move her furniture for her.

Will rolled his eyes. He almost said 'no', but Anna had told him she had some work she needed to get done, so it would be a good excuse to get out of her hair so she could concentrate.

He promised Marie he would be there as soon as he could and hung up. He walked into the kitchen, where Anna had just finished washing up. It had been her turn, seeing as he had cooked. They shared all the chores and there were never any arguments.

He kissed her on the cheek. "I'm going over to help her move some furniture. Apparently there will be a number of us there, so it shouldn't take too long."

"She does have a large house and a lot of furniture."

"I know, but with the amount of men she knows, it still shouldn't take long."

She dried her hands on a tea-towel and placed her arms around his neck. "Have fun, but not too much fun." She pecked him on the lips.

The glint in her eye told him she was teasing him. She had shown no hint of jealousy in regard to Marie since she her return, despite Will's fears that she would, and she didn't seem to mind that he was still friends with her.

He swatted her playfully on the bottom before putting his arms around her and pulling her closer so he could give her a proper goodbye kiss.

He released her and removed her arms from around his neck. "Gotta go. Enjoy doing your work."

He was retrieving his keys from their usual place near the door when she called out to him. "Behave."

"Always."

He was chuckling as he left the house.

There were a number of cars parked outside Marie's house when he arrived, some of which he recognised. She hadn't been kidding when she said she would be calling in a number of people.

There was no answer when he rang the bell, so he tried the door. She frequently left it unlocked, expecting visitors to let themselves in if she was too busy to answer the door. Today was no exception.

He didn't bother calling out as he entered. With so many people in the house, he wouldn't have any trouble finding them.

He went straight to the kitchen, but it was empty. As was the lounge, the dining room, the formal lounge, the study. He checked everywhere, but there was no sign of anyone.

As he climbed the stairs, he listened for sounds of conversation, or even footsteps, but could hear nothing.

The hairs on the back of his neck stood up. Something was wrong. He called out when he reached the second floor, but there was no answer. Where was everyone?

He ran from room to room, but all were empty. He looked out of each window, in case he could see someone in the gardens which surrounded the house, but they were deserted. Marie owned a lot of land around the house, so they could be anywhere, but why would they be outside if they were there to move furniture?

He took out his phone and called Marie, but there was no answer. He could hear her phone ringing and found it in the lounge. She never left the house without it, so either she was still in the grounds somewhere, or she had been taken against her will.

He tried calling the owners of a couple of the cars he recognised, but both calls went to voicemail. His concern was turning to real worry. He wouldn't put it past Marie to forget she had asked him to come over and go out, but not without her phone. And where was everyone else who had driven over?

The only room he hadn't tried was the basement, though why anyone would be down there, he had no clue.

When he opened the door, the light was on, illuminating the stairs. He listened carefully and could make out some sounds, indicating someone was down there.

He moved slowly down the steps, listening carefully with each step. Unlike in every horror movie he had seen, the stairs didn't creak, so he wasn't alerting whoever was down there of his presence.

When he stepped onto the basement floor, he stopped and listened once more. The entire basement was to the side and behind the stairs, meaning he would have to walk around them to see anything. It also meant anyone down there would see him before he saw them.

Taking a deep breath, he stepped to his right. And froze. The basement was half filled with nearly a dozen chairs, most of which had people sitting on them, their legs tied to the chair legs and their arms tied behind their backs. Will recognised everyone. They were all vampires. Everyone looked terrified. Everyone except Marie.

"Nice of you to join us, Will," a voice he recognised said.

He forced his eyes away from the captives and turned his attention to Joseph.

"Please, take a seat."

Will knew it wasn't a request. He also knew most of those being held captive could get out of their restraints if they wanted to, so something was keeping them in place. Was it fear? What had Joseph threatened to do to them?

Will didn't obey the command. He wanted to know what was going on and didn't think he would get any answers if he complied. "No."

Joseph laughed. It wasn't the maniacal sound Will was expecting; it was filled with genuine amusement.

"So you do have a backbone. And here was me thinking you were such a quiet little mouse."

"What do you want?" Will was impressed his voice didn't shake.

"I want Gabriel and you are going to help me get him."

Joseph sounded sure of himself. Will wondered what his plan was. His thoughts were interrupted by sounds coming from the seat Marie was sitting on. She was struggling against her ropes and yelling out in French. Will didn't understand everything she said, but he spoke enough of the language to know that she was calling Joseph some very unpleasant names.

"What is wrong my dear?" Joseph said in a mocking tone. "Did you really believe I just wanted to take my sister away and leave Gabriel free to enjoy life with you?"

267

The words told Will all he needed to know. That was exactly what Marie had thought and she had helped set him and everyone else up.

With a cry of rage, Marie twisted and turned so violently she managed to break the chair she was tied to. She made light work of freeing herself. Joseph looked on with an amused expression.

Once she had the ropes removed, she launched herself at him, her arms outstretched, her nails reaching for his face as though they were talons.

She moved so fast it would have been almost impossible for a human to see her, but Joseph managed to intercept her before she got to him, grabbing her by the throat and throwing her against the wall like a rag doll.

The crunch which echoed around the room was sickening. Looking at her body, slumped on the floor, Will wasn't sure if she was just unconscious or her neck had broken and he didn't care. She had abused his loyalty, the loyalty of all the hostages, just so she could get Gabriel. She probably didn't even realise that it wasn't Vivien that was keeping him from her; he just wasn't interested and taking Vivien away would do her no good.

In the past, he would have felt sorry for her, but that was before his feelings for Anna had helped him open his eyes to what she was really like.

He returned his attention to Joseph, who was straightening his sleeves.

"Now that her little temper tantrum is over, shall we continue? Where were we? Oh yes, Will was about to take a seat."

Joseph looked at him pointedly, waiting for him to comply. Will had no intention of giving him the satisfaction.

"Actually, no I wasn't. You were about to tell me your devious plan."

Did he sound sarcastic? He certainly hoped so.

"Oh it is quite simple. You are going to give me the number for Vivien or Gabriel and I am not going to kill everyone here."

Will forced himself not to look at his friends to see how they were reacting. Outwardly calm, but inwardly doing his best not to panic, he folded his arms and faked looking bored.

"I told you, they didn't give me their numbers."

"So you say, but I do not believe you. But it does not really matter. There are easier ways to accomplish my goal than forcing the truth out of you."

Before Will had chance to ask Joseph what he meant, he was standing in front of him, so close Will could feel his breath on his face.

"I am sick and tired of playing nice with you."

Will felt hands on either side of his head and it was twisted violently to the side. The last thing he heard before death claimed him was the sound of his neck breaking.

GO TO HELL

Anna looked at the clock once more. She hadn't believed Will when he said he wouldn't be long, but she hadn't expected him to be out this late. It wasn't that she thought he had lied to her, she was just sure that helping Marie move her furniture would take longer than he thought, no matter how many people were helping.

She was starting to get worried. She hadn't heard from him, which was unusual. She had expected him to phone her before now, to admit that she had been right and he had been wrong and he would be a while longer.

But he hadn't called, or replied to her text message. She wasn't sure if she should call him. She didn't want to come across as the sort of woman who always needed to know where her partner was and was constantly checking up on him. Will had the freedom to come and go as he pleased and didn't have to always let her know his whereabouts.

But she was worried. Did that justify her calling him? She was tired and thinking about going to bed, so a quick call to say goodnight wouldn't do any harm.

She selected his number in her phone and hit the dial button. She listened to it ringing and sighed in frustration when she heard his voicemail greeting.

"Hi, it's just Anna. I'm heading to bed so try not to wake me when you come in. Love you. Bye."

She hung up and thought over the message she had just left. Why she always had to say who it was when leaving a message she had no idea, as most of the time the person she was calling would see a missed call from her, but it was a habit she had always had.

Was it a mistake to say 'love you'? While she had said it to him a few times, she could never bring herself to put the 'I' in front of it. 'I love you' felt more serious that just 'love you'. It felt like a declaration rather than just a statement and she wasn't quite ready for that. Soon, but not yet.

Will, on the other hand, often told her he loved her. And showed her. She didn't doubt his honesty and her feelings for him were growing on a daily basis. She no longer felt she was betraying Luke by caring about another man, but something was still holding her back from falling in love with him.

Maybe she just needed time. And they had all the time in the world.

Dragging herself away from her thoughts, she changed into her nightclothes and brushed her teeth. She had just climbed into bed when her phone sounded. Someone was trying to call her using Messenger.

She reached over to where she had left it on her bedside table and smiled when she looked at it. Will's name filled the screen.

She answered it and turned the volume up.

"Hey, how's it going?"

Instead of seeing Will's face, all she could see was a brick wall. This didn't concern her as his phone had front and back facing cameras and he had probably switched the wrong one on. Again.

She didn't recognise the voice who answered her, but she could take a good guess at who it was.

"I am sorry Anna, but Will cannot come to the phone right now."

The image panned around so Anna could see a group of people tied to chairs. She recognised all of them. Most looked terrified. Marie's makeup was smeared with tears and there were two mascara trails down both sides of her face.

Will looked defiant.

"Don't give him what he wants," he shouted out.

Anna winced as an arm appeared on the screen and a fist punched Will in the face. His head was thrown to one side, but when he turned it back again, the defiant look was still there.

Then the phone was moved so Anna was looking at a man she assumed was Joseph. Her nemesis. The man she had sworn she would kill.

"I am sorry for what happened to Luke. It was not what I wanted, but I take full responsibility."

271

She didn't care. He could say whatever he wanted; it wouldn't stop her hating him and wanting him dead.

"What happens to Will, however, will be down to you. All I want is Vivien and Gabriel. I am sure you know how to get in contact with them."

Anna said nothing. She wasn't prepared to tell him the truth, but there was no point in lying to him.

Joseph didn't wait for her to respond. Maybe he knew she wasn't going to. Or maybe he didn't care what she had to say. "I am going to make this really easy for you. I do not want to kill everyone here, but I will. One by one until you give me what I want. I will save Will to last, so he can watch all his friends die."

"Go to Hell," Will yelled.

This time, Joseph ignored him.

"You will contact my sister and tell her what is going on. You will tell her that if she and Gabriel do not hand themselves over to me, everyone will die. And when I have finished here, I will find you and I will kill you too. Are you hearing me?"

"Yes," she stammered, hoping she sounded scared. Given the rage that filled her, it wasn't easy.

"You have until morning. Unless I hear from Vivien and she assures me she is on her way, as soon as the sun rises, I will start killing hostages and until I hear from her, I will kill one every hour. I will keep everyone imprisoned here with me until she and Gabriel turn up so you can tell them they had better not lie to me about coming here. Have you got all that?"

Again, all Anna said was, "Yes."

"Now before I go, I think I should give a demonstration of my sincerity."

Anna was shaking with rage as the view from the phone changed to show the ceiling. She assumed Joseph had put the phone onto the floor. The sound of something scraping along the floor reached her ears, but she had no way of knowing what it was.

Then she heard Joseph's voice, but he wasn't talking to her. She wondered what he would do if she hung up, but curiosity got the better of her. She knew she wasn't going to like his 'demonstration', but felt compelled to watch it.

Whoever he was speaking to was told to film what he was about to do. If any attempt to escape was made, the person wouldn't live to regret it.

Did Joseph realise all his captives were vampires? Of course he did, which meant that when he said he would kill someone, he meant he would kill them permanently; he was threatening to remove their heads. Anna couldn't suppress a shudder and she was no longer sure she should keep watching.

But something prevented her hitting the red button to end the call. Will's phone was positioned so she could see Joseph looking at his captives as though he was trying to decide which one to use in the demonstration. Anna knew them all, some better than others, and while some she would class as acquaintances rather than friends, she didn't want any of them harmed.

"I never have liked beards," Joseph said and walked up to Robbie, who had a large amount of facial hair. Then she noticed the knife Joseph was carrying.

Her mouth went dry as she watched, the image blurring as whoever was holding the phone failed to stop their arm from shaking.

Bile rose in her throat as Joseph took hold of Robbie's hair. Shouts and protests filled the room, but Joseph yelled for everyone to be quiet or he would slaughter them all. The silence that descended told Anna all the captives believed him.

She desperately wanted to turn away, but was unable to take her eyes off the screen.

Robbie was only part way through telling Joseph to do something to himself which Anna was sure was anatomically impossible when Joseph pulled back his head and cut his throat. Blood fountained out of the wound and Robbie's voice became a gurgle.

From somewhere in the background came the sound of retching.

The gruesome demonstration wasn't over. Not satisfied with just cutting Robbie's throat, Joseph sliced the knife across his neck again and again until he had cut through all the flesh and had severed his spinal cord. When there was nothing attaching Robbie's head to his body, Joseph held it up high before throwing it into the corner, where it landed with a sickening squelch.

"I am sorry you had to see that, Anna," Joseph called out. "But it had to be done. You have until morning before the next person dies."

The expected maniacal laughter didn't reach Anna's ears. But then again, Joseph wasn't a megalomaniac nor a sociopath. Anna didn't believe he was a psychopath either. While he was cold and methodical, he seemed to have a conscience. She had believed him when he said he regretted Luke's death. She didn't care, but she did believe him. He was just someone prepared to do anything to get what he wanted. And he wanted Gabriel. Preferably dead.

He walked up to whoever was holding the phone, took it from them, and disconnected the call.

For a while, all Anna could do was stare at the blank screen. Part of her didn't believe what she had just witnessed while the rest of her knew it had been all too real. She couldn't let her friends die, but on the other hand, she couldn't let Gabriel sacrifice himself in order to save them. And she had no doubt that was exactly what he would do if she contacted him.

She had to do something, but she wasn't sure what. Her need to kill Joseph had been replaced by a desire to save the hostages. Even Marie.

While her training had been going well and she was more than capable of looking after herself, her plans for killing Joseph relied on the element of surprise and he had taken that away. If she turned up at Marie's house, it was unlikely she would be able to accomplish anything.

She needed a plan, a strategy, and she just happened to know someone who was an excellent strategist.

Not caring that it was late at night, she called Elias. She wasn't in the least surprised when he answered after only two rings. He always seemed to stay up late, but never slept in in the morning. Maybe being 'infected' meant you didn't need as much sleep as humans. Or vampires.

He didn't question why she was calling so late and didn't sound unhappy about being disturbed. He asked how he could help her and she told him. She told him everything. She didn't describe what Joseph did in any detail, but there was no need. Elias had done similar things, and things which were much worse, so he would be able to picture the scene in his head.

When she finished, he didn't ask her any questions. He didn't want to know what she planned to do or why she had contacted him; he simply told her to head over to his place.

She dressed and drove straight there. The gate was standing open so she didn't need to stop and ask for admittance. As she pulled to a stop in front of the house, the front door opened and Elias walked out.

Instead of greeting her, he said, "Come inside. We need to start making plans. Have you called Vivien?"

Anna shook her head. "No. I didn't think it was a good idea. They will just sacrifice themselves."

"Good. Letting them know what's happening is the last thing you should do."

It was going to be a long night, so Elias led Anna to the kitchen, where he had already turned on his coffee machine. Patrice and Ben were also there, though the latter looked like he had just woken up. Anna offered her apologies for disturbing them, but neither of them minded. Or so they told her, anyway.

Planning didn't take as long as Anna had expected. The 'infected' had already discussed some options. A full-frontal assault would work, if the 'infected' were involved, but that option was also dangerous. They had no idea how many of the hostages would be harmed, or killed, before they managed to overpower Joseph. Plus, they wanted him taken alive, if possible. Anna didn't, but she kept her feelings to herself. She was willing to go along with the majority until everyone was safe. After that,

Elias would have to kill her, temporarily, to stop her removing Joseph's head.

Almost as if he could read her mind, Elias said, "Revenge isn't as sweet as you would think. For a long time I wanted my father dead. For what he did to me, but more for what he did to Nick. But when he was finally killed, I didn't feel glad. I was glad the internal war was over, but that was it. I felt numb inside. Part of me still does. After all, he was only doing what he thought was best for us. Initially anyway. And I know Nick still struggles with he was forced to do."

"This is different," Anna said. "You loved your father, once. I have never felt anything but hate for the monster who's responsible for Luke's death."

"Maybe. But believe me when I say Joseph's death won't give you the closure you're looking for."

Anna said nothing. What could she say? It wasn't that she didn't believe Elias, she just didn't care. Despite how it might look, she wasn't after revenge. She wanted Joseph dead so he wouldn't be a danger to anyone ever again. She could have explained that to those present, but she was sure none of them would believe her.

"It's late," Elias said when it was obvious Anna wasn't going to respond. "We should get some sleep. We have to be up in a few hours."

-------------------------∞-------------------------

The lack of sunlight streaming through the curtains told Anna it wasn't yet dawn when Elias woke her. She wasn't convinced his plan would work, but it was the best one they could come up with.

"Are you really sure about this?" she asked as she stood beside the car she had borrowed off Will. She hadn't eaten anything as the thought of food made her nauseous, but she had drunk some blood. A lot of blood. She couldn't remember the last time she had drunk that much blood in one go.

"I'm sure," Elias said. "You know what you need to do."

Anna nodded.

"Don't be scared. Everything is going to be alright."

"I'm not scared," she said, though the shaking of her hands betrayed her lie.

Elias didn't call her out, though the look on his face suggested he knew she was lying.

Nothing more needed to be said, so Anna got into her car and drove away.

There were a number of cars outside Marie's house when she arrived, including Will's. She pulled up beside it and got out. She walked slowly to the front door; she was in no hurry to meet Joseph. Elias was relying on her not to attack him on sight and she wasn't sure she would be able to stop herself.

She didn't ring the bell or knock on the door. She didn't believe for one moment she would be able to get into the basement without Joseph knowing she was there, but there was no point in announcing her arrival.

She assumed the hostages were still in the basement. The scenes she had seen on the phone told her that was where they were when Joseph had called her, but that didn't mean he hadn't moved them.

She let herself into the house and went straight to the basement door. There was no point in searching the house in case her assumption they were still under the house proved to be wrong. She could look for them if she didn't find them where they were most likely to be.

She put her hand on the doorhandle and stared at it. Willing it to stop shaking made no difference. It wasn't too late to back out. She could leave without anyone knowing she was ever there. But she had to see Will; she owed him that much.

As soon as she opened the door, her nostrils were assaulted by an unpleasant odour, which grew stronger as she descended the stairs. Stale air, mixed with sweat, vomit, urine and faeces. At least one person was going to have to change their underwear if they survived their ordeal.

It was eerily quiet. If the hostages were down there, they were not saying anything. There were no hushed voices, no moans, no shouts to be released. Was anyone left alive, or was she about to walk into a room full of dead bodies? There was only one way to find out. She took the final step off the stairs and moved around them.

Lots of eyes looked at her as she stepped closer, but nobody spoke, other than Will, who let out a soft, "Anna." He didn't sound pleased to see her. Or relieved. He didn't want her there. He wanted her safe and away from danger.

She surveyed the scene, taking in the defeated look on all the faces. Everyone was tied to chairs still. She did a quick mental count, but had no way of knowing if all the hostages, other than Robbie, were still alive.

"I was not expecting to see you in person," Joseph said, making her jump. She hadn't noticed him standing in the shadows. She took a deep breath before turning to face him.

The images she had seen the previous night on her phone hadn't focused well on him, so it was the first time she was really seeing him. She didn't notice if he was an attractive man. All she saw was a man she wanted to kill.

"So tell me, what did my dearest sister have to say? I am surprised I have not heard from her yet."

Anna braced herself before speaking. She wasn't sure how anyone was going to react to what she had to say.

"It's not really surprising, seeing as I haven't contacted her and I have no intention of doing so."

She willed herself to not look at Will, but her head automatically turned in his direction. She expected to see shock, uncertainly, maybe even a little anger, but she should have known better. He looked proud and a slight smile was forming on his face. He gave her a small nod of approval.

Joseph, however, was far from pleased.

"What did you just say? I must have misheard."

She turned her attention to Joseph once more. This time it was easier. She held her head high as she said, "Vivien did not give me her number. And even if she had, I wouldn't be calling her."

She chose her words carefully so as not to lie.

Joseph seemed confused. He had sounded so sure of himself when he had called her, so certain that his plan would work, but now he seemed uncertain as to what was happening. Was he even aware that he had already lost control of the situation? She almost felt sorry for him. He was a man who was used to everything going his way and now it wasn't.

"Are you telling me you are going to let me kill everyone here, just to save Vivien and Gabriel? Why are you even here?"

She ignored the first question and focused on the last. "I'm here to say goodbye to Will. And to get some blood before I leave."

"You are going to leave Will here to die?" The pitch of Joseph's voice told her he didn't believe what he was hearing.

She shrugged her shoulders. "Despite what you may have been led to believe, I'm not in love with him."

She turned her back on him and made her way over to Will, ignoring the glares she was receiving. Everyone was looking at her with open hostility. Everyone except Will and Marie, who stared in front of her as though she was in some sort of trance.

Will never took his eyes off her as she approached and sat on his lap, her legs straddling the chair. She was glad she was wearing trousers. It was a strange thing to think about, given the situation, and she forced herself to refocus on the task at hand.

The pain in his eyes broke her heart. She almost couldn't go through with what she needed to do, but Elias had convinced her it was necessary.

She looked him straight in the eye and said, "You will not say anything. You will not do anything. You will move your head to the side and let me take your blood."

He obeyed. "Trust me," she whispered before plunging her fangs into his neck.

I AM NOT AFRAID OF YOU

Joseph didn't understand what was happening. How could Anna be leaving? How could she be turning her back on all her friends when a simple call to his sister would save their lives?

Maybe she was calling his bluff, but the look Will was giving her suggested otherwise. She hadn't lied when she said she wasn't in love with Will, he was certain of that, and the statement had hurt Will deeply.

He looked at Marie, but she was staring into space. She had assured him Anna would do anything to help anyone. It looked like she had either been wrong or Anna thought betraying her friends, including Will, was a small price to pay for protecting Vivien and Gabriel.

His plans were falling apart and he had no idea what to do about it. He had to think quickly. He had to find a way to make Anna contact Vivien or Gabriel and he had to do it before she left Marie's house.

He could see her taking blood from Will. She hadn't lied about that and he was beginning to think she hadn't lied about anything. He had underestimated her. He had thought he had her right where he wanted her, but he was no longer sure that was the case.

Strangely, Will wasn't saying anything. He wasn't convincing her to stay or telling her she was doing the right thing by leaving. From what Marie had told him, Will would always put Anna's well-being above his own. It looked like Anna didn't feel the same about him.

He did his best to not let his concern show. He waited patiently, at least on the outside, while she drank her fill. She then kissed Will on the cheek. Still he said nothing, though the look he was giving her suggested he wanted to. Maybe he couldn't find the words. After all, what do you say to the woman you love when she is abandoning you and leaving you to die?

As soon as she moved away, Joseph spoke. "Do you honestly expect me to believe that not only are you walking away from everyone, but that you are going to do nothing to get your revenge on me?"

Anna turned to look at him. "Believe whatever you want. A good friend told me that revenge isn't worth it."

He watched her turn her back on him and walk away. He had no idea what he could say or do to get her to tell him where Vivien and Gabriel were before she left.

Before the shadows at the edge of the room consumed her, she stopped and looked back at him. She returned, stopping when she was close enough he could have stroked her cheek, had he the inclination.

She looked him straight in the eye and he found himself unable to look away. Not that he would; his pride wouldn't let him. He refused to be intimidated by anyone, especially a woman. There was a strange sort of fire in her eyes, one he had never seen before. It was mesmerising.

"One last thing," she said. "You will stay here until I tell you otherwise. You will not move and you will not speak."

A chuckle escaped his lips. Who did she think he was? Some stupid human who could be controlled by a small amount of venom? He was her superior in every way. There was nothing she could do to control him. She hadn't even bitten him.

He opened his mouth to tell her exactly how stupid she was, but no words came out, only a gagging noise. He tried again, to no avail. He attempted to grab hold of her, to shake her, to make her tell him what she had done to him, but his arms wouldn't move.

He didn't panic; he never panicked. But a feeling was creeping through him that was unfamiliar and he didn't like it.

"I'm sorry," she said, sounding anything but. "Did you want to say something?"

He couldn't speak, so he snarled. At least he was able to do that. However, it came out as more of a whimper than a sound of dominance.

Out of the corner of his eye, he could see some of the hostages looking at him. He wasn't the only one confused by what was happening. Why couldn't he speak? Why couldn't he move? It couldn't be because she had told him not to. Nobody could control someone like that, not without injecting them with venom and he would have seen and felt her doing it.

"I control you now," she said. It was a statement, not a boast. "I can make you do anything I want."

She looked around the room and spotted what she was looking for. She moved away, returning a moment later with the knife he used to behead one of the vampires. She held it up for him to see. It still had blood on it.

"I could make you cut off your fingers, one by one. Or other parts of your anatomy." She looked at his groin meaningfully.

He found himself glancing down and his body began to tremble. Now he knew how others felt when he threatened them. But he only ever threatened someone's life, never their manhood. Only a woman would stoop so low.

It wasn't the thought of being disfigured that terrified him, it was that he could be made to do it to himself. He didn't realise his bladder had released its contents until he saw a wet patch appearing at the front of his trousers. He had never felt so humiliated.

For the first time in his life, he was afraid he was going to die.

---------------------------∞--------------------------

Anna had only ever killed one person before, and that had been an accident. She had only been a greater vampire for a short while when a heavily pregnant Sarah was kidnapped by an ex-member of the hunter society. She hadn't had chance to get used to her new strength and speed and had reacted instinctively when the kidnapper had threatened Sarah with a gun. Anna had pushed her against the wall with enough force to split her skull. She had nightmares about it for weeks afterward.

But this situation was different. Anna was in control of herself and this man was responsible for Luke's death. He didn't deserve to live.

But Elias's words about revenge came back to haunt her. Killing Joseph wouldn't bring Luke back. And did Vivien want her brother dead, or just to leave her alone?

She had waited so long for this moment, trained hard day after day, but now it had finally arrived, she wasn't sure it was what she wanted.

She wasn't a murderer. Despite being a vampire, she had never killed anyone for their blood. Yet did what she had always planned to do count as murder? She wasn't sure.

And then there was Will. What would he think of her if she killed Joseph in cold blood? Even if she made him do it himself, she would still be responsible, just like Joseph was responsible for Luke's death, even though he hadn't been the one to do the actual deed.

She didn't know what to do.

She was so caught up in her thoughts, she jumped when Will spoke.

"Anna, sweetheart. What's going on?" There was a slight tremor in his voice. Was he scared of her? Well she did have control of Joseph, who terrified a lot of people, so the answer was probably yes.

She smiled at him. "I have a lot to explain. Firstly, I do love you. I'm not in love with you, yet, but I do love you and I'm sorry it has taken until now to say it."

The way his face lit up made her heart flutter.

"Let me get everyone untied, then I will tell you everything."

It felt strange to ignore Joseph, who was glaring at her as though she was something a dog had left in the corner of his bedroom, but he wasn't going anywhere and he didn't deserve her attention.

She untied the ropes on Will first and between them they freed everyone else. Most, she noticed, didn't thank her and moved away from her as soon as they could. One shook her hand, however, and another hugged her.

She left Marie to Will. She didn't even look at him as he undid her bindings. Once she was free, she didn't get up; she just

283

stayed sitting in the chair, staring into space, as though she wasn't aware she had been released.

There was something seriously wrong with her, but finding out would have to wait. First, she had a call to make.

She dialled Elias's number and the call was answered after the first ring.

"How did it go?" he asked.

"As you predicted."

His laugh sounded down the phone. "I knew you could do it. I never had a doubt."

That was a lie. Neither of them had been certain she would be able to control a greater vampire, seeing as she had never taken the opportunity to try.

"What are you going to do about Joseph?"

She admitted she didn't know, but told him she would let him know when she did. Then she thanked him for his help and hung up.

With that out of the way, all that was left was an explanation. It wasn't going to be easy. She wasn't sure anyone would believe her.

"I guess you all want to know what's going on," she said.

"Not me," one of the men said. "I'm going home. My wife will be worried about me."

"That's a good idea," someone else said. "And I need to find some clean clothes." Both men headed to the stairs, but the first one turned around before reaching them. "Promise me you will tell me later?"

Anna nodded. He gave her a quick smile before departing.

All the remaining ex-hostages, other than Marie, wanted to know details so after calling their loved ones and taking a much needed bathroom break, everyone met up in the lounge, where Anna and Will had set out mugs of coffee for people to help themselves to.

Someone had thought to guide Marie from the basement, but she took no notice of the conversation. Anna wasn't convinced she even knew where she was.

Joseph was ordered to accompany them. Not only did she want him to hear what she had to say, she also wanted to keep an eye on him. She would need to keep giving him orders if she wanted to make sure he remained under her control.

Once everyone was settled on the sofas, chairs, and even the floor, Anna began. Will sat beside her, holding her hand.

First she told them about Elias. She had received his permission to do so when he devised his plan. Not everyone believed her when she spoke about how easily he had beaten Gabriel in a fight, until Will backed her up. A few nervous glances were exchanged, causing Anna to reassure them that Elias was not a danger to them and would keep away from them as long as they kept away from him. After all, he had been living among them for a while and hadn't caused any trouble.

She didn't mention all the horrific things she knew he had done in the past; she told them only enough for them to understand what abilities he had.

She went on to describe the training she received from him and his housemates, including the reason why. Will was the only one this news seemed to shock. He couldn't understand how she had managed to keep it from him. It was something they would have to discuss later. While she hadn't actually lied to him about her visits to Elias's estate, she hadn't been open and honest and she hoped it wouldn't affect their relationship.

She spoke about experimenting with drinking Elias's blood. Everyone in the room knew she wasn't able to digest human blood and most had let her drink from them at least once.

She went on to explain how drinking the blood of any 'infected' made her stronger, faster, better in every way, but Elias's blood was more potent.

When she told them how an 'infected' was able to control someone without injecting them with venom, and that she temporarily inherited that ability when she drank their blood, there were more than a few sceptics until she demonstrated on them. She only had to take control of two people before everyone stopped doubting her.

"So why did you force me to stay silent when you drank my blood?" Will asked. "Come to think of it, why did you drink my blood? You didn't need it if you had already taken from a number of infected."

"I took your blood as an excuse to experiment on you. Until I tried it on you, I didn't know if I would be able to control any vampire, let alone a greater one."

Someone whistled. "You were taking a big risk. What if it hadn't worked?"

"Then I would have left and Elias and his friends would have taken over."

Something told her a number of people were glad the plan had worked. They had already stated they never wanted to meet Elias.

The whole time she was speaking, Anna was aware that Joseph was watching her carefully. She had a decision to make and she still had no idea what she was going to do.

"You may speak, Joseph."

The look he gave her was filled with hate. "I used to regret what I did to you. You were just an innocent victim of a mistake. Now I wish I had made you suffer more. You cannot hold me prisoner forever. I will escape and when I do, I will make you watch as I kill Will and Gabriel. Then it will be your turn and I will make sure it is slow and excruciating."

That made up her mind for her. She phoned Elias and said she had someone for him to collect.

Joseph laughed. "He will be no match for me."

"Oh, I think he will."

Hearing that Elias was on his way to Marie's house caused a number of people to make hasty retreats before he arrived. Others stayed. They were fascinated by what they had heard about him and wanted to see what he could do.

Will decided to stay, though he clearly didn't look happy about it. Anna wondered if he and Elias would ever be friends. She hoped so, but wouldn't be holding her breath.

When Elias arrived, he was inundated with questions, though Anna noticed everyone was keeping their distance. Elias promised to speak with everyone at a later date, but he had something to take care of.

He turned to look at Joseph, who sneered at him. "I am not afraid of you."

Elias shrugged his shoulders, indicating he didn't care. He walked up to him, looked him in the eye and said, "Come with me."

Like an obedient servant, Joseph followed him out of the room. Anna took Will's hand and they went with them. She didn't want to see what happened to Joseph, but she needed to.

They followed Elias's car back to his estate. Upon arrival, Joseph was taken into the grounds to a large clearing. Patrice and Ben were already there, waiting for them, along with another two 'infected' Anna knew, but not well. On a signal from Elias, they moved to the outside of the clearing, standing at the four compass points.

Elias addressed Joseph. "As a demonstration of why you should do as I say, we're going to have a fight. No rules. If you choose, instead, to run away, my four colleagues will stop you."

Joseph looked around him. Anna assumed he was working out how easy it would be to escape, given the gaps between the 'infected'. She knew from experience it wasn't going to be as easy as he thought.

When his attention returned to Elias, he smiled. "I hate getting my clothes dirty, but if that is what you want, I will make an exception."

Elias chucked softly. "I like a man who is confident in his abilities."

Before he had finished speaking, Joseph moved. Not at Elias, but at Patrice, who he may well have mistakenly thought was the weakest link. It didn't take him long to find out he was wrong.

She grabbed him by the neck and threw him onto the ground. Placing her foot on his chest, she leaned over him.

"Are you really that scared to fight him?"

Joseph tried to push her foot away, but was unable to move it.

"No. Just seeing how good you are."

Patrice laughed and stepped away.

Joseph got to his feet and straightened his clothes. He turned to look at Elias.

"Are you ready?"

Unlike his fight with Gabriel, Elias didn't play with Joseph. As soon as he came for him, he grabbed his arm, pulled it behind his back and pushed him to the floor. He knelt on him to prevent him moving and leant over so he could speak in his ear, just loud enough for those present to hear.

"I once pulled a man's arm off and beat him to death with it. Don't make me do it again."

He then released him and stood back, allowing him to get to his feet.

"Shall we carry on or do you now understand the position you are in?"

Joseph no longer looked so sure of himself. "If you want to kill me, just get it over with."

Elias shook his head. "I don't want to kill you, though I will if I have to. I think you will be a good asset. Give up your quest to kill Gabriel and imprison Vivien. Come and work for me."

"As your slave? I do not think so."

"No, as a free man. Prove to me that you can be trusted and I will give you your freedom."

Will looked at Anna with a raised eyebrow. She nodded. She was sure Elias was telling the truth.

"And you expect me to believe that?" Joseph asked.

Elias shrugged. "I'm a man of my word. Take the offer or leave it, it's up to you. But if you reject my offer, you won't be leaving this clearing alive."

Joseph immediately agreed, though Anna didn't believe a word he was saying.

Elias gave instructions for Joseph to be taken to the house and a room prepared for him. He also asked Patrice to arrange for his things to be collected from wherever he was staying.

As soon as Joseph was out of sight, Anna walked up to Elias. "You know he's lying, don't you?"

"Of course. But as soon as he's showered and changed, I'm going to let him know that the grounds are patrolled by my men and should he try to leave without my permission, their instructions are to kill first and ask questions later."

Anna thanked Elias for his help and then she and Will left. She had a call to make and she wasn't looking forward to it.

As soon as they reached home, Will put the kettle on. He said he felt like something stronger, but it was too early in the day. While he was in the kitchen, Anna called Gabriel. She should probably have called Vivien instead, but she felt more comfortable talking to her kind-of-brother-in-law.

He was driving with the phone on speaker, so she asked him to call her back when he found somewhere to pull over. What she had to tell him wasn't the sort of news that should be received while in control of a vehicle.

A few moments later, her phone rang. She was on the sofa, with her feet curled up under her and her phone beside her. She checked it was Gabriel before she answered.

After receiving confirmation Vivien was with him and she could hear everything that was said, she told him all that had happened, from Marie setting Will up, and the reasons why, to Robbie's beheading and Joseph's capture.

"Are you alright?" was the first thing Gabriel said.

She almost said yes, but realised that she wasn't. Everything had been moving so quickly, she hadn't had time to process it. Her anger had been hiding the shock of watching Joseph cut off Robbie's head and now everything was over, it was beginning to hit her.

She was cold and couldn't stop shaking. The hot drink Will had made her didn't help and he went off to get her a blanket. Tears streamed down her face as she admitted to Gabriel how she felt. They washed away all her hate for Joseph, leaving her feeling empty.

Vivien assured her that was normal and she should cry as much as she wanted to. She cried for the loss of Luke, for Robbie's death, for how scared she had felt but wouldn't let herself admit it. And finally she cried with relief that it was over.

289

Joseph wasn't dead, but he was safely under guard at Elias's place. Gabriel and Vivien could go home. Anna could go home.

As she thought those words, she realised she already was home.

I WISH THINGS HAD TURNED OUT DIFFERENTLY

Joseph took his time showering. He told himself it wasn't to avoid Elias, but he was lying. He wasn't scared of anyone, but that man terrified him. He couldn't understand how he had been so easily subdued. He should have been able to beat him.

And as for the woman, he should have been able to get past her. He was fast enough, faster than any greater vampire he had met. Then again, these people weren't vampires. They were something else, something much more deadly. It was an uncomfortable feeling for a predator to become the prey; he had no doubt in his mind that was what he had become.

When he finally made it out of the shower, he discovered his dirty clothes had been taken away and clean ones laid on the bed. They weren't his, but he supposed nobody had bothered to collect his things yet. They fitted well enough so he couldn't complain.

He was expecting to see a guard at the door, but when he opened it, there was nobody in sight. He wandered around the floor he was on, checking each door. Some were locked, but most weren't. He found nothing out of the ordinary; bedrooms, a large bathroom, a fully stocked linen closet.

There was nothing to hold his interest, so he made his way down the stairs. He looked toward the front door, wondering if it was worth opening it to see if anyone was guarding it, but decided he would be wasting his time.

He searched every room on the ground floor until he reached Elias's office. The door was standing open and Elias was seated at his desk, looking at his computer screen.

"Did you enjoy searching my house?" Elias asked without looking up.

Joseph shrugged. "You would have done the same."

Elias finished reading whatever was on his screen before turning his head to look at Joseph.

"Probably. Why don't you take a seat?" He gestured toward the chairs in front of his desk with his hand.

"Like I have a choice," Joseph mumbled as he sat down.

"You're not a prisoner here." Elias tilted his head slightly, as though he was thinking. "Actually, I suppose you are. Though how long for, is up to you."

He leaned back in his chair. "You and I are very much alike. Both men who will do whatever it takes to protect those we love. After all, that is all you were doing, wasn't it? Protecting Vivien."

Joseph opted for honesty. "Mostly. At least initially. When Vivien first left the protection I provided to run off with Gabriel, I was annoyed. But I got her back and he suffered for it. I would have left him alone if she hadn't run away again."

"That was hardly Gabriel's fault."

Joseph didn't want to admit he was right. "She left because of him."

Elias shrugged his shoulders, conceding the point. Either that or he didn't think it was worth arguing about.

Joseph continued. "It took me a long time to find her again. A very long time. She moved around a lot, trying to find where Gabriel was and whether he was still alive. If he cared for her, he would not have left. He would have stayed where he was, searching for her until he found her."

Elias leaned forward. "I've heard Gabriel's version of this story. He had no idea why she left. And he did search for her. For a lot longer than most people would have. Eventually he decided she didn't want to be found. It was a dark time in his life."

Joseph smirked and Elias scowled at him.

"You don't make it easy for people to like you, do you?"

He let the smile drop from his face, though he was still smiling on the inside. It wasn't a good idea to antagonise this man; not if he wanted to live.

"It was Luke who persuaded him to move on. You remember Luke, don't you? The man your hired assassin killed by mistake. The man Anna was bonded to."

Elias didn't sound like he was being sarcastic, but he must have been. Of course Joseph remembered; how could he ever forget? He had been responsible for a lot of deaths and most he felt no regret over, but this one he did. Everything he had heard about Luke told him he was a good man. It wasn't his fault he was related to Gabriel, but he had paid the price for that relationship.

"Can I ask you a question?" Elias said when Joseph remained silent.

He wondered how Elias would react if he said no, but wasn't brave enough to find out. He nodded.

"Why didn't you bother getting to know Gabriel, to see how he treats Vivien? Why did you just assume he couldn't take care of her?"

"I did not need to. It was obvious he did not know how to protect her. A woman like Vivien is very desirable to men. She needs to be kept away from them."

Elias looked shocked. "So you wanted to keep her locked up?"

"For her own safety, yes."

Elias relaxed back again, shaking his head. "No wonder she ran away from you. You can't keep anyone prisoner and expect them to be happy."

"You are planning on keeping me prisoner."

He didn't like the way Elias was smiling at him.

"But I don't care if you are happy or not. Besides, it's your choice to remain here. All you have to do is walk out the door. I'm not going to stop you."

"And how far would I get before one of your men kills me?"

Elias laughed. "Why don't you find out?"

Joseph wasn't stupid. That was one offer he wasn't going to take Elias up on. At least not yet. He had no intention of staying longer than he had to. He just needed to find out more about patrol schedules, that kind of thing. He intended to be the model prisoner until Elias and the other 'infected' became complacent.

Even thinking the word 'infected' made him shiver. He wanted to know more. No, he needed to know more. If he was going to escape with his life, he had to gather all the information he could.

"Tell me more about yourself, how you became 'infected' and what it actually means."

He expected Elias to refuse, but he seemed happy to discuss himself. It took a long time for him to go over his history. They took a break for lunch, but Joseph didn't feel like eating. After hearing some of the things Elias and his extended family had done, he didn't think he could keep anything down.

Elias admitted to performing some atrocious acts, but his father and step-siblings had been a lot worse. According to Elias, anyway. Joseph was grateful he hadn't met any of the 'infected' before their civil war. Then he realised he probably had met some; he just hadn't known it.

He found the entire conversation fascinating. It made him think about what humans must feel when they find out vampires are real.

Joseph believed everything Elias told him. The only part he found hard to understand was when Elias had a witch put him in suspended animation because he couldn't stop himself killing people. It wasn't something Joseph would ever consider doing. It didn't take him long to learn to take blood without killing, but if he hadn't, it wouldn't have stopped him. Sometimes death was necessary and if he had to kill people to keep himself alive, so be it.

When Elias finished detailing his life's history, he offered to give Joseph a tour of the grounds. Joseph couldn't believe his ears. Elias may be powerful, but he was an idiot; he was going to show him where and how to escape.

Or was that the idea? Was this a test to see how closely Joseph observed the escape routes and routines of Elias's men? Joseph had no idea and didn't care. Any reasonable person in his situation would want to take in all of their environment, so that was exactly what he did.

He wasn't aware of Elias watching him as they walked and Elias told him all he needed to know about the grounds. Nowhere was off limits, but the wall that surrounded the property was the border as far as Joseph was concerned; cross it without permission and there would be consequences.

Joseph didn't bother to ask what those consequences were; he could take a good guess.

Getting over the wall wouldn't be hard and there didn't seem to be any sort of patrol. Then again, he was with Elias. Would it be different if he was alone? He had a distinct feeling he would never be truly alone.

Feeling eyes watching him, he turned around, but there was nobody there. Could 'infected' move so fast that even he, a greater vampire, couldn't see them? He didn't think so, but wouldn't stake his life on it.

Before the tour was over, Elias got a phone call. He moved away from Joseph, far enough that he couldn't overhear the conversation.

Joseph didn't take advantage of his lack of attention. He looked at the wall, calculating how long it would take him to reach it, and then looked away. He was certain someone was watching him and would intercept him before he could escape and it wouldn't do him any good to show his desire to leave. At least not yet.

When Elias returned to where Joseph was patiently waiting for him, he had a look on his face that Joseph couldn't decipher.

"That was Anna. Vivien and Gabriel are on their way back and Vivien wants to meet with you. I'm not sure that's a good idea. What do you want to do?"

It wasn't something he had thought about. He didn't think his sister would want to see him or that the choice would be his. "I think I should see her," he said after thinking it over.

"Very well. They will be here tomorrow. Now I have business to attend to. Can you find your own way back to the house?"

Joseph couldn't believe what he was hearing. He was going to be left alone, unsupervised? Elias wasn't that stupid. It answered the question on whether he was being watched or not.

"No problem," he said.

Elias left him alone, without warning him not to try to escape. He obviously had great faith in his men. And women. An image of Patrice filled Joseph's mind. That was one woman he didn't want to cross again.

He had no problem finding his way back to the house; he had been mapping the route in his mind as they walked. He didn't see anyone following him, but he knew they were there, keeping an eye on him.

He didn't see Elias again that day, though he heard him working in his office. He spent some time in the library, perusing the books, until one of the 'infected', who introduced himself as Ben, asked if he knew how to play pool. He didn't, but had played snooker a number of times in his distant past.

He enjoyed himself and not once did he feel like he was a prisoner. After the sun had set, Elias joined them, along with Patrice, and they set up some doubles matches.

At one point, he found himself relaxing and wondering if he could be happy there. The thought made him wonder if that was the intention of the evening and he stiffened up. Was he being played or just shown what life on the estate was really like?

Not liking the feeling of uncertainty, he made his excuses and retired for the night, though it was a long time before he fell asleep.

He woke before the sun rose, but the house was already full of activity. He was offered breakfast, but declined. He ate when he had to, but had stopped enjoying it decades ago. He wasn't thirsty, but he remembered the effect 'infected' blood had on Anna and wondered if it would have the same effect on him. However, he was denied the opportunity to find out. When he mentioned he needed blood to one of the workers, he was politely but firmly told to speak to Elias.

Elias patiently heard him out, before calling him out on his lie, though he was smiling as he did so.

"Bullshit. You just want to try infected blood. Well sorry to disappoint you, but I have a number of humans working for me, though not on this estate, and I'm sure one of them will be happy to come here and donate some blood."

Joseph shook his head. How did Elias know? He was beginning to think there was a lot more to him than he first thought. This wasn't a man who relied on his superior strength and speed. He was astute and calculating and thought things through. He was going to be a tough opponent.

Mid-morning Vivien arrived. And Gabriel wasn't with her.

"It is good to see you," he said as she was shown into the lounge, where he had been told to wait for her.

"I wish I could say the same." She plonked herself down on a sofa in an unladylike fashion, making Joseph wince. This was one of the reasons she needed to live with him; she needed to be retaught some proper behaviours. His thinking may be old-fashioned, but that didn't mean it was wrong.

"How are you?" He took a seat opposite her, but not too close. She had always liked her space and didn't like to feel crowded. Except where Gabriel was concerned, of course.

Before answering, she looked at her escort and nodded. The man then left the room, closing the door behind him. Joseph hadn't been expecting privacy.

"Pissed," she said once they were alone.

Again Joseph winced. It seemed she needed to be taught appropriate language as well. Gabriel had a lot to answer for. But he couldn't entirely blame Gabriel. Vivien had been travelling without him for a long time and could have picked up her bad habits from others. As her significant other, though, it was Gabriel's responsibility to get her to break them.

"I love you, Vivien. I only want what is best for you," he said to her. He had to struggle to control his anger when she rolled her eyes at him.

"No, you want what you think is best for me, not what I think is best for me. I have the right to run my own life, not have you run it for me."

Joseph couldn't help laughing. After all these years, they were still having the same argument. When would she learn that he was right and she would be better off living with him, obeying his rules? He could turn her into the Lady she was meant to be, not some ordinary woman.

"Look at the way you are dressed," he said, indicating her jeans and t-shirt with his hand. "You are wearing men's clothes. Women should look feminine. That is one thing I will give Marie credit for. I do not have a lot of respect for her, but she knows how to dress like a proper woman."

It was Vivien's turn to laugh. "I used to think you were old-fashioned, but in reality you're just old."

Joseph sighed. Dealing with his little sister had always been hard work. She was too independent for her own good. She always had been. And she was reckless. It was her fault they were both vampires. After she fell in with the wrong crowd and they mesmerised her with how good life was when you became immortal, there was nothing he could do to stop her from going ahead with the change. All he could do was agree to join her. It was a decision he didn't regret, but he couldn't help wondering, sometimes, how different their lives would have been if they had stayed human.

"Why did you come to see me?" he asked. "You obviously have no intention of having a proper discussion."

All amusement left Vivien's body. She tensed up and leaned forward. "To tell you to stay out of my life. I don't need you in it and I don't want you in it. Once, I thought we could work things out, have a normal, functional, sibling relationship. But not anymore." She leaned back, as though all the energy had gone out of her. "Robbie was a friend of mine." She said it so quietly, Joseph hardly heard it.

"Who is Robbie?"

The question had been a mistake. When she raised her head and looked at him, there was steel in her eyes.

"Robbie was the man you killed as a demonstration." There was venom in her voice. And not just venom; he was sure he could detect a trace of hate. But that wasn't possible. Vivien was his sister and she loved him. No matter what happened between them, she could never hate him. Could she?

"It was necessary."

It was the wrong thing to say. Vivien jumped to her feet. "Necessary?" she shouted. "Necessary? It was far from necessary. All you had to do was talk to me, but no, that isn't good enough for you. You don't want to discuss things. You want to dictate and have people obey you. And you will do anything and everything to make sure that happens."

She was pacing the room, waving her arms about. Joseph pushed as far back in his chair as he could, putting a little more space between them. If it hadn't made him appear weak, he would have stood up and moved to the other end of the room.

"You are a monster and I hate you. If I never see you again, it will be too soon."

She stormed out of the room, slamming the door behind her. He had never seen her so angry. She was acting like a child, but then again, she always did whenever they had an argument. She had grown into a mature, sensible woman, except in her dealings with him.

He hadn't been expecting his meeting with his sister to go well, but could never have imagined it would go this badly. He had no idea if she would ever return, which made plotting his escape essential.

Elias entered the room.

"That didn't go well. I could hear her shouting at the other end of the house."

Joseph gave a wry smile. "Now you know what I am dealing with."

"She'll be back. Just give her time. Hopefully, next time she will be prepared to talk."

He would give her time alright. Just enough time to lull Elias into a false sense of security. He would convince him that he didn't want to escape, that he was happy staying on the estate and was no longer a danger to Gabriel or Vivien. Then he was going to pay his little sister a visit.

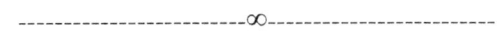

He gave it two weeks. He did everything Elias asked of him and played the perfect house guest. Outwardly he spent the time finding out about 'infected' and what Elias and his brother were doing to help them. He was openly fascinated with witches, having suspected they existed but never having proof.

Inwardly, however, he was planning his escape. He found out all he could about those who lived on the estate, what they did, what their routines were. Then he concentrated on the regular visitors, especially those who worked on the estate. He mentally documented their schedules.

He made no mention of escaping or going to visit his sister. He said he no longer wanted to take her away or kill Gabriel. He wasn't sure if anyone believed him, but he did nothing to make them doubt his word.

After he had been staying with Elias for twelve days, Elias drove him into the town. He said he had some shopping to do and Joseph was welcome to join him. He took the opportunity to look around, to plan where he would go when he escaped.

At one point, Elias said he had a private matter to take care of and Joseph should grab a coffee or something in one of the cafés and wait for him.

Joseph chose Cassidy's. She remembered him and seemed pleased to see him.

"You must be glad your sister is back," she said as she placed his coffee in front of him. He said he was and she smiled at him before going to check on customers at another table.

He wasn't aware of being watched by anyone, but didn't look for anyone who might be doing so. He didn't care if Elias had someone keeping an eye on him as he had no intention of doing anything wrong, at least not yet.

He was half-way through his drink when the shop door opened and someone entered. He looked up to see if it was Elias and saw Marie being escorted by a man he had never met before.

Their eyes locked and all colour drained from her face. She began to tremble violently. Cassidy ran over when the screaming started.

Both Cassidy and the man tried to calm Marie down, but she was too terrified to move. She seemed unable to look away and Joseph forced himself to do so.

Guilt, mixed with a bit of shame, flowed through him; it wasn't a pleasant feeling. He hadn't intended to scare her when he had killed her friend and it never occurred to him his actions would have long term psychological effects.

Cassidy and Marie's companion managed to coax her out of the café. Only then did the screaming stop.

He looked at what was left of his coffee and put the mug down. He no longer felt like drinking. Should he apologise to her? Probably, but if she reacted like that every time she saw him, it was going to be an impossible task.

He looked out of the window, watching the people walking by as he tried to take his mind off Marie. He didn't look around when the door opened once more, so he didn't know Elias had entered until he heard his voice beside him.

"Is that your doing?"

It was a question, not an accusation and he didn't need to ask what Elias was talking about.

"Unfortunately, yes. She started screaming as soon as she saw me."

Elias was surprisingly understanding. He placed his hand on Joseph's shoulder. "Come on. Let's get you out of here."

As they left the café, they passed close to where Marie was sitting at one of the outside tables, still visibly shaking. Elias positioned himself so his body partially shielded Joseph from Marie and both men were glad she didn't look up to see him.

"Are you alright?" Elias asked once they were in his car.

"Not really. Her reaction came as a bit of a shock."

"It's understandable though."

"Yes, it is."

The rest of the journey was made in silence. Joseph's mind was on escape. He needed to get away, as far away as he could, so Marie could start to rebuild her life.

A few nights later, he did just that. He waited until the darkness outside would hide his movements. Cloud cover prevented the moon from providing any light, so it was the perfect night to be out without being seen.

He had no trouble leaving the house. The front door was never locked and all the residents were in their rooms, presumably asleep.

Joseph checked his surroundings as he moved through the grounds, but there was no sign that anyone was watching or following him.

He made his way to the side of the estate instead of the front, which would have been the more logical choice. But if someone was patrolling the grounds, waiting for him to escape, the front was where they were more likely to be.

He jumped over the wall into the neighbouring property and breathed a sigh of relief. He was free!

He followed the wall toward the road and a feeling of elation flowed through him when he reached the front boundary wall and jumped over it. He followed the road east, toward the town.

It took a few hours for him to reach Will's house, turning off the road he was walking along before he reached the town. There were no lights on inside and no sign of movement, but he checked all around the house, just to make sure. There was also no sign of the dog.

The front door was locked, but the back wasn't. He let himself in and soon found the kitchen. Even in the dark, he managed to find a block of knives on the counter and he extracted the largest before making his way to the bedrooms. He tried two doors before he found Anna, peacefully sleeping. He no longer had ill intentions toward her, even though it was her fault he had ended up Elias's prisoner, so he left her in peace.

He discovered Will's room next and quickly exited it. He wasn't his target.

The last room he tried contained two people in a bed, both under the covers. It was too dark to see properly, but one of them was obviously a woman. Long hair flowed from her head. It was impossible to make out the colour, but it was most likely a dark brown or black, the colour of Vivien's hair. Not that Joseph was looking for confirmation; who else would be sleeping at Will's house?

The woman he assumed was Vivien stirred, but didn't wake. He would have to be quick. He thought about breaking her neck so she couldn't get in his way if she woke, but decided not to. He knew what to do and was confident he could get it done quickly.

A sharp turn of the head to kill Gabriel and then use the knife to decapitate him. His need to make him suffer had evaporated during the days he had spent with Elias, but not his desire to have Gabriel out of the way. Permanently.

He silently walked around the bed to Gabriel's side and placed his hands on either side of his head.

Then everything went wrong. Before he could break his neck, Gabriel moved, faster than should have been possible. One moment he was seemingly sleeping peacefully, the next he was standing beside Joseph.

Joseph stared at him, a frown covering his face. Even in the darkness he could see it wasn't Gabriel he was facing; the man had the wrong build. Realisation dawned, bringing a sinking feeling in the pit of his stomach.

Elias. It had to be Elias.

He turned around to find the woman was awake and out of bed. She removed her wig and smiled at him.

Patrice.

His legs gave way and he sank onto the bed. He had been stupid and overconfident. He hadn't fooled either of them. Despite his pretences, they both knew he still wanted Gabriel dead and would do something about it.

His life was over. There was nothing he could do or say to change that. He would have begged if he thought it would do any good.

"How are you here?" His voice sounded dead, devoid of all emotion. He was numb. He didn't feel scared; he didn't feel anything.

"We thought you might try to escape tonight, given the cloud cover, and arranged for your sister and Gabriel to stay at a friend's house. Will and Anna took a sleeping drug so they would sleep through the entire episode. After all, you would be suspicious if you didn't find them in the house."

If Joseph had been in Elias's position, he would have been gloating, but Elias wasn't; he was simply stating the facts in case Joseph was curious.

He didn't ask how they had known he would try to escape, what he had done to give himself away. There was no point; it wouldn't make any difference.

"What happens now?"

"Now we go back to my place."

'For my execution,' Joseph thought to himself, but couldn't bring himself to ask Elias for confirmation. He didn't want to hear the words.

He allowed himself to be led from the house. Trying to escape would be futile. He couldn't outrun either of his captors. Like a condemned man being walked to the gallows, he walked along the driveway.

It took a long time to reach Elias's estate. Nobody seemed to be in a hurry to get there. The gate stood open, awaiting its owner's return. Once they were through it, Patrice hit the button to close it. The clanging of it shutting had a ring of finality to it.

Joseph wondered how they would do it, and where. Inside the house was unlikely, given they would have to remove his head, which would result in a lot of blood being spilled.

Somewhere in the grounds then, but where exactly? Joseph had no idea why he was thinking about that, as the location made no difference to the outcome.

A desire to say goodbye to Vivien filled him, but he pushed it aside. Even if she was prepared to speak to him, he couldn't see Elias allowing it. No, Elias would get this over and done with before speaking to her.

He was led to the same clearing where Elias had demonstrated how weak greater vampires were compared to 'infected'. Just as he stepped out of the trees, the clouds moved, allowing the moon to fill the area with its light. It was almost as if the celestial body was giving its blessing to what was about to happen.

"I wish things had turned out differently," Elias said with what sounded like genuine regret. "If you had let go of your obsession with killing Gabriel and kidnapping Vivien, I think we could have been friends. But you couldn't and this has to end, here and now."

Joseph said nothing, waiting for Elias to ask him if he had any last words. He didn't. Instead, he said, "Are you ready, Pat?"

Joseph turned to her, waiting for her answer, but she didn't speak. Instead, she walked up to him and punched him in the chest.

Never before had he experienced such agony. He heard as well as felt his ribs break before something took hold of his heart and ripped it from his body. The last thing he saw was Patrice holding it in her hand before darkness took him.

His legs gave way and he was dead before he hit the ground.

He didn't hear Elias approach and felt nothing as his head was ripped from his body.

YOU HAD BETTER TAKE GOOD CARE OF HER

Anna looked at herself in the mirror. She had never been a vain person, but she couldn't help admiring herself. Marie had done a wonderful job with her hair and makeup.

Marie had come a long way in the last two years. The incident with Joseph had affected her badly. Not just because she had been held prisoner and had seen a friend brutally murdered, but also because it was the first time she had been used as a means to an end. It was a shock to her system that a man could sleep with her and it mean nothing to him, that he didn't worship the ground she walked on.

The news of Joseph's death went a long way toward her recovery, but the emotional scars his betrayal left her with lingered on. It wasn't until she settled down with a greater vampire who was more than happy to take care of her, that she began to emerge from the shell she had created around herself.

Her personality had changed. She no longer expected everyone to do her bidding and be at her beck and call. She now showed appreciation to those around her. Anna couldn't help thinking the incident had made her a better person. She seemed to be happy. Anna and Marie had become good friends.

There was a knock on the door and once given permission, Gabriel walked in.

"You look stunning," he said. "Luke would be happy for you."

It was exactly what she needed to hear. When Will had first proposed, she hadn't been sure what to say. It wasn't that she didn't want to marry him and agree to spend the rest of her life with him, but she wondered if it would be a betrayal of Luke's memory. Will had understood when she said she needed time to think about it. He accepted that she had fallen in love with him, but would never feel for him the way she had for Luke.

It had taken conversations with both Sarah, who had gone through the same thing, and Gabriel, who knew Luke better than anyone, for her to realise she was worrying about nothing and Luke would have wanted her to move on.

So she had said yes and wedding planning began in earnest. As Gabriel and Vivien had moved back home and all her friends from Sanctuary 14 lived nearby, it was decided the wedding should take place there, not where Anna and Will lived. JD spoke to the hunter society's local priest and he agreed to perform the ceremony in his church. He wasn't the only one to find it ironic that vampires would be marrying in a church for vampire hunters.

"Where's Vivien?" Anna asked.

Gabriel grinned. "Marie is still doing her makeup. She's never been a maid-of-honour before and wants to look perfect."

Anna had debated a long time about who to ask. While she and Marie had become close and she had been friends with Sarah for a lot longer, Vivien was family and had been a great support when she lost Luke.

Choosing a flower girl was easy. Young Charlotte had jumped at the chance and loved trying on different dresses until they found the right one. Nathan, Katie and Jonathon's son, was pageboy. Alexander had been asked, but he had flat out refused and nobody wanted to force him to do something he didn't want to.

Sanctuary 14 would be hosting the reception. A large marquee had been set up in the grounds. A lot of hunters would be attending, as well as numerous vampires, and Anna couldn't help being concerned there would be trouble. A few 'infected' would also be there and Elias had assured her any problems would be swiftly dealt with, even if he had to threaten to kill everyone. Anna hoped he had been joking, but wasn't entirely sure he was.

Anna, Vivien and Marie had spent the night at Sanctuary 14, while their partners had stayed at Gavin's place. Anna thought it was nonsense that the groom shouldn't see the bride in her wedding dress before the ceremony, but had been overruled by Will, Gabriel, Elias and just about everyone else.

Gabriel wasn't at the Sanctuary now to collect Vivien; a vintage car had been hired to take the maid-of-honour, flower girl and pageboy to the church. He was there to assure Anna she was doing the right thing, to quash any last minute doubts she might have been experiencing, and she appreciated it.

"How's Will?" she asked.

"Nervous. Not about marrying you, but about doing or saying something wrong. He's worried that if he makes any mistakes, Elias will make him regret it."

Anna couldn't help laughing. To the best of her knowledge, Elias had done nothing to make Will think that way; it was all in his head.

"Tell him to relax," she said.

"I will. He probably won't want me telling you this, but he went to the lake this morning, where we scattered Luke's ashes, to ask for his blessing."

Anna thought Gabriel was right. Will wouldn't have wanted her to know, but she was glad she had been told.

Gabriel glanced at his watch. "I suppose I should head back and get changed. While Will may have nothing to worry about as far as Elias is concerned, I'm not so sure he would be so lenient toward the best man if he let the groom arrive late."

He gave Anna a kiss on the top of her head before leaving her alone, though she wasn't alone for long. Almost as soon as he left, Sarah entered the room, checking if Anna needed anything.

"To be honest," she said when Anna assured her she was fine, "I had to get away from Charlotte. She's driving me crazy. She's so excited she won't sit still. I left her with her father."

Before Anna could respond, there was another knock on the door and Marie and Vivien walked in, holding a bottle of wine and four glasses.

"I thought I would find you here," Vivien said. "I think we have just enough time for a quick drink before we have to leave."

Anna didn't argue, though she didn't need it. She wasn't suffering from any of the pre-wedding jitters she had heard other brides talking about.

They were only half-way through the bottle when JD announced Elias had arrived with the wedding car and it was time for everyone except the bride to head over to the church.

When Anna had asked Elias if he would give her away, as both her parents were dead, he had enthusiastically accepted. She had thought about asking her brother, but it didn't feel right and he was happy that she had opted to go with Elias, stating he wouldn't have felt comfortable taking their father's place.

"Let's take a look at you then," Elias said as he walked into her room.

She stood up and he moved his finger in a swirling motion, indicating she should turn around. She obeyed.

"You'll do, I suppose." The glint in his eye told her he was winding her up and that, in reality, he thought she looked great.

Then he turned serious. "I'm really proud to be the one walking you down the aisle."

Smiling, she walked up to him and took both of his hands in hers.

"Thank you. It means a lot to me."

"Are you ready to go?"

Anna nodded and allowed him to escort her out of the house and down to his car. He owned a number of cars, including a vintage Rolls Royce, which was sitting on the driveway, an 'infected' in the driver's seat, dressed as a chauffeur.

It took longer to reach the church than it should have as the driver deliberately went slowly, saying it was good to make a groom wait. Anna didn't object.

The car park was packed when they finally arrived and Vivien was waiting outside the church, along with the flower girl, pageboy and their mothers.

Elias helped Anna from the car and escorted her to the door, where Vivien pulled down Anna's veil and rearranged her train, making sure it was flowing properly. Katie handed her son a purple velvet cushion and placed two gold rings on it. After instructing him not drop it or lose the rings, she went into the church to find her seat. Sarah handed a basket filled with flower petals to her daughter, kissed her on the cheek, told her to behave and then followed Katie into the church.

The sound of an organ playing the traditional bridal march sounded from inside, letting the bridal party know it was time to begin.

Nathan went first, walking slowly and steadily, making sure he didn't fall or drop his precious cargo. When he saw his father wink at him, his face lit up with a dazzling smile.

Charlotte followed him, concentrating hard on throwing the petals down in front of her.

"It's not too late to change your mind, you know," Elias whispered to Anna. "Are you sure he's the right man for you? After all, even after all these months, I still intimidate him just by being in the same room."

Anna gave him a friendly dig in the ribs with her elbow. "Everyone gets intimidated by you. It's just that most of us have learned to hide it from you."

Elias chuckled.

When Anna and Elias entered the church and looked down the aisle, she spotted Will at the other end. The smile he gave her the moment their eyes met would have erased all doubts, had she had any. She wanted to run to him, but Elias had a firm grip on her, preventing her from going faster than him.

As she walked down the aisle, Anna saw many friendly faces, all smiling at her. Her eyes fell on Natalie, who was seated next to Craig. The 'infected' who Nick had sent to help Craig, only to find his services were no longer required, had gone to see Natalie as soon as she was allowed visitors, but his attempts at fixing her failed. The first time Nick saw her, a few days after she had been released from hospital, he also tried to use his enzymes to mend her damaged spinal cord, but her injuries had been too severe.

She hadn't let her disability get her down, though. She soon mastered manoeuvring her wheelchair around and not once did she feel sorry for herself, or let anyone else do so.

Work had been done on Sanctuary 14 to turn three of the bedrooms into offices for Doc, JD and Sarah and their old offices were converted into a downstairs bedroom and bathroom. A lift was also installed, should Natalie ever wish to go upstairs for any reason.

The restaurant she worked at had been great. As soon as they found out she wanted to return to work, they rearranged the tables to make it easier for her to guide her wheelchair between them and she had recently been promoted to assistant manager.

With JD and Sarah's help, she exercised and remained fit and healthy. Anna had never seen anyone cope so well with such an injury. From the first moment she had found out she would never be able to walk again, Natalie had promised herself she wouldn't let it stand in her way and it was a promise she was keeping. A few days previous, she had announced she and Craig were expecting their second child.

On the other side of the aisle, Kurt was sitting with some of the other greater vampires. He had settled in well with Gavin's family, had gained control of his urges and was now dating Cassy.

Vivien followed Anna and Elias as they made their way to the altar, where the priest was waiting for them. He must have been in his late fifties, the greying of his hair showing his age, while the sparkle in his eyes left you wondering if he was, in fact, younger. He was the same man who had performed Sarah's wedding and Anna began to have doubts about her choice of venue; she had heard a lot about vampire hunter marriage ceremonies.

When they reached the end of the aisle, the two children moved to one side and Elias took Anna's hand and placed it on Will's arm.

"You are a lucky man," he said so quietly that only those at the altar could hear. "You had better take good care of her."

"I will."

Anna was impressed; there was no trace of a tremor in Will's voice.

Vivien raised Anna's veil and took her bouquet before stepping to the side to join Elias and the two children.

"You are beautiful," Will whispered to Anna, making her smile.

"We are gathered here today," the priest said, "to join together Anna and William in marriage. While this is not the first time I have performed this service for two non-hunters, it is the first time I have done so for a vampire."

JD coughed loudly, causing a few of the congregation to snigger.

The priest turned his attention to JD. "You don't count. You're a hunter first and a vampire second."

He returned his focus to the bride and groom and commenced the ceremony. While it wasn't quite what Anna had been expecting, it was a far cry from a typical hunter wedding, for which Anna was grateful. There was no slicing of palms and sharing of blood.

When it was time for the vows, Will went first. He turned to her, his eyes full of emotion.

"I love you Anna. It took you leaving for me to realise it and make me see what should have been obvious to me. I know I cannot replace Luke, in your heart, and I will never try to. All I ask is that you give me as much of yourself as you feel you are able to and allow me to treat you the way I think Luke would have wanted. I promise I will do all I can to keep you happy."

He looked around, allowing his gaze to drift around the room, falling on Gabriel, Elias, JD, Gavin, Craig and even Nick, before returning to Anna.

"I know there are plenty of people in this church who will make sure I keep that promise."

Anna felt a tear fall down her face and hoped it wasn't ruining her makeup. Will's words touched her more than she had been expecting.

Then it was her turn to say her vows.

"I promise to love you for the rest of my life and never make you feel second best to Luke. He would have liked you and this is what he would have wanted. I know he is watching us and giving us his blessing. I will never give you reason to regret choosing me and those people who will make sure you keep me happy, will be ensuring I do the same for you. For always and forever."

With a little encouragement from Gabriel, Nathan moved forward and held out his cushion to Will, who took the smallest ring and held it close to Anna's finger.

"William, do you take Anna to be your wife, to love, honour and cherish for the rest of your eternal life?" The priest failed to keep a straight face when he said 'eternal'.

"I do."

Anna had never heard Will sound so sure of himself. He slipped the ring onto her finger and kissed the back of her hand.

Anna took the other ring from the cushion and put it on the top of Will's finger, but didn't slip it into place.

"Anna, do you take William to be your husband, to love, honour and cherish for the rest of your eternal life?"

"I do."

She slid the ring all the way down his finger and he gripped her hand once it was in place.

"I now pronounce you man and wife."

The cheering almost drowned out the words that Anna had been waiting for.

"You may now kiss the bride."

From Trudie:

I hope that you enjoyed this book. Please help others have the same opportunity by leaving a review.